THE RIGHTFUL HEIRS

A NOVEL BY
TOM SCHUYLER

Copyright © 2010 by Tom Schuyler. All Rights Reserved. No part of this book may be reproduced or transmitted in any form or by any means, electronic or mechanical, including photocopying, recording, or by any information storage and retrieval system, without the written permission of the publisher except in the case of brief quotations, or except where permitted by law.

The information contained in this book is intended to be educational and not for diagnosis, prescription, or treatment of any health disorder whatsoever. This book is sold with the understanding that neither the author nor publisher is engaged in rendering any legal, psychological, or accounting advice. The publisher and author disclaim personal liability, directly or indirectly, for advice of information presented within. Although the author and publisher have prepared this manuscript with utmost care and diligence and have made every effort to ensure the accuracy and completeness of the information contained within, we assume no responsibility for errors, inaccuracies, omissions, or inconsistencies.

Library of Congress Control Number: 2010930240

ISBN-13: 9780615382845

THE RIGHTFUL HEIRS softcover edition 2010

Printed in the United States of America

For more information about special discounts for bulk purchases, please contact
3L Publishing at 916.300.8012 or log onto our website at www.3LPublishing.com.

Book design by Erin Pace

*To the memory of all the Holocaust victims
and their **Rightful Heirs**.*

> For my classmate Dale —
> Good to see you again —
> Hope you enjoy my story!
> "Class of '51"
> Tom Schuyler

FOREWORD

To this day nearly $5 billion lie in Swiss bank accounts belonging to victims of the Holocaust. This is the fictional story of six Italian Jews who deposited their combined fortunes in Switzerland just before World War II and the hell that followed them. It also is the story of three people whose search for **THE RIGHTFUL HEIRS** amidst a whirlwind of love, sex and murder, which must surely cause the reader to follow the money!

II THE RIGHTFUL HEIRS

ACKNOWLEDGEMENTS

To my wife Barbara whose encouragement and countless hours of corrections kept me on track.

A special thank you to the following people for historical and technical advice and encouragement along the way: Harv & Gwen Gadberry, Capt. James Ryan, USN Ret and his wife Marge, Michael Brown, Captain United Airlines, and last but not least, Don Oliver, NBC News.

IV THE RIGHTFUL HEIRS

ONE

JIM RILEY'S FEET HAD BARELY TOUCHED THE FLOOR when the muffled shots rang out, three in rapid succession and one a few seconds later. He wasn't sure if the shots woke him or if it was just a coincidence. In fact, he wasn't sure it was gunfire at all.

He rubbed his eyes and glanced at the large digital numbers on the alarm clock: 6:54. He frowned, showing some disgust at waking up so early. His first lesson wasn't until 10:00 a.m., and he needed only 30 minutes to get to the San Carlos airport. He thought of going out to breakfast but decided it was too much trouble. More importantly, he had only $20 to last until Saturday.

Jim Riley had been a flight instructor for Aero-One Flight Center at San Carlos Airport for nearly two months now and hated every minute of it. Sitting in the right seat of a Cessna 152 was a far cry from the spacious Beech Baron he had been flying up and down the San Joaquin Valley, chauffeuring the Windom Wine executives and their guests from the Modesto headquarters to SFO, Oakland International, Chico, San Jose, Livermore, and throughout the Napa Valley. On occasion, there would be a trip to Los Angeles or Santa Barbara and places that he couldn't recall.

For as long as he could remember, all he ever wanted to do was fly. Flying for Windom had been a sweet deal for more than four years, especially since the completion of his commitment to the Navy and the end of his marriage nearly two years ago.

After receiving a business degree from the University of Montana, he reported to Naval Air Station Pensacola in June of 1992. Upon reporting for duty, he was immediately met by the Hollywood version of the perfect marine drill instructor, with his full complement of bad attitude, spit-shined demeanor, and a very narrow band of tolerance. The brutish man introduced his attack plan by rolling the unit out of bed at 0400 on the first morning to more push-ups than a gorilla is capable of performing. Jim took it all in stride. He could only smile when the DI would single out a cadet caught slacking and stand him in the corner, demanding him to repeat, "I want my mommy." Jim, however, managed to keep a step ahead of the infamous DI.

Jim learned to fly in the Beech craft T-34, a forgiving two-place trainer. Jim soloed on his eleventh hop. His instructor had him land on an outlying field, got out, and told Jim to do some touch-and-goes. The excitement was without parallel. Before his solo, he knew that he was never totally in command of the airplane with the instructor on board, but now he knew. He was in control. "Damn, I've done it!" he had yelled at the top of his voice on his second touch-and-go.

From that point on, training went well for Jim and he became a distinguished graduate. This meant a regular commission and his choice of fleet airplanes. He chose the fighter community and the F-18 Hornet.

His Navy career seemed on track; he was soon flying the Hornet during his first deployment off the USS Constellation. "Connie" was a dream come true. He had nearly made up his mind to stay in the Navy until all was dashed on the rocks when he came back from his first cruise to a wife who was not happy with the Navy way of life. Shirley could not handle the pressures of naval aviation. They hung on for another two and a half years, because Jim found it necessary to meet his initial commitment. In an effort to save the marriage, he finally left the Navy; but it became quite apparent that even with his resignation, the marriage would not survive.

They had made the mistake of having been too eager and too careless, and Shirley became pregnant with their daughter Julie. Shirley's father was against the wedding, but Jim Riley persisted. They were married just three months before Julie arrived on the day Jim received his "wings of gold."

They separated by mutual agreement. Shirley filed for divorce two years later. It had more or less been a friendly divorce, and he continued to keep in touch with Shirley and his daughter. Jim applied for the airlines, but the pipeline was filled. The Windom job was a godsend and much less boring than driving a big sky bus.

Jim was free most weekends, except for an occasional wine show in San Francisco or somewhere in the Napa Valley. On those occasions, he would fly two or three buyers in for the exhibit. Life was simple and uncomplicated, and that's the way he wanted it — at least until he could develop some sense of direction.

* * *

THE UNDOING CAME ON A BLUSTERY TUESDAY MORNING just two days before Thanksgiving. Oliver Windom, founder of the Windom Wineries, was due in Chico at 11:30 a.m. The old man's Mercedes limo pulled up to his private hangar at the Modesto airport at 7:45 a.m. Oliver got out of the car and headed straight for the walk-through door where he knew Jerry Dunne, his mechanic, would be inside, dusting the Baron and washing the windshield. Dominic, Windom's younger brother, was with him, and stood quietly touching the Baron as he admired the beautiful plane.

Jerry was at the company wall safe with the locksmith. The thing was old and almost impossible to open. Finally Jerry had had enough and called a friend of his who was a safecracker in his other life. Jim was always amused at Jerry's embellishment of his friends' backgrounds. One plumber had been a "circus fat man" though he weighed barely 130 pounds now. Jerry and the "safecracker" had been good friends for several years. On one occasion, the man had called Jerry Dunne to bail him out of jail after a bar fight had gotten out of hand. Jerry paid the bail and made no further reference to the incident. Soon, the safe was opened and Jerry continued his daily routine.

It was almost a ritual. Oliver always arrived early for a flight. He loved to talk about his beautiful Beech Baron with Jerry Dunne. He owned two other planes, but this was his baby. It looked brand new, though it was nearly 20 years old. He had ordered it new with two 56 TC Lycoming engines instead of the standard IO 520 Continentals. It was a gas-guzzler, but it was the hottest thing available at the time. He had also ordered cherry wood paneling and Corinthian leather seats. Over the years, Jerry Dunne had added other goodies, including the custom paint job. The Windom crest — a brilliant gold oval with a lion standing on its hind feet on either side of the oval with its front paws resting at the top — consumed the entire vertical stabilizer. In the center of the crest, was a large green "W." Jim Riley thought it looked like the crest on a Philip Morris cigarette pack. However, it was elegant over the pure white paint. From the tail section running down the side to the nose were green and red stripes forming an elongated "W." Near the tail, just below the stripes, was the identification N777TR.

Windom himself was nearly as elegant as his airplane. A tall, willowy man in his late 70s with white curly hair, neatly trimmed, he appeared molded into a perfectly tailored navy-blue pinstriped suit with a white silk shirt and matching tie and pocket-handkerchief. His patent leather shoes flashed from the overhead lights as he moved. His eyes were deep brown and his skin a leathery tan. The man could not be ignored. His sheer demeanor and rugged good looks commanded a second glance from men and women alike. From his white hair and thin moustache to the soles of his shoes, the man was a page out of Esquire.

Oliver Windom was the elder of two brothers who had learned the business from his father in Milan, and was the real force behind the Windom Wineries. His younger brother had long ago become a full-fledged alcoholic, in and out of one sanitarium after another. Though Oliver could provide his brother with the very best of care, he was a greedy man and sought the least expensive care possible. Most people were unaware of the man's existence. Oliver, on the other hand, never drank anything but the family wines, and was clearly visible throughout the entire Napa Valley and anywhere where wines were likely to be marketed.

Jim Riley thought Oliver to be like Jekyll and Hyde. He never knew which one to expect. Oliver Windom could be soft-spoken and fatherly one minute and a vicious tyrant the next. It was impossible to know what would set him off. Today, he decided to be kind to his brother by taking him on one of his business trips. In more than four years, Jim was never comfortable around the man, and aside from Jerry Dunne, Oliver Windom had never made small talk with anyone. He was congenial yet cold, and Jim Riley had a gut feeling that there existed a very dark side to the man.

At 8:40, Jim crossed the tarmac as Jerry Dunne rolled the Baron out of the hangar. Oliver followed immediately behind the tail section with outstretched hands as if to protect the plane from hitting anything. The gold crest dazzled in the early morning sunlight, flashing off and on as the clouds passed overhead. Jim loved the Baron nearly as much as the old man did. He petted it gently as he passed by the wing tip.

"Morning, Jim," said Jerry.

"Morning, Jerry. Good morning, Mr. Windom."

"Jim," acknowledged Oliver. "Let's do it."

The preflight was completed by 9:00 a.m. Jim cranked the engines to life. They purred as usual, and within five minutes, Oliver Windom was aboard and on the phone to one of his associates. Dominic was fastened in and waiting patiently for takeoff.

Oliver was actually joking with his brother about having given Dunne a bad recommendation to one of the airlines in order to keep him from being hired. Jerry Dunne was his property.

The wind had picked up, and dust and debris were flying across the taxiway. Jim pulled the Baron slowly forward and began moving down the tarmac. He was busy checking gauges and did not see the old tail-dragger emerge from between the hangars. It was over in an instant. The Baron's left wing tip caught the prop of the Cessna and metal flew everywhere. Jim immediately killed the engines. The collision had stopped the tail-dragger's engine. For a moment, there was dead silence.

Oliver Windom suddenly jumped to his feet and rushed to the front of the cabin, his eyes darting back and forth. "What the hell was that?" He looked through the windshield. "Oh, my God, Riley! You son of a bitch, you've wrecked my airplane!" The old man reached out and slapped Jim Riley across the back of the head.

"Get off my airplane. Get out! Get out!"

Dominic could not believe what his brother had just done. Yet it was not unlike the older brother with whom he'd grown up.

Jim was stunned. He slowly folded his map into his flight case, picked it up, got out of the Baron, and slowly walked over to the crunched wingtip. In all of his flying, he had never even come close to an accident. He could only shake his head in disbelief, and almost aimlessly, he walked to his car and pulled out of the parking lot.

"Damn! Damn! Damn!" he muttered as he headed in the direction of the Red Lion Inn. He felt that he needed a stiff drink. As the barmaid set the gin and tonic in front of him, he began to gather his wits. He decided that it would be rather stupid to take a drink now. He paid his tab and returned to the airport FAA office. Riley filed his accident report in less than an hour and drove 12 miles southeast to the Windom mansion guesthouse. It was a great place for one person. He had lived there free of charge for the entire time he had flown for Windom Wineries. Now it was over. He packed all of his belongings in less than 15 minutes, loaded it all into his '81 Camaro, and headed north on 99 toward the 120 cutoff to the 205 and the Bay Area.

* * *

RELIVING THE EPISODE AS THE CAMARO SPED NORTH, he calculated the total damage to be somewhere around $50,000. He thought there would be very little to the investigation, and the FAA would probably tell the owners to file with their insurance companies. At this moment, he didn't really care, but he knew he'd better let someone know how to contact him. He pulled off the highway at Ripon and called Jerry Dunne at the hangar.

"Jerry Dunne," came the answer.

"Jerry, Jim Riley."

"Jim, where the hell are you? This place is buzzing with people, and the old man is screaming like a Comanche!"

"Jerry, listen to me. I've already filed the report. I'm heading to San Jose, and I wanted to make sure I can be reached. I'll call you tomorrow, and let you know where I am. I can't deal with Windom right now."

"Are you sure this is the right thing to do?"

"I'm not running away, Jerry. Other than bending the old man's airplane, it's not that big a deal. Make sure he knows I'll call tomorrow. This will give him a chance to cool down."

"Okay, Jim, I'll let him know … and take it easy, guy, it wasn't your fault. You had the right of way."

"Yeah, I know. Tell that to the old man!"

"I will. Gotta go. I'll talk to you tomorrow."

Jim picked up a coffee to go and eased back onto the freeway. It was over. He knew there would be no going back. Jim Riley's pride would not allow that, even if the old man forgave him.

TWO

JIM'S MIND WANDERED THROUGH THE EVENTS of the past four years with Windom, especially the David Steinmetz thing and that damned little leather book. It had happened less than three months ago. He remembered how nervous and frightened the young man had appeared on that terrible Friday morning following Labor Day. Steinmetz had been at the guesthouse since Tuesday, and had met with Oliver Windom at least five times that week, once well after midnight on Thursday. Jim thought he had heard old man Windom speaking very loudly several times that evening.

Jim and David had lunch together on Wednesday and became fairly well acquainted. Jim liked the man. He was rather shy, extremely brilliant, and avoided any reference to his purpose for being there. Jim was to fly him to Santa Barbara on Friday morning, wait for him, and fly him to Oakland International Airport for an evening flight back home to Boston.

They sat at the restaurant for nearly two hours after lunch talking about Jim's flying, his divorce, how proud he was of Julie, and of course, his ex-wife Shirley. Steinmetz was a good listener and seemed genuinely interested in what Jim had to say. He had revealed more about himself to this man in two hours than he had with anyone for the past year or so. David Steinmetz was easy to talk to. He, in turn, told Jim a great deal about himself, and how his grandfather had emigrated from Italy in 1940. Being Jewish, he had to get out or suffer the consequences. Mussolini was flexing his muscles, and Italy was becoming no safer for Jews than Germany. Fortunately, his grandfather had money and was able to pay the price necessary to get out.

"My grandfather landed at Ellis Island with thousands of other immigrants, and after the quarantine period and whatever else, they moved to Detroit and into the auto industry," David explained.

"You spoke of your grandfather. What about your grandmother? Had she passed away?" Jim asked.

"Yes, I'll just say that she didn't make it to America. I won't go into that now. However, to show you what kind of fanatics they were dealing with, my father told me that my great-grandmother had been murdered. The police in Milan claimed that she had stepped in front of a car, but he knew she had been deliberately run down for no reason at all. The police were seen by my great-grandparents' friends to be laughing as they drove away. You know, Jim, anti-Semitism was not Hitler's little invention. He and his puppet, Mussolini, just took it to the next level."

The men finished a small dessert and left the restaurant. David was almost late for another meeting with Oliver Windom. Jim dropped him off at the mansion and headed for the airport to check out a new transponder Jerry had installed in the Baron. Mr. Dunne would be pacing the floor.

* * *

JIM WAS WAITING IN THE HANGAR when David Steinmetz drove up in the Windom limo. Jim could see the moment Steinmetz stepped out of the car that he was a man in some state of panic. He fumbled with his suit bag and could hardly hold on to his carry-on. Jim knew he must have come directly from the old man's office at the mansion.

Jim had barely reached altitude when David slipped into the right seat. He pulled out his handkerchief and wiped the perspiration from his upper lip.

"Jim," he began, "you don't really know me, and you don't know why I'm here, but I think I've read you well enough to feel that I can trust you. In fact, I have no choice. I want to give you something and I don't want you to ask me why."

Jim raised his eyebrows, looked straight ahead, and said nothing. David reached into his suit pocket and brought out a small leather-bound book, approximately three-inches wide and four-inches high. It was barely a half-inch thick. Jim gave a quick glance and thought it looked quite old. The leather was scuffed and faded.

"What is this thing, anyway?" Jim asked.

"Please, Jim, don't ask any questions. You can look at it later. Obviously, you're more than curious. I know that."

"What do you want me to do with it?" Jim asked, totally confused.

"Nothing now. Just hold onto it. Someone who will identify himself as 'Ellis' will call and arrange to meet you. Give the book to him and nobody else. It's a matter of life and death, Jim."

"Whose?" Jim asked with wide-opened eyes. He knew the man meant it.

"Mine, Jim — and quite possibly, others. I won't lie to you about that, and I'll understand if you don't want to take the book."

Jim sat looking straight ahead for almost a minute and then slowly reached over and held out his hand. He took the book, and with his right hand, he thumbed through the pages. All he could see were a lot of numbers and letters mixed together, which made no sense whatsoever.

"It looks like a bunch of gibberish to me, David. Is it some sort of a code for something?"

"In a manner of speaking, it is, Jim, but believe me, if you knew what it represents, it would make your hair stand on end."

"Whew! I'll tell you what, David: I'll think about this one, and we'll discuss it on the way to Oakland. If it's as hot as you say, I'm not too sure I want anything to do with it!"

"Okay, Jim. Fair enough."

Jim slipped the book into his pocket, leaned over, set the trim tab, and eased back into his seat. David Steinmetz had moved back into the cabin, loosened his tie, leaned back, and closed his eyes. Jim glanced back. The man looked exhausted.

They touched down in Santa Barbara at 9:40 a.m. Jim pulled the Baron into the transient parking. David left his luggage aboard and caught a cab into town. Jim boarded a city bus to find a place for breakfast and then maybe a little sightseeing. He had nearly four hours to kill. He thought he might even bowl a few lines somewhere.

The cab pulled up in front of the offices of Goldman and Steinmetz. David paid the fare and headed for the elevator. He hadn't seen his uncle for almost a year and was looking forward to seeing him again. Uncle Aaron was his only remaining relative. Since David's father had passed away, Aaron Steinmetz had become father and brother to him.

They rarely agreed on anything, but they were family and David loved the man. Uncle Aaron had helped him financially to complete college at Boston University, and even supported him until his law practice got off the ground. He owed much to the man, and would not think of coming to California without seeing him. He also wished to ask Uncle Aaron about the book. David had been told most of the story by his father, which his grandfather had passed down. But there were some missing pieces to the puzzle that David needed to know about. He was not at all sure his uncle could help him, and more than that, he had some doubts that his uncle had ever known about the book. If not, it was certainly time to tell him. With his life in danger, it would only be fair.

The two men hugged each other and disappeared into Aaron Steinmetz's office. No more than a minute had passed and it happened. It was over in a matter of seconds. Two shots rang out. Goldman jumped from his office chair, ran to the reception room. His heart was pounding and he did not see the secretary.

"Oh my God!" he shouted, thinking something had happened to her.

At that moment, she appeared from the copy room. Her face showed no color, and she was shaking all over. Goldman thought he had heard the stairway door snap shut, and his nostrils filled with the smell of gunpowder.

"Mr. Goldman!" came the terrified voice of the secretary. "Did you hear that?"

Without answering, Goldman turned and walked slowly toward Aaron Steinmetz's half-opened office door. The secretary stood motionless, holding on to her desk for support. Her eyes were glued to Goldman. The man peered into the office and immediately vomited. The secretary was barely able to dial 911.

* * *

JIM BOWLED A 215 followed by a 126. He muttered something under his breath and decided he'd had enough of that. He paid for the bowling, went into the lounge, sat down, and began looking through the book. He noticed that the random numbers and letters seemed to be divided into a page or two, followed by a blank page and then another couple of pages of numbers, letters, delta signs, small triangles, another blank page, and the same format again. The only thing Jim could determine was that whatever the coded numbers meant, there were 24 distinct groupings. Other than that, the book made no sense whatever.

At 12:15, the bulletin came over the TV in the bowling center lounge. The local news anchor, obviously caught unprepared, began, "We interrupt our regularly scheduled program for this special bulletin. Word has just reached us that there has been an apparent shooting at the law offices of Goldman and Steinmetz in downtown Santa Barbara. Harry Long is on the scene now. Harry, can you hear me?"

"Yes, Frank, I can hear you," he answered as his picture appeared on the screen.

"Harry, can you tell us what has happened?"

"Well, Frank, details are still coming in, but according to Mr. Goldman, one of the general partners, someone entered Mr. Steinmetz's office about 40 minutes ago and shot both him and a second man in his office. The other man, I'm told by Mr. Goldman, is a nephew, a David Steinmetz. I cannot confirm this, however."

"Harry, can you confirm if the men are dead or alive?"

"No, not at just a minute. Ah … yes … Frank, it seems both men are dead."

"Are there any details as to why the men were shot? Is there any information regarding any suspect?"

"Not that I'm aware of, Frank. I was told a few minutes ago that according to one of the police officers, an Asian female was seen by a custodian running from the building. I don't know if this person is a suspect or not. The police, however, are searching the area now. Other officers are cordoning off the area at this time, and in fact, we are being asked to leave the area at once."

"Frank, you said that the police are searching the area now. Are they looking for the Asian woman?"

"Well, I'm not sure, but I would assume that is precisely who they're looking for. The building is closed off, and perhaps there are one or more suspects still inside —"

Jim was stunned. He immediately wanted to get back to the Baron and get the hell out of there. He waited nearly 15 minutes for a cab and headed for the airport. His mind was reeling. He paid the cabby and rushed quickly toward the Baron. He saw it before he stepped onto the wing. The door lock had been ripped open, and Jim Riley was not surprised. He had subconsciously expected it. He opened the cabin door and saw the clothes strewn everywhere.

"Oh my God! The luggage. Someone is looking for that damned book!"

He knew he'd better not leave now. He went to the flight office and called the Santa Barbara police. They were there in three minutes. Jim knew they would treat him as a suspect, but he was able to explain what his business was with David Steinmetz. That is, with the exception of the book. The police removed all the clothing and took all the ID information they needed from Jim. One of the detectives, a sergeant Lowe, gave him a business card and told him that they would be in touch if they needed him.

Jim Riley was an emotional wreck by the time he returned to Modesto. Oliver already knew about the shooting and assured Jim that he would answer any questions the police might ask. Jim was not contacted again.

He had tried many times to put the whole sickening episode behind him, but it was not possible. It would not leave his mind. He resented being caught up in events that didn't concern him and that he didn't care about, but fate had sucked him in and he knew this was not likely to be the end of it.

THREE

JIM SLIPPED ON HIS BIRKENSTOCKS, opened the refrigerator, grabbed the Minute Maid carton, and took a huge gulp, sloshing it in his mouth before swallowing.

What a hell of a night, he thought. He, Bill Talbot, and Ron George — the old-timers at the flight school — had lately spent Monday nights at the 94th Aero Squadron, watching *Monday Night Football* and drinking beer. This made Tuesday mornings pure hell. The thought of 360-degree turns and stalls made him instantly nauseated.

Remember, 12 hours between bottle and throttle, he thought to himself. He had learned it in ground school and all the instructors and students recited it at one time or another. Why he couldn't follow it he didn't know, except perhaps that becoming an aeronautical genius through beer talk was worth the price. He took the last piece of stale bread and tossed it into the toaster, picked up the phone, and dialed the flight school office.

"Aero One Flight Training," came the sweet voice at the other end. "This is Nancy. How may I help you?"

Jim immediately thought of several options, but said, "Hi, Nancy, this is Riley. Any other lesson for today besides Mary Rison?"

"Ah, let me see. Yes, you have Howard Davies at 11:30 and Donny Friend at 2:00."

"Oh, jeez, not Donny Friend on Tuesday. This must be my day to die. Why me, Lord?" he said under his breath.

"Did I just hear a discouraging word?" Nancy asked.

"No, just doing my morning Bible recitation. Has Mary Rison called in yet?"

"No, Jimmy, but she'll be here all right. She has the hots for you, or can't you tell?"

"Anyway, enough of this small talk," Jim said. "Why don't you close the office and we'll go to Reno for a couple of days?"

"This sounds like sexual harassment to me," she chuckled. "I'll talk to my lawyer and get back to you. Bye bye."

He hung up the phone and opened the refrigerator again. Peanut butter was the only edible substance left. He spread some on his toast, took a bite, and longed for one swallow of milk. Sirens were screaming to a stop in front of his apartment building. He stepped to the window and looked down. Apparently the commotion was coming from the Chinese apartment house across the street. He called it the "Chinese apartments" because the roof corners turned up like an oriental lantern. He had never seen anyone but Asians going in or out.

"Damn! I must have heard real shots."

Then he saw it — a white Mercedes limo with the unmistakable gold-crested rear door swing around the corner. There was no doubt about it: it was Oliver Windom's limo. He would know that car anywhere.

Why would Oliver Windom be outside my apartment building at 7:00 in the morning? Why would he be in San Jose at all? His mind was racing, and nothing made sense.

Why would old man Windom know or care where I live? What the hell is going on? Why all the cops? Something is really wrong here. It's like one of those dreams where the wrong people are in the wrong places, he thought wildly, trying to piece this idiotic puzzle together in his mind.

* * *

THEY MOVED RAPIDLY FROM ROOM TO ROOM. Jim could see one uniformed policeman and two guys in suits that he assumed were detectives.

The apartment was directly across from his on the third floor. One of the suits picked up the phone and was talking to someone with his hands waving, apparently describing the scene. Shortly, he hung up the phone and both suits were looking down at the floor. Jim guessed they were in the bedroom. The uniformed cop stood at the door in what looked like the living room.

He had met the young Asian couple who had recently moved into the unit. Karen Chen worked at a nearby deli.

Jim talked to her at the deli on a few occasions, and other than a small birthmark just below her right eye, she was quite attractive. The mark was shaped like an open boxing glove, quite faint and not particularly distracting. Louie Chen seemed to be the Asian version of a nerd, with thick glasses and a suit pocket full of pens and pencils. Jim guessed he probably worked in the Silicon Valley somewhere in the computer industry. He had never asked; he didn't really care.

Even though the limo stuck out like a sore thumb, apparently all the attention of the half-dozen onlookers was directed at the apartment house. No one noticed the Mercedes limo moving slowly south on El Camino Boulevard, before running the stop light at the first intersection and then quickly speeding away.

"Damn! What in the —?"

Jim jumped when the phone rang. He had the receiver in hand before the second ring.

"Hello, this is Jim Riley."

"Hi, Daddy. Happy birthday."

"Well, thank you, sweetheart. How's my best girl?"

"Fine."

"How come you're up so early?"

"I wanted to wish you happy birthday before you leave for work. Also, Mommy wants to talk to you. Are you coming home next week? I'm in a play at school. I'm going to be an Indian princess. I hope you can come and see it."

"Oh, honey, I can't … I'm sorry. Maybe Mommy can videotape it and you can send it to me for a birthday present."

"Okay. Bye, Daddy. Here's Mommy."

"Bye, Julie, I love you."

"I love you too."

"Jim?"

"Hi, Shirl. I guess you're wondering about the check, huh?"

"Yes, among other things. I really need the money, Jim. I had to buy material for Julie's costume and she needed another outfit for school. Since you didn't send money last month, I had to borrow a hundred from Dad. I don't like to do that. I don't need anymore 'I told you so's.'"

"Shirley, you know we've been through this a hundred times. I don't have a steady paycheck anymore. I get paid when I instruct students. I should be able to send you $250 on Saturday. I don't know what else to do."

"I know, Jimmy, I don't mean to be the mean bitch. I know you're doing the best you can. Anyway, happy birthday! Uh, Jim?"

"Huh?"

"I've met someone."

"Anyone I know?"

"No. He's from Scottsdale. I've been seeing him for about three weeks. I know it's not very long, but I really like him, Jim, and I think he feels the same way. He and Julie really hit it off."

Jim was silent for a moment, feeling a rock in the pit of his stomach. It was a mixture of relief and a sense of loss. He knew this day would come and he would be happy for Shirley, but he could not imagine some other man being a father to Julie.

"That's great, Shirl. I hope everything works out. Tell Julie I'll come the first chance I get. I really feel bad about the play."

"She understands, Jimmy. She has somehow accepted things the way they are, and aside from missing her daddy, she's fine. Anyway, I'll let you go now. Have a happy birthday, and I really mean that."

"I know you do, Shirley. I'll talk to you next week. Bye."

* * *

HE TURNED ON THE TV and began surfing through the channels, hoping to see or hear something about what was going on. Nothing. He turned up the sound and headed for the shower. The cool water felt good on his neck and back. Jim Riley never seemed to get a mean hangover with the splitting headache. He always felt queasiness in his stomach, and on more than one occasion, he had thrown up. That seemed to be the end of it.

All this business across the street brought back the David Steinmetz incident in Santa Barbara.

"Why hasn't 'Ellis' called?" he wondered. He stepped out of the shower, quickly brushed his teeth, skipped the shave, and slipped on a clean pair of Levi's and his favorite long-sleeved Gant shirt. He hurriedly put on a pair of old loafers and headed for the door. He hesitated, snapped his fingers, and returned to switch on his answering machine. There was still plenty of time. He couldn't understand why he was in such a hurry all of a sudden, other than feeling an urgent desire to get out of the apartment and get his mind on something other than gunshots, David Steinmetz, codebooks, limos, and peanut butter on stale toast.

The air was crisp and damp, and he could smell the distinct odor of roasting coffee beans from the MJB plant up the peninsula as he pulled onto the 101 and headed north for San Carlos Airport. The traffic was light going south and bumper-to-bumper heading north to San Francisco. He turned on the radio and listened to Frank and Mike's morning show.

Mary Rison was already at the flight school and had completed the preflight by the time Jim arrived. This was her routine, and he never worried about having to check her out on the preflight. She did it by the book and never missed a rivet. He knew it wouldn't be long before she qualified for her license, and he often wished to drag it out as long as possible. Most of the time, he had her run through a list of maneuvers and would only observe with casual interest. He was definitely going to miss her.

Jim completed some necessary paperwork. He was aware that Mary Rison was looking at him. He smiled to himself and gloated a bit knowing she had a schoolgirl crush (or so he thought).

"Okay, Mary, I guess we can do it. Are you ready?"

"Jim, I'm always ready." She smiled and headed out the door to the flight line.

Mary cranked up the 152, called ground control, and in few minutes, they were at the end of 3lR and ready for takeoff. She noticed that Jim had very little to say, and so for the moment, she said nothing. Control tower cleared her for takeoff, and soon she was at 1,500 feet over the Leslie salt flats. Without a word from Jim, she did a couple of 360-degree turns, a few takeoff and landing stalls, and circled back toward the airport for some touch-and-go landings.

"Jim?"

"Yeah."

"You're awfully quiet. Are you okay?"

"Yeah, I'm fine. I just didn't get off to a good start this morning. I have a few things on my mind."

"Do you want to talk about it? I'm a good listener."

"Mary, that's an understatement coming from you. Anyway, thanks for your interest. I'm okay."

"Why is it that men never want to talk about things that are bothering them? If the subject is football or something macho, you can't shut 'em up. Jim, I'm very interested in things that you think about, or can't you tell?"

"I'm sorry, Mary, and yes, I can tell that you care what I'm feeling or thinking about and I am truly flattered, believe me. I always look forward to seeing you, and not just because of flying lessons. You're a nice person to be around."

"Well, that's a first. I didn't think you knew I was alive outside of an airplane. I thought I might have to hit you over the head with a two-by-four to get your attention."

"Look, if things were different," Jim said, "and we were a little closer to the same age, I certainly would have made a move on you by now."

"What the hell is this 'age' stuff? Jim, wake up and smell the roses. I really resent that. I'm not a high school girl, you know!"

"See, we've barely started talking and already we're having a fight. I guess maybe that's why men don't talk more. We always end up putting our foot in our mouths."

Mary reached over and punched him lightly on the shoulder and smiled.

"You bastard, do you want me going through life a scorned woman?" she muttered in a shaky Katherine Hepburn imitation. "I'm not trying to get you into bed. I just want you to show a little interest. I'm not exactly ignored by guys, you know. That is, except for you."

"Okay, Mary, you got me. Will you marry me?"

"Well, we're making progress. No, but I'll buy dinner tonight at the Elephant Bar."

"Hey, wait a minute, I'm just kidding around."

"Jim Riley, I am very honorably asking you for a very honorable date at a very nice restaurant. If you refuse me, I shall plow the runway with this honorable airplane. Dinner or Kamikaze? Your call."

"Jeez, now I know what it means to get an offer you can't refuse. Well, Miss, excuse me, *Ms.* Rison, since you put it that way, I'd be delighted. Now will you land this thing before I make another error in judgment and open my mouth again?"

Mary taxied up to the tie-down, shut the engine off, and before Jim could loosen his seatbelt, she reached over and pecked him on the lips. Her mouth was warm and soft, and Jim Riley felt the sudden and distinct sensation that he would taste her again.

"I'll meet you at the Redwood City Elephant Bar at 7:30," she called back as she walked toward the parking lot.

"Whew!" was all that Jim Riley could conjure up. He could feel his pulse racing as he walked into the office.

Jim sat at a table at the far end of the office and made a few notes in Mary's file, put it away, and took out Howard Davies' folder. He sat and stared at it, but could not get his mind off of what had just happened. Obviously Nancy noticed Jim's preoccupation and called to him.

"Jim, are you in a trance? You're going to burn a hole in that folder with your eyeballs. Your face is kinda red too. What did Mary Rison do to you?"

Damn, he thought. *How do women always know everything? There must be some secret universal telepathy that men don't know about. Women's intuition, my ass; they just communicate to each other though the air,* he concluded.

"No, I'm just getting ready for Mr. Davies."

"Uh huh," said Nancy.

Howard Davies was on time for his lesson. They were back at the ramp by 12:20. Jim was feeling a little better by now. Howard always had a new joke or two to liven things up a little, but mostly to settle himself down. Jim was often surprised at the man's quick reflexes and soft touch on the controls for someone his age. He had no doubt that Howard Davies would become a good and safe pilot. He was cautious and thorough and never attempted any maneuver beyond his skill level. Jim liked the man and wished that more of his students paid as much attention to details.

He set up Howard's next appointment, jumped into the Camaro, and headed for the 94th Aero Squadron. He sat at the bar and ordered a tuna sandwich and iced tea. He wanted a cold beer but decided against it.

He finished his sandwich as *Days of Our Lives* was winding down on the TV set over the bar. He stared at the screen but was unaware of a single word of dialogue. His mind wandered over all the events of the past several months, and he could not stop thinking about David Steinmetz and that damn Windom limo in front of his apartment this morning. That bothered him more than the mess going on at the Chinese apartments.

And what about this 'Ellis' person? he thought to himself. *Christ, it's been four months and nothing.*

Jim wondered if the guy could even find him, and if he did, how would he know this was the right person? He was certain he didn't want to give the book to the wrong people, especially after Steinmetz had scared the hell out of him with the whole idea of life and death — which he had immediately discovered was not idle talk. David Steinmetz had punctuated that false notion with his own life.

Well, all I can do is wait, but I'm going to be damn sure I know what's go-

ing on before I give that book to anyone! he thought to himself.

He paid his check, waved to a couple guys near the door, and headed back to the flight school office to clean up some final paperwork before the infamous Donny Friend showed up for "destruction derby."

This life is so exciting, I think I'm going to puke, he was thinking to himself as Donny Friend blew through the door and flew the final three feet to his chair next to Jim.

"Hi, Jimbo! You ready for *Top Gun*?"

"Um hum, I wish I had one," Jim mumbled under his breath.

"Okay, let's hit the wild blue yonder, cowboy!"

"Lord, save me," Jim answered, a bit louder this time.

Donny did a perfect preflight, and Jim Riley thought there might be hope for the world after all. The boy followed with a respectable takeoff and headed out over the salt flats. Jim always allowed a little extra altitude with Donny and asked him to climb to 3,000 feet.

"Okay, Donny, let's try a power-on stall. Do you remember how to set it up?" Jim asked.

"I think so; here goes nothing," Donny answered with a little less arrogance.

Donny pulled the power back to idle, and then held the nose slightly up to bleed off speed. At 65 knots, he hit full power and pulled the nose high and held it for the stall warning, ready for the nose to break over.

"Ball in the center, ball in the center!" Jim admonished.

Donny looked at the ball, but held full left rudder. The 152 broke sharply with the left wingtip dipping, and immediately the plane was in a hard left spin.

"Cut the power!" Jim yelled. "Opposite rudder!"

Donny responded quickly. The airspeed showed only 45 knots, but they were plunging toward the ground almost straight down. Donny hit the right rudder and held it. The 152 stopped rotating to the left and began spinning to the right. Donny froze.

"Hands off. Let go, damn it let go!" Jim yelled. The altimeter was tumbling past 1,500 feet, and Donny Friend held tight!

"Donny! For God's sake, let go!"

It was apparent the young man was frozen in panic, totally unable to move or respond. By reflex alone, Jim reached over and hit Donny hard across the nose with the back of his hand. Donny recoiled into what looked like a fetal position as the blood began to trickle from his nose. Almost effortlessly, Jim stopped the spin, entered a shallow dive, and leveled off at 750 feet. The pungent smell in the cabin told the whole story.

Jim immediately did a 180 and landed as soon as he received clearance. Donny sat looking straight ahead with hands in his lap and feet flat on the floor, with tears coming down his cheeks and a small blood trail from his nostril to his lip.

"Look, Donny," Jim said with as much compassion as he could muster, "I'm sorry I had to do that, but when you think about it, you'll be glad I did. There's no disgrace for cross controlling. Most students do it at one time or another. How about if we try that maneuver again next time, only we'll talk through it first?" Jim taxied up to the flight school parking area and turned the engine off.

Donny Friend said nothing. He opened the door, left his materials, walked to the parking lot, got into his car, and drove away. Jim knew he would not see Donny again. He walked into the office and told Nancy he would see her tomorrow and left for his apartment, totally exhausted.

FOUR

THE TRAFFIC WAS LIGHT and Jim was home by four. It had started to drizzle and the apartment was cold. He kicked on the heat and hit the rewind button on the answering machine. It took several seconds for the tape to rewind; he figured it was probably Shirley with some minor tragedy or other.

"Hello, Mister Riley, my name is Ellis. I know you've been expecting me to call. I'm sure you have a world of questions, the least of which is how I was able to locate you. I'll explain all of that when we meet and answer all of your questions."

"Damn!" Jim muttered as the tape continued to the next message.

"Hi, Jim," came Mary's voice. "Can we make it at eight o'clock? My dad is coming into San Francisco Airport and I need to spend a half hour or so with him. I'll explain later. I changed the reservation at the Elephant Bar. Bye!"

"Jim, this is Ellis again. Please meet me on Saturday at 10:30 in the morning just inside the entrance to Marine World in Vallejo. Stay by the gate. It's very important that you be there and bring the ah … *item* … with you. Don't worry, I'll recognize you."

"Finally, the infamous Ellis shows up," Jim said aloud. "Now I can get that damn book out of my life."

Suddenly a sinking feeling hit the pit of his stomach.

How do I know this guy is the real Ellis? he thought. *If he can find me, he … Oh, what the hell, who else would know I have the book? Then again, who does know I have the book? How does he know what I look like? Jesus H. Christ! What did I get myself into?*

Jim reached down to get a pencil from the desk drawer beneath the phone and noticed it was partially opened. Jim Riley was not a neat person, but he never left a door or drawer opened. If it wasn't a compulsion, it was close to it. He had not opened that drawer in more than a week.

He quickly ran to the bedroom and looked in his overnight bag in the closet. The safe-deposit key was still there in a small pocket. He returned to the front door to see if there was any evidence of a break-in. Nothing!

He turned on the television as Oprah was winding down her show, something about battered women killing their husbands or boyfriends. It reminded him of tuning in to a soap opera after skipping two weeks: he hadn't missed a thing.

After an interminable string of commercials, the local anchorwoman came on. "Channel Four has been following a bizarre shooting story in North San Jose throughout the day, and this is our lead story on the early news."

"Laurie," chimed in her co-anchor, "without a doubt, this has to be one of the strangest homicides I have seen in a long time, that is, if it is indeed homicide. All we can say at this time is that there are two people dead, apparently a husband and wife. What police have told us is that the victims are of Asian descent."

"Yes, John, and what makes this case somewhat bizarre is that both victims were found shot to death with handguns in their possession or nearby. We asked Detective Sergeant Carl Ormsby of the San Jose Police Department what the preliminary investigation shows."

"At approximately 6:45 this morning, we were summoned to an apartment house on North El Camino Real," came the stern Ormsby's statement on the screen. "Residents had reported hearing gunshots fired, four to be exact. Our men arrived on the scene around seven o'clock and were directed to an apartment on the third floor. We were not able to get a response from inside the apartment, and so we forced our way in. There we found the victims dead in the bedroom unit."

"Pardon me for interrupting, Detective Ormsby, but our sources indicated that two handguns were found on or near the bodies. Can you comment on that for our viewers?"

"Yes, John, there were two guns found, both of which had been fired."

"Detective Ormsby, this is Laurie Santos. From this information, are we to assume that these two people somehow shot each other?"

"Well, I would not assume anything, but yes, that is a possibility."

"But it is our understanding that four shots were fired. How is that possible?"

"Well, the male victim had what looks like two wounds to the stomach and one in the left shoulder, and the female has a single entrance wound to the forehead."

"Then it's quite possible that the woman shot the male victim and he then was able to fire a shot at her before —"

"Yes, Laurie, that's quite possible, but it's too early to speculate. Sometimes the obvious can be very misleading."

"Detective Ormsby, can you tell us anything else at this time about who these people were? Were they U.S. citizens?"

"I'm sorry, I cannot comment on that."

"Detective Ormsby, one last question. Does there seem to be any connection between today's event and any other shootings in the Bay Area?"

"I really have no further comments."

The TV cameraman was left with a shot of the police detective walking away.

Jim Riley felt a sudden need to check another possible connection. Maybe Santa Barbara … maybe. He thumbed through his wallet for the business card from Sergeant Donald Lowe, Santa Barbara Police. He dialed the number.

"Santa Barbara Police."

"Yes, is Sergeant Lowe on duty please?"

"I think he might have left; just a minute."

"Lowe. Can I help you?"

"Yes, Sergeant Lowe. My name is Jim Riley. I was the pilot you questioned at the airport when a Mr. David Steinmetz was killed."

"Yes?"

"Do you remember me?"

"Yes, I remember you. What can I do for you?"

"Did you ever find the Asian woman you were looking for?"

There was a momentary pause. "Who wants to know?" asked Lowe.

"Well, there was an Asian woman killed near my apartment building this morning, and I was wondering if she might fit the description of the woman you were looking for."

"Well, it sounds to me like people get themselves killed around you."

"Sergeant, please. If you haven't found her, it's possible it could be the same person. Can you tell me what she looked like?"

"Mr. Riley, where are you?"

"I'm in San Jose, Northern California."

"Yeah. There was some indication that she was probably headed north, maybe to the Bay Area."

"Was there anything unusual about her appearance, a birthmark or anything?"

"No, not really. She was reported by the witness to have had a shiner on her right eye, but that would be cleared up by now."

"What about a reddish birthmark just below her right eye? It could have been mistaken for a black eye."

"Yes, I'm sure it could have. The witness had only a quick look at the woman and assumed she had a black eye. Mr. Riley, give me your telephone number. I may want to talk to you again."

Jim gave the officer his number and hung up the phone.

FIVE

MARY RISON WAS SITTING AT A WINDOW TABLE in the bar when Jim arrived just before eight. She had ordered a margarita and was busy looking out at the planes' lights as they descended into San Francisco Airport.

Jim had never seen her dressed up and could not believe what a striking woman she really was. She could have easily passed for a model. She was wearing a short, tight black dress that followed each and every curve, matching heels and dollar-sized, gold-caning loops. She wore no other jewelry. He noticed that her hair seemed a darker red, almost auburn in the evening light. Her simple elegance caused Jim to draw in a deep breath as he approached the table. He was glad he had thought to wear a sport coat, which for Jim Riley was a real sacrifice; however, wearing a tie would have been beyond the call of duty.

"Hi, Mary."

"Hello. Are you hungry?"

"Yeah, I am. You really look great."

"Thank you, sir, and so do you."

They decided to have dinner in the bar. Mary ordered the blackened swordfish and Jim ordered the New York steak.

"How'd you happen to be meeting your father in the airport?"

"Oh, we do this all the time. He is West Coast sales manager for a San Diego chemical company, and he passes through San Francisco once or twice a month. Whenever he has a layover, he calls me and we try to meet, usually for an hour or so."

"He must be doing pretty well to send a daughter to Stanford and pay for flying lessons at the same time."

"Well, the flying lessons are for my graduation present. I'm just getting a head start. Besides, my mom helps a little. She's an attorney in San Diego."

"Why are you learning to fly? How does that fit in with anything else you're doing?"

"Well, both my parents fly. We have half interest in a Mooney. I've always liked to fly and decided to get my license. That's all. It's no biggie."

"Maybe that's why all this flight training is so easy for you. Did you help your daddy fly?" Jim asked with pursed lips.

"As a matter of fact, I did, smart ass! I learned to do a barrel roll when I was 11. My dad taught me a few instrument maneuvers under the hood; I guess when I was about 14. I watched my dad do an Emelman turn, but he wouldn't let me try it. I think I could have done it."

"And?" asked Jim.

"And what?"

"What else am I not going to have to teach you?"

"Well, I learned to file flight plans. Aeronautical charts were a piece of cake. I could plug in Omni coordinances, track by beacon or fly dead reckoning. Which would you like?" she beamed.

"Now who's the smart ass?" Jim responded with a wrinkled nose. *She truly is fun to be with,* he thought, *and very sexy besides.*

"Are you going to be a lawyer too?" Jim asked.

"No way! I'm majoring in economics with a minor in history."

"Are you planning to teach?"

"No, I'm thinking more of government work of some kind. I'm not really sure, to tell the truth. What about you? Are you planning to continue instructing?"

"Hell, no! Not if I can help it. I hope to get back into corporate flying. Right now, there isn't anything out there, but I'm looking."

In the next 40 minutes, Jim Riley had revealed even more about himself than he had to David Steinmetz. Mary seemed intent on every word, and on more than one occasion, rested her hand on his. He liked it. He felt relaxed and comfortable with her and did not fail to notice her slight cleavage. She was quite aware that he noticed. Her smiles at those moments caused his face to flush, and he tried not to be so obvious.

Mary took the check from the waitress, who registered a slight surprise and immediately glanced at Jim Riley. Mary smiled and winked at Jim.

"She's probably wondering if I'm buying a night in the sack!" Mary whispered to Jim as the waitress walked away. "Come to think of it, that's not a bad idea," she said, jabbing Jim lightly with her elbow and raising her eyebrow.

"I thought you said you weren't trying to get me into bed." Jim smiled.

"Okay, so I lied."

As they walked down the stairs, Mary put her hand under his arm. They walked to her car.

"Jim?"

"Yeah?"

"I'm really not kidding. It isn't a bad idea. Can we go to your place? I want to spend the night with you."

"I'm not so sure this is a good idea. I've had a lot of things on my mind lately and I just don't know if I'm ready for this."

"Jim!"

"No, Mary, hear me out. I still have a problem with our age difference. I know it doesn't bother you, but it does me, and I haven't sorted it out yet. I care more about you than I have a right to and I don't know where it's going to lead."

"I haven't said one damn thing about any commitment. I haven't asked you for anything. I like you a lot and I want to make love to you. Now are you going to pass up the best night of your life, or shall we shut up and go to your place?"

Jim could not resist the desire to take her in his arms. Nor did he. The kiss was long, and Mary's lips were as soft and sweet as he had imagined. She could feel him beginning to rise to the occasion, and she responded with some slight moves of her own.

"Follow me," Jim whispered, finding it difficult to breathe.

"Okay," Mary answered. For a moment, their eyes met. She reached up and closed her mouth on his lower lip, turned and got into her VW Rabbit. Jim couldn't resist a chuckle as he read the word *Rabbit;* it was precisely how he felt.

Jim fumbled with the apartment key for a moment, opened the door, and led her inside. He closed the door and turned. Mary Rison's arms were around his neck. This time the kiss was not long and slow. The heat of their bodies and emotions was intense. His hands were on her breasts. She fumbled with the buttons on his shirt and she could feel that his manhood was in full glory.

"Jim, Jim," she repeated, as she pulled away. He was almost over the edge.

"What?" he answered, sounding slightly irritated.

"I want this to be a night that you can't forget."

"Are you kidding?"

"No, Jim. Indulge me, please." She led him to the desk chair and turned it around.

"Just sit here for a minute. I'll be right back. Where's the bathroom?"

With hardly an ounce of strength, he limply raised his arm in the direction of the bathroom. She was back in little more than a minute. He could see by the light coming through the window that she had removed her panty hose and shoes.

She slowly walked toward Jim to where he could see her clearly in the light. She began to slide her dress up over her hips and gently over her head in one rhythmic motion, revealing her smooth and perfect body. His eyes ran slowly from her head down to her bra, which supported the most beautifully shaped breasts he had ever seen. At that moment, she released them from their lacy corral. Jim's passion could stand very little more. He felt he would explode at any moment. She cupped them in her hands and touched each nipple gently. Then her hands began a downward movement. Jim followed with his eyes. The beauty below, protected by the sheerest of material, was overwhelming. He could stand no more. Jim reached his hands out to her and pulled her to him. She moved her legs apart over his and rested on his lap. Because of his condition, it both hurt a little and made him want to burst at the seams.

He gently picked her up and carried her to the bedroom. She was right. He was not likely to forget this night — not now, not ever.

Jim awoke at 6:15 a.m. to the sound of the shower running. He slipped on his shorts and walked to the bathroom. The door was open, and Mary's silhouette warmed his heart once again. He opened the shower door.

"Got room for one more?"

"Why, of course, sir. Be my guest."

Together, they added an exclamation point to the night of Jim's life. He felt as virile as a teenager. Mary was everything he had ever fantasized. He couldn't remember being happier. He had found a lover and a friend.

*　*　*

AT BREAKFAST, JIM TOLD HER all about the codebook, David Steinmetz, and "Ellis." He told about his meeting coming up on Saturday.

"Mary, I wonder if you could do something for me?"

"Sure, I'll try. What do you want me to do?"

"Would you consider going out to Marine World around 10:00 on Saturday with your camera? I want you to pretend you don't know me and take some pictures of this guy 'Ellis.'

"Also, I want you to hang on to the codebook for me. If I don't wave to you, don't even acknowledge me. I don't know why, but I may not be able to trust this guy. The way things seem to be happening, I gotta tell you; I'm a little bit scared. Just stay far enough away from me that no one can possibly notice you anywhere near me."

"Sure, no biggie. I'll have to skip an 11:00 seminar. It's a dumb course anyway. All the prof does is speak in a monotone and try to look up my dress. What a creep!"

"Mary, this is pretty heavy stuff. There really could be some danger."

"I know, Jim. This has been bothering you for a long time, hasn't it?"

"Yes, a lot"

"Don't worry, you'll give the guy the book and that will be the end of it."

"Jeez, I hope so."

"Gotta go, Jim. My roommate will be having 10 fits. Oh, by the way, in case you think I make a habit of sleeping around, I want you to know the only guy I ever made it with was my high school boyfriend. We met in our senior year and dated for a year and a half."

"Who's asking?" he smiled.

"Probably the same guy who's been wondering all night! See ya, lover! I'll be there Saturday. Mum's the word."

Jim watched her drive away. She waved as she pulled onto the street. He waved back, got into his Camaro, and headed for the San Jose airport. Today was Wednesday and he thought he would pick up the book on Friday from the safe-deposit box.

* * *

JIM FELT A SICKENING LIGHTHEADEDNESS as he looked in the box.

The codebook was gone.

Oh, Christ! What do I tell Ellis? he thought.

"Holy crap! I'm not only scared, but I'm starting to get pissed!" he muttered to himself as he slammed the box shut. "It's time to get some answers. I'm gonna nail that Ellis to the cross if he doesn't have some good reasons for all this scary shit!" he concluded.

Jim immediately went to the nearest bank teller. "Would you please get the manager here now?"

Without hesitation, the teller scurried over to a nearby desk. She muttered to the person at the desk and the lady motioned Riley to her.

"May I help you?" she asked.

"Lady, can you tell me how someone other than myself can get into my safe-deposit box?"

"Oh, that's not possible, sir. As you know, we have one key and you have the other. It takes one of our tellers along with you to gain entry," she said.

"Yeah, I know the routine. How come I wasn't present when it was opened?" asked Riley.

"Sir, I'm sure you are mistaken. That kind of thing simply can't happen."

"Well, lady, it can and it did. Now I want to know who opened my safe-deposit box!"

"Well, Mr. ...?"

"Riley, James Riley." He had been longing to do this James Bond imitation for some time. It wasn't the time or place, but he might not get another chance.

She didn't appreciate his attempt at being funny. "Well, Mr. Riley," she said with slight disgust, "let's check the sign-in register." The manager walked to the tellers' counter and opened what appeared to be a logbook. "Do you have any idea when this might have taken place, Mr. Riley?"

"In the last few days, I'm sure."

"Oh, my goodness!" the lady remarked.

"What's the matter?" Jim asked

"Mr. Riley. I'm terribly embarrassed. It appears that a Jane Doe has signed into the log. I cannot imagine how such a thing could happen."

"Well, unless you can produce Jane Doe, I'd say your bank is in a heap of crap!" Jim concluded. "Anyhow, I'll have to deal with this later." He stormed out of the bank.

SIX

JIM COULD SEE MARY RISON standing with her back to him as he walked through the gate. She appeared to be the tourist with her camera over her shoulder, eating a bag of popcorn. She made one full circle, and appeared not to see him.

What an actress, Jim thought to himself. *She really likes this. I only wish she understood how serious it was.* Above all, he did not want anything to happen to her.

He seemed to come from nowhere; the frail little man in his mid-seventies nudged Jim on the elbow.

"Mr. Riley, thank you for coming on such short notice," Ellis said with what appeared to be a Southern accent. Jim turned quickly to face the man.

"I'm sorry ... you startled me," Jim responded. "I didn't see you come in the gate." Ellis was not at all what Jim had expected. From the sound of his voice on the answering machine, Jim had imagined a very tall man with beady eyes in a well-tailored, three-piece suit, much like Hollywood's version of Eliot Ness. Instead, he found himself looking down at a gentle man in his mid-seventies — though he looked much younger — with soft blue eyes and a slightly balding head of salt-and-pepper hair. He was wearing a St. Louis Cardinals jacket, faded Levi's, and tennis shoes.

Ellis peered directly into Jim's eyes, and Jim had the feeling the man was looking right into his soul. Jim Riley, in turn, could sense wisdom and deep secrets behind the man's gaze. Jim felt an immediate bond with him, and thought to himself that the man must be a marvelous interrogator. It would be almost impossible to lie to those probing eyes.

"I've been here for some time, Mr. Riley. I much prefer to see the other guy show up. I'm seldom surprised that way. And by the way, your young lady friend is quite good, you know. She seems to be enjoying her role."

"But how did you know —"

"Mr. Riley, when you've been hiding in the shadows as long as I have, you've seen it all. You sense things, and most of all you observe. People are predictable, and quite honestly, I would have been disappointed had you walked straight in here trusting me just because I said you should. You also telegraph your punches. You've glanced in the direction of your young lady twice since we've been standing here. A word of advice, Mr. Riley: beware of using an accomplice you care about personally. A moment of concern can be deadly."

"Mr. Ellis, I appreciate the advice, but I hardly see how it concerns me."

"Yes, of course, you're right, Mr. Riley. Please forgive me. I tend to be somewhat instructive with people, and it smacks of rudeness. And now, may I have the pleasure of meeting your young friend?"

Jim motioned for Mary to come join them, but she pretended not to notice, playing the game to the hilt. Again, Jim motioned to her and softly called her name.

"Come on over, Mary; he knows we're in cahoots."

Mary cautiously approached Ellis and Jim. She was glaring at Jim, suggesting that perhaps he had lost his marbles. She was also a bit disappointed that her acting career had been cut short. She said nothing.

"Mary," Jim began, "this is Mr. Ellis. Mr. Ellis, Mary Rison."

"I'm very pleased to meet you, Miss Rison. Ah, perhaps I should begin by telling you that my name is not Ellis; it's Rolly Hunter."

"What's with the fictitious name?" Jim asked.

"I will explain all that later. Right now, I'm interested in obtaining the item in question. I assume you have brought it with you?"

"Well, Mr. Ellis, er, Mr. Hunter, I'm afraid we have a little problem."

Hunter's eyes narrowed as he stared at Jim. Both men appeared instantly uneasy as Jim tried to assess the danger by telling the man what he obviously did not want to hear.

"I went to my safe-deposit box on Friday and the book was not there."

Hunter's eyes did not move.

"I'm not sure, but I think my apartment had also been broken into. The key was not taken, so I don't know how anyone could have opened the safe-deposit box."

"Unless they knew that you had a box, suspected what it contained, somehow made a copy of your key, and had access to the vault," Hunter replied. "A lot of unlikely ifs, should you ask me. Mr. Riley, are you sure?"

"Now wait just a damned minute, Hunter. What reason would I have for doing anything with the friggin' book except to get it out of my sight? I have no idea what it is! I think I've almost been killed because of it! I was asked by someone I hardly knew to give it to someone I've never met, who gives me a different name, and what's more, I have no clue at all as to who you are or why David Steinmetz was killed because of the stupid book! Now I have the feeling that you're looking at me as though I'm some kind of idiot! I'm sorry, Mr. Hunter, but I'm starting to get a little pissed off."

Hunter continued his stare for a moment. "Yes, yes, Mr. Riley, I must apologize. It has been a long, long road to this point, since 1968 to be exact, and I must admit, I still have a long way to go. But I owe you some explanation, obviously. I'll tell you this for now. It is quite possible that someone has tried to take your life, and you are still in much danger."

"What the hell is the book all about, Mr. Hunter, that people can get killed over the damned thing?"

"Jim — may I call you Jim?" Riley nodded. "Call me Rolly. You, too, Miss Rison. I will tell you, perhaps this evening, a rather bizarre and complicated story in which I have been a key player almost daily for nearly the past 40 years. You will most assuredly know why the book is so important and why your life is in danger. For right now, we need to break this off. I have one last question. Did you tell anyone about your safe-deposit box, either in or outside the bank?"

Jim told Hunter about Karen Chen, and what had happened at the apartment house across the street from his and how strange it was for Windom to drive by at the exact time of the shooting.

"Holy Jesus!" Hunter responded. "Now it makes sense, Jim. What took place at Chen's apartment was no accident. It is all directly related to your having had the book. I'll explain this evening. We must meet right away. I'm at the Radisson on 101 right near your place, room 702. Be there at 7:30. You might as well come too, Miss Rison. You may also be in danger. Oh, by the way, Jim, do you happen to have the safe-deposit key with you?"

"Yes."

"Good, do you mind if I take it? I'd like to see if there are any traces of wax on it. That will tell us if someone made an impression for a duplicate key. Your unlikely ifs may not be so unlikely after all."

Jim handed the key to Hunter, took Mary's arm, and hurried out the front exit to the parking lot. Hunter followed several minutes later. As he drove back to his hotel, his mind wandered over the past 30-plus years. He was getting close to the end of it, but now a new wrinkle appeared.

When does the payoff come? he wondered to himself.

SEVEN

ROLLY HUNTER WAS A STUDENT at City College in Kansas City in 1951. In February of 1952, at age 18, he decided to join the Army. While still in high school, Hunter had decided to major in foreign language and perhaps teach at the high school level. His emphasis would be in French and Italian.

He had taken Spanish and French in his junior and senior years, but really wanted to learn Italian. Since it was not offered, he studied on his own and was quite adept at picking up both the spoken and written language.

Hunter had considered seeking a deferment but decided against it. It would be easier to serve the time and get it over with. He could then get on with his life without future interruption. Later, however, he would find that events were to change the course of his life for good. Hunter reported to Fort Jackson, South Carolina, where he began 16 weeks of advanced infantry basic training. He had been told that Ft. Jackson was as tough as it gets.

Twenty-five-mile hikes were commonplace. With full packs, all 200 men followed the same routine: run a hundred yards, walk a hundred, and so on for the full 25. A full pack meant more than carrying an M-1 rifle. Rather, it was BAR's, bazookas, and mortars, and always at a gallop. He quickly learned to sleep during the entire 10 minutes of the hourly breaks, as did many of the others.

Hunter certainly didn't fall in love with the army, but there was something rewarding about being able to endure the constant harassment and aching body parts. This trainee kept his mouth shut, didn't volunteer for anything, and kept a low profile. Fortunately, Hunter had inherited a sense of humor from his father and actually found things to laugh about.

During the course of basic training, recruits were interviewed for officers' candidate school and other tech schools for which aptitude might be discovered. He took the battery of tests seriously and did his best. He knew his IQ was above average and perhaps he could get a better deal if he did well on the tests. He was right. Out of the 200 men in his company, six were singled out for schools. The remaining 194 were given two weeks' leave and handed orders to report to Camp Stollman at Pittsburg, California for immediate ship-out to Korea.

Hunter had some mixed feelings but tremendous emotional relief at being spared, for the present at least. He had been selected for the Counter-Intelligence School at Ft. Holabird, Maryland, in Dundalk, a suburb of Baltimore. Whatever it meant, he knew he had 12 weeks' reprieve. All students and instructors were cleared for top-secret status, and Hunter found the school to be interesting and challenging. He didn't like the part he anticipated was to follow, however. The training in counter-intelligence would surely mean a quick trip to Korea, where he would find himself in harm's way as an operative. He was amazed and even morbidly amused to find that the instruction included methods of torturing the enemy for information without leaving a mark on the victim.

In the years that followed, he had often chuckled as he remembered four methods in particular:

"Snap the bristles of a toothbrush against a man's arm many times and he will tell you anything you want to know," the instructor would say.

"The Chinese water torture is also a very effective device; just tie a man on his back and let one drop of water at a time hit his forehead, and it will drive him insane."

Hunter liked the water bucket and baton best. "Place an empty pail over the man's head, bang on it with a baton at irregular intervals, and the prisoner is sure to spill his guts."

The ultimate, however, was to kill a man without leaving a mark on him. Place a phone book against the side of his head and beat the man to death with a stick against the book.

"He will appear to have suffered a brain aneurysm," the instructor proudly hailed.

Hunter smiled broadly as he heard that one. He wondered what he would do if he didn't have a phone book handy and needed to kill someone.

There had been very little connection between classroom instruction and reality (and somehow, Hunter could not imagine himself in Korea — let alone behind enemy lines, though the entire class was reminded of it daily). Moreover, since the U.N. forces had been driven back to Pusan, there probably wouldn't be any enemy lines anyway. Nevertheless, he liked most of the instructors and found them to be bright, knowledgeable people. They were, in fact, the cream of the crop. Hunter had always been inspired by intelligent people, whatever the subject or occasion.

The school groups were treated rather liberally with weekend passes, and Hunter and a buddy or two liked to go out to Sparrow's Point, away from the bars and strip joints likely to be found on every corner in Baltimore and Dundalk. He had easily gotten his fill of that and preferred to get away. Sparrow's Point was the perfect place: quite rural, with small taverns and quiet houses as opposed to the row houses and clatter and clanging of Baltimore and Dundalk.

Bethlehem Steel was the reason for Sparrow's Point. The village was inhabited almost totally by Polish-Catholic families. The taverns were quiet, and family-style food was usually served on Friday and Saturday nights. Hunter loved the people, and they treated the GIs like royalty. Parents also looked for future sons-in-law. The place was lovely and rustic and a million miles from counter-intelligence school. Hunter never grew tired of being there.

Hunter had dated a woman named Maria Havlecek for several weeks, but he felt the parents (as well as Maria) were far too anxious to have him in their family. He began to make excuses for not having so many free weekends. Several weeks later, however, he ran into Maria and a girlfriend at one of the bars in Dundalk. He could see the pain in her face as she tried to make friendly conversation, but the tears began to trickle down her cheeks. She turned and left the bar. Hunter never returned to Sparrow's Point. He did not see Maria again.

* * *

HUNTER GRADUATED FROM CIC WITH HONORS (such as they were). A special-achievement ribbon and a handshake from the captain seemed to catch it. The GIs all fled the base for Baltimore and a wild weekend of celebration. Orders were to be cut and posted the following Monday morning. No one was curious; they all knew that they were going to Korea anyway. It was the first time since high school graduation that Rolly Hunter had gotten drunk. He wanted to find a prostitute, but Stokes and two of his buddies thought he was too drunk to enjoy it. They took his wallet so he couldn't get mugged. For that, he thanked them several times on Sunday, once between each glass of Bromo Seltzer. Most of the afternoon was spent in writing letters and reading the *Baltimore Sun* and *Washington Post*. Several of the men started a poker game around 7:00 p.m. and played until nearly 2:00 a.m.

Hunter brushed his teeth and slipped into bed. He was restless, and began thinking about his orders. He had never really taken the time to figure out what Truman's police action was all about, because until this moment, he did not feel that it had anything to do with him.

* * *

EVERYONE WAS MILLING AROUND in front of the company office, waiting for the orders to be posted. Finally a snippy lieutenant with a nasty smirk marched up to the door and posted the list. Hunter could not believe his eyes. The first 56 names on the list all said the same thing: CAMP STOLMAN, CALIFORNIA. Hunter knew that meant Korea. The other four names were listed:

Pvt. Marion Wells, Kansas City, Ks. U.S. Army Meat Inspection Station, Kansas City Stockyard Station.

Pvt. Mark Anderson, USO Special Services, Los Angeles, Ca.

Pvt. Rolland Hunter
Pvt. Raymond Stokes, Counter Intelligence Corps, Ft. Holabird, Maryland, Pentagon.

"Well, I'll be ..." Stokes said aloud to no one in particular. "I'm staying right here. Jeez, Wells and Anderson have been washed out."

Many of the men had expected it. Marion Wells had been a meat inspector before being drafted, and now was going back to the very same job he held as a civilian. Private Anderson was a trumpet player in high school and evidentially impressed someone in Special Services. As for himself, Hunter was stunned. He knew that Ray Stokes was a very intelligent individual and guessed that the two of them must be the smartest of the bunch. He was humbled to be on the same list with Stokes.

All 60 men were handed their official orders, and each went off to his own corner to study them. Reality had set in and Hunter could see hanging heads everywhere. Two or three GIs glanced in Hunter's direction with some disdain. It was not a clearly happy moment for Hunter, but he could not contain his joy. The emotion he felt at being spared was not possible to hide, nor did he.

"What the hell you cryin' about, Hunter? If you want to go that bad, you can take my place," came the voice of a GI passing by.

Hunter felt sudden humiliation, guilt and sympathy for his buddies, and yes, a sense of relief. He could not control his emotions. He turned quickly toward refuge in the barracks.

"Hunter!" shouted the lieutenant. "Get your ass back here. I want to talk to you!"

It was all he could do to turn toward the other faces. He felt the stares of 56 men.

"Get your gear ready. You have about 40 minutes," snipped the lieutenant.

"Where am I going, sir?" asked Hunter.

"Well, they tell me you and Stokes are moving to the BOQ. I can't believe they're going to pamper you pansies. Also, remove all your insignias and chuck 'em,"

"Stokes, get over here," barked the lieutenant.

"Yes, sir!"

"Did you hear what I said to Hunter?"

"Yes, sir!"

Well, that goes for you too. Get your candy asses over to the barracks, pack your gear, and I want you back here in 35 minutes. Got that?"

"Yes, sir!" both men said in unison.

They were standing in front of the company office in less than 30 minutes. The others had all wandered away, and Hunter was glad for that. Not one of the other men had said one word to Hunter or Stokes in parting. He couldn't blame them. He felt that he probably would have done the same thing.

The jeep pulled up to the front of the office. Hunter looked and immediately saw the gold star and the fender flags. He recognized it to be General Bergstrom's jeep, but only the driver was aboard. He had seen him many times.

The young sergeant stepped out of the jeep and looked as though he had just slipped off an ironing board. He was creased and pressed beyond the call of duty, and his spit-shined boots glistened in the sunlight. His brass insignias were polished to the brightness of gold. The blue and white braid circling through his left epaulet and under his arm gave him an air of importance far beyond his rank.

My God! What must the general look like? Hunter thought to himself. *I hope he's here to get that nasty little lieutenant.*

To Hunter's surprise, the sergeant walked straight toward him. "Are you

Hunter, sir?"

Hunter's mouth fell open. He and Stokes looked at each other in disbelief. "Yes, I'm Hunter," he said, unable to believe the man had called him "sir."

"And you must be Stokes?"

"Yes, sir, ah, err, Sergeant."

"Gentlemen, please toss your gear aboard and hop in, please."

The men moved quickly, and as the jeep turned around, Hunter could see the lieutenant peer from the office window. He smiled to himself.

Salutes were flying from everywhere. Stokes and Hunter looked at each other, smiling. They began returning salutes. It was amusing, but Hunter knew that nobody was going to treat a private this way for very long, so he decided to enjoy it while it lasted.

"Where in the hell are we going?" he whispered to Stokes.

"Damned if I know. Maybe we're gonna be guinea pigs for some new chemical weapon."

The jeep swung into the general's parking space at HQ.

A corporal moved quickly from the top step and confronted the two men.

"Gentlemen, please follow Corporal Siffer. I'll see that your gear is placed in your quarters and return to pick you up shortly."

The driver was out of the parking lot before the men reached the top of the stairs.

* * *

THE HALLWAY SMELLED OF OLD VARNISH. The warped wooden floors shone brightly, while the boards complained with each footstep. Hunter noticed that there was not a single sign on any door, no pictures on the walls, and aside from a single plant at the end of the hallway, it appeared to be completely deserted.

The corporal knocked on the last door and heard a deep voice say, "Come!"

Siffer opened the door, turned, and disappeared back down the hallway. *What is this cloak-and-dagger stuff, anyway?* Hunter wondered to himself. The office was nicely furnished with two identical leather chairs and a matching sofa. There were numerous pictures of military people on the wall and even one with what appeared to be General Bergstrum, President Truman, and another officer. The remainder of the decor consisted of an American flag, a very clean desk with only a small American eagle, an intercom, a pen in a marble holder, and a two-level basket with signs for IN and OUT. There was one sheet in the OUT file basket and nothing in the IN file basket.

Stokes whispered to Hunter, "It sure as hell doesn't look like they do much work here, does it?"

"I think they do a lot of polishing," responded Hunter.

"Hunter, is this supposed to be part of the Eighth Army? I don't see any signs anywhere. Come to think of it, there wasn't a damned thing on that jeep but the general's star. Hell, maybe it isn't even the Army at all. Christ a 'mighty, talk about your cloak-and-dagger stuff."

Hunter heard a toilet flush as the handle turned on the door leading off what they believed to be the general's office.

"I think we're about to find out."

Not knowing whom to expect, both men snapped to attention and stared at the door.

A short, fat man appeared through the door, drying his hands on a paper towel. At once, both men could see the star on each side of the tan dress shirt. Wide olive drab suspenders held up the green wool trousers. There was no necktie and there were no other insignias of any kind on the man's clothing. He was totally bald with a dark shadow (which led Hunter to believe the man had shaved his head and was probably not really bald at all).

"Damned shithouse," the man muttered without looking at the two men. "It takes three flushes to down one small turd! Are you Rolland Hunter and Raymond Stokes?"

"Yes, sir!" the men said with one voice.

"Well, sit down. Want some coffee or something?"

"No, sir," the men replied. It was obvious that they responded correctly.

The general was not used to waiting on privates, and they picked up on his empty gesture. Each took one of the twin chairs. The cushions were deep and the men sank uncomfortably low.

"Don't mind those damned chairs. They've broken down after years of lard-asses up and down on 'em, and shit, I can't even get new ones because nobody's supposed to know I'm here. I don't have a fucking budget, and unless my guys steal things, I'm shit outta luck for replacements. The only thing I got is my Jeep, and I'll shoot the first son of a bitch that tries to steal it from me!"

Both men sat in utter amazement, trying to figure out just who this nutcase was supposed to be, and what kind of hell they were in for. It didn't take the general long to get down to business.

"All right, gentlemen, I know what you're thinking. Right now you're wondering what kind of cornball outfit you've run into, right?"

Neither man moved.

"Well, it's still the army, so I don't want you to forget that. Now then, believe it or not, we do have a job here, and it's an important one. You don't see any army designation because we serve all of them — the First, Third, Fifth, Eighth, and so on."

"Yes, sir," said Stokes.

"Son, you don't have to answer me all the way through this. Otherwise, we'll be here all night. Now listen to me. Every army has its own intelligence, understand, and maybe the Third Army is gathering intelligence on the same person as the Eighth Army. Neither one of them knows what the other one is doing. Our job is very simple. We have a warehouse near the train station here at Holabird where all the different army files of all the intelligence is sent. We simply go through all the files and combine them into a single dossier and it becomes a single intelligence file. Understand?"

Both men nodded.

"Now, we have so many files that they have become practically useless unless they're condensed and filed into a single location. The information in these folders is then moved to the basement of the Pentagon and put on punch cards so we can call up damned near anybody in the world. Hell, we got information on important people all over the globe: military, civilian, world leaders, former Nazis, Communists, you name it. You ever heard of Senator McCarthy? This one I need an answer from you, boys."

"Yes, sir!" said Hunter.

The general glared at Stokes."Yes, sir!" Stokes answered.

"Now, you boys have been cleared for top secret, and that's just what we're talking about here. You could get your asses shot off if you leaked half of what I've told you so far. You do understand that, don't you?"

"Yes, sir, we do," Stokes responded.

"Yes, sir," Hunter concurred.

"Good, then I don't think we need to bring that up again. Now, this Senator McCarthy seems to be looking under every rock for Communists. He thinks they're everywhere, and hell, maybe they are, for all I know. The point is it has become a priority for our little group to red flag any dossier that smells of a possible Communist. Now here's your job, plain and simple: The files are dusty and the warehouse is dirty, so you will wear only fatigues to work; no insignias or rank will be displayed at any time. That means you don't wear any other uniform at any time, on base or on pass. Got that?"

They both nodded.

"Now, then, you'll be staying in the bachelor officers' quarters. You won't be on K.P. You don't stand inspection, and you don't march in parades. You will answer only to me and no one else unless you hear me tell you otherwise. Can I make it plainer than that?"

Again, the men nodded.

"What?" yelled the general.

"We mean no sir!"

"All of the files arrive at the Ft. Holabird warehouse, boxcars full, where they are condensed and all duplicate information is shredded. Now then, the new files are to be taken to the basement of the Pentagon on army trucks with armed escorts. A rather stupid idea, if you ask me, but nobody did, so the files will be delivered by armed escort.

"You boys, by the way, will also serve as armed guards. Once the files are safely at the Pentagon, the information will be computer punched and available for eyes only at the touch of a button. Can you believe that? It's not like the old army, I'll tell you that. Hell, today we don't even know who the enemy is or if there really is one. We used to shoot the bastards because we knew who they were and why they were the enemy. Now we just keep files on them. Isn't that the shits? Either of you boys play tennis?"

"I played some in high school," Stokes answered. Hunter indicated that he had not.

"Well, I used to be pretty good. I played at the academy. I've tried to keep it up as much as possible. Don't let this fat little body fool you. I can still kick some butt. Anyway, Stokes, maybe we can have a match one of these days."

"Yes, sir, I'd like that," responded Stokes.

"Now, then," continued Bergstrum, "we have 76 people in our little family: 16 GIs counting myself, the corporal, the sergeant, and 59 civilians. Twelve of those people are strictly counter-intelligence agents assigned to our group. A pretty fancy name for people who go around making records of other people's bathroom habits. Anyway, those fellows use the files, they don't work on them. Now that leaves 47 men and women plus the 13 of you to do all the file work. It doesn't take a genius to know that we couldn't complete the project in a thousand years, but what we do is this: Each Army G-2 office at the Pentagon prints out a weekly, or sometimes a daily, priority list if there is a lot of shit going on, and these receive immediate attention. When you've completed these lists each month, you go back to the possible subversives. Right now, that means Communists.

"Gentlemen, you're going to work your butts off, but I think you'll find your efforts quite rewarding. Part of my job is to keep everybody else off your ass, and believe me, there will be lots of those occasions. You'll be at the Pentagon as much as you are at the warehouse. Now there is brass all over the place. Full-bird colonels are a dime a dozen, and it will drive them crazy trying to figure who you are and what you are doing there, and some will even try to put you on some detail or another. If you are harassed by anyone, I want you to hand them this card."

The general handed Hunter and Stokes each a business card:

Brig. General J. P. Bergstrum
U.S. Army, Ft. Holabird, Maryland.
631-4478

"You just hand them one of these cards and tell them they need to call me. Corporal Siffer will see that you have plenty. Any questions?"

Both men slowly nodded a no.

The general continued, "When you need me in a hurry, I want you to call the number on the card and ask for 'Pony.' It will most likely be Siffer on the line. Just tell him where you are, and he knows how to find me. Under no circumstances are you to tell anyone what you are doing."

"Yes, sir," resounded Stokes.

"Ponich happens to be my middle name, and I've had the tag of Pony ever since I can remember. I kinda like it and I much prefer it to 'the Old Man,' or 'Fat Ass,' or whatever other names you might think of."

"Sir," asked Hunter, "is there someone we need to report to at the warehouse?"

"Don't worry about that. Someone will know who you are and get you started. Any other questions?"

"No, sir."

"All right then, you might as well get your gear unpacked. Breakfast is at *0630* at the camp mess hall. The warehouse is a short walk from there. That'll about do it."

General Bergstrum immediately walked behind his desk, picked up the telephone handset, and began dialing. Hunter and Stokes wriggled out of the chairs, stood at attention, and saluted. The general gave a limp wave of the hand and the men headed for the door.

"Just a minute, boys. I forgot to tell you that on occasion, you might be assigned to one of the agents for some investigations. It won't be often, but it does break the monotony."

Hunter nodded that they understood and then turned and left the building to the waiting Jeep and driver. Neither spoke as they made the short drive to the BOQ.

* * *

HUNTER AND STOKES quickly got into the routine, and time passed quickly. All the CIC military staff carried class-A passes, and anytime they were not on duty, they were free to come and go without asking anyone. Hunter and Stokes became very close and did everything together. It was rare to see one without the other. Stokes taught Hunter the basics of tennis, and on occasion, Pony would take on one or the other.

The files generally contained irrelevant notes, reports of nasty habits, and once in a while there would be juicy intelligence that made for good reading. Some files contained only one item, and some would be three-inches thick by the time they were compiled from several Army G-2s. All in all, it was fascinating work and a far cry from Korea.

Less than six months had passed when Pony called Hunter and Stokes into his office. "Boys," he said, "I didn't want you to hear this from any other source, but I have some rather bad news. Your entire advanced infantry unit except for 22 men has been wiped out just above Seoul. I don't know any of the details, but I thought you would want to know. I can get a list of names and addresses in case you want to write some letters. It's up to you."

The two men sat dumbfounded, unable to hold back the tears.

"Boys, I'm going over to the BOQ. Why don't you sit here for a while. Siffer will be outside, and he'll lock up when you leave."

"Thank you, sir," Stokes responded. "And thank you for telling us. We appreciate it."

"I know you do, boys. If there is anything you need, just let Siffer know. He'll take care of it."

"Yes, sir, we will."

The general left without another word, and Hunter and Stokes talked about some of the men in the outfit who they guessed might have made it and who probably didn't. They shared their grief for nearly an hour in the general's office before returning to the warehouse. They needed to get back to work. They did not want to think about it further.

* * *

GENERAL BERGSTRUM CALLED A MEETING for the military people the following week. The men gathered in the upstairs office at the warehouse. Corporal Siffer had his hands full of folders and was arranging them in some sort of order.

"Boys," began the general, "you know we've been moving pretty fast here at the warehouse, and we have a hell of a lot of dossiers at the Pentagon now. We have quite a few civilians over there who are going to need some training on the use of the files, and some of you people are going to be responsible for that training. This necessitates your moving over to Ft. Myers North Post. From there, it's just a short walk through the tunnel to the Pentagon. Now, I'm not going to do this democratically. We've already decided who's going over. These are the people I think can do the best job. Stokes, Hunter, Garibaldi, and Brown. I want you fellas to get your shit packed, and Corporal Siffer will have a van waiting for you at the BOQ in about two hours. The rest of you will continue here at Holabird. I'm looking for four replacements now. When you boys get over to North Post, you're going to see lots of brass. To them, you're gonna look like privates, smell like privates, and they're gonna treat you like privates. They will try to get you on K.P. and other details. They will quickly find out, however, what a terrible price there will be to pay for such goings-on. Just don't smartass anyone, and I'll do the rest. Are there any questions?"

No one responded.

"All right then, you four people stay here for a minute and the rest of you are dismissed."

As soon as the others had left, the general began. "Now then, boys, there's a little more to your going over to North Post than I needed to share with the others. You four men have done your work well and the reports I get suggest that you are careful and thorough. You remember I told you when you came in that some of you might be assigned to work with the agents in the field? Well, you will be doing the training for a few weeks. The agents have reviewed your records and you four have each been assigned to an agent for field work. Hunter, you are going out right away. I want you to stay here for a few minutes. The rest of you can go and get packed."

The three men left quickly and the general sat down next to Hunter. Almost immediately, a tall man in civilian clothes entered the office. The man was very ordinary in appearance, and Hunter knew at once that he was a CIC agent.

"Hunter, this is Agent Earl Collins. He knows more about you than you do. You're going to be working closely together for the next few months on a case out in California."

"Glad to meet you, Private Hunter."

"The same, sir," answered Hunter.

"Now let me tell you what we've got here, Hunter. It seems that there is a little Russian actress out in Hollywood who defected through Romania about a year ago. Our intelligence doesn't show any record of her ever having been an actress in Russia. Now that in itself doesn't mean much, but it tells us we ought to check her out. We'll follow her around for a while and see if she's up to anything. It probably wouldn't even matter except the request comes from Senator McCarthy's office, so it's now a priority."

"Yes, sir."

"I'm gonna leave you here with Agent Collins and he'll give you the details."

The general and Corporal Siffer left quickly, as Hunter looked closely at his new companion. He felt a twinge of awe to think he was sitting next to a real spy. He also felt an urge to giggle, but held it.

"Private Hunter, let's start by getting rid of the formalities. Call me Hal, and I'll call you Rolly. We're going to be like two peas in a pod for the next several months. Other than sleeping and going to the bathroom, we will become inseparable. This is a pretty ordinary assignment to get your feet wet on, so don't look for a lot of thrills. You may find it a little boring, as a matter of fact."

"I'm looking forward to it, Mr. Collins — Hal."

"We'll be taking a train for L.A. next Tuesday. One thing about the government travel, it's pretty good. Once we get there, we will be checking in at the Beverly Wilshire, and that will be our home for a while. Not bad for a couple of guys feeding out of the public trough, huh?"

"It sounds pretty good to me, Hal. I never thought I'd ever see Hollywood."

"We've prepared a bunch of phony background, making me a sort of New York producer type looking for some specific talent in Hollywood for a new play I'm producing in New York. That will bring people out of the woodwork to aid in our investigation."

"Who exactly are we investigating?"

"Her name is Ursula Kolenckov. Her Hollywood name is Greta Orndoff. I guess they're trying to pass her off as a Swede."

"If you're a producer, Hal, what's my role?"

"You're my playboy son. You'll get outfitted with a couple $400 suits, some nice watches, and we'll be ready to play."

Hunter was astounded. Hal Collins spoke as though they were young children planning a pretend game. It hardly seemed at all serious, but like a child Hunter was ready to play.

EIGHT

CORPORAL SIFFER STOPPED AT HUNTER'S QUARTERS early Tuesday morning to announce that Rolly Hunter was now Private First Class Hunter, which meant nothing more than a few extra dollars per month. Hunter was nevertheless pleased at the promotion. He finished his packing, shaved and showered, and dressed in his civvies for the train ride to L.A. He was excited and was anxious to be on his way to Hollywood.

It was a peaceful four-day trip with nothing to do but eat, read, and loaf in the club car. He enjoyed the ride and was almost sad to see the train pull into the Los Angeles station. The men hailed a cab and headed for the Beverly Wilshire. It was not nearly as elegant as Hunter imagined it to be. The restaurant prices were quite elegant, however.

Collins and Hunter quickly settled in and got down to work. They made their first contact with the actress at a hair salon on Rodeo Drive. Collins knew from her dossier that this place was a regular stop for Greta Orndoff. From that point on, it was just a matter of following the woman day and night, making notes of her comings and goings as much as possible.

In less than a week, Hunter determined that the spy business was not what he had hoped it would be. He grew quite tired of the many trips to Rodeo Drive and her other favorite hangouts — and never once to anyplace resembling a movie studio.

Collins had often left him alone, presumably to set up phone taps and bug her apartment. Hunter, on the other hand, had to concentrate on keeping complete notes. At times, he longed for the warehouse at Holabird where at least there would be occasional exciting and meaningful intelligence information.

Agent Collins had concluded that nothing subversive was occurring with the aspiring actress and had notified Pony that they probably would be through in a few days. There had been one call to the actress from a Hollywood director; a priority name on McCarthy's list that Collins felt was worth a look. Hunter thought it might be interesting. She was to meet him on Friday night for dinner at Cicero's in Hollywood, and if nothing came of that meeting, Collins intended to end the investigation.

It was decided that Hunter would sit at the bar and observe the couple's table, and Collins would see if he could find anything at the man's Beverly Hills apartment. Hunter was to phone the apartment when the couple left to allow Collins time to get out. They assumed that he probably would be bringing her there.

With more than 29 movie stars seated in the dining room, Cicero's was a showplace, with lengthy tablecloths, candelabras, and beautiful silver and china. Hunter watched the couple at a corner table for nearly an hour. They each had several cocktails, and the noise level rose throughout the restaurant with each passing drink. He was in awe at the sheer excitement of it all. He had turned his head only for a moment, and when he looked back, the woman had disappeared. He glued his eyes on the table and could not believe what he was observing. The man had his hands placed on the table with stiffened arms and his head was thrashing about wildly. He bit his lip and could not sit still.

My God, thought Hunter. *Could that woman be under the table doing what I think she's doing?* In a few moments, the man placed both his hands over his mouth, made an expression of pain or ecstasy, and suddenly relaxed and smiled broadly. As Hunter suspected, the woman re-appeared from beneath the table, also with a sheepish grin. The man proceeded to light a cigar and took a couple of satisfying puffs.

Hunter had had enough. He could not believe he had come all the way from D.C. to witness some airhead give a blowjob in a high-class Hollywood nightclub. He went to the payphone and dialed the number that Collins had given him. There was no answer, so Hunter knew that Collins had finished. He folded his notes and took a cab back to the Beverly Wilshire for a much-needed cold shower.

*　*　*

COLLINS FINISHED READING HUNTER'S REPORT and slowly laid it on the coffee table and looked up at Hunter shaking his head in disbelief. The report read as follows:

8:04 p.m.	Couple arrived at Cicero's restaurant — sat at corner table
8:04 – 8:54 p.m.	Four drinks consumed by each
9:06 p.m.	Female disappeared.
9:07 p.m.	Male began to experience seizure/arms stiff against table, eyes opening and closing, head thrashing about as though suffering neck or back pain, eyes rolling back showing signs of convulsions … evidence of shuddering motions … seizure grew more intense as man placed both hands over his mouth in an apparent effort to stifle painful screams … seizure ended abruptly. Man seemed relieved as pain subsided.
9:23 p.m.	Final note: It was concluded by this investigator that the situation ended reasonably well, and it was not necessary to summon the maitre d' to call an ambulance.

"Hunter, what kinda crap is this?" demanded Collins. "You're certainly not going to submit this as your report?"

"Why not? It's exactly what I observed," Hunter responded.

"Oh, come on Hunter, fun's fun, but this is not the kind of report you want to submit to Pony. He'll eat you for lunch. No pun intended." Collins started to giggle as he realized what he had said. Both men began to laugh loudly, as Collins tried to read the report aloud.

"Okay, Hunter, I'm going to turn it in to Pony just like this, and if you get your ass sent off to Korea, it'll be your own fault."

Collins finished his notes and told Hunter to start packing. They would be leaving in the morning for Baltimore on TWA. Rolly liked that idea.

* * *

IT DID NOT TAKE GENERAL BERGSTRUM LONG to call Hunter into his office.

"What kinda bull crap is this, Hunter? I suppose you think that was pretty funny to go out to California at Uncle Sam's expense, and write up a piece of pornography and call it an intelligence report."

"No, sir! Like I told agent Collins, it's exactly what I observed. I just tried to add a little style to it, sir. It was a rather boring assignment. I didn't think it would do any harm."

"Well, you're wrong. I don't like that kinda horseshit. I had more faith in you than that."

"Yes, sir."

"Well, I'll give you this much: it was quite funny. As a matter of fact, I laughed my butt off, but that's not what I called you in for."

"Sir?" responded Hunter.

"I see in your file that you speak Italian. Is that right?"

"Yes, sir. I think I can get by quite well."

"You've managed to keep it up?"

"Well, I might be a bit rusty, General, but it wouldn't take me long to get it back. I've always had a knack for languages," Hunter responded, furrowing his brow, as he wondered where the general was going with all this.

"Good! You ever been to Italy?"

"Italy, sir?"

"Yes, Italy! Can you hear me all right, Hunter?"

"Yes, sir … you sort of took me by surprise, General Bergstrum."

"Uh huh. Well PFC Hunter, you're about to have the adventure of your life."

Hunter could only stare at the general with his mouth wide open. Bergstrum continued, "When the American Fifth Army and the British Eighth moved through Rome and Milan in '45, there was a great deal of art and other treasures left behind by the fascists and the Nazis. Now then, a small detachment of the Fifth and British Eighth were left to sniff out any remaining Axis sympathizers and to begin to log all the captured treasures. To this day, very few people know they were even there. Well, they were and are still there working with the embassy trying to sort it all out, locate lost items, and get everything returned to the rightful places. You get the idea?"

"Yes, sir," replied Hunter.

"Son, I'm going to send you over there to join that little group. How would you like that?"

"Very much, General, very much indeed."

"I thought you probably would. Here's the picture. You will be staying at a hotel near the embassy and doing most of your work at the embassy. You will, however, as I understand it, be all over the place: museums, libraries, offices, and banks. Well, you get the picture."

"Yes, sir, I do"

"Good. You will have a 30 day furlough and report back here when you return. How does that sound?"

Hunter seemed uneasy for a moment and then responded, "Sir, I would just as soon skip the furlough. I really don't have anyone but my aunt and a couple of cousins in Atlanta. Is it possible that I could go now and spend some extra time looking around the country? I have saved quite a bit of my pay. I'd really prefer it, sir."

"Well, I don't know, Hunter. I guess I can look into it, if that's what you want."

"Yes, sir, it would be great."

"All right, I'll check it out. In the meantime, you can go back to North Post and continue training the new civilians at the Pentagon."

"Yes, sir!"

Hunter waited patiently for nearly two weeks for his orders to be cut. He could not get over the idea of being a spy in the Counter Intelligence

Corps at the ripe old age of 22. He had already been in the CIC and felt like a veteran. Stokes was still a rookie.

Stokes had received orders for West Germany. The Soviets were getting quite nasty, and a lot of U.S. intelligence people were going over. They decided they would try to get together somewhere in Europe once they were both settled. The two spent one final weekend in Baltimore before Hunter was to leave.

General Bergstrum sent Hunter off with a set of corporal's stripes and a Sunday afternoon dinner for him and Stokes at Little Italy in Baltimore. The man was beginning to enjoy army life. Korea was on another planet.

NINE

JIM AND MARY SPENT THE AFTERNOON at his apartment, sharing a pizza, making some love, and playing a few games of Scrabble. At 7:15, they drove to Hunter's hotel and were knocking at his door by 7:25.

"Good evening, Mr. Riley and Miss Rison. Thank you for coming. Please come in. Would either of you care for anything to drink? I have beer and Pepsi."

Riley took a beer and Mary opened a Pepsi and sat down on the sofa next to Jim. Neither said a word but looked at Hunter in great anticipation.

Hunter began, "Well, let's see now, where to begin? I guess the best place to start is with all the mystery surrounding the Karen Chen incident. I might as well tell you, Jim, that woman was not a bank teller by profession, nor was her supposed husband a gentle, harmless man. I spent the afternoon checking some very special sources, and I can tell you they were extremely dangerous people. They were not married, and in fact, they hardly knew one another."

"How do you know all of this, Mr. Hunter?" Mary asked.

"Well, as I said, I have some very special sources. I'll get into that in a few minutes. As I was saying, they were indeed dangerous. Have you ever heard of the Tongs?"

Both indicated that they hadn't. Hunter continued, "The Tongs are like a Chinese mafia, headquartered in Hong Kong. These are extremely vicious people and will do anything for money or to strengthen their own organization. They promote terror, drugs, prostitution, and things that you can't even imagine."

"And these people were Tongs?" Jim asked.

"Well, we're sure that he was. He had quite a track record. She, on the other hand, well, I'm not so sure. It seems to me that the Tongs are a male-dominated outfit and they use women if it suits their purpose. That's probably where she came in."

"Rolly, how does this relate to me?" Jim asked.

"Jim, Mary, I'd like to give you a little scenario, which I believe is not far a field from what actually occurred. I might be missing some of the words, but the music is pretty close. Mr. Riley, someone had made an impression of your bank deposit key. There were traces of wax on it. Now this is not a key one can take to a locksmith. There are certain keys they won't make, and this is one of them, that is, unless the locksmith was paid a lot of money under the table. Well, in either case, they did that or were able to make their own key. In any event, a key was made.

"As you know, Jim, it had to be Karen Chen. No one else could have had the opportunity to go to the vault, even if they had a key. I'd now like to take you back to David Steinmetz's murder. Tell me everything you can about the day he was killed, and anything you can about Karen Chen."

Riley related the whole story, beginning with his meeting David Steinmetz.

"All right, Jim, from the news reports I got, and what you're saying, I think I've pieced it together. I believe that someone had hired the Tongs, who in turn set up Karen Chen to murder Steinmetz and take the codebook. It should have been simple, except David Steinmetz didn't have the book in his possession when he was killed. Since it was not among his luggage, there could only be one place the book could be: in your hands."

"So all this bit with Karen and Louie Chen, her working at the bank, was all an elaborate scheme to get to me?"

"Yes, Jim."

"Why? Wouldn't it have been easier to just stick a gun in my face and take it from me?"

"Oh, no! You know too much, Jim. I think you were supposed to be killed. The person wanting the book didn't know what David Steinmetz might have told you, which could lead back to him or her. The perpetrator had gone too far."

Mary chimed in. "Mr. Hunter, why were you going by Ellis?"

"Well, Miss Rison, I'm sure you've heard of Ellis Island." She nodded that she had.

"My direct involvement with David Steinmetz's father, Mica, really began with records from Ellis Island, which you will understand shortly. Before David's father died, he assigned me a power of attorney together with specific instructions to make withdrawals from any or all of the Swiss banks as a safeguard against anything happening to David or any heirs he might have. I continued working with, actually for, David. This all began about 1988 or '89."

"What were you doing all those years from the 1950s to 1988?" Jim asked. "And how did you know David's father? Also, how did you ever find Windom? And what in the hell is this Ellis business?"

"Ellis was our code word for anything relating to what I'm going to tell you. It was not in anyone's best interest to have my name associated with the Steinmetz family. Can we defer your other questions for a while, Jim?"

"I'm ready to hear your scenario, Rolly."

"Yes, of course. I know that it was Oliver Windom who wanted you killed. He had hired Karen Chen, with or without the Tongs' blessing, simply to murder David Steinmetz, take the codebook, and deliver it to him for a large sum of money. When the book was not there, attention was directed toward you. This is where Louie Chen comes in. He was nothing but decoration. They set up the whole scheme to move in across the street as a married couple, determine that you had the book, bump you off, and deliver the book to Windom. You caused a bit of a problem by placing it in a safe-deposit box. Karen Chen went to work for the bank just to have a reason to keep close tabs on you until the time was right to get the book."

"Now, wait a minute. How did she know I planned to get a box at the bank and just happened to be the one to set it up for me?"

"Well, I don't know the answer to that, except that since you knew that you were in some sort of danger, it might be logical that you would do just that. She probably figured you wouldn't want it lying around your apartment, since David had been killed because of it. I assume you were followed into the bank on several occasions."

"What about the two shooting each other? That doesn't make any sense at all," Mary asked Hunter.

"Yes it does, Mary. If you were going to receive a lot of money for killing several people, you might not want to share it. Remember, Jim, you saw Windom's limo pull around the corner about the time the shooting occurred?" Hunter asked.

"Uh huh!" Jim responded. "I'm sure he thought I was already dead!"

"So Karen Chen had already stolen your copy of the book, and all that was left was to make the hit on you, hand the book over to Windom as he drove up, and most likely get an envelope full of cash. Only thing is, the woman didn't feel the need to share anything with Louie, so she decided to kill him just before coming across the street to wait for you to leave your apartment, and bang! It would all be over; she could collect her money and be gone for God-knows-where. Windom would have what he wanted and everyone but you and Louie could live happily ever after," Hunter summarized.

"Unfortunately, Karen Chen was not too accurate and didn't get the job done on Louie before he had time to get off one fatal shot. This leaves Windom with no book and his hit lady shot to death, just when he was supposed to drive up, collect the codebook, pay off Chen, and be on his way. It must have been quite a shock to Windom to suddenly find himself in the midst of a street full of cops with his gold-crested limo shining like a neon sign. I'm sure he wanted to get out of there rather quickly."

"Well, what about the book? Karen Chen obviously didn't deliver it," Mary said.

"My, my, Mary. You're way ahead of me, aren't you? Where do you think it is?" Hunter asked.

"Damn! It's still in the apartment, isn't it?" Jim responded as he jumped to his feet.

"Well, maybe," interjected Hunter. "If the police haven't found it. They certainly had no reason to be looking for it. We need to find out, don't we?" Hunter teased.

Mary and Jim looked at each other and shrugged in agreement.

"How do we do that, Mr. Hunter?" Mary asked.

"I have some ideas. I used to be a spy, you know." Hunter smiled.

"You mean like a CIA spy?" Mary asked with eyes wide open.

"Kind of like that. Only it was an army organization called CIC, which stood for Counter Intelligence Corps. Later, I did become a CIA agent."

"Whew!" Mary reacted, obviously impressed.

"Mr. Hunter … Rolly, you had promised to tell us why that damned book is so important. What the hell is it anyway?" Jim asked, becoming more than a little impatient.

"All right, Jim, it's time that you know the whole story. I haven't meant to keep you in suspense. In fact, I hadn't meant to tell you at all — that is, until it became apparent you had become a new player in the entire mess. Here it is, then."

Hunter began, "In January of 1954, I was stationed in Milan, Italy. My job there was to work with the American Embassy to locate, log, and facilitate the return of art treasures, government assets, rare books, documents of all kinds, and military records for review by the American Fifth Army and the British Eighth. It was most interesting and with my top-secret clearance, I was able to view many highly classified files.

"I had been there about three months when I ran across a rather obscure file on a Professor Gino DiNapoli, an economics teacher at Milan University, and a wine hobbyist. He had a small vineyard where he grew some varietal grapes. I'm only telling you this because it has a definite bearing on what was to come later. In that file was a 16mm documentary film prepared by a woman named Vernita Carter as part of a doctoral dissertation. Naturally, I watched the film. Several times, as a matter of fact. She had been studying under a fellowship from Cal Berkeley. Her research had been quite thorough, and she discovered that this DiNapoli fellow was advisor and friend to at least six very powerful Jewish industrialists. These people virtually controlled a large portion of the Italian economy. They were very wealthy people indeed. They were into textiles, clothing, shoes, automobiles, and other manufacturing enterprises."

Jim and Mary sat in silence.

"The film went on to suggest that their friendships extended beyond business. Many family gatherings were verified, and DiNapoli was accepted into their group as one of them, as was his wife Sophia and younger son Dominic. The elder son, Octavio, however, was considered a renegade. At 18, he had been smitten with all the Nazi and fascist propaganda spreading across the country. DiNapoli was humiliated by his son's activities, which included passing out anti-Semitic literature, attending hate rallies, and actual destruction of private property. The boy was proud to extol the names of Adolf Hitler and Benito Mussolini."

"How could anyone know this stuff?" Jim asked.

"That's why it's called research, Jim!" He continued, "Gino DiNapoli was to the Jewish families, however, a gentile, and his inclusion was limited. He, on the other hand, had many friends and acquaintances outside the Jewish community. Their association, nevertheless, was honest and sincere, and his economic advice was well received by the Jewish leaders.

"It was at this time, 1937 and beyond, that Il Duce and his fascists were coming into total power. In fact, in September of 1938, Mussolini held a boisterous rally in Rome to announce his recently passed anti-Semitic legislation. Together with the signing of the Pact of Steel on May 22, the obvious evil alignment left no further doubt in the minds of the Jewish community as to where events were headed. As a rule, the Italian people accepted the Jews at the very least as human beings, and many were later to aid the Jews in their efforts to evade the fascists and Nazis.

"There were actually two Jewish friends of DiNapoli who attended that rally. One was Isaiah Cohen, and the other was Franz Steinmetz, a German

Jew who had become a prominent textile manufacturer in Italy."

"Steinmetz, did you say?" Riley asked.

"Yes, Jim. That would have been David Steinmetz's grandfather."

"Why in the name of heaven would a Jewish man have attended a fascist rally?" Mary asked.

"Well, Mary, you have to look at the political climate at the time. Benito Mussolini didn't have anything in particular against the Jews personally. It wasn't until his Axis ally, Adolf Hitler, began in earnest to persecute the Jews that he joined in the parade. Prior to about 1937, he actually had friends and acquaintances who were Jews. He had worked with them when he was a journalist — apparently quite a good one. I don't think Cohen or Steinmetz were quite expecting the turn of events that was to occur at that well-orchestrated rally. It would be my guess that they came away quite shaken."

"You mean there hadn't been any persecution of Jews in Italy before that meeting?" Jim asked.

"No, I didn't say that. Jews have always been persecuted everywhere in the world. It just hadn't reached the fever pitch that it had in Germany," Hunter explained. "At this time, even the Jews outside Germany could only guess at the extent to which the Nazis were turning up the heat."

"So, what happened after that first meeting?" Mary inquired.

"Well," began Hunter, "let's analyze that for a moment. Here I am, a wealthy Jewish entrepreneur, in a country about to turn on my people. What do I do? The only non-Jewish person I can turn to is Professor DiNapoli. This, they did. And why? To try to get their money out of Italy, of course."

"I would think so," said Riley.

"Now then, that was not going to be so easy, was it? Every Jew with anything at all was already targeted and could not simply close his accounts and leave the country. No, there had to be another way. How about soliciting the aid of a highly respected college professor with a name like DiNapoli? It was their only hope. He was a man who had traveled extensively and was virtually free to come and go as he pleased. He had made countless trips to

Zurich, Switzerland, both by car and train. He was absolutely the man who could help these Jews get money out of Milan and into Switzerland."

"And did he?" Mary asked.

"Yes, Mary, and he had very good reason, or so he thought."

"What do you mean, 'So he thought?'" Jim asked, now totally absorbed in Hunter's story.

"Well, Jim, there is good evidence that the men discussed the signs of the gathering military storm. There were notes found by the woman doing the research for her thesis, notes written by DiNapoli that suggested they were very concerned that Italy was about to fall into financial and social chaos. They knew there would be no stopping it, and therefore had reviewed all their options and indeed fell upon a plan which was only meant to be a temporary measure."

"It was hardly temporary," Mary interjected. "Nineteen thirty-eight to 1945 could hardly be considered a long weekend."

"You're right, Mary, and this is where they miscalculated. You see, there was no way they could possibly imagine the terror and devastation that was about to beset them. The men had generally agreed that it would last perhaps a year or two, and then it would be over. They could then begin to rebuild. This was DiNapoli's motive for wanting to help. He felt that whatever happened, Italy would need the power and wealth of these leaders to put their economy back together. A plan was devised. There were two problems however; first, the plan had to be put together and executed quickly. Secondly, the plan must be short range. Two years was their target."

"I think it is becoming quite obvious just what you're getting at, Rolly," Jim said. "They planned to have DiNapoli take their money to Switzerland, and the codebook was some sort of identification for the location of the money."

"That's right, Jim. Only it was a bit more involved than that. You see, even though Professor DiNapoli was a good and trusted friend, you must realize that trust can only go so far. Can you imagine how those men must have felt, handing over everything to one man? No, they needed some sort of method to prevent DiNapoli from succumbing to overwhelming temptation."

"Well, how could they have their cake and eat it too?" Mary asked.

"Well put, Mary. Here's how they did it. Let me see, by way of example, did either of you ever devise a code when you were in junior high school, where you changed numbers for letters, and perhaps used some signs to represent vowels or maybe numbers so the teacher couldn't read your notes?"

Mary laughed and Jim nodded.

"Well, this is essentially what these men did. Jim, we have only talked about one codebook, right?"

Jim opened his eyes wide and nodded; showing disbelief at what Hunter was about to say. "Don't tell me there's another book, for God's sake?"

"Yes, there is another book, my friend, and it worked like this. One book — the one you had in your possession — contains a list of coded accounts with names of signatories, amounts, whether cash, bonds, or other securities, and of course, the name of the bank. Each account named the contact person at the bank. In short, all the relative information required to withdraw funds."

"Now, the obvious question," Mary said. "What was the other book for?"

"Well, if you have a codebook, there must be a key to read it, right?"

"So the other book is nothing more than a key to decode all the names and accounts in the book held by the Steinmetz family?" Jim asked, suddenly beginning to get the picture.

"That's correct, Jim. It was decided that DiNapoli would hold on to the decoding book, and one of the six men would retain the actual book of accounts and names. I'm pretty sure that there are no less than 24 bank accounts involved."

"That accounts for the blank pages between each set of code numbers. I noticed that right away when I thumbed through the book," Jim responded.

"That validates my search," Hunter concurred.

"How do you suppose the men did all of this? They were certainly not code experts," Mary wondered.

"No, they were not. But they didn't have to be. The code was very simple, unsophisticated, but quite effective. It appeared to me after many, many hours of studying the Steinmetz book that they had simply used random numbers, probably drawn out of a hat. In addition to that, they threw in some arrows, punctuation marks, triangles, just like, as I said, a junior high school student might do."

"And that's it? It's that simple?" Jim asked. "Couldn't a code like that be easily broken?"

"That's what I'm wondering," Mary agreed.

"Well, for one thing, there doesn't seem to be any patterning. For instance, a number like say 24, might be the vowel A in one word but not another, and apparently from what I can tell, not even necessarily when an A appears a second or third time in the same word. It's true that it is an amateurish code, but quite honestly, I have not been able to decipher it, and I've studied it many times in the last 30 years."

"Why haven't you taken it to some sort of cryptographer?"

"I could have done that, but I'm not sure I would want anyone to know what is in the Steinmetz book, would you?" Hunter asked, looking at both Jim and Mary.

"Yeah, I guess you're right there, Rolly, but 30 years, for Christ's sake? I would have thought you might have stumbled on to some pattern, at least partially." Jim was astounded.

"I told you I had been a spy, Jim. I never said I was a genius," Hunter snapped. "These guys were a pretty intelligent group. I'm sure they had a system, but I'll be damned if I can figure it out. Both David Steinmetz and his father spent as much time as I did trying to break the darned code. None of us had any success. Supposing that I could have broken some of the code — remember these are numbered accounts — get just one number wrong and you've got nothing." Hunter was beginning to show a little of his long-held frustration, and Mary and Jim were noticing that he had had enough for the time being.

"Just one more question, Mr. Hunter," Mary asked. "Do you have any idea how much money, or securities, or whatever there actually was?"

"Not *was,* Mary, *is!*"

"My God, Rolly, you mean it's still there after over 50 years?" Jim's hands were shaking.

"Well, let's see now. In order for the Swiss bankers to issue numbered accounts, a deposit must have been well over $100,000. Contrary to what you might think, Jim, all this mystery about numbered Swiss bank accounts is mostly fairy-tale stuff. Swiss banks are like any other banks around the world. The real difference is that they are located in a neutral country. That makes them safe, we think. All during World War II, Nazi spies hung around the banks like flies, trying to confiscate any accounts that might belong to Jews. They were generally unsuccessful, however. Secrecy in the banking business in Switzerland is not just policy; it's part of their damned culture. Yet there were occasions where accounts were tapped and totally confiscated by the Nazis. The Swiss were afraid of them. Something else you might want to remember, Mary, if an account in the United States remains inactive for seven years, I believe, the account is closed and all deposits are turned over to the state's general fund. That's not true in Switzerland, however. An account will remain indefinitely, drawing interest all the while."

"You mean all that money has been drawing interest for over 50 years, Mr. Hunter?" Mary asked.

"That's right, Mary, and if we're looking at simple interest on savings, at the 50-year average of a six percent inflation factor, that money is doubling about every eleven years. A hundred dollars deposited in, say, 1938 would be worth somewhere in the neighborhood of $3,200 today. Not bad, huh?"

"So, how much do you think they had, Rolly?" Jim asked.

"From all the doctoral research and the information I have gathered over the years, it had to have been somewhere between three and a half to five-million dollars."

"Holy Jesus!" Jim shouted.

"I think if you run the numbers, Mr. Riley, say four-million dollars, you should come up somewhere in the neighborhood of 73 million for the first 50 years, give or take a few dollars. Now it almost doubles in the next seven years. I make that out to be nearly $140 million, give or take a few million.

This, of course, is the incidental money and does not account for what some of the securities and stocks might be worth after 57 years. According to what I was able to find out, in addition to the research the woman had done, at least two of the men owned stocks in the U.S. auto industry. One that we know of owned 1,100 shares of Murphy's Oil stock. You probably recognize their present name of Standard Oil of New Jersey. It is also apparent that Steinmetz owned numerous shares of a company called International Business Machines. You probably know it as IBM. I think the list is quite extensive."

"I'm sorry, Mr. Hunter," Mary said, hardly able to catch her breath, "What was supposed to be in this for you?"

"If I can, or could, get the money home, my share is five percent of everything."

"That's well over a million dollars of the cash alone, give or take a few dollars," Jim said with a smile from ear to ear.

"So, Mr. Hunter, do you think Oliver Windom has the other codebook?"

"Of course he does, or at least knows where it is."

"How can you be so sure?" Jim asked.

"That's the easy part. The Steinmetz's and I have known about Mr. Windom for over 10 years. Actually, I've known about him for over 25 years. It took a bit of time to find out that his name was Windom."

"How did you find that out, Mr. Hunter?" Mary asked.

"Just a bit of detective work, actually. I went to the Hall of Records in New York and searched records of all ships entering New York Harbor in 1938 and '39. This took some time to complete. I knew, of course, that many immigrants had changed their names upon arriving in the United States. I had suspected this when after finding the ship and passenger manifest; I checked the records to find that the DiNapolis had changed their name to Windom. It wasn't that difficult. What was difficult was picking up the trail of Windom. It was easy to track the Steinmetz family with a copy of a sponsor letter in the record file. This pointed to Santa Barbara, California. After trying every source I could imagine, I had decided to give up on Windom until I happened to read an article in a United Airlines flight magazine while flying to California. Here was an article about Windom Wines in the Central Valley, with a bio of Oliver Windom who had grown up in Milan, Italy. I wasted no time in contacting David Steinmetz. We devised a plan to get him into Windom's life and pursue this codebook business."

"Was he somehow connected to all the events surrounding the DiNapolis and the others? He could only have been a young man or a boy at that time."

"That's true, in his late teens or early twenties."

"How does he fit into the picture?" Jim asked.

"Well, that's a long story. I'm just a little tired now, so if we can hold that until our next meeting, I'll fill you in on the rest then. I'll leave you with this. It began with one hell of scary night in July at a fascist rally."

Jim and Mary left quickly, thanking Hunter for beginning to clarify the whole mystery. Hunter kicked off his shoes, opened the honor fridge, picked out a Bud Light, hit the power switch on the TV remote, stacked two pillows on the bed, lay down, and began to channel surf. Unaware of the pictures flipping on the screen, Hunter's mind was doing some surfing of its own. Telling the story to Jim and Mary had excited his memory of the past 30 years and all that had taken place before. So many times, he had imagined the scenarios that must have occurred in that volcanic time and space.

Jim and Mary hardly spoke a word as they left Hunter's hotel. The story had been breathtaking, and to realize that they were suddenly cast as characters in a play, and that they were about to become entangled in a web of intrigue and danger left them almost speechless.

"Jim?" Mary asked quietly.

"Hmm?" Jim did not look at her as he pulled his Camaro out of the hotel parking lot.

"Are you scared?"

"Hell yes, I'm scared! Aren't you?"

"I don't know. It's just too unreal. I feel like I'm watching a Humphrey Bogart movie, and that we are not really a part of this thing. But yes, I guess I am afraid."

"Mary, you know the thought has been occurring to me that old man Windom is really Professor DiNapoli's son. He has to be. There is no other way that all of this codebook stuff makes sense."

"Yes, Jim, I think it is fairly obvious. I was just waiting for Mr. Hunter to say it."

Jim dropped her off at her apartment, gave her a peck on the cheek, and drove home exhausted. He fell asleep in his overstuffed chair trying to watch the 11:00 o'clock news. He woke up about 1:30 a.m., undressed, and fell into bed.

Mary could not get to sleep. She paced the floor of her apartment for well over two hours, her mind ablaze with what-ifs and who all the players would turn out to be in this maze of financial espionage. Finally, her mind shut down. She lay on the bed, covered up with her afghan, and drifted off into a fitful slumber.

* * *

JIM AWOKE AND SAW THE ANSWERING MACHINE flashing. He had not even noticed it when he returned from Hunter's hotel. He picked up the phone and heard Shirley's voice.

"Jim, I hope you're sitting down. I'm getting married next week. I know it's sudden but I am in love and it's the right thing to do. You remember when I told you about the guy from Scottsdale? His name is Ted Foster. We've been dating for several months now, and, well … I know he's the one! You will like him a lot. Here is the good part. Can you come to the wedding? Julie is going to be the flower girl. You will enjoy that. Then we can celebrate her birthday at the reception. There will be about 20 people all together. You'll know most of them. We're only going to have a long weekend honeymoon. If you would like, you can spend the weekend with Julie. If not, my mom will do it. Call me back, and please be happy for me! Oh, by the way, I have reserved a room at the Country Inn just off the 202 at Scottsdale Boulevard."

This was perfect timing for Jim Riley. He was exhausted from all that was happening and valued the time to get away and put it all aside for a while.

He called Shirley and said that he would be there. They agreed to meet at Bandera's up the street from the Country Inn on the following Thursday for dinner. This would give him the opportunity to meet Foster before the wedding. He longed to hug little Julie. He also wanted to see how she got on with her soon-to-be step dad.

Jim called the flight school to reschedule some of his lessons and told Nancy that he would be back on Tuesday.

THE BEGINNING

TEN

IT WAS A HOT, HUMID EVENING IN MID-JULY OF 1938; Franz Steinmetz and Isaiah Cohen stood at the edge of the crowd of black-and-brown shirts beneath the balcony of Mussolini's Palazzo Venetia in Rome. The train ride had been hot and muggy. They were uncomfortable; they could smell their own sweat. They had stopped to refresh at a local shop near the railway station, but to no avail. The humidity had seemed to increase as each mile brought them closer to Rome. Their discomfort was stressful and caused them to perspire profusely. They also sensed an air of anxiety as the train drew closer, and each man expressed it to the other. They had been encouraged by their friend Professor Gino DiNapoli to attend this important rally. The fascists were gaining power by the day and there were many rumblings of awful things to come for the Italian-Jewish community. They wanted to hear firsthand if their fears were justified.

* * *

IL DUCE STOOD ON THE BALCONY in full black-shirted regalia gesturing wildly, ranting and raving about his utter disgust for King Victor Emanuel. The man was Italy's old and tired sovereign. Mussolini hated the man with a passion, not only for his politics, but because he had relegated Mussolini to a non-entity during Hitler's regal entry into Rome. He continued his tirade suggesting that the king was "too short," and could not possibly portray the strong military image that Il Duce had desired. Mussolini himself could hardly be considered a big man, except in his own mind. It was a mixture of madness and egomania, to say the least.

"Look, Franz," Cohen said softly to Steinmetz, as he pointed to a young brown-shirted boy less than fifteen feet away. Franz Steinmetz gasped in disbelief.

"My God, it's Octavio DiNapoli!"

The men moved away and pretended not to have noticed young DiNapoli.

"Franz, what will we say to Gino? Do you suppose that he knows about his son's activities? I knew the boy was not like his father, but I never imagined this."

"Nor did I," Steinmetz responded.

Mussolini quickly turned his attack toward the Jews in Rome and the need to purge the nation of such people. Like a parrot, he began to regurgitate Hitler's exact words. Isaiah Cohen felt an attack of hyperventilation coming on and needed to get far away from this place as soon as possible. Mussolini's casual but powerful attack on the Jews jutted like a knife deep into Franz's very soul. However, he attempted to show no outward emotion to his friend.

Steinmetz could see that this was all too much for his friend. He took him by the arm and led him away in the direction of the train station. Neither man spoke until the train was nearly ten miles out of the city.

"What will we say to DiNapoli?" were all the words Isaiah Cohen could muster.

"I don't know. Perhaps it is better to say nothing at all," responded Steinmetz.

"We must meet with our group right away, Franz. I do not think we have much time."

"Yes, Isaiah, you are right, of course. We must ask Professor DiNapoli for his counsel. He will know what we should do."

"He is a good man, and a good friend," Isaiah said, "but can we put our trust in him totally?"

"My friend, Isaiah, think about it. What choice do we have? Decisions that we should have made some time ago, for whatever reasons were not made and now I fear it is too late. We must meet with DiNapoli now. He will not let us down. I am sure of that."

"What about the others, Franz? Will they be willing to listen to DiNapoli?"

"Yes, I think they will, once they understand what has transpired in Rome tonight. Like us, they must realize we have no choice. We must put our trust in Professor DiNapoli's hands, and we must do it now."

"Thank you, Franz."

"For what, my friend?"

"For always knowing the right thing to do. I have never told you, but the many times you have advised me in business matters always seemed to steer me on the right track. I will never forget those times, Franz."

"Isaiah, you sound like a dead man talking. Listen to me: We are neither dead nor defeated. I promise you here and now that we shall survive, and we shall be the better for the ordeal we now face. Look at it as a temporary setback. We must lay low for the next couple of years, and once these mad people have come to their senses, life will be better than ever. After all, we are human beings. What do you think these people can do to us anyway?"

"Yes, you're right. I just wish I were as strong as you. You always manage to see the good side of everything. I envy you for that."

"Now, I will drop you at your home, and you must call Wetzel and Gold to meet at my office tomorrow morning at nine. I'll call Professor DiNapoli, Dussell, and Sukin. Remind each man to come separately and not to park near the office."

"Yes, of course. I'll call them right away."

It was well past 5:00 a.m. when the train squealed and ground to a stop at the Milan station. Both men were ruffled and tired from a fitful night on the train. No food had been served, and they hadn't even noticed their hunger.

As the men drove through Milan, neither spoke while they passed by one aroma after another as the morning meals were being prepared across the city. Each smell seemed to bring back a vivid memory of a past event. Life had been good to them, and they were beginning to feel it slipping away.

Both men realized that they had not eaten in nearly 12 hours. They were physically exhausted, emotionally drained, and famished. A mixture of sweet and pungent smoke curled its way through the narrow streets, drawing the men to the fleeting safety of their homes again.

ELEVEN

THE SIX FAMILIES HAD BEEN CLOSE in both business and personal affairs. Though they had many acquaintances, they rarely included others in their social lives. Even in the synagogue, they were referred to as *the clique*. They were all in their mid-forties, and except for Franz Steinmetz (who had emigrated from Germany in 1931), they had been friends since their early twenties. Franz was outgoing, intelligent, and somewhat prankish, and the others readily accepted him into their group.

Franz Steinmetz was 29 when he left Germany. The rest of his family — mother, father, and younger brother Heinrich — had applied for their Visas to the United States and were awaiting final approval from the German officials.

It was agreed that Franz would hear from his father within six months via a letter to the Jewish synagogue in Milan. Franz became worried about his family because he had heard nothing for more than eight months. Finally, a letter arrived. They had spent three weeks at Ellis Island, where they met many new immigrants like themselves. It was a happy time, though they wanted to leave Ellis and begin their new lives. Surprisingly, while there they received a local sponsorship from a Long Island Jewish family who had known the Steinmetz family in Berlin. The sponsorship accelerated the customs process immensely. Franz answered their letter and agreed to stay in touch.

* * *

FRANZ STEINMETZ HAD BEEN EDUCATED in Berlin and graduated with a degree in mechanical engineering. He admired the Italian automakers, and after 16 years with Mercedes-Benz in Germany (along with a healthy bank account), he moved his wife, Gilda, their two daughters, Ethel and Sheila, and their son, Mica, to Milan. There, he joined the Alpha Romeo Corporation as a designer. This turned out to be a disappointment to him as well as the company, so Franz quit his lucrative position, rented a small warehouse, and began developing carburetor systems. This enterprise shortly propelled him into a five-figure income. Automakers from around the world clambered for his products. Within two years, he outgrew his space and built his own large plant facility. In another year, he doubled the size of his plant, and shortly thereafter, was well into a six-figure income. He was quoted in all the trade journals and mechanical publications.

Isaiah Cohen lived with his wife Estelle and one son, Howie. The boy was not particularly bright. He had fallen madly in love with Sheila Steinmetz the moment he laid eyes upon her, and because of his limited skills, Franz hired the boy as a parts cleaner and general custodian. If Sheila were to return his love, the boy was guaranteed to be a good provider. Franz would see to that.

Isaiah began at the age of 17 in his uncle's fabric and tailor shop as an apprentice. When he was not at the sewing machine, he was rolling bolts of material or delivering newly sewn garments to customers throughout the city. It was a good job, and by the time he was 21, he had become a master tailor. The money was not great, but he knew he would never starve. Two days before his 23rd birthday, his uncle died suddenly, and with no immediate family, he had left everything — including a tidy sum of money — to Isaiah. In that same year, Isaiah met and married Estelle Steinman.

Benjamin Wetzel answered Isaiah Cohen's ad for an experienced tailor. The two men worked well together, and it was not long before other employees were needed. The business grew steadily, and many designers from other countries were calling upon Isaiah to develop his own line of clothing for department stores, especially in New York City. He had begun to create stylish men's clothing that gave the Italian designers a run for their money. Benjamin Wetzel seemed to be drawn toward the design of women's clothing, experimenting with new fabrics and creating his own styles.

One French department-store buyer had convinced the men that they should have a show in Paris. In the summer of 1925, the men set up a display of seven suits and 22 dresses in the back room of the Bon Iviarchette department store in Paris, hoping to get a reasonable order, at least to cover their expenses. The head buyer had sent out invitations to some of the more important customers. Needless to say, the word got out and the men were deluged with orders and contracts for exclusive designs.

Upon their return to Milan, Isaiah offered Benjamin a full partnership. Papers were signed and the two men began to look for a large building to house the Cohen/Wetzel garment factory.

Within one year, they had employed nearly 300 garment workers. In the spring of 1927, Benjamin's wife became ill with Parkinson's disease and was confined to a wheelchair. Fortunately, there were four girls and two boys to look after their mother. Benjamin had lost some of his enthusiasm for business and spent a great deal of time with his wife. Business did not let up, however, and the money rolled in.

Samuel Gold seemed to have more money than his small rubber company appeared to produce. He manufactured syringes, hot water bottles, rubber hoses, fan belts, and an endless list of other products. It was suspected by the others that he had a side business of producing condoms in Belgium, though no one was certain, nor would they ask. Sam had no children, and lived alone with his wife, Estelle. He and Franz Steinmetz had become good friends through the synagogue, and Estelle Gold and Gilda Steinmetz were inseparable. Nobody ever asked Sam Gold why he traveled so much, nor did he tell anyone, especially Estelle.

Not only was Sam Gold a wealthy man, but also he had become something of a statesman throughout the country. Because of his extensive travel, Gold had collected a wide variety of political friends. He offended no one, and wined and dined everyone. He was in demand at colleges as a speaker on such subjects as manufacturing and marketing, economics in particular, and he never failed to put on a good show. His name was well known, and politicians all over Italy sought his endorsements and advice. Rumor had it that Mussolini had once interviewed him for an ambassadorship to Spain. Political climate had caused Il Duce to reconsider the wisdom of such a move, however. Sam was not disappointed, to say the least. He had been considering moving his entire operation to New York, and had actually signed a lease on a large facility in Lower Manhattan. He planned to become a United States citizen and spend the rest of his life in America. Fate was about to intervene as the war clouds continued to gather.

Peter Dussell and Harry Sukin were second cousins emanating from a long line of shoemakers spanning all of Europe for more than two centuries. Both men had worked and played together since childhood. They served their apprenticeships together as young boys, and continued as friends and workmates into adult life. They were craftsmen and developed shoe lines of the highest quality for both men and women. The brand name Roma was considered the finest Italian shoe on the market. Like the others, success was abundant with financial rewards to match.

Though they were part of the clique, the Dussells and Sukins spent very little time with the others. They and their families worked together and vacationed together. It was strange, however, to hear the two men talk business. One would think that they thoroughly disliked one another, but such was not the case.

TWELVE

IT WAS 9:05 P.M. WHEN PETER DUSSELL pulled into a deserted alley near the Steinmetz plant. He stepped out of his car and looked cautiously in all directions to make sure he had not drawn attention to himself. A gust of wind caught his hat, and he chased it for nearly a hundred feet before he could place his foot on it. He picked it up, began dusting it off, and reshaped the brim. All the while, he continued to look around for some unseen danger. He chuckled to himself as he thought how indiscreet he appeared.

Dust and debris continued to blow against the side of the building as he peered through the office door. Holding his hat tight to his head with one hand, he cupped his other for a better look. He wondered if he had misunderstood the directions. There was no sign of anyone else around. Just then he saw the silhouette of Franz Steinmetz coming toward the door. Dussell backed up a step as Steinmetz opened the door.

"Peter, we were beginning to get concerned," Steinmetz commented.

"Where are the others, Franz? I didn't see any cars. Is anyone else here?"

"The others are all upstairs. We need to get started. Come in! Come in!"

The men sat nervously around a large oak conference table. They were engaged in conversation and took no notice of Peter Dussell.

"Friends," Steinmetz began, "I know this is short notice, and I'm sure you're wondering about the urgency of this meeting." They all stared at

Franz in anticipation of his purpose in calling the group together.

"As you know, we have discussed the present political situation in the country many times, and what it may mean to us and our families as time goes on. Well, gentlemen, it appears to me, and Isaiah Cohen as well, that perhaps we have been involved in too much discussion — and not enough planning."

"What do you mean by that?" Sam Gold chimed in. "Have you discovered something that we are not aware of? I know we are not the most popular people on Earth, but why this sudden need to do something? More importantly, to do what?"

"Please, Sam, hear me out. As you know, Isaiah and I just returned from Rome, where we listened to Mussolini speak about many things, not the least of which dealt with the future of the Jews in Italy. I can tell you, it was not comforting."

"What is he planning to do, hang us all?" quipped Sukin. Three or four of the men chuckled softly. Benjamin Wetzel did not chuckle. His face turned ashen as he fumbled with a pencil, and with eyes shifting wildly, he waited for Franz to continue.

Franz was about to speak when he heard a car outside. He motioned for the men to be still as he peered out the corner of the window. There it was, an unmistakable Buggatti with military paint, occupied by two brown shirts with helmet liners, looking at the building and slowly moving around the corner toward the alley where Dussell had parked. Soon, the group heard a distant, loud knocking at the door below. They remained frozen until the car drove off. Franz decided all was clear.

Steinmetz quickly related his trip to Rome with Isaiah Cohen. He did not mention that he had seen Professor DiNapoli's son, however. He cleared his throat and began, "We have all been friends for a long time. We have trusted one another, depended on one another, laughed together, and yes, have cried together. You all accepted me and my family when we arrived in Milan, and now I'm going to ask that you trust me more than you can imagine." He waited for comment. No one moved or spoke.

"I will tell you this: We are in the midst of a political conflict with a dim outlook that could actually propel Europe into war, and we — by which I mean the Jews — are once again a focal point in this conflict for ridicule and God knows what else. I am convinced that we are in for hard times, and we must take immediate action to protect ourselves and our families."

"What can we do, Franz?" asked Benjamin. "We are only six men. Surely you don't expect that we can stop what is going on, do you?"

"No, of course not, Benjamin. What we must do is to protect our financial resources. I have talked to Professor DiNapoli." The men immediately began to fidget and mumble.

"Please listen to me," Franz protested. "The professor agrees with me that we must take action at once. We are not poor men, and DiNapoli feels that our combined financial strength will be necessary to get the country going again when this mess blows over. He has a plan and would like to present it to us."

"Why, in God's name do we need DiNapoli to help us protect our own money?" Sam Gold demanded. "It seems a little strange to me that a group of Jews must turn to a gentile to help save our asses. I don't like it."

"Neither do I," Sukin joined in.

"Gentlemen, please, please! This is not the time to talk about Jew and gentile. We have a good friend we can depend upon. He is willing to help us, and let's face it, we are not left with a lot of options," Isaiah Cohen declared. "Listen to Franz."

"Let me see if I understand just what you're leading up to, Franz," one of the men commented. "Somehow, we're going to put all our money into DiNapoli's hands and then wait a year or two to see if he gives it back. Is that correct?"

"No! No! Now you're talking like a child. First of all, we do need to put our money and other securities in his hands. But he assures me that he has a plan that protects us. Will you at least hear his ideas?"

The men talked back and forth for five to ten minutes, and finally Sam Gold turned to Franz and said, "You are right, Franz. Now is not the time to discuss our heritage. Gino DiNapoli has been a good friend to all of us, and I for one trust him and I trust his judgment. I just have one question, however. Why can't we close our accounts here and just make transfers to Zurich or New York, or some other safe place?"

"Well, Sam, part of that plan is workable. At the present time, we can still close all our accounts. The problem is that if we try to transfer monies to foreign banks, a red flag will go up, and Mussolini's people will be on us like a pack of dogs."

"What's to prevent us from simply going over to Zurich and depositing our monies?" Wetzel wanted to know.

"Because, Peter, we are Jews, and Hitler's guard dogs are all over the place. I doubt that any one of us could make it to the front door of any bank in Switzerland. Everything would be fine once you get into the bank. The problem is that we must use several banks, and that lowers our odds of making it. Sam Gold, here would probably have the best chance, but even that is stretching it. No, we need someone who looks Italian and has a name like DiNapoli. He has been in and out of every bank in Zurich, is well known, and would not arouse suspicion. The Swiss banks are completely confidential, and quite honestly, I think it's our only chance to do this thing right."

After a great deal of muttering, the men all agreed to listen to DiNapoli's plan. They were running out of time and they knew it. It was time to act.

"All right, my good friends, forgive me for anticipating your wishes in this matter, but I have already taken the liberty of speaking to Gino. He has been preparing for this turn of events for some time. In fact, he discussed it with me over a month ago. At that time, I felt no need to consider such drastic action as he is proposing. I was wrong."

"What do we do next, Franz?" Sukin asked.

"We are to meet with DiNapoli Monday night at seven in the conference room of the university library. There will be people everywhere, so we should not draw undue attention to ourselves. I wish to warn you all that this meeting is not only to hear the professor's plan, but that we must be ready to put it into action immediately. I cannot impress upon you enough the urgency that faces us all. Now, we have been here long enough. Please leave the building one at a time. The brown shirts may still be snooping around; be careful. Thank you all for coming on such short notice. It is a terrible thing to spend the Sabbath talking of such things. Certainly, Jehovah will understand." The men continued departing until the last man had left the building ahead of Steinmetz.

Military vehicles seemed to be everywhere. Eyes were watching every move of anyone who remotely appeared Jewish. Fear was mounting daily. The Jewish community was showing signs of fatigue. Jews were beginning to be arrested for minor infractions without letup. Yards and houses were targeted for graffiti. Decomposing butchered animals were left to rot in yards and on porches. All manner of evil acts were perpetrated against the Jews. Police ignored all acts of vandalism. More than a few men had left for work, never to be seen again. Indiscriminate murders were commonplace. Parents were afraid to send their children to school.

THIRTEEN

PROFESSOR DINAPOLI WAS PACING THE FLOOR AS THE SIX MEN ARRIVED, one at a time over a period of ten minutes. He wasted no time in getting started.

"My good friends," he began, "thank you for coming. I'm sure you must have many questions and thoughts going through your minds, and I hope to clarify everything in just a few minutes." He paced slowly back and forth seemingly interminably to Sam Gold and Benjamin Wetzel. They were not known for their patience.

DiNapoli continued. "The best way to present my plan is to tell you exactly what each of you must do and when you must act. As you're probably aware, the Italian military is watching anything that the Jewish community is doing, more so than any other group. Therefore, what we do must be done quickly and efficiently. Timing is everything.

"I'm sure that in our discussions, I have revealed my feelings on the upcoming economic crisis which is going to face Italy, if not all of Europe. My plan is to see that you men are able to get your financial resources out of the country so that when the time comes in a year or two, three at the most, you will be in a position to help rebuild the economic structure of Italy.

"I know that each of you has both cash and securities needing protection, and here's how we must do it. First of all, should you all withdraw extremely large amounts of cash at the same time from a number of banks in Milan, a signal would go out to Mussolini's people, and you would certainly be under suspicion, if not arrested. Naturally, our intent is to get your monies out of Italy. To do this, timing and cover-up are the two elements necessary. There will be a great deal of trust required of you to carry out the plan."

Sukin and Cohen leaned forward on the table. Wetzel and Gold did not move. Franz Steinmetz made eye contact with Dussell, who made no expression whatsoever.

"First is the cover. I have here a letterhead with the name of SOA Development Company. I have printed each of your names as general partners. I would like each of you to sign at the appropriate spot, and I will file it with the court here in the city tomorrow."

"What in the hell does SOA stand for?" Gold asked.

"For anyone outside this group, it stands for Suits of Armor," Gino replied. "Think of it this way: Wouldn't it be nice if a group of patriotic Jewish fellows pooled their capital to set up an enterprise to design and develop such needed items as uniforms, boots, and other military equipment in the hopes of remaining in the good graces of Il Duce?"

The men chuckled and welcomed a moment of released tension.

DiNapoli continued. "Benjamin, how difficult would it be for you and Isaiah to design three or four colorful uniforms to display in your office?"

"Not too difficult. Give us a week or two, and we can have two or three ready."

"How about a day or two?" Gino pursued.

Isaiah and Benjamin looked at each other and shrugged, looked back at him, and nodded.

"That is if you promise not to ship them to Paris for a fashion critique," Cohen chided. Again, the men laughed softly. They were beginning to relax, and they seemed fascinated as to where DiNapoli was going with all of this.

"Now, then, Peter and Harry, I would be most disappointed if you could not design the appropriate footwear for the well-dressed Italian soldier of

1938. I would propose that you use mannequins and a spot in your showroom to display three to four, just in case someone wants to check us out." DiNapoli was on a roll and continued.

"Sam, I would imagine that you and Franz can provide us with some interesting research items for our little company. Something in rubber, perhaps, or a new military application for your carburetor system, Franz." The men indicated that they would be able to come up with something by Wednesday or Thursday.

"Now, Sam, this is where we need you. I know you have a lot of political friends in Rome who owe you favors. I want you to send a cable to someone who is not too strong or in very good favor with Il Duce. Give him one sentence about our little company, and ask if he can get us in to see some high military personnel sometime late next week. It may backfire on us if we are actually granted an interview, however. In either case, we will have accomplished our goal … that of appearing to be out in the open with SOA Development Company, and thus accounting for large bank withdrawals to fund the company. The problem is that bank inspectors always look at large withdrawals, especially if the monies are not redeposited somewhere. I realize it's a lame attempt at a cover-up, but time does not allow us to do any serious planning. Maybe, just maybe, should something happen, the Mussolini people might buy it, and save somebody's neck if the rest of the plan gets fouled up."

"These people are probably arrogant enough to believe that we are trying to save our hides with this charade," Sukin surmised.

"Gino," Isaiah interrupted, "how do we avoid drawing the attention of the examiners?"

"All right, Isaiah, this is the next step, and the critical one. Beginning Monday morning, two of you need to make withdrawals no larger than your normal amounts, which the banks are used to. You must get cashier's checks. Some of your withdrawals can be made out to cash, most to SOA Development Company. You need to coordinate this together, so that throughout the week, you will not all be bombarding the banks at the same time.

"By Friday afternoon, about an hour before bank closing time, you must make your final withdrawal. Under no circumstances are any accounts to be completely closed. This would certainly raise the red flag. Maintain enough balance in each account to continue to operate your business and provide for your families. Remember, you will have to provide for yourselves for a year at the least, perhaps up to two. Allow a little extra."

"What about our stocks and other securities, Professor?" Dussell asked.

"Peter, I want each of you to bring all of your bonds and securities to our next meeting. List every item that you have and bring it with you. Do not keep a list for yourself. I think it would be very dangerous to do so. Isaiah and Franz have agreed to be here to receive everything. I suggest that you work out a schedule of every 15 minutes per man."

"But how are we to be assured that our securities are protected?" Sam Gold asked. "I have a lot of negotiable bonds and other stocks easily disposed of by anyone."

"Samuel!" Isaiah said with an offended tone in his voice. "You think that one of us would steal from you?"

"No, of course not."

"Then perhaps the good professor intends to steal your securities?"

"Isaiah, do not talk to me like a child. I have concerns, as I'm sure we all do. It is not a matter of distrust."

"Then, let us not talk in this manner again. We agreed in Franz's office that we must do this thing. The matter should be closed."

Gino DiNapoli interrupted, sensing the tension mounting. "Please, gentlemen, I understand your concerns, and I do not feel that any of you truly distrusts me or my intentions in this matter. We have been friends far too long for that. It is difficult to sort things out when time does not permit. I think when I am finished; you will all feel more comfortable. May I continue?"

The men all quickly responded with their desire to press on.

"I'm sure that you have all guessed that the most sensible and safest place to hide your money is, of course, Switzerland, and that is precisely what I have planned."

There were no surprised responses. DiNapoli continued, "First, it would be impractical to separate your bonds and securities or to do anything other than place them in one safe-deposit box in one bank. Therefore, I have provided Isaiah with a satchel that is just small enough to fit into a twelve-by-eight-by-fourteen-inch box. Once your securities are safely locked inside the satchel together with a list of each of your holdings, the key will be removed and given to Franz to hold until we decide where it shall be kept. That meeting will take place at exactly four o'clock on Friday in Franz Steinmetz's office. Isaiah will bring the satchel, and all of you men will bring your cashier's checks."

"Will we be given a receipt for our money?" asked Sam Gold, looking at Isaiah, who in turn responded with a dirty look.

"No, but we'll do better than that, Sam. I think you can remember from Friday until Wednesday how much you will have entrusted to me. I, in turn, will trust your memory." DiNapoli chuckled, thinking he had made a pretty good joke. Only Isaiah Cohen laughed. The others didn't respond. Gino was a little disappointed. He continued, "I'm going to hand you each a copy of the letter that will be the instructions for each of the banks in Zurich. There is nothing complicated about it. As I deposit your monies in each of 24 banks, I will be assigned to a particular officer who services the account. This is done with this simple instruction letter on the SOA letterhead. We will be using numbered accounts only, which is typical for large depositors."

"How do the banks keep records of numbered accounts?" Dussell asked.

"Just like any other account, Peter. The only difference is that once an account has been designated a numbered-only account, the name on the account is filed in the bank president's office, and from there on, the account is referred to by number alone. Not too mysterious, is it?"

"You mean our name is kept in an office for prying eyes?" Gold wanted to know.

"That's right, Sam. Remember, secrecy in Swiss banking is a way of life. I assure you, no prying eyes shall ever see anything. Now, let's get back to the letter of instruction."

The men studied the letter, which read as follows:

SOA Development Company
A Partnership
11104 Plazio Marrianni
Milan, Italy

Gentlemen:
Each of the following individuals listed herein, by their signatures or those of proven heirs, shall be entitled to severally or individually act for all in any and all dispensations, deposits, and withdrawals of account numbers listed herein.

They shall further be entitled to present to this bank, on their behalf a power of attorney of another person/s whose signature/s are duly notarized together with a signed copy of instruction from that partner or partners.

The bank is further instructed that no withdrawals shall be made for any reason prior to July 1, 1940.

Following the instructions, each man's name was printed with a line above for his signature. DiNapoli handed them another 23 copies of the same letter, which they quickly signed.

"Now, gentlemen," DiNapoli began, "the reason I have asked you to make your final withdrawals late Friday afternoon is so that I can be on my way to Zurich in order to be there when the banks open Monday. By the time the Milanese people have a chance to smell anything, the deed will be done. Then, let's hope that our cover-up will work if need be."

"Gino," Wetzel interjected, "no one has thought to ask why you are taking such a personal risk. Should all of this create problems for us, it will certainly rain down on you."

"Thank you, my friend, for your concern. I have thought much about the risks. It appears to me, however, that since I have a record of consulting you men in the past, what I'm advising you to do now is not actually against the law. No one has said that you are not allowed to deposit your money wherever you wish. There is no written mandate limiting your actions. I must play the role of the good citizen who follows the law and begs forgiveness for any ignorance that I may possess."

"Gino," Dussell began, "what happens after the deposits are made and you return from Switzerland? Do we meet again?"

"Yes, Peter, we do. I should be back in Milan no later than Wednesday night. We will do nothing until after you all meet at the synagogue on Friday night. This will allow us to see which way the wind is blowing. Assuming that everything is safe, we will meet at the Café Romano at 8:30 p.m. This will allow you to see your families home and return."

"Must we meet on Friday again? I do not have a good feeling about that, Gino," Isaiah remarked with much concern.

"I am sorry for that, Isaiah. But it is the time that others would not expect you to be meeting on business matters. It is the safest time. Now for the matter of what happens next. I have devised a simple code system, which involves using two books. One will contain all the coded account numbers and their locations. Each of your names will be placed in a hat, and the name drawn will be the custodian of the codebook. Should you worry about that individual having such access, I propose another book that will contain the decoding method. This book I will keep in my possession. I obviously can do nothing with it except to decipher the book, which one of you shall have. Therefore, as a safeguard, it will require that both books are needed for anyone to do anything."

"How does the code work, professor?" Sam Gold asked.

"It will not be complicated, just a bit confusing. One book will mean nothing without the other one. My plan is to place double numbers from 10 to 99 and one set of the English alphabet letters into a hat. We simply take the bank names in alphabetical order by the last word of the bank name, rather than the first. A piece of paper is pulled from the hat. It doesn't matter if it is a letter or a number; it will represent the first letter of the last word of the bank's name. There will be no spaces. Numbers and letters will all run together. After the code for the bank's name is drawn, we continue to draw from the hat for the account number. Only the bank name and account numbers will be used. Let's take an example. Say the first bank is Bank of Zurich and the account number is 81168. We start drawing from the hat. Say the first item drawn is the number 33. That represents the letter Z. Then we might draw the letter K. This represents U, and so forth, until we have drawn the bank's name and account number. In the actual codebook, the bank and account could look like this." He began to write on the chalkboard: 33k162lpsl27556mtb14s44hj-meaning Zurich Bank of 81168.

"We might even interject some arrows, asterisks, some equal signs, pound signs, and so on, all of which have no meaning whatsoever, but serve to confuse someone trying to break the code. So our first entry might look like this." Again, DiNapoli went to the board and wrote: >33#**k1621-->ps^127556+mtb14s44<hj.'

"As the code is being deciphered, one need simply ignore anything but the numbers and letters. All the other stuff is interjected at random so that no pattern is formed and hopefully confuses any prying eyes."

"Professor DiNapoli," Steinmetz inquired, "isn't it possible to pick up a pattern if say, the number 33 is always the letter Z?"

"Yes, Franz, you are absolutely correct. Therefore, for each bank and account, we simply put the items back in the hat and repeat the process. Should we draw the number 33 again, it might represent the letter M or W. Unfortunately, this process must be repeated 24 times. I know it's time-consuming, unsophisticated, and well, just damned amateurish, but by God, it should work. Are there any questions so far?"

"Yes, Gino, I have one," Sukin replied. "I noticed in the example you gave, you have run the numbers 127556 together. How do we know if we're looking at one, 27, and 55, or 12, 75, and 5? You know what I mean?"

"That's easy. Remember, we are using only double digits ... a single-digit number never appears. That way, you know that the division must be 12, 75, 56."

"What about the other book that deciphers the code, Gino? How does that work?" Sam Gold inquired.

"Well, Sam, all we do is record the real letters and numbers that are represented by the letters and numbers drawn from the hat to determine the code for each bank and account number. When we are finished, as I have suggested, I will keep the deciphering book and one of you will be in charge of the actual codes. We will place six pieces of paper in the hat, five blank and one with an X. Whoever draws the X will be custodian of the codebook. Fair enough?"

The men all nodded in agreement.

Peter Dussell spoke. "Professor, speaking for myself, and I assume the other men here, I cannot thank you enough for all your help and genuine concern in this matter, and I personally would like to see your name listed on the SOA letterhead. If, God forbid, something should happen that we cannot foresee, I know you will see to our families."

To a man, they all agreed and applauded quietly.

"Friends," DiNapoli began in an obviously emotional manner, "thank you for your trust, and most especially your friendship. I do not know where this will all end, but I assure you that I will be there for you and your families. Thank you again. And now, I think we have been here long enough. If all goes well, I'll see you at 8:30 on Friday. Oh, by the way, let me leave you with this. Just so you can remember the name of our little company, to me SOA was always meant to stand for Sons of Abraham."

The men filed out of the library, one at a time, Isaiah Cohen and Peter Dussell turning to wipe their eyes.

* * *

THE ENSUING WEEK WENT PRETTY MUCH AS PLANNED. Each man made several large withdrawals and the banks took no apparent notice. At noon on Friday, Dussell and Sukin arrived at the same bank. Not wishing to arouse suspicion, Sukin turned and walked into a small shop next door. Upon seeing Dussell leaving the bank, Sukin proceeded to go in and make his final withdrawal. The plan had gone rather smoothly.

Everyone was at Steinmetz's office well ahead of the appointed time. Soon, DiNapoli arrived. The men quickly gathered into a small conference room at the rear of the office and got down to business. Isaiah set the small satchel on the table. Each man placed a stack of bonds and securities on the table with an accounting sheet of contents. DiNapoli began.

"All right my friends, I will now pick up your securities with the content sheet and give them to Isaiah to place into the case. If you have any doubts or second thoughts, now is the time to express them. Once they have been placed into the satchel, you will not see them again until at least 1940."

They all chuckled and pushed their stacks forward. Isaiah Cohen slipped them into a large waxy brown paper bag, placed it into the case, snapped the lock shut, turned the tiny key, and handed it to Franz. Franz kissed the key and held it up for a moment and then slipped it into his vest pocket.

"Now then," DiNapoli continued, "I will collect your cashier's checks. You know how much you are depositing, and that alone is your record."

* * *

ALL OF THE MONEY WAS COUNTED and separated into 24 stacks. The total count was $4,872,356.00, counting bonds and assuming the value of their combined stocks. As DiNapoli announced the total, there was a unanimous sigh of amazement. Each of the stacks of checks was placed into a large envelope with the bank name written in English on the outside. Once the funds were deposited, Professor DiNapoli would be issued one numbered account from that bank, one account per bank. They all agreed to the appointed meeting at the Cafe' Romano the following Friday to prepare the codebooks. Each knew that there would be no turning back.

Once again, they filed out one at a time, some five minutes apart. An old paint-peeled green military vehicle drove past as Sam Gold left the building. The two black-shirted passengers studied him closely as they continued down the darkening street. Sam felt the hair stand up on the back of his neck, much as one senses fear when a barking dog leaps out from a nearby yard. DiNapoli was the last to leave ahead of Franz. His eyes were drawn and his complexion pale from the stress of the last several weeks. He worried about Octavio, whom he loved more than he could express, and yet a son whose political leanings were breaking his heart, day-by-day, piece-by-piece.

FOURTEEN

THOUGH BARELY 140 MILES separated Professor DiNapoli from his appointed destination, the trip would be harrowing enough as he wound his way through the rugged Italian Alps, climbing to nearly 9,000 feet before descending into Switzerland and Zurich. Soldiers would be stopping him several times along the way. They would be asking questions about his destination and business. Gino checked his coat pocket to make sure his papers were there. He shook his head, realizing it was merely a nervous gesture. He was sure that the trip would take all day, perhaps eight to 10 hours or more — and if he should encounter car trouble, even longer.

As the sounds of the city faded behind him, he made his way through Monza, Sorano, and Lombardy. As he began his ascent to the summit, his mind wandered back to the beautiful days of his childhood, and the utter enchantment of the Italian Alps. He had spent his early years near Voghera at the foot of Monte Rosa, rising over 15,000 feet.

From the surrounding luscious green hills and gentle valleys to the majestic heights of Monte Rosa and the Matter horn, the sights and sounds would overflow his senses; yet at times, the utter beauty had seemed almost surreal. *This must be what heaven looks like,* he had often thought.

Everyone loved the Alps. Skiers longed for winter and the breathtaking downhill slopes. Children sped down the hills on their sleds. Girls and boys giggled and squealed, shouting until they became hoarse. Serious cross-country skiers glided across the upland plains, and mountaineers of summer could climb to almost inaccessible paths that would take them to within an inch of infinity.

* * *

THE DRIVE WAS MOSTLY UNEVENTFUL except for occasional military vehicles along the route to the Swiss border, whose passengers glared at the professor's car with the utmost suspicion. Never once did he take his eyes from the road to acknowledge their penetrating glances. His left foot routinely shook each time he engaged the clutch as he shifted up and down the valleys and hills. His nervousness was prompted more from the sheer magnitude of his exotic cargo than from some imagined fear of being caught.

The professor had made the trip in record time, just under eight hours. He checked into his favorite haunt, a small bed-and-breakfast home on the outskirts of Zurich. DiNapoli had known the owners for nearly 10 years and had stayed with them many times. A second-floor corner room overlooking the city — his favorite — was available, and he was soon settled in. Two small satchels were placed under the bed. There was imagined security in this innocuous performance.

His sleep was restless, however, and he was up several times in the night in nervous anticipation of his appointed rounds to come at daylight. *Twenty-four banks, 24 accounts* ran like a record in his brain over and over until he could tolerate it no longer.

Gino got out of bed, drew a tub of water, climbed into the bathtub, and slowly sank up to his neck in the warm water. Now he was able to doze.

As the water began to cool, he awoke. Quietly, he found himself humming some obscure aria and leisurely shaving his face. He dressed and headed downstairs to a breakfast of eggs and sausage. He made the usual small talk with the caretakers. He thought he needed to cover his purpose for being in the city. For no apparent reason, he had summoned some unused hidden courage, feeling confident that all should go well. He began his rounds.

FIFTEEN

BY 2:00 P.M. ON WEDNESDAY, DiNapoli had made all deposits and was on his way home. All had gone well; each bank had been eager to accept the deposits. The managers knew precisely why the money was being deposited and they did not care.

Gino knew that some of this money could be intercepted by the Nazis to finance the Third Reich, but the chance had to be taken. Spies and subversives were everywhere and they surrounded the banks like hungry dogs waiting for a juicy bone. DiNapoli was not a Jew and looked deeply Italian. He was well known in the financial community and was satisfied that he rose above suspicion.

It would be close to midnight before he reached home. Though quite exhausted, the adrenaline kept him alert. He was quite proud of his plan so far. Now, all that remained was to meet with his friends and set up the codebooks.

* * *

FIVE OF THE SIX MEN showed up at the Café Romano right on time. Harry Sukin was not among them. The other men's faces spoke volumes. Gino DiNapoli drew in a deep breath. He knew he had to ask.

"Where is Harry?" he asked, his voice barely audible. The men looked knowingly at one another and then to Sam Gold, who Gino determined had been selected spokesman by the others.

"Gino, my friend, our friend, we are in shock. Harry Sukin is dead!"

"Dead?" responded DiNapoli. "Why? What?"

"Shot by the fascists. Evidentially one of the tellers at his bank, we think, suspected that he was trying to purge his assets. They dragged him to the shed behind his own house and murdered him. The bastards just left him there." Beginning to weep, he continued, "His wife called me, and I called Peter. We went to the house and found him." Now unashamedly crying, he said, "He had at least 15 bullets in his body. These people are barbarians! We called the police and told them what happened. It took 45 minutes for them to show. Damn them to hell, they didn't even take a report. They said we should call our local undertaker. God Almighty, has it begun?"

No one spoke for at least five minutes; then Gino slowly rose to his feet. He paced back and forth for a few seconds and then spoke.

"Has it started? Perhaps," Gino began. "I don't know, but I will tell you this: It didn't start here. This can only be the beginning of another horrid chapter." He continued, "I have no words of wisdom at a time like this. I can only pledge to you my utmost loyalty and friendship. Now, forgive me, but I must ask that we continue with our business — or would you prefer to postpone until later in the week? I'm sure you will need this time to grieve for our friend."

Benjamin reached beside his chair and brought up a sack of rugelahs, small, sweet rollups. He tore the sides of the sack down and exposed the delightfully aromatic treat. He explained that the rugelahs were developed in Austria during Hanukkah in honor of the heroism of Judah.

Benjamin concluded, "I would like to honor the heroism of our brother, Harry, as well as to seek the strength we're going to need in the coming days."

How little do they know, thought Gino, sensing some impending nightmare.

Peter Dussell spoke. "Friends, I know this may seem disrespectful to our beloved brother, but we must make haste to protect our families. Rumors of dire persecution are abounding in Germany. Jews are being singled out and even required to wear the Star of David like a target on their outer clothing. We cannot wait to begin our own personal plans. I say that we conclude all the necessary arrangements regarding the codes right now!" The men all agreed, and Gino rose to speak.

"Very well. Here I have a list of 24 banks, which is divided into 24 sections, each representing one bank and one account number to which I made one deposit. Secondly, here is the book that allows you to decipher the code of accounts; also 24 sections corresponding to the other book. All we have to do is enter a digit or letter for every bank letter and account number, as we discussed. Franz Steinmetz has agreed to assist me in this endeavor. Following that, we will proceed to the other book to replace the actual banks and account numbers with the new codes."

"How are we going to guarantee that this code business will all work out?" Sam Gold interjected. "What if one book is lost, or worse yet, both are lost?"

"Gentlemen," responded Gino, "I cannot express enough that this must not happen! We have this one chance and we must not ruin it!"

Isaiah Cohen rose to his feet. "Friends, I think we know what is at stake here; let's get on with it, please!"

"With that, I suggest we decide on the caretakers of the codebooks," Gino said. They all nodded in agreement.

"If I may," Dussell offered, "I suggest that Professor DiNapoli be selected to hold one of the books."

"Yes! Yes! Of course," Gold cried. "And I think that should be the book that deciphers the codes!"

"My friends, no!" DiNapoli protested. "This is not my business. You must rely upon each other."

"Nonsense!" shouted Benjamin Wetzel. "Think about it, men. Who is the least likely of us to be in danger for the foreseeable future? And if we cannot trust Mr. DiNapoli, then were are in deeper trouble than I imagined."

"I agree with Wetzel," Gold interjected. The men verbally assented.

"If you feel that strongly, then I will agree," DiNapoli responded.

"Franz, you have been rather silent," said DiNapoli. "Do you agree with the others?"

"Yes, yes I do," Franz said softly.

"All right then," Gino continued. "Who would you gentlemen choose to keep the accounts code?"

"I vote for Franz Steinmetz!" declared Sam Gold with great certainty. To a man, they agreed.

The men then settled in to the monotonous work of setting up the books. It took nearly four hours. Professor DiNapoli then handed the completed codebook to Franz Steinmetz and kept the other book as agreed. With that, the men shook hands and departed their separate ways, hoping to forestall the hell which was sure to follow.

SIXTEEN

THE PHONE RANG SEVERAL TIMES before Jim could get himself awake. He had hardly slept at all until almost daylight.

"Hello?"

"Jim," Mary called, "I've got an idea how we can get the book out of that Asian woman's room if it is still there."

"Jeez, what time is it anyway?"

"It's after seven, why?"

"Oh, no reason, just wondering how you can be so chatty."

"I couldn't sleep. I've been up for hours. Now did you hear what I said?" Mary asked with mild concern in her voice.

"Yeah. What do we do, hit the guard over the head?"

"No, nothing like that. I was thinking more of the feminine approach."

"Umm hmm, why am I not surprised? Tell me more."

"Just call Hunter, Jim. Tell him to meet us at your place right away. I'll explain then."

"Mary, you know what you're saying, don't you? You're suggesting that we jump into this thing and stick our butts out just to see if we end up dead or alive. Are you sure that this is what you want?"

"Jim, you tell me you don't want to go any further and I'll shut up and never mention it again … not too often anyway … at least today."

"You may be right, Mary. I couldn't think of anything else when I got home. But I'm not very hot on the idea of you sticking your neck out, however."

"Don't you worry about me, big fella. Hell, let's call this Jim and Mary's excellent adventure!"

"Damn, Mary, last night you told me you were afraid. I sure as hell don't hear any fear in your voice this morning. What changed?"

"Oh, I don't know; daylight, intrigue, maybe the fear itself is exciting. I just know that I don't want it to stop here."

"Okay, I'll call Hunter and see you at your place in about an hour. Bye!"

* * *

HUNTER PULLED UP TO JIM'S apartment a few minutes late. Mary was already there.

"What's up? Do we have a super plan hatching?" mused Hunter.

Mary immediately spoke up. "Are there stairs at both ends of the Asian's apartment building?"

"I don't know, I suppose so," Jim interjected. "Why?"

"What if you and Mr. Hunter position yourselves just below the head of the stairs nearest the apartment? I'll come up at opposite side carrying a sack of, oh, apples"

Chuckling, Hunter said, "Apples? Apples? Okay, Miss Rison, then what do we do with the–ah-er apples?" He was patronizing her.

"I'll cough or make some slight noise to attract the guard's attention when I reach the top of the stairs. When he looks, I pretend not to notice him. I'll raise my skirt and adjust my pantyhose ... I'm sure that will disarm him — no pun intended."

"All right, so you've created a horny guard," Jim responded. "Now what?"

"I drop the sack of fruit. At that point, with my skirt raised and apples rolling everywhere, don't you think he would be inclined to help a lady in distress?"

Jim and Mr. Hunter looked at each other with no expression whatsoever.

"Well, what do you think?" Mary asked, quite proud of her little covert plan.

"Oughta work," Jim said, tilting his head and shrugging his shoulders. "The guard might be thrown by the sight of a non-Asian woman in the building. But then again, he would have no reason to suspect that only Asians live in the building, right?"

"How do you feel, Mr. Hunter? Do you think it can work? And will you be able to get into the room?"

"Not a problem, Mary. I've picked some mean locks over the years, and yes, it's just simple enough that I think it will work," responded Hunter. "The key is to get in and out in a matter of seconds." His face was showing some signs of doubt.

They agreed to execute the plan the following day around 1:00 p.m., hoping that most foot traffic would be gone from the building.

* * *

JIM HAD THREE LESSONS before meeting with Mary and Hunter. He grabbed a Starbucks on the way to the airport and headed on in.

"What have I got this morning?" he asked Nancy.

"Would you believe? Donny Friend called yesterday and wanted to schedule another lesson."

"You got to be kidding! What did you tell him?"

"I just told him it would be up to you. So he's coming in this morning. I hope that was okay." Nancy made a funny pursing shape with her mouth.

"Yeah, it's all right. I don't have a clue what I'm going to say to him."

"I'm sure it will be just the right thing," Nancy said and smiled.

"Why don't wives talk like you do?" Jim said with a smile. "There'd sure as hell be a lot less divorces."

Jim went into the common office, updated his logbook, and reviewed his lesson plans for the day. Mary wasn't due for her lesson until later in the week.

He completed his flights in plenty of time to meet Mary and Rolly Hunter.

SEVENTEEN

JIM RILEY HAD ARRIVED AT the Asian apartment house at 12:55 p.m. Mary and Hunter showed up minutes later. They quickly discovered that there were indeed stairs at both ends of the hallways. Mary had her paper sack of apples. Hunter chuckled. Jim checked her legs to see if she had her pantyhose on. She did. *My God, what a pair of legs!* he lustfully observe.

"Are we sure that the guard is on duty?" Mary asked.

"Let me check," responded Jim.

He softly took the steps two at a time. It was a matter of seconds before he returned. Breathing rapidly, he reported in. "He's there, all right. About a third of the way down on this side."

"Okay," Mary chimed in. "I'll head to the other end and see you at the top. I guess its show time!"

Jim merely shook his head at her. He couldn't decide if it was her acting or her self-assurance that made her such a piece of work. Whatever it was, he liked it!

Jim peeked around the corner. The guard was engaged in a folded magazine. Mary tipped her index finger at the other end. Plan A was underway. Mary Rison began to play her part with an Academy Award-worthy performance. The guard responded in the predictable way Mary had foretold.

She stopped at the top of the stairs. With one hand, she slid one side of her skirt up and over her hip and said aloud with pretended modesty, "Oh damn!"

The guard played his role on cue. He jerked his head up and turned to look at Mary. He dropped his magazine and stared wide-eyed at this magnificent sight down the hall. Holding the apples in one hand, and her lifted skirt in the other, she let the apples drop. The guard was on the scene in an instant.

Hunter worked like a surgeon on the police lock attached to the doorjamb. It was no match for his years in the business.

They had agreed to spend no more than 45 seconds, and they would look only in the most obvious places such as desk drawers and dresser tops. They had no reason to believe that the book would be hidden.

The plan was rewarded. The book lay in open sight on the bedroom dresser beside a wallet, a plastic toothpick holder, and two condoms. Hunter quickly placed the book into his coat pocket and they were at the door.

Jim opened the door a crack. The guard was on his hands and knees, picking up apples. His back was toward the door. Both of Mary's arms were waving and gesticulating and she was talking a mile a minute to the guard, raising her eyes on occasion to see what the two men were doing.

Jim and Hunter rushed down the stairs and waited out of sight outside the building for Mary. Nearly 10 minutes passed before she appeared.

"What happened?" Jim asked.

"Well, you can't just drop the curtain. You have to end the play. I asked him about his family, and you know, small talk. Then I told him I had forgotten something in the car and walked back down the stairs. I knew he couldn't leave the floor."

"Let's go to my hotel," Rolly Hunter said.

Jim and Mary nodded in agreement.

EIGHTEEN

"HELLO, MR. WI, THIS IS Oliver Windom ... Yes, you asshole! Windom! No! Don't give me that crap! I know exactly what happened! Haven't you seen the news, for Christ's sake?"

"Uh huh," yelled Windom, following a barrage of Korean epithets from the other end.

"Now let me tell you something. If your stooges hadn't been so damned greedy, this thing would be over and done! Now I've got so many tracks to cover, I'll be lucky to get out of this with my hide. God knows who might have seen my car there."

"You must still pay as agreed, Mr. Windom, only now, you pay me," came the voice from the other end of the line.

"Pay? My ass! First of all, you didn't deliver. Then your little trigger-happy friend's self-destruction exposed me to I don't know what the hell. I will pay as agreed for the Santa Barbara thing, but that's it! Check the drop spot on Wednesday morning. And by the way, I wouldn't consider some sort of revenge or blackmail if I were you! I don't think you would like my response."

"Mr. Windom, may I conclude with a little saying where I come from which allows, 'All deserved things will come in their own time.' I'm a very patient man, Mr. Windom. I will wait, but my turn will come. You may count on it!"

"Yeah, whatever," responded Windom. He slammed down the phone.

Oliver Windom had been more angry than worried about any repercussions that he might endure at being spotted outside the double shooting. He wondered if Jim Riley had somehow looked out of his window. Indeed, there was nothing he could do about spilled milk now. He must operate with the idea that Riley knew he had been there. What worried him most was how much David Steinmetz might have told Riley when they were together. Now Jim Riley must be considered dangerous. He still felt that Riley must be eliminated.

Windom could not let the thought go. How close he was to having both books in his hands. So many years, so many prices paid. How he had paved the road to this moment, only to have it slip from his grasp.

* * *

HIS MIND TRAVELED BACK to June of 1940 and the morning he had boarded the freighter *Algiers* with his younger brother, his mother, and his father, Gino DiNapoli.

His father had not spoken to him in nearly a year. The boy had brought so much shame to the family through his flirting with the fascists, and yet, he loved the boy so much that he felt he must get him out of Italy altogether. He must go to America, away from those pigs.

Gino had paid a lot of money to have his son literally kidnapped by a group of thugs and brought to the pier. He prayed that he could undo the brainwashing Octavio had received at the hands of the fascists. Time would tell.

The *Algiers* was a rotting tub of steel, yet the passenger staterooms were quite acceptable. There were seven in all, each exactly like the others. The DiNapolis had a porthole of their own. Gino had added a few extra lira to the ticket price during negotiations with the captain. Gino had even been allowed to bring aboard 22 carefully contained grape roots. They were placed out of the way on the bridge. Gino's son Octavio would know how to tend to them during the long crossing. Even though Octavio hated his father, he had always loved tending the tiny family vineyard.

Next to the DiNapolis was a family named Henderson who had not yet arrived. All other passengers were aboard and busy with their unpacking. The captain was quite irritated and paced back and forth across the bridge.

Finally, they showed up. Gino DiNapoli drew a deep breath in disbelief. He did not need to see the man's face. The familiar walk was enough. It was Franz Steinmetz and his family.

"Good morning, Mr. Henderson," shouted the captain from the bridge as the Steinmetz family ascended the gangway.

Steinmetz, not raising his head, held up his left hand and waved with a weak circling of his wrist.

How in God's name was Franz able to wrangle this? thought DiNapoli. The military goons had checked and searched his family from stem to stern. They looked at Octavio DiNapoli as a possible deserter from Mussolini's chosen. Gino made up an on-the-spot story about his son going to America to learn fluent English and exclaimed how the military would profit from his son's experience. Gino was sure that they hadn't believed the story, but let him go when Gino handed them a few lira. Franz Steinmetz must have paid through the nose to make this happen.

By noon, the *Algiers* was out of the harbor and laboring its way toward America. The bunker fuel was billowing its smoke a hundred feet into the air. The old vessel complained with every turn of the screw. The weather, on the other hand, was beautiful and lunch was far better than anyone had expected.

Soon, everyone had settled into a spot for viewing, snoozing, or reading. Some of the passengers became a bit seasick, but no one had to vomit.

The ship moved slowly south down the Ligurian Sea into the Mediterranean, west to the Straits of Gibraltar, and eventually out toward the Atlantic and America.

Within six hours, there was nothing but water and waves. Octavio, his father, and Franz Steinmetz could not possibly know what was about to befall them in a matter of a few weeks.

* * *

GINO DINAPOLI AND FRANZ STEINMETZ had spent most of their

days sitting on the fantail of the *Algiers,* talking about all that had happened since the murder of Harry Sukin, and the fear it had generated among all the Jewish families.

"Franz, I am astounded," Gino announced on the first morning out of the harbor. "How in the name of God were you able to get your family out of Milan?"

"It was not easy, my friend. The last two months have been a nightmare, to say the least."

"In what way a nightmare, Franz?"

"To begin with, all of my family members and I have been followed day and night. Not once was I able to go to work or to the emporium without at least one black shirt in sight, always staring accusingly at me. The same was true for all of my family!"

"I am so sorry, Franz. That was not fair."

"I tell you, Gino, we all nearly died of pure fright!"

"So what did you do to get out of the city?" Gino asked. "How did you get your family on this boat, and all safe?"

"After nearly one month of this constant fear, I decided that I must do something. We could not live in Milan any longer. To do otherwise would have been a death sentence to my family."

"Yes?" replied Gino.

"As you know, Gino, I do have many connections throughout Europe, and yes, America. I cannot trust that my family would be safe anywhere else but the United States. I contacted a client in New Jersey, Abel Weiner. I explained that I must get my family out of Italy. I asked that he retain my last half-dozen invoices to his company until I could see him in person and collect. He understood and I can tell you, Gino, it is enough to last until I can make other arrangements."

NINETEEN

THE SUN HAD JUST RISEN ABOVE THE HORIZON. The *Algiers* steamed its way well into the mid-Atlantic westward toward America. All aboard were moving about, having breakfast, walking the decks, and generally feeling free. They were somewhat giddy as they contemplated their final destination.

Then it began. The white watery torpedo trails were unmistakable. A loud thud followed by a sudden uplifting of the entire port side of the ship, accompanied by a deafening explosion.

"What in the hell?" yelled Gino from the opposite side of the ship as it settled back to level for only an instant. Suddenly, the explosion repeated itself. This time, the bow appeared to Franz to literally fly apart. The ship rolled and shuddered so violently that passengers could not stand. The shudder was felt in their very bones. People were falling and stumbling everywhere. Franz could hear Mica screaming, "Papa! Papa! I need you!"

As he moved toward the source of his son's voice, he glanced toward the sunrise. He could barely make out the undeniable shape of a small vessel on the surface. He thought how black and evil it looked. He knew in an instant: It was a U-boat. Several crew and passengers saw it simultaneously. It turned broadside in what seemed like an arrogant snubbing of the sinking *Algiers*. The numbers shown against its black background color were U-61.

Gino thought to himself, *I'll remember that number forever!* Then he yelled, "God damn you all to hell!" as some flying debris hit him in the face and belly. He went down instantly.

Minor explosions emitted from deep in the bowels of the ship from bow to stern. The heat and smoke were overpowering. Franz Steinmetz tried to remain on his feet. The stench of burning flesh made him nauseated. Panic and fear welled up in his brain. He turned his mind toward Gilda and the girls. Gino DiNapoli lay unconscious at his feet, bleeding from his nose and chin.

Franz felt the blood on his brow as he swiped the back of his hand across his eyes. He felt no pain. Trying to shake the cobwebs from his mind, he gazed across the burning, twisted steel and cargo, which in no way resembled a ship.

Franz realized the ship was sinking. He ran as fast as he could to the family's cabin. No one was inside. He grabbed only an old briefcase containing the agreements and deposit records of the six men.

By the time he returned to deck side, he noticed that the ship had continued to list to starboard, making it impossible for anyone to stand upright. He reached for whatever was not burning and tried to make his way forward to where he had last seen members of his family. Holding tightly to the briefcase, he called out, "Gilda! Ethel! Sheila! Mica!" Suddenly hit by a flying piece of debris, he fell to the deck unconscious.

The ship continued to shudder and emit strange noises like a dying animal in its final death throes. People were screaming. Some were trying to get to the bow and others were scampering toward the stern.

The U-boat circled like a vulture around to the port side. Its crew raised the hateful swastika. It blew in the breeze as a final insult.

Two members of the *Algiers* crew screamed at Gilda. "Missus. You must come to the lifeboat! Now!"

"Where is my husband?" she cried in anguish.

"Do not worry, Missus. We will find him. Now you must get in the lifeboat! Please, Madam! We have no time!"

"My boy, please! My boy!" she cried.

She could not see or hear Mica or Franz. She could only trust the crew to rescue the two. With great hesitation, she and the girls boarded the life raft. Shelia had been close to one of the many explosions. Her clothes were torn away above her waist. Only the cuffs of her blouse remained attached to her upper body. The crewman handed her a canvas tarp to wrap around herself as she entered the lifeboat. The second crewmember began to lower the small boat. However, the ship was listing so badly, the lifeboat slid slowly down the side of the ship with a terrible screeching and bumping noise.

As the lifeboat neared the water, the U-boat opened fire, riddling the boat to splinters. All that remained was blood, flesh, and bits of clothing splattered along the side of the sinking ship.

Franz awoke and began calling frantically for Mica. He continued calling his name. He picked up the briefcase as he stumbled his way toward Mica's earlier call. He saw him several feet away, near what remained of the bow. Twisted steel and burning cargo prevented forward progress toward his son. Mica was wedged between a wooden cargo box and a bulkhead girder. His father thought him to be unconscious. Then Mica moved slightly and looked toward his father.

"Papa! Papa!" the boy yelled. "Please!"

Franz tried moving debris out of his way, cutting and burning his fingers and arms while holding tight to the briefcase. He could not give up.

Another explosion came from the aft portion of the ship, which shook the twisted metal in front of Franz. It allowed him to move enough wreckage to get through to his son. At first glance, the boy's arm appeared broken, but Mica assured his father that it did not hurt much.

Franz dropped the briefcase and picked up a steel bar, enabling him to pry the carton from the girder. He cried as he held his son. The sudden thought of losing his wife and daughters flooded his mind with anguish. He had last seen them in the dining area just below the bridge. It had all been blown apart. Everything above the main deck was totally destroyed.

The ship was now listing nearly 30 degrees. Franz was certain that she would roll over at any moment. He picked up the briefcase and handed it to his son.

"Do not let go of this case, my son, no matter what happens."

He and the boy made their way to the highest point of the vessel. As he looked out, he saw debris everywhere. Less than a thousand yards beyond the wreckage lay the fearsome U-boat. He could swear he saw a smiling face looking at him from the deck. Spotting a large wooden crate floating just a few feet from the ship, he immediately acted.

"Mica! We must slide down the side of the ship and get to that crate in the water. Do you understand?"

Mica nodded in response. Without hesitation, Franz grasped his son by the waist. With briefcase in hand, he lifted his legs over the side. They began kicking and sliding down the side. They hit the water hard. Franz felt something snap in his shoulder. He screamed with pain but held on to his son. Nearly exhausted, Franz Steinmetz dog-paddled his way to the carton while holding tightly to his son.

It was perfect for the moment, about two feet thick and roughly a four-by-eight-foot rectangular crate. Drawing his last ounce of strength, Mica was able to help himself aboard, careful not to drop the briefcase. He reached for his father's good arm and pulled him close enough to grasp one of one of the wrapping bands. With his son's help, he was able to get aboard the ready-made raft. Franz grasped the old briefcase, now waterlogged, and slipped into unconsciousness from the unbearable pain in his shoulder.

* * *

GINO DINAPOLI COULD HEAR the captain's voice screaming at him as he slowly regained consciousness.

"Mr. DiNapoli! Mr. DiNapoli! Please, wake up, sir! You must get off the ship, now!"

"Yes, yes, where is my family? Are they safe?"

"Mr. DiNapoli, your wife and youngest son are safely aboard one of the lifeboats. We have not seen your elder son. Now, please let me assist you aft where you may abandon ship!"

"All right. Please look for my son!" Gino demanded.

"Yes, but we have less than five minutes before the ship sinks. I will do my best."

The captain lifted Gino to his feet and forced him into a lifejacket. He guided him through the rubble toward the rear of the ship. The ship was now tilting more than 45 degrees and Gino was just able to slip under the guardrail and into the icy water. He barely felt the cold as he moved away from the ship as quickly as his tired body would allow.

DiNapoli paddled for what seemed like hours, scanning the water for any signs of a lifeboat. Nothing! As he looked back, he saw that he was barely 50 yards from the *Algiers*. He felt a slight bump at his back from a section of one of the lifeboats. He turned and saw that it had either been blown up by a torpedo or destroyed by gunfire from the U-boat. All that remained was the port-bow section. It floated, and it was enough.

Gino hooked his finger into the bow's tie ring. He swung himself around and clung to the vessel. At almost the same moment, his eldest son Octavio grasped the same piece of floating wood.

"Octavio! Thank God you're safe!" Gino cried. "What about your mother and Dominic? Have you seen them?"

"No! I jumped from the ship a few minutes ago and I saw no one," Octavio answered while water sputtered from him mouth.

A sudden screeching sound rose behind them. As they looked, the ship rolled over. What was left of the bow squealed for help as it pointed to the sky; the *Algiers* slipped beneath the surface, fan tail first. It made no further sound as it disappeared.

Within seconds, the water began to swirl as it sucked against the float. Octavio and his father hung on tightly as they felt the powerful tug toward the gaping whirlpool. Oddly, as they looked, they were able to see another boat being drawn toward them from the other side of the pool. There was no doubt: it was Franz Steinmetz and a child.

Almost as quickly as it started, the whirling water settled, followed by an eerie calm over the scene. In the distance, a black boat turned and slithered beneath the ocean. Life stood still for several moments.

Gino began to have trouble holding on to the jagged piece of boat. With one hand, he reached into his pocket and pulled out a small, wet black book. He said to his son, "Octavio, you must listen to me. What I have in my hand is more valuable than my own life!"

"What is it?" asked Octavio.

"I want to tell you a story without much detail, and you will see what I mean," Gino said with much hard breathing. The boy looked into his father's eyes and said nothing.

Gino began, "Son, I know that you have been involved in a very hateful and dangerous circle. I know how angry you are with me for forcing you away from those awful fascists. This makes it much more difficult for me to count on you to follow my instructions."

The boy looked at him with some defiance, but Gino knew that he must continue. "I have to trust you, son. Please do not defame me with any idea that may hatch in your mind. You will know what I mean."

Octavio nodded in reluctant compliance, his lips tightly pursed. For nearly two years, because of his activity in the fascist youth movement, Octavio had been angry with his father. His father had vehemently opposed his participation. How often he had thought that his father humiliated the family with his close friendship to those hated Jews.

Octavio's father then told his son of the codebooks and what lay behind their meaning. Octavio was stunned. It was incomprehensible to him that his own father would put his family's lives in jeopardy for a few rotten Jews.

"See that Mr. Steinmetz gets this book!" Gino uttered, now barely able to speak. "You must promise me! Should he not make it out of this mess, give the book to one of his family. They will know what to do."

The boy became silent for a few moments and then reluctantly assured his father that he would do as he was asked. He squeezed the wetness from the book and slipped it into his jacket pocket.

Octavio had not had time to secure a life vest before leaving the ship.

Nevertheless, he exhibited considerable strength and was able to hold tightly to the makeshift raft. Gino, on the other hand, was losing his strength. His arm was aching and he felt himself slipping. He was unbearably cold. He could see blood seeping from beneath his vest. His mouth was dry and he could not breathe. Soon, he lost his grip. He closed his eyes. Gino DiNapoli fell away from their temporary haven. The son turned his head from the father. He would not look back. The last words from his father burned into his brain.

"Octavio, promise me!"

He began to scan the debris field, trying to spot his mother and younger brother Dominic.

* * *

FROM A HUNDRED YARDS AWAY, the lifeboat crewman spotted a small crate floating with two people aboard. He rowed the boat toward them, calling out. "Ahoy there! Ahoy! I'm coming alongside! Reach out for the line! Now then, mates. That's it! Gotcha!"

The crewman, with the help of Sophia DiNapoli, pulled Franz and Mica aboard. They were exhausted but glad to be safely aboard the lifeboat.

Franz looked at Sophia with anguish. She returned the look, slowly moving her head back and forth, affirming the worst. Franz's eyes welled up as he hugged Mica. He began to cry softly. Mica patted his father on the back.

"Do you know what happened?" Franz finally asked.

Sophia and the crewman exchanged glances. She turned to Franz and placed her hand on his arm.

"It was the gunfire from the German boat. They just blew it up. So barbaric. So barbaric."

Franz said nothing and continued to hold tightly to his son.

"I'm sure it's no consolation, Mr. Steinmetz," came the crewman's voice, "but it was quick. I do not think your family suffered."

"Thank you," Franz responded. "I'm glad to know that."

The passengers continued to scan the surrounding water for any signs of life. Soon they heard the call of Octavio DiNapoli coming from a distance. Sophia cried out in response, "Octavio! We're coming, we're coming! Hold on, sweetheart!"

They rowed their way to the source of the call. Indeed, it was Octavio alone. He was helped aboard. His mother hugged him tightly, both laughing and crying.

"Have you seen your father?" she asked.

"No," he lied.

They searched the immediate area. Nothing was found but an empty lifevest, several mattresses, and miscellaneous bits and pieces of ruined lives. Finally, the crewman stopped rowing and announced, "We need to take inventory of our supplies. We do not know if the ship's radio operator was able to send a distress signal after the first attack. There is no telling how long we will be here." They began their inventory, knowing full well it was probably an exercise in futility. The boatman opened the small emergency rations hatch and determined that they could survive perhaps three days, certainly no more than five.

Most important of all, they needed to dry their clothes. A few disrobed and lay their clothing over the rail as modestly as the situation would allow. Sophia DiNapoli turned her back and shared as much of her dry outerwear as possible with the others. The crewmember shed his jacket for one of the men.

"We must try to maintain our present position," Franz managed to suggest.

"It is our best hope," the crewman affirmed.

* * *

THE FIRST AND SECOND DAYS were calm and clear. During the second day, while most of the survivors were dozing, Franz moved to Octavio's side and asked him, "Octavio, did your father ever say anything to you about a small book he was carrying?"

"No," was the one-word reply. Franz knew he was lying and that he would not be able to trust him further.

Franz made his way to the other side of the boat next to Octavio's brother

Dominic. They spoke quietly for several minutes. The very thought angered Octavio, but he said nothing.

On the afternoon of the third day, Octavio shouted, "There! On the horizon! Don't you see?"

"Yes, Oh yes! I see the smoke rising! It must be coming this way!"

Everyone began to chatter at once. A new hope sprang up within the little group. A collective sigh of relief fell over them.

Soon the shape of the vessel began to show, and minute by minute, grew larger. All began to shout and wave. Shortly they could hear a half-dozen blasts of the ship's horn. It was music to their ears.

As the ship neared, some mouths fell agape! *Americaland* shone brightly on her bow. She flew the flag of Sweden.

"How ironic," said Franz. "Must we indeed be in God's hands? Such an omen!"

Captain Hermann Rauch stood on the bridge to welcome the survivors. Little did he know that his fate would come in February of 1942 at the hands of U-106. But for now, he would deliver his embattled cargo to New York Harbor. Two books in separate pockets made their way to America. Five souls were to embark upon a life that many could only dream of.

* * *

BY THE EARLY '40s THERE WAS A FEEDING FRENZY all over Italy. Jews were being indiscriminately shot or rounded up for delivery to Nazi death camps. War was exploding everywhere. America was responding to Pearl Harbor. General Doolittle was soon to lift the American spirit with a bombing run over Tokyo. The entire world was at war.

Samuel Gold and his family were arrested while trying to make their way to Southern Italy and consequently transported to Auschwitz.

The Wetzel-Cohen plant was burned to the ground. The two men were clubbed and killed while trying to fend off looters. The black shirts stood by and watched. The Wetzel and Cohen families seemed to disappear from the face of the earth.

TWENTY

THE PORT AUTHORITY PILOT made his way to the bridge of the *Americaland* as she circled Sea Gate. The ship made her way through the Narrows past Fort Wadsworth on the left and Fort Hamilton on the right. Soon the shape of Miss Liberty grew larger on the left. Sophia DiNapoli and her two sons stood viewing the unbelievable sight as it came into view. Sophia cried softly, "Gino, Gino, how you would love this sight!"

Dominic held his brother's hand and gazed without expression. Octavio looked defiant, like a soldier taken prisoner.

Franz Steinmetz held tightly to Mica and cried aloud for his family. Yet not all tears were sorrow. He knew he would soon regroup with the other family members, whose faces he could barely recall. First of all, he must contact Abel Weiner to arrange a meeting in New York as quickly as possible. Captain Rauch offered a ship-to-shore connection, and soon Franz was talking with his client and friend. They agreed that Abel would meet him at Ellis Island. It would not be necessary for Franz to call. Abel would contact the information center at Ellis and track him down.

Soon the lines were thrown and *Americaland* was secure against the dock at the Manhattan Piers.

With all the thank yous said, the passengers disembarked. With wide eyes, they were directed to one of the ferryboats docked at Battery Park.

Customs agents checked what few papers had survived the attack and soon the five were on their way down the Hudson to Ellis Island. Sophia DiNapoli and Franz Steinmetz felt fear and excitement.

* * *

AS THE IMMIGRANTS ARRIVED in the Ellis Island Great Hall, exhausted and overwhelmed from their long journey, they were herded through inspections. Captain Rauch had told them early on that in order to gain entry to the United States, they needed to be disease-free and prove their ability to earn their way in their new home.

Sophia DiNapoli had no worries financially. She knew her husband had taken care of those details. He had given her all the necessary information required to make her way in America should something happen to him. Gino had heard horror stories of others who had come before — money stolen or lost, family members getting separated after leaving Ellis Island, children getting into the wrong situations. Gino DiNapoli had taken no chances.

Franz Steinmetz, on the other hand, had lost everything but a single old water-drenched briefcase with the sinking of the *Algiers*. It held the key to his past and possibly his future. He knew he would need the help of the Italian Embassy, if indeed it still existed, with Italy continuing to chum up with the Nazis. He knew that at best, it would be a matter of time before the embassy had to vacate the United States. He would have to deal with it. Perhaps his client Abel Weiner could run interference with the customs people.

Inspectors began immediately. They were looking for any sign of illness, and those were marked with colored chalk: an X for mentally handicapped, a K for hernia, SC for scalp disease, or H for heart problems. Xs were returned to their homeland at the ship's expense. Either the whole family could return or send the affected member home. There were no exceptions.

Many were detained for various reasons, and some had to have relatives claim them. Families were forced to decide on the spot whether to split up or return home.

* * *

ABEL WEINER ARRIVED AT ELLIS, where Franz was waiting patiently. Together they met with the customs agents. It was clearly understood and forgiven that Franz Steinmetz had no papers. He did have a wallet, two signed receipts from a local bank in Milan, and a hard-to-read receipt from the U.S. Embassy in Milan. It was immediately obvious that his wallet had been quite wet. In another pocket, Franz produced a small black book that contained only gibberish. It was damp and showed signs of deterioration. To further help matters, Weiner agreed to sponsor Franz and his son. It proved to be no disadvantage that Franz was Jewish. His reason for leaving Italy was all-too-well understood by the Customs agents. There were no chalk marks on either him or his son. All necessary papers were processed, and Franz and Mica left Ellis Island for the streets of New York. He would soon try to contact his younger brother, whom he believed to be living near Santa Barbara, California. Even though his only correspondence from his family went down with the *Algiers*, he had remembered the postmark from Santa Barbara, California. He and Gilda had found it on a United States map and had looked at it many times. They would visit the family there someday.

What a beautiful place it must be," they had often commented to each other. It was urgent that Franz and his son make their way to California. However, it held no excitement for him now without his Gilda and the girls.

"Mica, America is our new home now. We must always remember your mother and your sisters, but we must go on to our new lives. You know they would have wanted that."

"Yes, Papa," returned Mica.

* * *

THINGS WOULD NOT GO AS WELL for Sophia DiNapoli and her sons. They had been questioned at length several times. Always the same questions: "How long had your husband been a professor? How much did he earn? To what organizations did he belong? Who were his associates? What did they do? How long did you live in Milan? How much money do you have? How will you support yourselves?"

It was always obvious to Sophia DiNapoli. Why didn't they ask the only question that mattered? *"Mrs. DiNapoli, was your husband a member of the Fascist Party, or did he sympathize with them?"*

That question was never asked. This routine continued for nearly a week. She was advised that she must remain at Ellis Island until they could verify exactly who Professor Gino DiNapoli was, and if not, Sophia and her sons would be deported back to Italy. The customs agents were not so tolerant of their lost Visas and passports as they were for the Steinmetz's.

Mrs. DiNapoli was informed that a communiqué had been sent to the U.S. Embassy in Milan seeking information about Professor DiNapoli, but they would not offer hope that the embassy would respond or was even still operating. They would simply have to wait. Octavio DiNapoli studied the strange little black book. It made no sense, yet he was not a stupid boy. He was reasonably sure it had something to do with finances and the Jews his father befriended so closely. Otherwise, why was he asked to give the book to Mr. Steinmetz?

It was not a good time for Europeans to be emigrating to the United States of America. Italy was about to be cut off, as were immigrants from Germany and Japan.

Sophia called her two sons together.

"Octavio, Dominic, I would like to ask you something … well I guess tell you something. As you can see, we are not being made to feel welcome in America. Do you know why?"

"Yes, ma'am," Octavio replied. "We are Italian!"

"Of course, honey, but more than that, we are being looked at as though we are a part of those awful people who are trying to destroy our country."

Octavio responded, "They are not awful people, Mama! They …"

Sophia slapped his face hard.

"Do not ever say that to me!" she shouted. "Now listen to me. Our name is going to become a problem in America if we're allowed to stay."

"Are we going to change our name?" Dominic asked.

"I'm not sure. Dominic, would you like that?" she asked.

"Can I be Superman?" he responded.

"No, sweetheart, I don't think that would be a very good name." She looked quizzically at Octavio but did not speak.

"Do whatever you want. I don't like any of this," was his retort.

"In talking to others here at Ellis Island, I have heard of several people who have changed their names for all kinds of reasons."

"Are you ashamed of who we are, Mama?" Octavio asked.

"No, Octavio. We will always honor the name of your father. It's just that we must begin a new life here, and we do not need ridicule or worse. Do you understand, my dears?"

Octavio pursed his lips and gave a quick, unenthusiastic nod. Dominic imitated his brother.

"What name are you thinking, Mama?" asked Octavio.

"Oh, I'm not sure. I guess any name that sounds American. She noticed a newspaper sitting on the bench near them. The headline read, *WINDOM OFFICE COMPLEX TO SPEND THOUSANDS FOR RENOVATION*.

"How do you like Windom?" she smiled.

She continued to peruse the article, something about an Oliver Windom spending a lot of money to fix up an old building in New York City.

"How do you like that, Octavio, Oliver Windom? Sounds pretty sophisticated to me."

"Whatever you want, ma'am," he answered.

"Dominic, I think you should keep your name. I do love it so!"

"Dominic Windom?" he said, curling up his nose.

"It's settled then. We are the Windom's," Sophia stated emphatically. "Now, I must have a first name." She went to the phone booth and began thumbing through the pages.

"There, that's it! Dorothy. Dorothy Windom," she pronounced in her very broken English. "I think it is very American," she said with a laugh. It was the first time in weeks.

None of the immigrants at Ellis bothered to question another's business. If someone wanted to change his name, it mattered not to anyone. This was the place and time for it.

* * *

AS THEY WAITED FOR SOME RESPONSE from the embassy in Italy, Sophia used the time to become friends with other immigrants, discussing their plans and hopes for their future in America.

There were several fellow Italians who talked of the great Central Valley in California, perfect for growing wine grapes. She found this to be most intriguing. She and her son Octavio — Oliver — knew a good deal about grapes and winemaking. If they were to use their knowledge and expand their thinking, it might just be possible to make a living. She would think more about this idea. Fortunately, she had retained all banking documents in her handbag, which survived the sinking, along with $400 in U.S. currency. She would certainly have no trouble in gaining access to her money through their Italian sister bank in New York City. She knew that she must move quickly before assets could be frozen, if they were not already.

After nearly two weeks, Sophia was summoned into the Customs Office.

"Mrs. DiNapoli," the man began, "I'm happy to inform you that we have heard from our embassy in Milan regarding your husband."

"Yes?" she responded.

"Professor DiNapoli was quite well known and respected in your homeland, Mrs. DiNapoli."

"Thank you," she said.

"Our embassy verifies his financial and social standing in his community. Further, he was a stalwart voice against the fascist regime."

"Yes, sometimes to the detriment of his family," Sophia responded.

"Well, you might be happy to know that the embassy also sent a letter of recommendation for your husband, along with some copies of legal documents tracing his activities for the last several months. You should be quite proud."

"Yes, I'm very proud to have been a part of his life. I loved him very much."

"Mrs. DiNapoli, I certainly don't want to throw water on all this, but there is some information regarding your elder son that does not sit well with our inspectors."

"I know where you're going with this, but believe me, my son is not now involved nor is he sympathetic to those horrible people who have stolen our country."

"I understand, Mrs. DiNapoli, but hear me, please. There are those who want to deport him at once."

"No! Please, no!" she protested.

"Now, now, don't get excited. I simply said that there is that feeling among some."

"And you, Officer?" she replied.

"Well, as far as I am concerned, I would much rather see him here instead of in the middle of an enemy nation where he would represent more danger than in your hands here in the United States."

"Thank you," she said

"Our decision is to let you pass, with the understanding that you will, without exception, report to us where you are going and notify us of any change of address for the next five years. Any violation of this requirement will mean immediate deportation. Do you understand?"

"Yes, Officer —" looking at his badge, "Hanlon. You may be sure that I will comply."

"Well, then, Mrs. DiNapoli, may I be the first to welcome you to the United States of America. You are free to leave any time."

"Thank you for your help, Officer Hanlon. I do have a question for you."

"Yes, ma'am?"

"If one were to consider a name change, how would he go about it?"

"Well, I know that it is common thought that many people change their names here at the island, but actually very few have. I would suggest that you go to the Superior Court Building in downtown Manhattan and file for a legal name change."

"That's all?"

"Yes, ma'am, I think so, or perhaps easier than that is to apply for a social security card and use whatever name you wish to continue using. It's not official, but as far as the government is concerned, it is. Over a period of time, it will become your name."

With that, Sophia DiNapoli, now Dorothy Windom gathered her two children and their belongings and boarded a ferry for New Jersey. A small town called Modesto would be their final destination. Mrs. Dorothy Windom and her sons Oliver and Dominic shortly boarded a train for the West Coast of America. Soon they would be home.

* * *

THEY INDEED MADE THEIR WAY to Modesto. Sophia DiNapoli (now Dorothy Windom) died within two years. She made Octavio (now Oliver) promise to take care of Dominic. By now, Dominic was a teenager. Oliver was busy with his winemaking and paid little attention to his brother. He took care of his basic needs but little beyond. It would be only a matter of time until Dominic would be into mischief and in trouble with the law.

Dominic spent his early twenties steeped in drugs and women. Oliver threatened to disown him if he didn't settle down. Dominic could not, and Oliver did what he promised. By now, Oliver Windom was becoming a noteworthy member of society. With the help of a local lawyer, it required very little effort to have his brother committed to a rehab center, from which he would not be released. Dominic had run away twice and now was on permanent lockdown. Oliver padded the monthly payment to see that his brother was well cared for — and more importantly, locked up.

* * *

"MY GOD, HAS IT BEEN SO LONG?" Windom spoke out loud to himself. It had happened more than 50 years ago, and yet it seemed like yesterday to this tall, ruggedly handsome yet sorrowful man.

He had lost nearly 20 pounds since firing Jim Riley. His weight loss made him appear taller, yet his face now looked bony and sallow, rather than the chiseled Marlboro Man.

He got up from his desk and walked slowly out onto his massive redwood deck. He stood silently surveying the fluffy cloud formations. Slowly, he dropped his eyes and began to pore over his beautiful vineyards. That sight alone brought him solitude and made him feel complete. Yet he cried softly to himself. There was pain in the solitude of his murmuring.

* * *

FRANZ STEINMETZ AND HIS YOUNG SON had spent several weeks in New York before heading west to Detroit. There, Franz would be welcomed by General Motors as a fuel mechanics engineer. Mica soon learned English and achieved above-average grades in school.

He met a lovely gentile girl, Susan Anderson, in his senior year. They were married on Mica's 19th birthday. Susan had been pregnant for six months at the time of the wedding. Though Franz felt some shame at his son's lack of judgment, he nevertheless treated Susan as his own daughter. He loved his new grandson, Isaac, and he hoped they would have a daughter. Such was not the case. He soon became the grandfather of a second boy, Aaron. Things did not go well with the pregnancy, and Susan spent many weeks in bed. She nearly lost the boy on two occasions. She died three days after a difficult birth. The diagnosis was massive hemorrhaging with no further explanation. It was totally unexpected. She had felt no symptoms of danger aside from normal postpartum problems. Nonetheless, it happened.

Mica vowed that he would not find another partner. His father had given him the down payment on a small deli in the Motor City. It became quite successful. Mica raised his sons with all that a father could give.

The boys were close friends and rarely had disagreements. Aaron idolized his older brother and loved his role as a "me too" brother.

Mica told the boys about the codebook. His father had given it to him for safekeeping until he would hear from some descendant of the original families. No word came. Mica had tried to find Octavio DiNapoli, whom his father told him he must find. No such name could be located. He told the boys that Isaac was to become the custodian of the codebook. Isaac promised to assume the responsibility.

Time passed, and the boys grew to become respectable adults. Aaron attended UCLA Law School, and soon after joined the firm of Goldman Law

Offices in Santa Barbara.

Isaac continued the male offspring. His son David, his only heir, was given the codebook for safekeeping. He was admonished by his father to contact the Holocaust Foundation and any other source to aggressively find an heir of Gino DiNapoli. David Steinmetz promised to pursue the search. Knowing that it was unlikely for a gentile name to show up in any records, he would continue to investigate every possibility.

He would begin with the Ellis Island Historical Records Foundation. He knew that DiNapoli must show up. He would follow the trail from there. Most likely, if the family had changed their name, it would have been without formality at Ellis Island, or legally in Manhattan. The Hall of Records would reveal any such action. David Steinmetz began his long and arduous journey.

TWENTY-ONE

MARY HAD ONE MORE DUAL CROSS-COUNTRY hop to complete and a couple of solo cross-country flights before her final check ride with the FAA inspector.

Jim met her at 9:30. She had filed her flight plan, and her pre-flight was completed. Jim knew it was not necessary to double-check her.

Unlike Donny Friend and others he could not trust, Mary had always been flawless. He had often observed her from his office window. Her procedure was exemplary. He had never known anyone else who could make a pre-flight inspection look sexy, but she did.

On several occasions, Jim had asked Mary to show Donny how to do a proper pre-flight. It was a lost cause. Finally, she refused any further attempts.

Mary strapped herself into the left seat, and Jim climbed into the right side. Jim reviewed her flight plan. Her plan was to fly to Livermore, southeast to Stockton, on to Los Banos, do a touch-and-go, and head straight back to San Carlos.

Mary called "Clear," and immediately started the engine. She did her taxi clearance and headed to the end of the runway. She did her engine run-up, received her clearance, and they were off. She rotated at 65 knots and swung out to the east, sailed past Moffett Field to the 880, climbing to 3,000 feet, and then turned toward Livermore.

Jim was looking at the *San Jose Mercury News*, only glancing occasionally to see where they were. There was some cloudiness, and Jim thought it might be a good time to see Mary's performance under the hood. They would do some cloud flying as well. They were well clear of traffic.

"Want to try some hood work?" he asked Mary as he reached back for the headgear.

Mary readily nodded. She slipped the hood on and looked only at the instruments. Jim took her through some standard stalls and turns. Mary soon became bored and asked her instructor if she could do a loop.

"It's not legal, you know. Oh well, what the hell?" Jim responded. "Do you need me to talk you through the setup?"

"No, thank you, sir," came the answer.

"Okay, Miss Smarty Pants, take it away. It's show time!"

Mary leveled off for a moment, wiggled her butt to get comfortable, got her wings straight and level, and checked her heading. She gently increased to full power and began a shallow dive. At 130 knots, with the motor whining, she eased the wheel back and continued until it was against her chest. Her eyes were glued to the ball, trying to keep the rudder and ailerons centered. The power bled off as she climbed straight up and over. Just as the stall warning sounded, she was over the top and into a steep dive. She immediately relaxed back pressure and pulled her power to idle and eased the wheel forward enough to ease into a shallow dive. She leveled off, looked at her heading, and squealed, "I'm dead-on heading!"

"That's great, Mary," Jim concurred, "and all under the hood! That was a classic inside loop! Nice work, sweetie." She had performed the loop like a seasoned professional. He could not have done better. Her father had taught her well.

"Excuse me, Mr. Riley, what did you call me? Have I just been insulted, patronized, or verbally kissed?" Mary squirmed with excitement.

"You choose. That was sweet, and it was most certainly not an insult."

They flew in and out of some small clouds, and Jim gave her pointers as to what happens when the weather suddenly closes in on you and requires some immediate decisions.

Jim and Mary did not discuss anything related to Rolly Hunter, codebooks, or anything that had been going on lately. They were not ready to talk about their next move for one simple reason: They had no idea what the next move would be.

Mary touched down at Los Banos. She was battling a 15 mph cross wind. Jim thought for a moment that he would have to take over. However, with his confidence in Mary's unique ability, he would hold off as long as possible.

It was ugly, but she hit the centerline halfway down the runway, gunned the engine, and whisked her way back into the air with a steady hand and a Mona Lisa smile on her face. Jim could only shake his head in utter respect and amazement.

She had completed one of her final requirements as they returned to San Carlos, hardly speaking a word. Both Jim and Mary independently knew what they wanted to do next — this day, at least.

Jim walked Mary to her car. She unlocked the door, got in, and rolled down the window. Jim placed his hands on the door, reached his head in, and gave Mary a short kiss. She responded without hesitation.

"Would you like to come to my place tonight?" Jim asked.

"Uh huh," she answered. "I have a class at 4:00 this afternoon. Then nothing until 10:00 tomorrow. Will that work into your plans?"

"I'll have to think about that. Okay, I thought about it. That plan will definitely work."

Jim looked up as the Subaru passed down the next lane.

The Asian man peered straight into his eyes from the driver's side. The man formed a pistol with his thumb and index finger. He pointed the pretend weapon at Jim and moved his lips to further pretend a gunshot. He then sped out of the parking lot and onto the 101 north. Jim tried to get the license number, but the car was too fast. He thought that there were two passengers besides the driver in the car. Mary saw the car, but she made no comment. She rolled up the window, left the parking lot, and pulled onto the 101 south.

Jim returned to the flight office and his next appointment: Andy Rivers, a new student in his early twenties, fresh out of the marines. Riley was looking forward to the meeting.

* * *

ANDY RIVERS SHOWED UP ON TIME for his first meeting with Jim Riley. Riley explained the flight program, took Rivers for a familiarization ride, completed his morning flights, and left for home. He was on the 101 south as the Subaru pulled alongside. In an instant, his peripheral vision took over. He spotted the Smith and Wesson aiming at his head. Behind the trigger was a scar-faced man. The picture burned into Riley's brain. A rugged scar ran from under his right eye, across his nose, and down to his upper lip on the left side of his face. Jim hit the brakes and swerved as he heard the shot. Riley lost control of his Camaro, slammed into the concrete divider, flipped twice, and landed on the driver's side in the far right lane. At the same time, the car continued turning as it slid along the pavement, finally resting hood-down in the barrow pit. The right front wheel continued turning for several seconds. Cars were screeching behind the wreck.

Police and other emergency vehicles quickly arrived on the scene and began their work. Jim Riley was not moving. Firemen pulled out the Jaws of Life and began ripping the passenger door apart. Upon completion, one of the EMTs crawled inside with a neck brace in hand.

Within a few minutes, Jim Riley was extracted from his car and loaded into the waiting ambulance. He remained unconscious and was bleeding from the forehead. His shoulder was twisted into an unnatural position. The ambulance screamed its way to Kaiser Memorial Hospital emergency trauma center. A practiced team of doctors and nurses swung into action. In a matter of minutes, Riley was embedded in a mass of tubes and electronic monitoring equipment.

As standard operating procedure dictated, Jim's pockets were emptied by the attendants in search of a contact person. Mary Rison's phone number was folded inside his wallet.

"Someone want to call this number?" asked the head ER nurse. One of the nurses took the number and left the room. The time was 1:13 p.m.

TWENTY-TWO

AT 3:00 P.M., Mary Rison hurried into the hospital waiting room. She approached the information desk and inquired as to Jim Riley's situation.

"Mr. Riley is still in surgery, miss," answered the elderly woman. "Let me call the nurses' station to see when they expect him to be transferred to recovery."

After a few moments on the phone, the woman turned to Mary. "They expect to finish in another half hour or so. Would you care to wait in the recovery waiting room? Also, there is a cafeteria down the hall on the left."

"Thank you, I think I'll wait in the recovery area," Mary replied.

The woman gave her directions and Mary moved quickly to the elevator.

* * *

IT WAS 5:30 P.M. WHEN THE NURSE shook her shoulder softly. "Are you Mrs. Riley?" she asked.

"No, just a good friend," Mary answered, rubbing her eyes.

"Oh, well he is resting comfortably, but he'll be quite groggy for several hours. He should be fine, though."

Mary left for the cafeteria and some supper, though she had no appetite. Mostly, she had no intention of leaving until Jim would wake up and assure her that he was all right.

After dinner and back in his room, she saw him begin to move while uttering incoherent sounds. Mary jumped to his side and laid her hand on his hair.

"Jim, Jim, can you hear me?"

"Yeah," he finally managed to respond. "What happened?"

"Jim, you've been in a car accident. Do you remember?"

"No, but I think someone shot at me," Jim answered.

"Oh my God! Have you been shot?"

"I'm not sure. I saw this guy point a gun. That's all I remember."

Mary rolled his sheet back to find any evidence of a gunshot wound. She quickly realized she wouldn't recognize it if she saw it. She could see that his shoulder was wrapped together with his left arm and securely in a sling.

"Just a minute!" she said as she hurried out the door to go to the nurses' station.

Shortly, she returned to Jim's bed. "You have not been shot, thank God!" she exclaimed.

"What's all this cast stuff?"

"The nurse said you suffered a dislocated shoulder and a bump on the head."

"Oh, is that all?" Jim replied.

"Well, it could have been a lot worse, Mr. Smarty Pants!" came her retort.

Jim dozed off. Mary held on to his hand and ran her fingers through his hair.

By 8:00, Jim had been moved to his own room and was resting comfortably. Mary called Hunter's number to explain what had happened.

Hunter answered, "I'll be over as soon as I can. Whatever you do, don't leave his side!"

"You think this has something to do with those damn books?" Mary asked Hunter.

"I don't know, Mary, but we're going to find out! Now keep your eye on him. Watch everybody who comes into his room. I'll be there soon." He hung up the phone.

* * *

ROLLY HUNTER MADE HIS WAY up the elevator and through the nurses' station to Jim Riley's room. Mary was sitting in the visitor's chair, reading an obscure medical magazine.

"Hello, Mary," Hunter said.

"Mr. Hunter! Thank you for coming. I don't know what to make of all this shooting business, do you?"

"Not just yet, Mary, but I intend to find out. This is not a case of road rage; I am sure of that!"

"Do you think someone suspects that Jim has the codebook?" Mary asked.

"Well, look at it this way," Hunter answered. "Jim said that he saw the Windom limo outside the apartment house when the Asians killed each other. I think Windom knew that they had retrieved the book."

"Then why is someone trying to kill Jim?"

"Not someone, Mary — Windom," Hunter clarified.

"Well, if Windom latched on to the second book, why would he care what Jim does?"

"The Santa Barbara murder, Mary. Jim could easily tie Windom to that killing. I think it was a hired hit and it was to include Jim Riley. You know, clean up the whole mess with one contract."

Jim was beginning to awaken.

"Jim … Jim? Wake up, Mr. Sleepy Head. How are you feeling?" Mary asked.

"I don't know. I can't seem to wake up," Jim responded. He recognized Hunter. "Hi, Mr. Hunter. How come you're here?" Jim sleepily inquired.

"Hello, Jim. I'd like to ask you the same thing. What are *you* doing here?"

"Well, Mary probably told you. Some nut tried to shoot me."

"Did you recognize the guy or have any idea why someone would try to shoot you?"

"Mary and I saw that same car in a parking lot earlier. I'm not sure about the driver."

"Jim, I need to find out if the guy meant to kill you or just scare the hell out of you. I'll find out where they took your car. I want to see if there is a bullet hole anywhere."

"I can't imagine that Windom would want me dead until he has both books in his hands. I don't think he could have known that the Asians had it," Jim surmised.

"Yeah. Maybe you're right, Jim," Hunter answered. "And I do think that if there's a bullet hole near your car window, we should assume that someone was trying to kill you," he concluded.

The three discussed other possibilities and concluded that they would follow the bullet theory. They agreed that whatever it was, Windom was behind it.

Mary gave Jim a quick peck on the cheek and said, "We need to let you get some rest. I'll be back in the morning, Jim. Sweet dreams."

"Yeah, right!" he mumbled as he gave her a limp wave. Jim was sound asleep as Mary and Hunter left the room.

* * *

HUNTER CALLED THE SAN CARLOS POLICE DEPARTMENT the following day to get permission to view the car. He was given the name of a local garage and proceeded to look at the car. It was sitting on its wheels. He could view the driver's side clearly. It was covered with dents and scratches, but just above the window, he could detect the unmistakable pattern of a bullet hole.

"Those bastards *were* trying to kill Riley!" he said aloud to himself. "Why would they do that without knowing where the friggin' book was?" he wondered.

Then the obvious struck him: *There was a contract on Jim Riley and somebody didn't know it had been cancelled!*

"Who in the hell are these people who seem constantly to know where Riley is?" Hunter muttered to himself.

First the Windom limo in front of his apartment. That is understandable, he thought, *but out of the blue they spot him in a parking lot. I don't think so!*

Hunter felt an urgency to talk to Jim Riley alone. He did not want Mary Rison to be there. Somewhere in the back of his mind, Hunter was getting an uncomfortable feeling.

Something smells in Denmark! he thought to himself.

TWENTY-THREE

HUNTER PULLED INTO THE HOSPITAL parking lot a little before noon. He entered Jim's room a little uneasy about what he was thinking.

He did not expect to see Mary sitting there, but it didn't surprise him either.

"Hi, Mr. Hunter!" she said cheerfully. "Look at our patient. He's crabby as hell, so I think he's doing quite well, wouldn't you say?"

"Umm, yeah, he looks all right to me. How about it, buddy, how are you doing?"

"Well, I'll be doing a lot better when I'm outta here, I can tell you that," Jim answered.

Hunter continued the usual hospital small talk. He would have to wait until a more opportune time could present itself. In his heart, he hoped he would be wrong. Right now, it seemed unlikely.

Mary's cell phone rang.

"Hello, this is Mary," she answered, walking toward the door. She stepped outside.

The men could hear her talking. Jim paid no attention, but Hunter was trying to catch anything while listening to Jim Riley.

"Yes, I know. I'll meet you at the usual place in about an hour." She concluded the call.

Hunter felt a sense of concern. "The usual place." He had heard it clearly.

"Hey, guys, I have to go. My roommate has lost her key and needs to get in."

Mary went to Jim's bedside and pecked him on the cheek.

"I'll be back tonight. Bye!" she called as she left the room.

Rolly Hunter slowly paced the room, looking for just the right words. Then he began, "Jim, how well do you know Mary?"

"What?"

"How well do you know her?"

"What in the hell are you asking me that for?" Jim asked in total puzzlement.

"Jim, have you been to her place? Have you met either of her parents?" Hunter continued.

"Now wait just a minute, Rolly. I don't know where you're going with this, but I really don't like it."

"Have you ever figured out how Windom knew where you lived?" Hunter pursued. "Jim, I know how you feel about Mary, and I don't blame you, but I've got to tell you, someone knows your whereabouts all the time. The only two who should know are Mary and I."

"So what?" Jim responded, now getting irritated.

"Jim, please bear with me for a few minutes, okay?"

"All right, but I'm not liking this."

"Jim, have you wondered how someone just happened to know that you were in my hotel parking lot?"

"Well, maybe someone has been following me, I guess."

"Have you seen anyone following you? Have you looked?"

"As a matter of fact, I have. After those guys in the parking lot, I have really been watching."

"And yet, you didn't see them coming on the freeway!"

"No ... but I'm not sure that means anything," Jim said.

"Maybe not, Jim, but I think it's time to consider the possibility. Remember, somebody, most likely Windom, thinks you have the codebook."

"Yeah! But to try to shoot me?"

"Hey, remember, we're talking about millions of dollars here!" Hunter interjected.

"Okay, Rolly, if I buy this cockeyed idea, what do we do next?"

"Well, I'm going to do a little snooping of my own. In the meantime, don't do or say anything to alert Mary."

"I guess I'm due to get outta here in a couple days. We'll need to talk then."

"Don't worry, I'll get back to you. I won't try to see you until then. I'm going to be busy."

"I'll be fine. I still don't know whether I should just slug you and be done with it," Riley concluded.

Hunter quickly left Jim Riley's room.

Jim was suddenly startled as his phone rang loudly.

"Hello?" he answered.

"Hi, Jim! Guess who?" Mary's voice sounded.

Riley was so taken aback that he had no words, but began stuttering slightly.

"Jim Riley, what the heck's the matter with you? Is that bump on your head getting worse?"

"No, I'm just surprised. You just left here. I didn't expect you to be calling me."

"I was just curious. When we got the book from the apartment house, who ended up with it, you or Mr. Hunter?"

Jim Riley was stunned. "Why do you want to know that?" he asked, sounding almost angry.

"Oh, no reason. I guess I just wanted to talk to you again. I'll be glad when you are out of that smelly place!"

"We'll talk about the book when I get out. It should be by tomorrow afternoon," Jim said.

"All right then, you take it easy, big boy, and I'll see you tomorrow. By the way, I can't stop by tonight. My roommate is having more problems than a lost key. Tell ya later!" Her cell phone clicked off.

Jim was starting to sweat. *Is it possible that Hunter is on to something?* he thought.

He needed to call Nancy at the flight center. She would be beside herself wondering why he had just disappeared. He dozed off before he could make the call.

It was nearly 4:30 p.m. when he woke to the sound of his phone. He knew it could only be one of two people. He was wrong.

"Hello?" Jim answered.

"Hello, Jim?" came the voice from the other end.

"Yeah, this is Jim."

"Jim, this is Oliver Windom."

"Mr. Windom?"

"Yes, Jim. I heard that you were in the hospital and I was concerned and wanted to see how you're doing."

Jim Riley said nothing.

"I know how surprised you must be, considering how we parted and all." Jim was silent.

"Jim, you know me well enough to know that I don't hold a grudge. I'm sure you may not even be over it yet. That's okay, but I was concerned and needed to call."

"Who told you I was here?"

"Some young lady called me yesterday and thought I might like to know that you were in the hospital."

My God, he thought, *Mary!* Riley decided not to ask any further questions for the present. He was almost breathless.

"Thank you, Mr. Windom. I'm doing fine and should be out of this place tomorrow."

"That's good, Jim! I would like to get together with you when you're feeling better. I wanted to talk to you about David Steinmetz."

"David Steinmetz? I don't understand," he lied.

"Well, it's nothing really. I just have a couple of questions I'd like to ask you," he said, not wanting to overplay his hand.

"That's fine, Mr. Windom. Be glad to," Jim lied.

"Glad you're feeling all right, Jim. I'll call in a few days."

"Thanks for calling, Mr. Windom." He hung up the phone.

He immediately picked it up again and dialed the flight school number.

"Flight school, this is Nancy. How may I help you?"

"Nancy, this is Jim."

"Jim, how are you doing? I was just about to call you!"

"How am I doing? Well, let me put it this way, I'm in the hospital."

"Yes, I know. Mary Rison told me right after the accident. She's called every day. I have your hospital phone number. Honestly, I was going to call you before I leave work today. What do think of that?"

"I think I'm either stupid or mentally handicapped. Stuff is going on around me that I feel I should know, but I don't."

"What are you talking about, Jim?"

"Never mind; you wouldn't understand," Jim said, shaking his head.

"By the way, I took the liberty of calling the Windom Wineries to let someone know about your accident. I guess I actually talked to Mr. Windom himself."

"Thank you, Nancy, thank you!"

"For what?"

"Nothing, just thank you!" Jim replied.

Jim was relieved that Mary had not been the one to call Oliver Windom. She would know better. All he could think about were the things that Hunter had asked him about Mary. His mind would not let him believe that Mary could be part of anything to do with Windom. His dinner arrived, but he ate nothing. He found himself wanting to talk to Hunter, so he decided to call him.

"Hello, this is Rolly Hunter. I can't come to the phone right now. Leave a message. I'll get back to you."

Jim hung up the phone, sat up on the edge of the bed, wincing from the bumps and bruises he felt. He put his feet on the floor, stood up, and stretched for a few minutes. He walked out into the hallway and began to circle the nurses' station. Walking actually felt good, and for a few minutes, he was able to put aside his worst fears — but only for a few minutes.

His phone was ringing as he returned to his room. Somewhat out of breath, he answered, "Hello?"

"Jim, Hunter!"

"Hi, Rolly," he said slowly.

"I know why you called, Jim," he answered.

"Yeah, but I'm not sure I want to hear what you have to say!"

"Well, all I can tell you now is that I found the name of a Donald Rison from my Washington connections. He *is* a sales distributor for several wineries in Northern California."

"And?" Jim interjected.

"And, they are all vintners for, are you ready, Windom Wineries!"

"Oh my God! This can't be!"

"Jim, let me ask you a question," Hunter said.

"Yes?"

"I've heard you talk about Mary's flying ability —"

"Good God! What now?" Jim asked, obviously shaken.

"Well, it may be nothing, but I also found out that at least one of Windom's pilots is a woman."

"Oh no! For Christ's sake!"

"I really didn't want to tell you until I find out for sure. I guess you have a right to know whatever I find out. I'll know by the time you are released tomorrow. I'm sorry, Jim."

"I know," Jim answered. "I'll see you tomorrow."

* * *

MARY AND ROLLY HUNTER MET in the hospital cafeteria at 11:00 a.m. They decided to have lunch while waiting for the medical people to complete all the discharge paperwork for Jim.

"Mary," Hunter jumped right in, "Jim thinks you're an unusually fine flyer!"

"Yeah, I guess I get that from my dad," she said.

"I guess I really haven't asked you much about your family, with all this codebook stuff going on. I apologize."

"Why would you apologize?" she asked.

"Oh, I don't know, just common courtesy, I guess." He realized the comment sounded a bit stupid. He decided to go no further with it.

The nurse had just assisted Jim into the wheelchair when Mary and Rolly entered his room.

"Hey, let's get out of the place!" Jim stated with glee.

Mary pulled her car up to the ER exit. Jim got in, feeling very uncomfortable. The three left the hospital and agreed to meet at Jim's apartment.

Jim hardly spoke as they drove to his place.

"You're awfully quiet, Jim. Are you feeling okay?"

"Oh yeah, I'm fine. Just glad to get out of there."

He was trying to be careful not to say anything that might make her suspicious. At the same time, he felt an overwhelming sense of guilt that he could even be thinking that Mary could be part of some scheme prompted by the likes of Oliver Windom.

They continued on. Neither spoke; each was trying to be the coy one. They pulled into the parking lot and headed up to Jim's apartment.

Hunter was waiting for them.

TWENTY-FOUR

JIM LAID AROUND HIS APARTMENT for several days. He had not heard from Hunter, and he couldn't help wondering if Hunter did not want to deliver the inevitable message. "Mary is not who she claims to be!"

I can't stand it, Jim thought, *but I've got to know!*

Mary had called a couple times in the last few days but did not want to come by his apartment. He thought he should drive by her place to see where she lived, but he thought, *I don't have a clue where she lives! No wonder women think men are so dumb!* Anyway, it didn't matter. He could barely move his arm and shoulder. He definitely wasn't ready to drive. Besides, he had nothing to drive.

Can it be that Mary is sensing something going on? Jim thought. *I've got to settle this once and for all.*

Jim picked up the phone and, with some difficulty, punched in Hunter's hotel room.

"Hunter!" came the answer.

"Rolly, this is Jim!"

"Jim, I'm glad you called. I think we need to talk, but not on the phone."

"You going to come over now?"

"In a little while. I have a few more calls to make. How about I see you in a couple hours?"

"Yeah, okay, I'll see you then!"

"Can I pick up some chicken or something?"

"Yeah, fine, see ya!" Jim hung up the phone.

His message light came on.

"Hello, Jim! It's me. Call me on my cell phone, okay?"

Damn! I don't want her to come over! he thought. *I need to talk to Hunter.*

He dialed Mary's number.

"Hi, Jim. Who were you talking to just now?"

"Nobody, just my girlfriend," he answered, trying to appear funny.

"Yeah, sure! What are you doing now? I thought I could come over and take you to dinner."

"Ah … gosh, I don't think so, Mary. I feel kinda tired right now. I think I'll have a bowl of soup and hit the sack." He nearly choked on his words.

"Okay, I'll see you tomorrow then." She hung up.

Jim knew this was not going well.

The chips will have to roll, he thought.

Hunter showed up as planned.

"How you doing, Jim?" he asked.

"I'll know better after we talk," Jim returned.

"Well, you better stay seated, my friend!" Jim's face turned a shade of white.

"First of all, Mary is not a student at Stanford," Hunter began. "Secondly, she is 29, not 23." He hesitated to go further.

"Come on, Rolly, give me the rest of it." He looked down to the floor.

"Jim, I contacted the FFA office in Washington for a list of licenses issued in the last 10 years."

"How'd you pull that one?" Jim asked.

"Once connected, always connected! That's the government. Anyway, here's the scoop: Mary Rison took her private flight program at Reid-Hillview in San Jose starting in June of '93. She completed her check ride and was signed off by the FAA inspector in November of the same year. She completed her multi-engine rating and IFR rating in January of '94. That was at

Stockton Airport. That's where she met Windom through her father."

"I guess I don't need to ask how she did," Jim quipped.

"I talked to one of her instructors at Stockton. He just said she was a natural."

"That figures," Jim interjected, looking totally exhausted. Hunter knew Jim was devastated.

"Well, it was as we guessed, Jim. She is a pilot, or *was* a pilot for Windom … I'm sorry," Hunter said reluctantly. He was surprised at Jim's response.

"Yeah, okay, what do we do now?"

"What do you mean, Jim?"

"Do I confront her with this or do nothing?"

"Oh, we'll do something, all right. But I suggest we say nothing for now. Follow me on this."

Jim said nothing.

"Mary may be just the one to get us to Windom and maybe inadvertently help us get the other codebook."

"How is that going to work?" Jim asked.

"I'm not sure at this point, but in the spy world, it always helps to infiltrate the enemy's camp!"

"Rolly, that's dumb! I think she needs to know that we know. I couldn't carry it off anyway."

"You know, Jim, we've never discussed our reason for doing any of this code stuff. We need to ask what we are doing this for! Are you expecting to get something out of this treasure hunt?"

"You're damn right! I've nearly been killed, ended up in the hospital, and have just found out that a beautiful lady that I'm falling in love with is nothing but a lying … whatever. Besides that, I never asked to get involved in this shit in the first place! I'm mad as hell now and just maybe I'm entitled to something for it!"

"I think so too, Jim. However, it won't do either of us any good if we screw it up! You don't think Windom will gladly hand over his book, do you?"

"Oh, hell no! But I don't know how I'm going to fool Mary with this little charade."

"You'll have to, Buddy, for a little while."

"All right, Rolly, like I asked before, where do we go from here?"

"Well, let's just say nothing for now and see where Mary leads us. It should be toward Windom. We can blow the lid whenever it suits us. In the meantime, we're the ones armed with the most secrets."

"Okay, I'm in for the ride, I guess. I've got to tell you, though, my heart ain't in it right now!"

"I know, Jim. I wish there was something I could say."

"Well, I'm not convinced it was going to work out with Mary anyway. Now my gut aches and it hurts to think that I've lost her. I believe my divorce was easier than this is going to be."

"I want you to take this key," Rolly said. "It's for a safe deposit box at U.S. Bank, up the street from your place," he continued.

"What's this for?" Jim asked.

"I have moved my bank from Wells Fargo to U.S. Bank. I opened a safe deposit box. Sound familiar, Jim?"

"Yeah, I think I've been there, done that!" Riley responded.

"Well, it's still the best thing to do. I've placed our copy of the codebook there for good reason! I'm sure that Windom knows who I am, thanks to Mary."

"And?" Jim asked.

"And, he knows that one of us has the book! I had two keys made, and your name is authorized with mine. Of course Mary doesn't know. She'll be trying to find out where the book is. She must not know!"

Jim's doorbell rang. Hunter pulled a gun from behind his belt and hurried to the side of the door.

"My God, Hunter! What in the hell are you doing?" Jim shouted.

Hunter motioned for him to get away from the sofa and touched his finger to his lips.

Jim ducked behind the easy chair and Hunter slowly opened the door.

Mary stood holding two double lattés, staring into what seemed to be an empty room.

"Anybody home?" she asked, peeking around the door.

She spotted Hunter and wondered why he was acting so sneaky. Jim looked up from behind the chair. Mary started laughing.

"How's the hide-and-seek game going, guys?" she asked.

"I guess I'm still a little nervous from this last trauma," Jim said with a shrug.

"You thought somebody was coming here to finish the job?"

"Mary," Hunter interjected, "it's not very funny if you think about it, or hadn't you noticed?"

"I'm sorry, Jim. I just wasn't thinking. I really am sorry. What happens now?"

Hunter responded, not wanting to tip his hand. "Well, there really isn't much we can do right now. We just need to see what Windom plans to do."

"Are you sure it's Windom behind all this?" Mary asked.

"Come on, Mary! What do you think?" Jim snapped.

"Well, excuse me for asking!"

"I didn't mean it like that! I'm pretty spooked at the moment. I guess you noticed."

"Hmm," was her response.

It was hardly possible to continue a conversation with Mary. Jim was looking closely at her, trying to see the six-year difference in her age. She still looked twenty-three.

"Anyway, I thought you might like a latté, James."

"Ah … yeah, sure, Mary. That sounds good."

"Can I get you one, Mr. Hunter? Starbucks is just around the corner."

"Oh, no thanks, Mary. I don't care much for that stuff. Besides, I've got to go. I'll see you two later!" He left without waiting for goodbyes.

Jim was starting to sweat. *How in the hell am I going to pretend this?* he thought.

"How's school going, Mary?"

That was stupid, he thought.

"Fine, why?" Mary asked. "Are you all right?"

"Sure! Why do you ask?"

"I don't know; something seems different."

There goes that damned woman's intuition shit! he thought. *I can't do this! I know I'm gonna blow!*

Mary sensed Jim's uneasiness and felt she should leave.

For a moment, Jim thought he would explode. He wanted to hit Mary with everything he had, but he knew that Hunter was right. Now was not the time. But he would have to confront her sooner or later, probably sooner. For now he would leave it alone. He wondered how he could pretend another day.

"Jim," she said coyly, "I was thinking that I might just as well spend the night. I don't have anything urgent at school, and well, maybe we both could use some relaxation. And besides, I'm feeling kind of hot!"

"How do you suppose I'm going to do anything about that?" There was no way he would rise to this occasion.

"Jim, you must know by now that I'm quite creative. I don't think you're going to suffer at all!" She began to rub her hand on his thigh. He sucked in his breath.

This can't happen! he yelled silently in his head. *My God! She's a lying bitch! She might be the one trying to have me killed!* His face was reddening, and he certainly wasn't standing up to the task Mary was offering.

Nonetheless, Mary found her way to his groin, and like most men he had ever known, the battle was over.

Jim Riley made love to her with as much anger as passion. He squeezed her so hard, she had to complain.

"Jim! You're hurting me!"

"I'm sorry," he returned.

While she finished with a wild, "Oh, yes! Yes!" He uttered no sound.

Mary sat up. "Well, thank you very much for your approval, Mr. Riley." Her feelings were obviously quite hurt.

Jim felt angry because he let it happen. He wanted to be mad as hell at her, yet somewhere deep inside he was grasping with a hope that he would awaken from a terrible dream and it would all be gone.

God, I do love her, he thought.

He watched her as she walked to the bathroom. Her slightly sweaty body glistened as the light shone through the apartment window. He admired her beautifully slim hips and rounded behind. *What a beautiful woman!* he thought.

Jim could go no further. She needed to leave.

"Mary!" he called to her in the bathroom. "You know, I'm feeling really tired right now. Do you mind if we don't make it a sleepover?"

Mary returned from the bathroom with the look on her face like a little girl who had just been slapped. She slipped on her clothes quickly without a word. Jim could only look at her hurt expression as she picked up her purse and walked out the door.

Jim Riley had always prided himself in being a tough, macho guy, but the tears ran down his cheeks, and he nearly cried out loud. He turned on the television set with the volume high enough to almost drown out his feelings. He didn't hear a word.

This is nuts! he decided. *I'll talk to Hunter in the morning and we'll get this damn thing over.*

In the midst of his wild thoughts, it occurred to him that Mary Rison might even be flying his old Baron. He did miss the wonderful days with Windom. No problems, good money, lots of time off. "Ah, shit!" he said aloud. He turned off the TV and rolled into bed.

TWENTY-FIVE

JIM WOKE TO A LOUD KNOCKING at the door. It was well after 9:00 a.m. His shoulder was killing him. Last night's frolicking had taken its toll.

He jumped out of bed like the place was on fire. From outside the door, Hunter was shouting, "Jim! Open the door; it's me, Rolly!"

"Rolly! What the …!" He opened the door.

Rolly Hunter stood like a ghost at the door. His left arm was bleeding from the elbow down. Blood was dripping on the floor. He was holding his wrist with his right hand. He had wrapped a towel around his arm, but it was soaked. He was losing serious blood.

"Wait a second, Rolly!" Jim said. He went to the bathroom and grabbed a bath towel. "Here, put this around your arm. Let's go into the toilet."

Rolly followed Jim into the bathroom. Jim turned on the water in the sink and slowly unwrapped his arm. It looked to Jim like about an eighth-inch gouge ran across his arm, just below the elbow.

"What the hell happened, Rolly?" Jim asked.

"Buddy, you're not the only one who somebody wants to hurt!"

"Kill, you mean! Man that looks ugly!"

"Nobody is trying to kill us, Jim. If so, we'd both be dead by now!" Rolly said.

"Then what is this bullshit going on?"

"Trying to scare us, Jim, that's all. How would we be good to anyone dead?" Rolly continued.

"Hmm … yeah. They're sure as hell doing it. I can tell you that! Somebody must be either a marksman or a lousy shot to graze you like this."

Hunter began to turn white. He was looking sweaty, and Jim knew he was about to faint. He reached around Rolly with his good arm and sat him down on the sofa. Rolly passed out.

Jim reached for a damp washcloth and put it on his friend's forehead.

In a few seconds, Rolly came around. Jim thought he needed to get to a hospital. It was apparent that he would go into shock at any moment.

"Rolly, gimme your car keys! You need some medical attention right now."

Hunter pointed to his pocket; Jim reached in and retrieved his keys. With much difficulty, Jim put on his sweats and they left his apartment for Kaiser Hospital.

Because Rolly was bleeding, the nurse on duty took him right into the ER. Jim was trying to put a story together about his buddy being shot. It involves more than a patch-and-go visit when a gunshot is involved. Jim knew this and was planning the whopper in his mind. He decided on the old "cleaning-the-gun" story. It would have to do. He couldn't think of anything else.

Hunter was being cared for as the nurse grilled him on the cause of the injury. It was an obvious gunshot graze as far as the ER doctor was concerned. He did not care, however, to pursue the reason. The ER was packed and no one cared or had time to continue questioning.

In the midst of all the action, Jim realized that Mary had made no attempt to contact him.

It's time to talk to her and get this over, he thought. Hunter continued to urge Jim to wait until they could see what Windom was planning next.

"I'll hold off if I can," Jim said. "But don't blame me if she tries to pretend everything is hunky dory. I'm hurt and mad as hell!"

"I know, Jim. I assure you it won't be long before we find out exactly what's going on! I'm waiting for one of my former co-ops to call me. He's been nosing around the Windom headquarters. He should get back to me any time now." He felt his cell phone vibrate. They moved outside in order to get a better signal.

"Hello, this is Hunter. Umm. Okay, thanks John." Hunter disconnected.

"Well?" Jim asked.

"My guy says that Mary was not a regular pilot for Windom, and the rumor is that she quit or may have been fired."

"Jesus, now where does that leave us, Rolly?" Jim asked.

"Well, probably not as bad as you were thinking. Maybe she didn't know what had really been going on," Hunter suggested.

"Oh hell, Rolly, she had to know about everything! She didn't just accidentally run into me!"

"I know, I'm not trying to simplify matters. It just might be possible that she didn't know she would eventually be playing with fire!"

"She had to, for Christ's sake!"

"Wait a minute, Jim! Do you think when Oliver set up the plan for her to cozy up to you, that he told her he was willing to have you killed for the book? This is big-boy stuff!"

"Well, no, but …"

"But nothing! I've spent my adult life dealing with all kinds of people, good and bad. Maybe I'm a little naive, but I don't think she connected all the dots! I think it was all a game to her until bullets began to fly."

"But why didn't she tell me then?" Jim asked.

"I don't know, Jim. But I would give her a chance to explain her side of things. She got in way over her head and probably didn't know how to tell you."

"But she lied to me, Rolly! How could she do that?"

"All right, I wanted to put this off for a while, to see if she would lead us back to Windom, but I can see that you can't wait, so we'll confront her with it and let the chips fall where they may," Hunter replied.

They decided to go back to Rolly's hotel and call Mary to come over. Neither man spoke as they drove to the hotel.

TWENTY-SIX

JIM DIALED MARY'S NUMBER. "Hi! This is Mary. I can't come to the phone right now. Please leave a message." Jim hung up the phone.

"Whew!" Jim said, relieved that Mary was not home. "What now?" he asked.

"Jim, you know we have never discussed what would happen if we were to get our hands on Windom's codebook."

"Yeah, I know. I haven't thought much about what happens after we get his copy. I'm sorry, but I've been occupied with staying alive!"

"I guess that goes for both of us now!" Hunter agreed.

"Rolly, suppose we do get both codebooks and decipher them. Now we know where all the money is located, along with all the account numbers. You don't think we're just going to fly over the Switzerland and pick it up, do you?" Jim asked.

"Well, as a matter of fact, yes! That's pretty much it!"

"What? We just walk into a bunch of banks and pretend to be legal heirs to a fortune?"

"Not exactly that simple, Jim," Hunter said. "There are some hoops to jump through, but they are not insurmountable."

"Now, supposing we get the books and are able to recover some or all of the money. What did you have in mind as far as disposing of it? It really doesn't belong to any of us!" Jim interjected.

"In a sense that's true, Jim, but think about it. Windom, as far as we know, is an heir of Professor DiNapoli, but then DiNapoli was never expected to gain access to any of the money. Not only that, his son has tried to kill you and me both for something that doesn't belong to him in the first place!"

"That's true," Jim said, "but there's David Steinmetz on the other side. What about his family?"

"As far as we know, David and his uncle Aaron were the only surviving heirs of Franz Steinmetz."

"So who does the money belong to?"

"David gave you the book to hand off to me, right?"

"Yes, but you never did tell me how you knew David Steinmetz, or why he wanted you to have the book," Jim added.

"Well, it was quite easy to track the Steinmetz family genealogy to David and his uncle," Hunter continued.

"I arranged a meeting with David in Boston and informed him about Oliver Windom's real identity and the companion book. I assumed that he would contact Windom, and together they would recover the assets and perhaps share equally. I would get my percentage as a finder's fee and that would be it."

"So why did he ask me to give you the book?" Jim asked.

"When David met with Windom, he realized that Windom had no intention of sharing the wealth, and further threatened David if he did not turn over the other codebook. When David realized his life was in danger, he called me and said he would try to get the book into my hands. Thus, along comes Jim Riley! You, my friend!"

"Well, it all makes sense now," Jim said.

"We'll talk more about how the money is retrieved later, Jim," Hunter concluded. "Now we need to settle everything with Mary."

"God, I hate this part!"

"I know, Jim; so do I!"

Both men jumped when the phone rang. Hunter leaped to his feet.

"Hello, this is Rolly."

"Mr. Hunter, is everything all right? You didn't leave a message!" Mary said.

"I knew you'd see it was me on your caller ID. It was Jim who called. Here's Jim."

"Jim, what the heck is going on? You've been acting very strange for several days now! Have I done something?"

"Mary, Rolly and I would like to come over to your place and talk about a couple of things."

"My place? Ah … no, that wouldn't be a very good idea. You know, my roommate and all. I'll come over there. It won't take me but a few minutes!" Mary hung up the phone.

"Well, Rolly, she obviously didn't want us to come to her place! What's she hiding?" Jim asked.

"Probably that fact that there is no roommate, for one thing, would be my guess," Hunter said.

Mary arrived in less than 15 minutes. Hunter answered the door.

"What's all this about, guys? Mr. Hunter, what in the world happened to you?"

"Well, Mary," Hunter said, "maybe you can tell us what's going on, other than your boss is trying to kill us!"

Mary stood with her mouth wide open.

"Mr. Hunter, Jim … I can explain!" Mary protested.

"Explain?" Jim shouted. "Cut the crap, Mary. How could you be such a damned liar? And why, for God's sake?"

"Jim, please! Listen to me!"

"Listen, hell! I want to puke!"

"Hey!" Hunter shouted. "Stop, both of you! Sit down, Jim, and give her a chance!" he demanded.

Jim sat on the bed and said nothing. Mary began. "Jim, I'm sure if you know anything, you know everything. You know that I have been flying for Windom. I'm sorry for making you go through all the flight instruction, but

I did love every minute of it, Jim. I really mean that!"

"Yeah, yeah! Sure. You made me look like an ass!" Jim said.

"No, Jim! I'm the one who looks like the ass!"

"Well, I'm not going to argue that point!"

"Okay, I deserved that one," Mary said quietly. "Now will you let me explain?" Mary begged.

"Come on, Jim, let her talk," Hunter said.

Jim said nothing. He shrugged his shoulders and sat motionless. Mary continued. "I was planning to enter flight training for the airlines when my dad told me that Windom was looking for a pilot to replace one he had just fired. This was the guy he employed after you left, Jim."

"Ummm ..." Jim acknowledged with a bit of sarcasm.

"Anyway, I interviewed and he hired me on the spot. I figured I could do this for a year or 18 months at the most. That would give me all I needed to complete my airline training." She waited for a response. Jim said nothing.

"At first it was a blast," Mary said. "I loved the Baron. I know you must have also, Jim." She paused. "Everything went well for nearly two months. Then Windom approached me with something that made sense at the time."

"What was that, Mary?" Hunter asked.

"Windom explained that a former pilot — you, Jim — had been privy to some very sensitive conversations that could have been serious enough to be life-threatening to some of his associates.

"I asked him what he wanted me to do," Mary continued. "He said he would pay me a significant bonus if I could make contact and get to know you. My job was to probe for answers about a certain 'little black book,' which contained the so-called 'sensitive information.' I had no idea what that was, nor did he offer to tell me."

"Who hatched the flight training scheme?" Jim asked.

"I did, Jim. I felt I could pull it off and get the information Mr. Windom wanted. I had no idea what he was really up to, Jim, I swear!"

Jim Riley was beginning to relax a bit, but still was furious with Mary.

"Mary, I can't believe that you screwed with my mind like this! How did you think this was all going to end? Were we supposed to ride off in the sunset and live happily ever after, for heaven's sake?"

"No, of course not! But once I got into this mess, I began to realize that I was falling in love with you. That was not supposed to happen, damn it! And I never suspected that Windom had plans to hurt you or anyone else. I was not a party to any of it."

"Then why didn't you quit when you saw what was happening?"

"If you two spies had bothered to complete your work, you would have learned that I *did* quit!"

"When did that happen, Mary?" Hunter asked.

"Right after the parking lot episode. I went to Windom, mad as hell, and asked him outright if he was trying to kill Jim Riley! He didn't really answer, but it was obvious."

"Is that when you gave notice?" Jim asked.

"No, Jim, and I'm so sorry. I tried to rationalize that he just wanted to scare you. It wasn't until your wreck that I knew how far he was planning to go. I didn't even go back to collect the money he owes me. The bastard can shove it up his butt, as far as I'm concerned! I didn't bargain for any of this crap!" Mary sat on the bed and began to sob quietly.

Jim knew her contrition was real. In an odd sense, he felt more in love with her now.

I'm going to get that son of a bitch! he thought to himself, without the slightest clue as to how it would be accomplished.

"This may prove to be advantageous!" Hunter interjected into the silence.

Mary and Jim looked up and said nothing. They waited for Hunter to continue.

"Mary, you didn't actually quit, as it seems to me," Hunter continued.

"Well, I guess not," Mary answered.

"Then I think you need to continue working for Windom. It keeps us connected. It may be our path to securing the other codebook," Hunter concluded. "That is if you want to be part of this."

"I certainly do!" Mary quickly responded. "I've been used by that bastard, and I resent it! Yes, Mr. Hunter, I'm in!"

"Mary," Jim asked, "this is off the subject, but where are you living?"

"I'm living in Palo Alto, so I guess you could loosely say Stanford. I don't have a roommate either. I'm sorry, Jim." She placed her hand on Jim's wrist.

"I suppose the stuff you told me about your folks is baloney too," Jim said.

"No, Jim, it's all true. I just didn't tell you that my dad worked for Windom Wineries," she said.

"All right, you two. I don't mean to put an end to this little love fest, but I've got a few things to do!" Hunter announced. "Mary, can you give Mr. Riley a ride home?"

"I thought you'd never ask! Okay with you, Jim?"

"Sure, why not?" Jim answered with some degree of enthusiasm.

TWENTY-SEVEN

WINDOM WAS RANTING on his office phone. "Damn you people, I want you in my office today!" he shouted at the listener.

"Yes, of course, Mr. Windom. Shall we say one o'clock?"

"That's fine. I'll call the gate to let you in."

Windom called his secretary into his office. "Mrs. Jordon, have you heard from Miss Rison in the last couple of days?"

"She just called this morning, Mr. Windom. It was to ask you if you needed her this week."

"Call her back. Tell her that I need to go to Napa tomorrow afternoon. Have her bring the Baron into Stockton. I'll meet her there at eleven thirty."

The secretary agreed, left the room, and called Mary Rison. Mary was satisfied that Windom had not found it strange that she seemed to disappear for a few days.

The Tongs arrived precisely at 1:00. There were three, K.C. Wi, Henry Wong, and a scarred-faced Lonny Kim. Windom was pacing the floor. K.C. Wi spoke first. He was twiddling a 50-cent piece between his fingers. This, he thought, would create the effect of a very confident individual. It helped him control his nervousness. Wi was never comfortable in the presence of occidentals. He was quite dark and showed some features of African-American descent. He had earlier revealed to Windom that his grandfather was indeed a black American from the Korean War.

"Mr. Windom," he began, "we seem to be at some stage of misunderstanding regarding Mr. Riley."

"No, Mr. Wi, as I told you before, you did not complete our contract, therefore I owed you nothing! Now that is all changed," Windom continued.

"I presume that our original contract is in effect, then?" responded Wi.

"Yes, Mr. Wi. However, the problem is that I'm no longer sure where the 'item' is located. Eliminating Riley would only complicate matters."

"And what do you propose that we do?" asked Wi.

"I am adding five percent to your contract if you can devise a plan to extract the codebook from Riley or his cohorts. Following that, you may proceed with the rest of the contract. But there is no contract unless I secure the book!"

"Mr. Windom," Wi responded, "my friends and I will attempt to do as you say, but should we fail in securing the book, I must remind you in the strongest of terms, do not dismiss us!"

"Well, Mr. Wi, let's see where we go! Now I believe that completes our discussion. Thank you for coming, and we will not meet until our task is done."

Windom did not rise from his desk. He dismissed the men with the flick of his wrist.

Oliver Windom went to his bedroom armoire, reached in, and pulled out the small black codebook given to him by his father more than 50 years earlier. He quickly thumbed through its contents. *Once I have the other book, I can embark upon a treasure hunt beyond my wildest dreams!* he conjured up in his mind.

Money itself was of no particular value to Windom. He had enough. It had always been about the journey to wealth that motivated his life. To reach it had always proved anticlimactic. The man was unalterably alone. Too many memories plagued his mind. He found satisfaction in very little. Perhaps a new vine graft, a vintage year, a new varietal wine. But these were fleeting things. The void in his soul was too deep. If only he could relive those days of his youth, perhaps things would have been different. He found himself missing his father, Gino DiNapoli. Time was running out. Soon he would be too old and tired to continue the quest. By his own logic, there was no one else more qualified to inherit a fortune than he. The man was becoming consumed by his own terrible destiny.

TWENTY-EIGHT

JIM, MARY, AND ROLLY HUNTER began devising their plan to relieve Windom of his codebook as they sipped mochas at Starbucks. Rolly had still not acquired a taste for Starbucks. Mary would have to find a way to locate the book at Windom's residence. Then a little Hunter spy work could take place. Beyond that idea, very little thought was given toward what they would do after recovering Windom's book. Certainly the assumption was that they would try to recover some of the assets from Switzerland. That in and of itself would be a monumental, if not impossible, task. Some questions needed answering: Did he still have the book? The three could only suppose that he did. Is it on the property? How would Mary gain access to it?

Jim had a question of his own for Hunter. "What makes you think it is still possible to gain access to the banks even if we have both books?"

"Jim, let me explain that in a roundabout way, if I can," Hunter began. "I have an article here written on March 7, 1997 titled, "Swiss still stingy on Holocaust," written by Bernard Kaplan, a foreign affairs writer for the Hearst papers. He made several important points. Let me summarize," Hunter continued. "The gold held in Swiss bank vaults turned Switzerland into the world's postwar financial center. The Swiss government just announced after months of wrangling, a $5 billion Holocaust survivors' fund.

This is a really good deal for the Swiss, since $5 billion is at the lower end of the scale of what was deposited between 1933 and 1945. Sixty billion would be a closer amount of the real value. Guess what a lot of that money was used for, my friends?" Hunter asked.

"I thought it couldn't be used for anything! Didn't you say that was the nature of Swiss banking?" Mary asked.

"Well, yes and no, Mary," he continued. "Yes, except for the pressure of the Nazis during the war. Now here is the terrible irony of this. Kaplan goes on to explain that according to historian Francoise Guillemaud of the University of Paris, 'Switzerland was virtually the exclusive source of hard currency needed by the German war effort to purchase such vital material as Swedish iron ore.' This financing contained money deposited by the likes of Franz Steinmetz, Isaiah Cohen and the other Jewish families. Can you imagine?" asked Hunter, "that the very people who were murdered by the Nazis had in part inadvertently financed their own holocaust? This is evil at its worst!"

Tears began flowing down Mary's cheeks. She could only shake her head. Jim gently patted her hand.

"Guillemaud continued," Hunter stated, "Swiss officials knew what was going on but shut their eyes, either because there was a lot of profit in the business or they were afraid of what the Germans would do if they stopped it.

"In Kaplan's article, he concluded with a reference to New York and New Jersey threatening to suspend the licenses of Swiss banks to operate in their states unless they ponied up the $5 billion for a Holocaust survivors' fund."

"So this is where the money comes from for the six families' heirs?" Jim asked.

"No, Jim, most of that money is designated for a general fund. It has nothing to do with deposits," Hunter answered.

"Then where does the money come from?" asked Mary.

"Sixty-five million of the $5 billion is to be available to Jewish families who had deposits, according to Kaplan's article," Hunter concluded.

"Didn't you say that the Jewish families' assets were in excess of $100 million? And that's just one such story!" Jim said.

"Yes, I did, and that bridge will have to be crossed when we come to it!" Hunter answered.

"When we come to it?" Mary asked with raised eyebrows.

Hunter smiled and nodded.

"Then I have two questions, Mr. Hunter," Mary interjected. "First of all, why are we going to continue this treasure hunt? And secondly, how are we going to get the money if we do continue? None of us is an heir!"

"I'll answer the second question first, Mary. Remember I told you about David's father and the power of attorney he granted to me. That power of attorney was never rescinded."

"I guess that means you can act totally as an heir if you have all the paperwork?" Jim said.

"That's right, Jim. The job here is to trace David back to his grandfather's life in Italy and his participation as one of the six original depositors. Now I'll address the first question, Mary. Why are we going to continue the treasure hunt, as you call it? I can give you two reasons. First, I made some promises to David's father. In turn, I was to receive a reasonable fee for expediting the money's return to its rightful owners or their descendants."

"Was that fee amount determined?" Mary asked.

"No, it wasn't, Mary. It was left to my discretion."

"Wow! That's a trusting soul!" Jim stated.

"Well, I had a very good relationship with Mica Steinmetz. He did trust me."

"And you need us to make it happen!" Mary said.

"Yes, I do, Mary. It would be virtually impossible without your help. Now, can we get started?" Hunter asked.

"What would you like us to do, Mr. Hunter?" Mary replied.

"Well, Mary, are you up to getting a little friendlier with Mr. Windom?" Hunter asked.

"Excuse me?" Mary exclaimed.

"I'm sorry, Mary, I don't mean to suggest any hanky panky! I'm just suggesting that you try to become more of a confidant to him. I have a feeling that he may be a very lonely man."

"I think I can do that," she answered. "As a matter of fact, Windom has invited some very important buyers to his mansion for wine tasting and a tour of the facilities next week. For whatever it means, he is going to be completely occupied. All the employees are required to be there. Maybe I can disappear long enough to snoop around his quarters," she continued.

Hunter chimed in, "No harm in trying, Mary. There is really nothing more we can do until we get our hands on Windom's book. I have to believe that this will happen eventually. With that in mind, I'm off to Switzerland. I will contact you two in a couple of weeks. Jim, watch your back. I think Windom might be running out of patience!"

* * *

ALL THE BUYERS were at the mansion and busily talking and tasting, with the usual wine lingo.

"This has an unusual bouquet! Woody with lots of apple and pear, with hints of orange and peach," ad nauseum.

Mary chuckled as she made her way through the crowd. With her untrained palate, it was all quite comical. She counted the actual number of adjectives the guests could derive, just to avoid total boredom. She made the small talk that the employees were expected to make.

Windom soon became engaged with a few of his guests. Mary knew he would be busy for some time. She slowly slipped her way past others, into the foyer of the mansion. There was only muffled talking coming from what Mary believed to be the kitchen. She had seen very little of the place.

She made her way down the long entryway leading to the huge dining room. She stopped and hugged the wall. Two women dressed in server uniforms were busy setting the table. They giggled, and Mary was sure that they were imitating Windom's pompous gestures and mannerisms. Mary smiled as she recognized the old man.

The ladies left the room, still giggling. Mary passed the long table and moved off to the right, where a long circular staircase rose to the upper floor.

Its gold-colored wrought iron railing flowed ornately as it wound its way to the second floor. At the top was a set of double doors, beautifully carved in dark red cherrywood. Inset in each was the Windom crest. It seemed totally out of place for a bedroom door. She decided it was not a woman's interior design; it was strictly a man's thing.

She turned the knob slowly, and the giant door moved like a feather. She stepped inside and stood still. Her eyes moved slowly across the room from left to right. A large Thomas Kincaid of San Francisco's wharf hung over the bed. *How beautiful,* she thought. She smiled as she observed that a few locations had been moved into the scene from a block or two away. She hadn't remembered any cable cars running down the Embarcadero, but the painting was nonetheless a beautiful piece of art.

What she could not understand was why the man would not have possessed more expensive art, such as a Picasso or two. At least one or two of the masters would be more fitting for a man of his station.

The bedspread had the appearance of gold weave, and shone brightly with the bedroom sunlight shining through. The gaudy Windom crest adorned the center of the spread.

Moving her eyes to the right, she encountered a large trunk. It appeared quite old, and she presumed it might contain a 60-year-old keepsake — more specifically, an old codebook. She moved her eyes to the left and viewed the large armoire. Its décor did not fit the rest of the furniture. Perhaps the treasure may reside behind its antique doors. She would look there. Next to the armoire was a two-way loveseat. A lacy doily rested on its back. Mary decided that a woman's touch had been present after all. It had never dawned on Mary that there may have been a lady in Windom's past.

Her eyes continued to move past a tall, thin mirrored dresser to a set of folding doors.

A closet! Yes, I need to look there, she thought. This brought her around to a single contemporary chair. Behind it was a second Kincaid painting. It appeared to represent a Napa Valley wine country scene. Again she admired its great detail.

Now she knew she must move quickly. She lifted the corner of the painting over the bed, looked under the bed, and moved around the foot to the large trunk. It squeaked as she opened it.

In the upper box shelf were a myriad of tiny knickknacks that could only have been saved by a woman. *His mother,* Mary concluded. She lifted the upper box and placed it carefully onto the bed. In the bottom were very old clothes, along with some copies of Italian newspapers dated 1940. She could read only a few words.

She put the box back into the trunk, smoothed the bedspread, and moved to the armoire. She opened it quickly and found only an assortment of work clothes. She had seen Windom wearing the coveralls that hung there. Mary closed the doors quietly and opened each drawer beneath the doors. They contained nothing of significance. There were numerous envelopes, letters, and legal papers, none of which Mary felt were important to her search.

She opened the folding doors. On one side she saw gowns, dresses, coats, and women's shoes. These were very old and had obviously belonged to Windom's mother. *This must have been her bedroom,* Mary concluded. The other side of the closet contained what had to be Windom's present wardrobe.

Mary quickly opened several shoeboxes on the upper shelf. Nothing caught her attention. She moved on to the dresser, opening drawers and trying not to make a mess of things, shuffling with a specific target in mind.

She suddenly heard a door opening close by. Mary quickly opened the folding doors and slipped inside. She could hear the bedroom door open. One of the house staff entered the room and walked past the closet doors. Mary could imagine the intruder moving about. She heard what she knew to be the armoire door closing rather loudly. She heard the bedroom door close.

Mary breathed a sigh of relief, left the closet, and continued looking for her treasure. She passed the chair and headed for the door. She stood, turned around, and surveyed the room once more. As her eyes met the second painting, she realized she had not tried to look behind it. She walked over to the painting, felt around the frame with both hands, and pulled slightly. The picture was hinged on the left side. Mary continued to swing it out. There, behind the picture, was a home safe, very old, very ornate.

Damn! This has to be it! she almost said out loud.

She tried to turn the handle, knowing full well it had to be locked.

She had been gone long enough. Quickly she moved the painting into place and tiptoed out of the room, and then made her way carefully down the stairs and out into the garden.

"Mary! Where the hell have you been?" Windom said as he approached her. "I've been looking for you everywhere!"

"I'm sorry, Mr. Windom. I've been in the restroom. It's just a woman problem," she lied. She felt pride in her ability to adlib so easily.

Oliver, obviously embarrassed, responded, "Yes, well, Mary, you need to pack a bag for a four-day trip to Yakima, Washington. We'll be leaving at nine tomorrow morning. I'll be taking two people with me. Set up enough provisions for us. You can coordinate with the kitchen staff while you are here today."

"Very well, Mr. Windom, I'll get right on it! I need to make a couple of calls. Do you want me to call Jerry Dunne at the hangar?"

"Yeah, Mary, please take care of all the details."

Mary left the lanai area for the guest house to pack and do all the other flight planning. She would need to call Jim Riley at once.

* * *

MARY CALLED JIM RILEY AS SOON AS SHE reached the guest house. She told him that she was taking Windom to Washington and let him know of her scavenger hunt at the mansion.

"Jim, I'm almost sure that the book has to be in the bedroom safe. I'd bet money on it! The problem is, how do we get into a locked safe in the mansion?" she asked.

"Hmm," Jim thought aloud, "I've got an idea, Mary. I guess you're going to be seeing Jerry Dunne before you leave?"

"Yes, I'm going to call him as soon as we're finished talking. What do you want me to do?" Mary asked.

"I want you to give my number to Jerry and ask him to call me. Tell him not to use his cell phone. I don't want it ever to come out that we talked."

"He's going to want to know what it's about. What shall I tell him?" asked Mary.

"I don't want you to tell him anything, Mary. I don't even want him to know that you and I are acquainted. I don't want any trouble for Jerry. Just say that there was a message from me on the phone at the guest house."

"Okay, Jim, talk to you later. I'll be back up there on Sunday. See you then."

TWENTY-NINE

THE INSURANCE COMPANY TOTALED JIM RILEY'S CAMARO. He was able to buy a used Firebird straight across for the cash he had received. His shoulder was still sore, but he was able to drive with very little trouble.

He was anxiously waiting for Jerry Dunne's phone call. They had been good friends, and he was sure Jerry would not let him down. He had concocted the scenario in his mind. *Will Jerry buy it?* he wondered. He knew it would take a special trust on Jerry's part to go along with the plan.

Jim didn't have to wait long for Jerry Dunne to return his call.

"Hi, Jim. It's Jerry."

Jim responded with the usual small talk and then approached the real subject.

"Jerry, do you remember one day at the hangar, you had a locksmith working on the safe?"

"Yeah, what about it, Jim?"

"I remember that you said he had been a safecracker. Was that true?" he asked Dunne.

"What the hell you want to know something like that for?"

"Well, stick with me a minute and I'll tell you. Was he really a safecracker?" Jim pursued.

"Oh, I don't think so, Jim. You know me. I was just horsing around. Why?"

"Do you think he's pretty good, Jerry?"

"Hell yes, he's good. He opened that safe just by listening to the tumblers. I'd say he's good!"

"Jerry, how you getting along with Windom these days?"

There was a long pause, and then Jerry asked, "Why, do you know something I don't, Jim?"

"No, but it's kind of important that I know how you feel about Windom."

"Sounds like you're about to offer me some kind of new job!" he chuckled.

"You know, Jerry, as a matter of fact, you're right, loosely speaking, of course!"

"Are we going to continue 20 questions or do you have something to say?" Jerry sounded as if he had had enough of the trivial pursuit. "I will tell you this: I have the word out that I'm looking for another job. I am burned out here. Nothing against Windom. Also, I can make a lot more money up near the San Jose area."

"Jerry, I'd like to make a proposition to you. It can mean a lot of money if we're successful, but nothing but your time if we're not," Jim continued. "You have to trust me. Okay, Jerry?" Jim said with much uncertainty.

"All right, Jim. I trust you. What you got?"

"Are you familiar with the Windom house?" Jim asked.

"Well, more or less, I guess. I've been there a few times," Jerry answered.

"You remember at the top of the stairway is a double door?" Jim asked.

"Where in the hell are you going with this, Jim?"

"Stay with me, buddy. Inside is a wall safe behind the painting over the chair," Jim continued.

"Yeah?" Jerry answered quizzically.

"I want you to get your safecracker friend to open it up!"

"My God! Then what?"

"I think there is a small black book inside, probably water worn. I need that book, Jerry!"

"That's it? A black book? What the hell is it?" Jerry asked.

"I'll tell you all about it later, Jerry. For now, I need your help. I don't think you'll regret it," Jim concluded.

"I'm sorry, Jim. I can't do anything like that. There are lots of things I would do, but breaking and entering is not one of them!"

Jim responded, "Jerry, I would meet with you right now to convince you if I had the time. I don't, so here goes." Jim took a deep breath and continued, "You might want to know something about Windom that you didn't know."

"What the hell are you talking about, Jim?" he asked.

Jim related the conversation that he had heard between Windom and one of his associates, killing Jerry's chance for a job with the airlines. For a few moments, Jerry said nothing; then he continued, "Son of a … all right, Jim. I know you wouldn't ask me to do this if it wasn't important. When do you want me to do it?"

"Windom is going to be gone for a few days next week, isn't he?" Jim asked.

"Yeah, he's leaving Monday morning, but how would you know that?" Jerry asked.

"I'll explain that later too. Can you get in without the service staff knowing it?"

"Oh, I think so. Shouldn't be too hard."

"Okay, Jerry, call me after you have opened the safe."

"You got it, Jim! I'll be calling. You know Windom is going to go ballistic when he finds the thing missing. That is if it's in there!"

"Oh, I know that! He'll rip the shit out of everyone in the house. But I can't worry about that now. I'll talk to you later, Jerry."

Jim hung up with a slight flip of his fist. "Yeah!" he whispered. He called Mary and filled her in on his call to Jerry. They were pleased once again that a smooth plan was unfolding. Jim wanted to hold her again. He had forgiven her for not being honest with him, but he understood and thought to himself that he might have done the same. He wanted to make love to her. She could tell it in his voice.

"Do I detect some lechery in your voice, Jim?" she asked.

"Well, like they say, 'dirty old men need love too!'" he laughed.

"Jim, I'd love nothing more, as you know, but I just don't have the time to come up there and still get back in time to take Windom to Washington. How about if we take a rain check until I get back? You won't be disappointed. Have you heard from Mr. Hunter yet? What do you suppose he is doing in Switzerland?" she asked.

"He's going to be searching for any possible descendants of the original families. He will be checking several random banks to get an idea of how money is being drawn from long-standing Holocaust accounts. Then he plans to look at court records in Rome and Milan, and I guess wherever his trail leads him. He's expecting that we will get the other book in the meantime."

"Sounds like you're going to be a little busy yourself, cowboy!" Mary said.

"Yeah! I hope it works out with the safecracking!" Jim answered.

"I would really be surprised if the book isn't there, Jim. Wouldn't you?"

"For sure! I don't think there's any doubt. But we're about to find out."

* * *

IT WAS NEARLY NOON WHEN JERRY DUNNE AND THE SAFE-CRACKER made their way to the Windom mansion. Jerry parked his car several hundred yards down the lane, blocked by the row of eucalyptus trees lining the long drive from the county road to the house. The trees were especially nauseous at this time of year. The pungent smell reminded Jerry of cough drops.

They were soon at the front door. The safecracker slipped a credit card between the door and jamb. The door opened smoothly. The men stepped inside and moved to an indented space in the entryway. A slight noise emanated from the kitchen area. They slithered along the wall of the dining room, across to the spiral staircase. One maid moved across the room and up the stairs into the target bedroom.

The men waited patiently, breathing as quietly as possible. Shortly, the woman returned with her hands full of soiled linens. She moved down the stairs and into the kitchen area. There were no other sounds detected.

They made their way to the top of the stairs and quickly into the bedroom. Jerry pointed to the picture over the chair. Both men slipped on latex gloves. The safecracker moved quickly to the painting, swung it open, and gazed at the wall safe. He studied it for several moments while rubbing his thumb and forefinger together. The man gently touched the tumbler dial and put his ear against his hand so that he could both hear and feel the tumblers as they dropped. Twice he stopped to turn the handle. The door did not open. He backed away, took a few deep breaths, and removed a long, skinny tube-looking apparatus from the vest of his coveralls. The tube had a wire and earpiece. He inserted the earpiece and touched the end of the tube against the safe door. As he turned the dial, he moved the tube to various positions.

Jerry heard a small click. The man stopped turning the dial, looked at Jerry, and smiled. He motioned to Jerry to take the honor of opening the safe. Jerry moved to the safe and turned the handle. The door opened. He gazed into the open safe. The safecracker's cell phone suddenly began playing "Yankee Doodle Dandy," with the volume on high. He removed his right-hand glove, fumbled with his vest-pocket button, and finally retrieved the phone. He shut it off and slipped it under his armpit, hoping to silence the damned thing. That action brought another musical interlude, as it turned off. He looked at Jerry and shrugged an "I'm sorry!"

It was too late. The woman's voice came from downstairs. "Who's up there?" she cried.

Jerry closed the safe door, and the safecracker, without thought, swung the picture closed with his naked hand. Jerry motioned to the safecracker to get into the closet. They quickly disappeared behind the woman's clothing.

The maid entered the room, looked around, and listened. She shook her head slightly and assumed that nothing was amiss. She left the room and returned to the kitchen.

The men remained silent for several minutes before re-entering the bedroom. Jerry moved quickly to the painting, swung the picture out of the way, and turned the handle of the safe once again.

Before touching anything, he let his eyes move about the contents. Nothing the size of a small book was in his sight. He saw what appeared to be a small statue of the Virgin Mary holding a baby Jesus, which he assumed to be a family treasure. He spotted two medals with ribbons, which had to be exhibit prizes. There was a small metal box.

This must be it! Jerry thought. He lifted the lid with his index finger. He saw several rings, a gold pocket watch, and some other trinkets, but no black book.

Next he spotted an envelope addressed to Octavio DiNapoli. The return address was from The Aryan World Order. There was a small swastika above the return address. He replaced it as he turned aside and pretended to spit.

The last item was a large tan envelope. Dunne removed it and untwisted the string tie. The flap was tacky and he could not get the latex-gloved finger under it. He needed his fingernail. He removed his right glove and carefully lifted the flap. As he raised it, his thumb rested on the inside glue strip. He swiped across the print with the back of his index finger. He placed his hand inside the envelope and felt a small book! He removed a small black book that had the appearance of water damage.

In his excitement, Dunne opened the book to a page at random. He looked at the first item. "A=R, 2=b, m=t." *What nonsense is this?* He closed the book, put it in his pocket, retied the envelope string, and replaced it back in the exact spot where it had been.

The men left the house as stealthily as they had entered. They made their way to Jerry's car and left the premises.

Jerry called Jim and reported that he had indeed found what he believed was the book in question. Jim thanked him and arranged to meet him in Ripon. Jim called Mary on her cell phone. Both were obviously excited. They were anxious to get together to study the book.

"I'll call you as soon as I get back to Palo Alto, Jim," Mary said. "Remember, we have another reason to get together. I'm getting hot just thinking about it!" she added.

"You're getting hot? You ought to see my Levi's right now just talking about it!" Jim responded. "I'm apt to explode any minute now!"

"Well, I guess you'll just have to take a ride on the unicycle until I get back. Anyway, gotta go! Bye, sweet cheeks!"

* * *

WINDOM MET MARY AT THE HANGAR. She loaded his bags, and as usual, Windom was quickly at his work on the plane. Mary fired up the Baron and taxied out to the runway. She called the tower and was cleared for takeoff. Soon she reached altitude, set the autopilot, and began thinking of Jim and what would happen after all this codebook and money stuff was over. She knew that she had indeed fallen in love with him and was sure that he felt the same.

We'll probably get married and have a bunch of kids! she fantasized. *Let's see, how old will Jim be when they reach college? What if I can't have children? I've never found out! Maybe it's too late! No, thirty isn't too old. Perhaps there is only time for one kid!*

Her mind wandered back to other things: the codebooks, the millions of dollars that must be waiting in a bunch of Swiss banks. *My God!* she thought. *What if all this stuff is true?*

The flight attendant brought her a prepared salad and half sandwich. Mary ate her lunch, drank a Diet Pepsi, and settled in for the three-and-a-half-hour flight.

* * *

JIM RILEY AND JERRY DUNNE met at the appointed time. Jerry asked Jim, "Why is this damned book so important, Jim? Isn't that the item you told me about that had something to do with David Steinmetz's murder?"

"Yes it is, Jerry. David was killed for the twin of this book."

"You mean there's another one like this?" Dunne asked.

"That's right, there are two of them," Jim continued. "David had the other book with him when he met with Windom. Windom would have had him killed right there if he thought he could have gotten away with it."

"Holy Christ!" Jerry exclaimed. "I could have lost my ass for stealing this little bugger!"

"Not yet, Jerry. Wait until Windom finds out it's missing. The shit will really hit the fan then!"

"Do you suppose he's going to suspect me?" Jerry gulped.

"Jerry, he's going to suspect anyone and everyone. I hope you used gloves," Jim said casually.

"Shit! Now you tell me!"

"Well, I wouldn't worry about it. He really has no reason to look your way. He will more than likely target the household staff."

"What did you mean when you said I wouldn't regret the commission of this little burglary?" Dunne asked.

"Well, I won't go into detail, Jerry, but I can tell you this. If I and a couple other people are successful, there will be a ton of money at the end of the rainbow!"

"Where you getting all this money, Jim?"

"That's not important right now, Jerry. In fact, it may not happen at all. Just consider it an investment in your future. Some work out, others don't."

"Gee thanks, Jim. I can hardly wait!"

"Honest, Jerry, the chances are pretty good that you may see some return. I just can't promise it."

The men finished with small talk and parted.

Riley was hoping there would be a phone message from Hunter.

THIRTY

"HELLO, JIM, IT'S ROLLY HUNTER," the answering machine droned. "I'm in Naples and will be leaving this afternoon for Haifa, Israel. I think I'm on the trail of a pair of twins who are direct descendants of Harry Sukin. Remember, he was one of the original six men who had been shot by the fascists. Anyway, are you having any luck with finding the other book? I'll try to call you around 8:00 p.m. your time today. Don't hold your breath waiting for me."

Another message was left by Mary. "Jim, had a good trip so far. I hope all went well with the treasure hunt! See ya soon! I love you, sport! Bye!"

Jim could not deny the warm and fuzzy feeling that came over him with Mary's comments. "I love you too, Mary!" he said out loud.

Now he had to consider what to do about the bad guys who had been trying to kill him. He knew he was not going to continue to do nothing. If they were to try again to hurt him, he would surely fight back. At this point, he didn't know *whom* to strike at, however. He would have to be ready for whatever came his way. He would probably have to prime the pump a little with Windom to get these creeps out into the open. He knew he was playing a deadly game. Somehow he would have to devise a plan that would cause Windom to suspect him as the codebook thief. That would bring the rats out of the woodwork.

Jim had kept a .22-caliber target pistol in his nightstand for several years. He had almost forgotten about it. It was time to dust her off. Even though he had no license to carry a concealed weapon, he was going to keep a concealed weapon. He only hoped he wouldn't get caught with it. *Maybe it will be enough to scare them off*, he thought. He had no intention of shooting anybody.

He walked to Starbucks, ordered a mocha, and sat down to once again review the book. It was obvious that some of the pages had been stuck together from the water-logging. Someone, probably Windom, had carefully pulled them apart. Only one page was nearly impossible to read. The ink had been badly smeared. All of the other pages had been smeared but were quite legible. He was anxious for Hunter's return so the two books could once again speak to each other.

The thought of some financial reward was quite removed from Jim's mind. The chase would bring excitement and perhaps he could be part of something that would turn out to be something bigger than himself. A deserving treasure for one or more descendants of the six families would bring more satisfaction than he could hope for.

Now he wanted Mary back. He shuddered to think how close he had come to losing her. He ordered another mocha.

Mary spent the rest of her free time shopping. *Hardly a place for high fashion*, she thought. *But then again, why would I be shopping for high fashion?* She decided a bikini would do the trick. *Something hot to entice Mr. Riley*, she decided. She could hardly wait to get back home. It had only been three days and it seemed much longer.

Windom completed his business by late evening and informed Mary that he wanted to leave early in the morning. She was pleased and let him know that she would have the pre-flight completed by 8:00 a.m. They would be back at the Stockton airport by noon.

Mary had decided that she would go directly to Jim's place from the airport. Windom would not need her for a few days, and she and Jim could spend some real time together.

Jim was conducting the final dual cross-country with Howard Davies. It would be a relaxed, uneventful trip. He too was thinking of Mary and longed to spend some time together. His shoulder was no longer hurting, Rolly Hunter was not around, both codebooks were in hand, and he was feeling quite horny. He felt like some sort of marathon winner who had just completed the last mile of the Bay to Breakers run.

* * *

WINDOM'S LIMO PULLED IN FRONT OF THE HOUSE at 1:30 p.m. As was his custom, the staff were instructed to stand just inside the door upon his return from a business trip and either answer questions, get instructions, or both.

"Everything go along all right, Tilley?" he asked.

"I believe so, Mr. Windom," she answered.

"What do mean, you believe so?" he demanded.

"Well, it was probably nothing, sir, but yesterday, I thought I heard what sounded like someone stirring around upstairs." Windom's eyes were wide and wild. "But I checked it, Mr. Windom, and everything seemed fine."

Windom dashed for the stairs, rushed up, and slammed the door open. He went straight to the wall painting, swung it out, and opened his safe. Several minutes passed and then suddenly and violently he called out, "Tilley, get your goddamned ass up here now!"

Tilley ran as fast as she could. Windom was facing her at the top of the stairs.

"So you think everything is all right, do you? Well let me tell you something, you bitch! Everything is not all right! Now tell me about checking things out before I throw you down the fucking stairs!"

Tilley began to cry openly, blubbering some incoherent, disconnected words.

"Aw, shut up!" Windom yelled. "Somebody get Jerry Dunne on the phone. The rest of you go on downstairs! Tilley, I'll talk to you later."

All the staff scurried down the stairs and disappeared into the kitchen. Windom picked up the phone. "Jerry, this is Windom. I want you to find me a private detective, someone that is connected to the fingerprinting business, and I need him as soon as you can locate somebody."

Jerry Dunne felt a lump in his throat and could barely respond, but managed to confirm his instructions.

What the hell have I let myself get into? he thought.

"Well, I can't worry about spilled milk now," he concluded. He began thumbing through the Yellow Pages and calling until he located a female private investigator who fit the bill. She was a former sheriff's deputy who fingerprinted inmates at the Stanislaus County Jail. She had filed and run down many suspect prints. It was her area of expertise.

Jerry Dunne set up an appointment with her to meet with Oliver Windom at 10:00 a.m. the next morning. She confirmed that she would be there. Dunne called Windom and asked if he should attend.

"No, that's not necessary, Jerry. I'll handle it."

Jerry Dunne sucked in his breath and knew it would only be a matter of time until Windom discovered what had happened. It was definitely time to update his résumé.

*   *   *

THE LADY SHOWED UP AT THE WINDOM MANSION with her fingerprinting kit and other paraphernalia. "Hello, Mr. Windom," she began in a whiny voice. "I'm Lydia Langston. I think you are interested in identifying some fingerprints?"

"Yes, Ms. Langston, that is precisely what I want!"

"I believe my secretary discussed my fee schedule?"

"Yes, yes, that's fine. Let me show you what I want."

The detective followed Windom into the house and upstairs to the bedroom. He showed her the safe.

"I'm reasonably sure that there are fingerprints on the face of the safe besides mine. I want you to find them and tell me whose they are!"

"Very well, Mr. Windom, let's take a look."

The lady took nearly an hour and found one print on the inside flap of a large envelope inside the safe. She lifted it and moved to the picture frame. She dusted for prints and lifted what looked to be one smudged unidentifiable print.

"Mr. Windom, could I have the right thumbprint from you, so that I can separate you from others?"

Windom touched the inkpad and rolled his thumbprint onto the private detective's pad.

"If there's nothing else, Mr. Windom, I'll go back to my lab and see who has been playing with your toys!" She giggled. Windom frowned and the lady hurried down the stairs.

"I'll be calling tomorrow afternoon!" she called back from the front door. Windom retreated to his bedroom office, slamming the door behind him.

* * *

JIM ANSWERED THE DOOR. Mary began removing her blouse as she entered. Jim closed the door and embraced her roughly. He was a man with serious semen backup. She was a woman who needed to be laid. Together they were out of their clothes instantly. Jim picked her up in his arms and moved to the bedroom. She fondled his firm erection and he felt the softness between her thighs. Sooner than either had wished, it was over with a loud double eruption of passion.

They lay embracing for more than a half hour before repeating the lovemaking with much more civility. It was long, intense, and gentle, yet with passion. It was the first time that Jim said, "I do love you, Mary," while looking into her eyes. Tears flowed as she confirmed that Jim had indeed fallen in love with her.

"Jim," Mary began, "what do you think this is going to mean to us when it's all over?"

"Well, I don't think either of us will have to work again if it actually happens. I think with what we're going through, we are certainly entitled to a finder's fee. I have no desire to keep any more than a reasonable amount."

"What about Jerry Dunne? How does he come out?"

"The same as us, Mary. He has put his ass on the line, knowing full well that he could lose it. He's probably not entitled to the same compensation as us, but I don't think we should receive the same as Hunter either. None of this could have happened without him. Anyway it's all conjecture. The odds of pulling this off are pretty slim, even if Hunter finds some authentic heirs."

The phone rang, startling both Jim and Mary.

"Hello, Jim?" came Jerry Dunne's voice.

"Hi, Jerry, it's me!"

"Jim, the shit is about to hit the fan just like I promised! Oliver has a private investigator looking for prints on the safe! Mine will be all over the envelope! I'm a dead man, Jim, for Christ's sake! What am I going to do?"

"Just hang in there, Jerry. I'm really sorry that I got you into this mess!"

"Oh hell, I'm a big boy, Jim. I should be able to take care of myself. You know it's not the thought of getting fired that bothers me, but I believe the son of a bitch will try to kill me," Dunne concluded.

Mary began to fondle his manhood. It immediately stood at attention.

"I know, Jerry, but we'll just have to stop him before he gets a chance! We'll talk later." Jim hung up the phone and turned back to Mary.

He kissed her on the neck and let his lips move to her earlobe. He moved his tongue lightly around her ear. Mary could feel her nipples getting hard and wanted him to touch them. He heard her thoughts. He played with her erect nipples with his fingers and tongue until she could stand it no more.

"If you don't stop that now, Jim Riley, I'm going to come," she said in her sexiest voice. "I don't want to do that yet."

Jim Riley yielded and moved to another target. They continued for another half hour until both were totally spent and hungry.

"Let's get dressed and find a hamburger somewhere," Jim announced.

"I'll buy that!" Mary responded. She gave Jim a long, sensual kiss before hopping off the bed. Jim loved to watch her walk to the bathroom naked. He had never met anyone who could arouse his animal desire like Mary Rison. Not even Shirley could keep him heated for so long.

THIRTY-ONE

"MR. WINDOM," CAME THE VOICE over the phone. "This is Lydia Langston."

"Yes?" answered Windom.

"Mr. Windom, there are two sets of prints in addition to yours on the safe."

"And?" prompted Windom.

"Well, sir, I have identified only one set found on the face of the safe. Those inside have not yet been completed. I thought you would want to know what I have discovered."

"Yes, thank you, Ms. Langston, I do!"

"The prints on the outside of the safe belong to a Roger Wills. Does that name mean anything to you?" she asked.

"No, should it?"

"Well, it seems that Mr. Wills is a locksmith in Turlock." She giggled slightly as she said, "Turlock Locks. He was the party who opened your safe. Now, the real perp is someone else."

"So have you talked to this Wills guy?" Windom asked.

"Not yet. I'll be going down there this afternoon."

"You better let him know that he doesn't want to play games with me!"

"Don't worry, Mr. Windom. I still remember, 'good cop, bad cop.' He'll tell me who put him up to this!"

"Miss Langston, I damn well know who is behind this theft. I just need to verify it. Then I'll take it from there."

"Mr. Windom, I can't be a party to anything illegal or shady!"

"That will not happen, Ms. Langston. Your job will be over when you find the name of the bastard that broke into my house! On second thought, I may need you to locate the item that was stolen from me. We'll talk about it later."

"Very well, Mr. Windom. I'm on my way to Turlock Locks." She chuckled her way out the front door.

Windom picked up the phone and dialed his Asian contact. "Mr. Wi, this is Windom … No, now wait a minute! I'm not calling to raise hell. I just want to add a little to our original proposition."

"Very, well, Mr. Windom. What are you proposing?" Wi asked.

"How would you like your contract fee doubled?" asked Windom.

"I would like that very much! And how does that happen?"

"First of all, I *do* want Riley dead, along with one or more others. I don't know their identities yet, but it shouldn't take long. I don't want any of them eliminated until I have recovered a couple items. Otherwise, killing the bastards would be of no value to me. Do you understand?"

"Yes, I do understand, Mr. Windom. Can you give me any information as to where these objects might be?"

"That's affirmative, Mr. Wi. I believe the items, two small black books, are in the hands of Jim Riley, or in close proximity to him. You may have to rough him up a little. He'll talk!" Windom concluded.

"I do understand, Mr. Windom. I think you will be pleased with our performance!"

"Yes, I'm sure I will. I'll call you with the names of the other perpetrators involved when I have them. But Riley is the one behind all of this! Start there!"

"That will be no problem, Mr. Windom. You have a nice day," he declared, hanging up the phone.

* * *

"HELLO! IS THERE ANYONE HERE?" asked Lydia Langston as she stood in the graphite-scented locksmith shop. It reminded her of the old shoe shops of her childhood. She took in the smell and found it rather pleasant. It brought back special memories long past.

"Yes? What can I do for you?" asked the little man. She smiled, as she was sure that she was looking at Danny DeVito.

"Are you the owner?" Lydia asked.

"Yeah, I'm owner, janitor, driver, and the only employee. Why are you asking?"

"Mr. Wills," she began, as his eyes widened, "I am a private investigator, and I'm working on a case in which I believe you to be deeply involved!"

"Bullshit! Who the hell do you think you are, coming in here to give me a ration of shit about anything you're working on?" he demanded. "Besides that, how do you know my name?"

"Mr. Wills, I said I am a private investigator. How difficult would it be for me to find out your name, particularly when I have your fingerprints?"

"Now wait just a damn minute! First of all, I don't have a clue what you're talking about! Besides that, my fingerprints are all over this town and as far north as Stockton. Now, what's this all about?"

"Mr. Wills, you opened a safe at the Windom mansion recently, and by the way, not at the request of Mr. Windom."

"So what? I get asked all the time to open safes, doors, and cars. Big deal! I assumed it was an employee who had the authority. I don't ask a lot of questions."

"Well, Mr. Wills, I think in this case, you should have asked a few questions." Wills stood staring at her.

"Unless you plan a jail vacation, I would ask that you tell me now who hired you to open the safe!" Wills could see that she meant business.

"I'm not saying anything. I'm calling my lawyer. Now you get the hell out of my store, lady!"

Lydia Langston immediately turned on her heels and left the establishment without a word.

She returned to her car and dialed Windom's phone number. She related what had just happened and assured Windom that she was on the trail. She told him that she would need to go to Stockton to get access to the more sophisticated fingerprinting equipment.

Roger Wills immediately dialed Jerry Dunne at the hangar office.

"Jerry! They know I opened the safe! Now you're going to have to get me out of this mess. You got to tell them that you hired me! I'm not going to jail for burglary!"

"Nobody is going to jail for anything, Roger! Even if Windom finds out about me, he can't do anything but fire me. And I'll be quitting before that anyhow!"

"Yeah, but robbery is still a crime!" Roger said.

"I don't think Windom will file any charges against me. He won't like the skeletons that I can dig up. Windom also has a hit out on a friend of mine. He probably wouldn't like that to come out in court!"

"All right, Jerry, but just remember, I'm not going to jail for you or anyone else!"

"So noted, Roger. We'll talk to you later."

Jerry Dunne dialed Jim Riley's number.

"Jim," he said to Riley's answering machine. "We've got a bit of a problem. The locksmith is about to spill his guts to Windom. What do you want me to do?" Dunne hung up the phone and immediately went to his locker at the hangar. He began to pack all his belongings into an empty Tide box. He gathered all his loose tools, placed them into his tool chest, and padlocked it shut.

I might as well haul this junk out now, he thought. *Windom probably won't let me anywhere near this place once he finds out what happened.* He loaded the box and his tool chest into his van and headed north. He would plan to meet Jim in the Bay Area tomorrow.

THIRTY-TWO

ROLLY HUNTER MADE HIS WAY from Haifa Airport to Haifa University, noted for its modern planning and three graduate buildings. Before beginning any business, Hunter proceeded to the main building housing the Eshkol Tower. He had heard of the breathtaking sight overlooking Haifa and the bay. He was not disappointed. Its beauty was rare.

Hunter was to meet his guide atop the tower at 1:00 p.m. It was now 12:47 p.m. The man approached him.

"Mr. Hunter?" he asked.

"Yes, I'm Rolly Hunter. Mr. Kayemeth?" Hunter asked.

"That's correct. I can see, Mr. Hunter, that you are sufficiently impressed with the view."

"I have tried to imagine, but I had no idea that a place like this in the desert could be so beautiful!"

"Mr. Hunter, I am somewhat limited for time today. Would you like to see the art gallery first?"

"Yes, yes, I would," Hunter answered enthusiastically.

The gallery displayed works by artists and victims of the Holocaust. This was precisely Hunter's target. He ignored the modern artists' paintings and made his way to a special section of the gallery that contained nearly 300 charcoal drawings.

As Hunter viewed the artwork, a feeling of dread and evil seemed to come over him. He touched the edge of one painting. He immediately felt emotionally drained. It was impossible to contain his tears. He felt embarrassed, even though he knew it was a natural expression.

He continued to dwell on the drawing. He began at the top. A single light cord hung from the ceiling and ended with a naked bulb. Below the light were two sets of bunk beds stacked four high. At the edge of one bed stood two small boys. They were the same size and looked identical. They could not have been older than a year or so. Their dark, sunken eyes and skeletal bodies spoke volumes about their plight.

Hunter removed a small magnifying glass from his pocket and moved it around the lower section. There it appeared, almost illegible: "M. Sukin 6/9/43."

As he studied the drawing, he confirmed what he believed to be true. The boys were twins, probably born a year earlier. Definitely born in a concentration camp barracks.

"Mr. Kayemeth, can you tell me how the gallery acquired this drawing?"

"Mr. Hunter, please follow me to the administration office. I think I may be able to help you."

Hunter's guide did not ask questions. Many persons pass through the gallery. So many emotions are displayed that the gallery's policy is to say nothing unless asked, and then to offer no more information than is requested.

The gallery went so far as to provide a sort of grief counselor just outside the exit. Episodes of fainting were a common occurrence.

After 20 to 30 minutes, Kayemeth returned from an office cubicle with several sheets of official-looking documents. He stood before Hunter and arranged them into some sort of presentation.

"Mr. Hunter, I have here one document that details the following information regarding this drawing. The document was recovered on August 22, 1945. It was located at the Ascetic compound, building C-1, bunk 11, by a Staff Sergeant Phillip Rodriguez. It was transported to Central Command on the 23rd. From there it was logged into the Army records for transport to the U.S. It was not determined as to the final disposition of the drawing.

"The artist was not determined. Only three children and their mother were incarcerated. No information on the father. The records show a daughter and a set of twin boys. Sergeant Rodriguez moved the boys to the Army Evac for transport to the nearest military hospital in England." Kayemeth concluded, "I show no further record of them."

"What do you suggest that I do to locate the twins, if they're still alive?"

"Well, until recently, the Holocaust archives were nearly inaccessible. They were records collected by the Red Cross from concentration camps, hospitals, and other parts of the Nazi regime after the war. Anne Frank's files are there, and so is a list of the people saved by Oskar Schindler.

"These records were, and still are, in the small German town of Bad Arolsen. As a result of the overwhelming demands, Bad Arolsen has opened its doors to the world. Digital copies of the archive will be circulated around the world, if it hasn't already been done. A complete copy will be made available to the Holocaust Museum in Washington, D.C. I suggest that you start there."

"How much information is in this list? I mean, what kind of information?" Hunter asked.

"From what I'm told, the files are extensive. The Nazis recorded the smallest details, such as which specific individuals had head lice, and even the size of the head lice seemed important."

"My God! What was the matter with those people?"

Mr. Kayemeth simply shrugged his shoulders. "Now Mr. Hunter, I must go. I hope you have made headway in your quest."

"Oh, no doubt!" responded Hunter. "I thank you for your time on such short notice. I can let myself out."

Kayemeth turned and left the main building. Hunter returned to his rental car and the airport. Next stop: Washington, D.C.

THIRTY-THREE

RILEY HEARD THE KNOCK AT HIS DOOR. He waited for the second knock before easing toward the door. He slowly opened the door and immediately felt a fist directly on the bridge of his nose. With blood flowing liberally, he staggered back and ended up on his sofa. As the Korean man approached, Riley leapt from his sofa and plowed his head into the man's stomach. Another man grabbed him by the sore shoulder, causing him to utter a sound of pain.

Riley whirled 180 degrees and caught the man square on the jaw, sending him plummeting to the floor.

As the first man came toward him, he kicked him in the crotch and hit him hard as his body bent forward from the intense pain in his groin. He collapsed in a fetal-positioned lump onto the floor.

Ignoring the pain in his shoulder, Jim picked up the other man by the belt and collar and threw him against the half-opened door. The man bounced, making a sound against the door much like a golf ball smacking a tree. The other man crawled quickly to the door and fled.

"Damn! This feels good!" Jim said aloud as he realized Windom was getting serious. But he knew this was only a scare tactic. He and Hunter held all the cards. Windom would not actually try to kill him now until both books were safely in his hands. Windom had been outflanked and he knew it.

Jim picked the scar-faced fellow from the floor and held him by the collar. "Now listen to me, you little shit. I want you to deliver a message to old man Windom!" The man looked and said nothing. "You tell Windom if he keeps this up, I'm going to tear his fucking house down! I've had all I plan to take from you bastards! Do you hear what I'm saying?"

The man was beginning to turn blue and could only nod slightly in the affirmative.

"Now get your ass out of my home before I rip that scar right off your face, and don't let me see you again!" The man rushed past the elevator and began taking the stairs two and three at a time.

Only now did Jim realize that his shirt was completely covered with blood. He quickly reached for a wet washcloth, sat down, laid his head back, and placed the cloth over his still bleeding nose. He began to laugh out loud.

* * *

WINDOM ANALYZED HIS OWN SITUATION. Undoubtedly Riley was behind the whole thing. *But who is working with him?* the man thought to himself. *He certainly could not carry this off alone,* Windom deduced. He knew it would be easy enough to figure it all out.

Windom's phone rang. "Hello," he answered.

"Mr. Windom, it's Lydia Langston."

"Yes, Miss Langston, this is Windom."

"The one set of fingerprints that I located on the picture frame are those of a Mr. Dunne."

"Oh my God! You don't mean Jerry Dunne?"

"Yes, Mr. Windom, that is the man."

Windom placed his right hand on his forehead and slowly let it slide down his face as if to erase this terrible news. He said nothing.

"Mr. Windom? Are you there?" she asked.

"Yes, yes, Miss Langston. Thank you."

"What would you like me to do now, Mr. Windom?" she inquired.

"Nothing for now, Miss Langston. I'll get back to you later. I'll keep your number handy. Goodbye for now."

Windom hung up the phone and called for his car.

As always, it was ready and waiting by the time he reached the portico.

"Where to?" asked the chauffeur.

"Take me to the hangar, George. Quickly, please!"

"Yes, sir!" He sped the great white limo down the long driveway and onto the 99.

Windom knew immediately as he approached the hangar that Jerry had fled. The doors were closed. They were always open when Jerry Dunne was on duty. He should have been there.

Windom opened the small side door and entered. As he made his way to Jerry's workbench, it was confirmed. Dunne was gone and so were his hand tools.

"That traitorous son of a bitch!" he yelled. "How could he do this to me?" The man was truly hurt. He had considered Jerry Dunne not only a loyal employee but the only person he had called a friend. He shook his head and left the hangar and returned to the mansion. He spoke to none of the staff but went directly to his study, picked up the phone, and dialed Jerry Dunne's cell phone number.

After several rings he heard, "Hello, this is Jerry."

"Hello, Jerry!" said Windom.

"Mr. Windom, I … I …"

"Jerry, let me do the talking," Windom commanded.

"Yes, sir," responded Dunne.

"Jerry, I don't know what prompted you to do what you did, and I'm not even going to ask. I will tell you this, however: you are fired, which I assumed you guessed, and I guarantee you that you won't work in any other shop in California. Now, having said that, I'm going to make you an offer that you should consider!"

"And that is?" Dunne interrupted.

"And that is, that you pretend to keep in cahoots with that bastard Jim Riley and let me know exactly what's going on …"

"Going on with what, Oliver?"

"Come on, Jerry, don't insult me, you ungrateful son of a bitch. You know exactly what I mean!"

Jerry Dunne said nothing.

"Now listen to me, Jerry, and don't interrupt me again, damn it!"

The phone was silent.

"Here's what I want you to do. First of all, say nothing to Riley other than I called and fired you in a hail of F-bombs. Secondly, I want you to stay close to him and whoever is working with him. I want names, and you had better give me all of them. Third, you may or may not know that there are two books; neither is good without the other. I need to know where they are exactly. Don't tell me you can't find out. You had better find both of them because I know Jim Riley has both!"

"And what do I get, Oliver?"

"Oh my, Jerry, that's a good question. Let me see now, what's in it for you? How about if I don't have you killed, Jerry? Is that a pretty good deal for you?"

"Mr. Windom, let me tell you something …"

"Be careful there, Jerry!" Windom responded.

"Oh, I'll be careful, all right. You can be sure of that! As for your threat to kill me, you need to get in line. I'm no cherry there, I can assure you! As far as squealing on Riley, I wouldn't think of it. He's been more of a friend to me than anyone I've ever met. And you know something, Windom, I've *never* trusted you! Half the time I showed up at the hangar, I fully expected to get fired for some damned thing or other."

"I'm sorry you feel this way, Jerry. I'm really not going to enjoy whatever comes your way next!" he concluded and slammed down the phone.

* * *

MARY HAD RETURNED TO THE WINDOM GUEST HOUSE. She was quite nervous. It was clear that Windom was getting close to discovering the whole scheme and she would have to fall on the sword soon. She wondered if he would hit her or even try to seriously hurt her, or worse yet, try to kill her.

She decided it wasn't worth worrying about now.

It will be what it will be, she thought. She would take her chances with Windom. *Not a pretty sight to come,* she thought.

Mary changed her clothes and walked up to the mansion. She preferred to enter through the kitchen door rather than up front. She was, however, the only employee besides Jerry Dunne who was invited to enter through the front door.

A member of the staff let her in and let her know that Windom was in the study. She walked in breathlessly.

"Hi, Mr. Windom," Mary greeted him.

"Oh, Mary, glad to see you. Listen, I need to run up to Oakland tomorrow. Jerry isn't around to fill up the tanks in the plane. Do you suppose that you can handle it?"

"No problem, Mr. Windom. I can run over there right now and check everything out," Mary said with a sigh of relief.

"Are you going to stay in the guest house tonight, Mary?" he asked.

"Yes, of course. I'll be ready anytime you want to leave."

"Good, I won't know until around seven in the morning. Thanks, Mary!" She started to leave, until he called out, "Mary!"

"Yes?" she answered.

"Mary, you remember why you were faking flying lessons from Jim Riley?"

"Of course, Mr. Windom. Why would you ask?"

"Well, it's cost me a lot of money, and you really haven't reported anything to me. Have you gotten to know him?"

"Yes, I've run into him at several flight-school functions. We've had lunch a couple of times. We conversed about the Baron and that kind of stuff."

"Did you talk about anything else?" he asked. "Did he ever mention a little black book or anything like that?"

"Nooo ..." she lied. "Is there anything else, Mr. Windom?"

"No, Mary. That's all, thank you." He turned back to his desk. Mary hurried out of the mansion.

There was no doubt in Mary's mind that Windom was on to something and knew that she was not beyond suspicion. It was just a matter of time until the whole caper unfolded.

It would take an idiot not to figure it out, she determined.

Furthermore, she thought to herself, *I hope to hell I'm not around Windom when he finally concludes that Jim, Jerry, and I are all in this together. At this point, only Rolly Hunter is unknown to Windom.*

For no apparent reason, her mind turned to Jim's ex-wife. She wondered what the woman was like. She wondered why they really divorced. She wondered about his daughter. If she and Jim were to get together, or better yet marry, would they spend time with Jim's girl? Mary certainly hoped so. She loved children and hoped she would have some of her own eventually. She realized that her biological clock was ticking and she would have to make something happen soon, if at all. Nonetheless, she knew she would love Jim's daughter, simply because she belonged to him.

She jumped as her cell phone rang.

"Hi, good lookin'," came Jim's voice at the other end.

"Hi, sweetie!" Mary answered. "I miss you already."

"Yeah, me too. It's been almost five hours," Jim said.

"So to what do I owe the pleasure of this call?" she asked.

"Oh, I just wanted to tell you I just got a call from Hunter. He's on his way to D.C."

"D.C., why?" she asked

"Well, he's on the trail of some of the families' descendants. The information he needs is in Washington."

"Do we know when he is coming back?" she asked.

"Not yet. He doesn't know if he might be led somewhere else."

"Did he tell you how to get hold of the other book?"

"No, he just said that it's safe and we'll get both books together when he gets here."

"Wow! It's starting to get exciting, huh?"

"You're telling me! I'm anxious to decode this thing if I don't get killed first."

"What, a big boy like you? I don't think so. I guess I do worry a little, however. Anyway, I have to get over to the hangar. I'll talk to you later. I love you!"

"Me too! Bye!"

As she drove to the Windom hangar, Mary tried to imagine Windom's reaction to her being part of the plot. She visualized his head literally exploding when the news hit his brain. She chuckled at the picture, but quickly felt a cold chill as she imagined what he was capable of doing. It occurred to her that she really preferred not to be in his presence when the dung hit the rotator. She had to get her mind off Windom and on to something more to her liking.

It dawned on her that she and Jim had not spent a complete night together since their first sexual encounter. There was no reason; things just seemed to happen to interrupt their passion. It wasn't a big deal.

She thought for the first time what it might be like to have real money. *I can buy 15 pairs of shoes and not bat an eye,* she thought. She smiled as she pulled into the hangar's parking space. She shut off the engine and spent the next half hour checking the Baron. She thanked Jerry Dunne in her mind. The tanks were full. He always filled the tanks before putting the plane away. He had only forgotten to place the chocks under the wheels. After finishing a complete walk-around, Mary drove back to the guesthouse with much trepidation. Windom truly frightened her.

THIRTY-FOUR

HUNTER STEPPED OFF THE PLANE AT DULLES Airport and made his way to the taxi signs. He had not had to check any baggage. Hunter traveled light.

He gave the cab driver his destination. "Holocaust Museum, please."

The driver was quite familiar with the location. "Checking on a family member?" he asked.

Hunter had never considered how he should think of the people he now represented. After a moment, he responded, "No, I'm just representing a family from Milan, Italy."

"Where did they end up?" he asked.

"Auschwitz, I think," Hunter told the man.

"Wow, I didn't know anybody from Italy was ever sent there! I always thought they were Germans or Polacks."

"Most of them were," Hunter responded. "But somewhere between 7,500 and 8,000 were Italian Jews."

"That many, huh?" the cabbie said.

"You might be surprised to know that Jews were not the only Holocaust victims!" Hunter continued.

"Really?" asked the driver.

Hunter was beginning to take note of the man's appearance for the first time. He was definitely Middle Eastern, probably an Arab or Iranian, maybe Pakistani. In any case, it was odd to think he would be interested in the plight of any Jew. Nonetheless he continued, "Yes, did you know that half a million Gypsies were murdered?" The cabbie shook his head. "There were 250,000 mentally and physically disabled in the mix of victims. Three million Russian prisoners of war were executed. Jehovah's Witnesses, homosexuals, Communists, Polish intelligentsia, and trade unionists were all included in the genocide," Hunter concluded.

"Man, those were some bad people!" said the cabbie.

"Yes, they were, Mr. Ah ..." Hunter looked at the tag on the visor — Raj Goyal. "Mr. Goyal, are you East Indian? You don't seem to have an accent."

"My father is East Indian and my mother was Palestinian. She has passed away. I suspect you are asking because I am interested in the fate of some Jews?"

"Well, the thought had crossed my mind," Hunter answered.

"Personally, I never cared much for any religion. My father was a Catholic and my mother a Muslim. They both converted to the Methodist or Baptist, or one of those funny Christian churches."

Hunter wanted to go no further. It was time to change the subject. The men made small talk for a few minutes until the cab driver pulled up to the museum. Hunter paid the fare and walked toward the entrance.

Within a few minutes, he was directed to the office of a Vera Moats. The sign on her door read *Registry of Holocaust Survivors*. The woman's secretary was most gracious and led Hunter to her inner office.

"Good afternoon, Mr. Hunter. I'm Vera Moats. How may I help you?"

Hunter gave a general synopsis of his mission without all of the pertinent details. He did not think of himself as a fortune hunter, nor did he want anyone else of get that idea. He couched and parsed his words carefully, so as not to reveal his final purpose. Miss Moats was impressed.

"I'm trying to locate a set of male twins by the name of Sukin. I don't know if they're alive or dead or where they might be. When I was with the

Army, stationed in Italy, I did some research on the family. I would like very much to make contact."

"Well, Mr. Hunter," she began officiously, "unless you are a direct descendant, I'm really not at liberty to give you any information. I'm sure you can understand my position."

"Yes, ma'am, I do," responded Hunter.

Her manner changed to pleasant sympathy. "I will tell you this, Mr. Hunter. We are beginning to receive a great deal of digital information from Bad Arolsen, Germany, which I understand will be completely opened to the public at some point in time."

"Is there anything I can do in the meantime?" asked Hunter.

"I suggest that you contact the International Red Cross headquarters. They have an organization called The Holocaust and War Victims Tracing Center. I would call their office right here in D.C."

"Thank you very much, Ms. Moats. You have been quite helpful." Hunter nodded in what could be taken as an abbreviated bow. He left the building and hailed a cab. It was nearly 5:00 p.m., and Hunter thought he had better get a fresh start in the morning. He asked the driver to take him to the nearest Marriott Hotel. He would call Jim Riley when he was settled for the night.

* * *

JIM RILEY WAS BUSY STUDYING the Windom codebook. It made no real sense, but he could see that it was laid out exactly like the other one that had been given to him by David Steinmetz. Twenty-four individual pages of nonsense.

It did differ in one respect: every letter or number had an equals sign that meant it stood for something else, just like Hunter had explained. The very first item on the first page appeared as d=2,4,7,9.<. Jim deciphered it to mean the first time "d" showed on the page it represented the number two. The second time it was to mean the number four, and so on to seven and nine. Then it was to repeat. For example, if the letter "d" appeared a fifth time, it would mean "two" again.

Riley thought perhaps the men went a little overboard with their code. Nevertheless, he sat in awe, looking at the book, trying to imagine six Jewish men, along with their friend, the professor, sitting in some dingy room nearly 60 years ago, devising a silly code system that they could not possibly dream would represent an unimaginable amount of wealth. How many more such stories existed he could only imagine.

He was already missing Mary, and he began to wonder what was taking Hunter so darned long. Jim was ready to get on with the decoding.

* * *

RILEY'S PHONE RANG SHORTLY THEREAFTER. It was Hunter.

"Jim, how you doing, my friend? It's Rolly!"

"Mr. Hunter. Where the hell are you?" asked Jim. "I thought you were going to call me back."

"It didn't work out. I'm in Washington D.C. I just wanted to check in with you. How are we doing with Windom's copy of the codebook?"

"I have it, Rolly."

"How did you manage that?"

"It's a long story. I'll tell you when you get back."

"Good! Just hang tight. I'll be back next week and we'll get to work on decoding!"

"How are you coming along at your end, Rolly?"

"Oh, I'm moving forward, I guess. Nothing exciting to report yet," Hunter answered. "Does old man Windom know that he has been relieved of his copy?"

"I'll say he does! I've already had a couple of his goons knock my door down, and they damn near broke my nose in the process!"

"Be careful, Jim. This guy is capable of anything!"

"Tell me about it! Anyway, I'm careful."

"Okay, Jim. I guess I'll see you next week."

"Sounds good, Rolly. Bye!" Jim hung up the phone.

* * *

HUNTER ARRIVED AT THE RED CROSS HEADQUARTERS at

9:00 a.m. sharp. He approached the information desk and was directed to the library, where several Yiddish-speaking women and men moved about. Some had nametags; Hunter supposed they were research people.

"Excuse me," he said to a man with a nametag. "Could you help me, please?"

"I hope so, sir! What can I do for you?"

"I'm not sure that you can help me, so I'll just tell you what I'm searching for."

"Very well!" said the man. "I am Jacob Moffat. And what shall I call you, sir?"

Hunter introduced himself and told the man about the twins and where their records had stopped.

"Since they were turned over to the Red Cross, the records are still intact, I assure you!" Moffat said.

"What is really interesting is the fact that they were twins. This makes it much easier for us to locate them. We have records of multiple-birth children, both twins and triplets, alphabetically listed." The man walked to a large desk with pigeonholed shelving. He ran his fingers up and down the rows until he stopped at a large "S." He reached in and retrieved a small canister containing a roll of microfilm. Hunter was amazed that this old-fashioned method of record storage was being used in the age of computers.

Moffat, seeing the disbelief on Hunter's face, spoke. "Mr. Hunter, we do use computers extensively. However, we find it helpful to use our old records first. Quite often, we have located exactly what we're looking for."

He loaded the film into the projector and began a methodical rolling of the information. After several minutes, he settled on one document. He began to read as Hunter viewed the information on the screen.

"Let's see," he began. "Simon, Salzmann, Suberman, Sukin. Here we are! There seems to be at least 20 Sukins. Where were they from?" asked Moffat.

"Milan, Italy," Hunter answered. "Is there an M. Sukin?"

"Ah ... I, J, K, L, M. M! Miriam Sukin. Milan, Italy. Arrested in January of 1942. Three children, a girl, 12, and two boys, infants, twins."

So it was the mother who was the artist of the twins' pencil drawings? Hunter thought to himself.

"So now how do we find out what happened to them?" asked Hunter.

"Now we can go to our computer!" Moffat said. "Let's begin by entering the name *M. Sukin*."

In a matter of seconds, the monitor screen filled with the charcoal drawing that Hunter had seen in Haifa, along with the record of Sgt. Martinez turning the twins over to Central Command and to the Red Cross.

"Can I bring this up on my own computer?" asked Hunter.

"No, Mr. Hunter. This is a special program available to very few organizations. It would not be wise to have this kind of information floating over the Internet. I'm sure you can understand why," Moffat responded.

"Yes, I can, Mr. Moffat. So what do I do now?"

"There are several pages of documents here. I will give you a printout and you can use it as you wish," Moffat concluded.

"Thank you. I'm sure I can find something of value."

Moffat ran the printer and gave Hunter the pages. Hunter slipped them into a small briefcase, left quickly, and returned to his hotel.

He spent the next hour perusing the documents. According to the records, SS officers had raped the daughter on several occasions. She had been one of many females that were kept healthy, solely for the pleasure of the Nazis. Just before the Allied forces overran the compound, the girl along with other special women were quickly shot and abandoned into a shallow grave. The retreating guards had no time to cover the pit. Her body was never identified. There was little doubt that her life ended there. Miriam Sukin was believed but not proven to have died in the gas chamber.

The documents continued to reveal information regarding the twin boys. Their names were Myron and Isaiah Sukin. At the time of their mother's arrest, the boys were less than a year old. Hunter determined that if alive, the boys would be in their sixties by now. There were no records of the father.

Hunter had never discovered the fate of Harry Sukin. This information confirmed to Hunter that Sukin had not lived long enough to be arrested. He continued reading.

The twins were taken from the Red Cross office near Auschwitz and transferred to what amounted to a foster home in England, near Liverpool. The Red Cross did not feel it wise to send Jews immediately back to Italy following the war. No one knew how they would be regarded or treated. It would take some time to sort things out. In the interim, many families were separated and transported to various sanctuaries around the world, many to the United States. Records had been kept as methodically as possible.

The boys were raised by a "reasonably tolerant" family by the name of James, with whom they remained until their 21st birthday. They had worked hard in their teen years and managed to save nearly a thousand pounds. The boys had obtained passports, and on their birthday sailed for New York aboard the *Queen Mary*. Here the records stop.

Without hesitation, Hunter determined his next step. He was able to determine the year of the boys' 21st birthday. They had to have sailed from England in 1962. He merely needed to contact the shipping company and ask for their passenger list to determine the boys' final destination. He could narrow down the sailing date if it were possible to contact the Hall of Records in Milan to get the actual date of the boys' births.

Hunter went to the hotel lobby and the Internet desk. After acquiring online service, he entered "Hall of Records, Milan, Italy." Within seconds, he was on the Web site. For $39.95 he could access almost any information. He entered his request along with his Visa number. Within two minutes, the Sukin twins' information appeared. They were born at 12:02 on August 14, 1941. They had not yet been named, but they were registered as the infants of Harry and Miriam Sukin. The first-born was difficult to deliver and suffered from oxygen deprivation for several minutes. It could not be determined if he had suffered any brain damage. The second child was fine, per the midwife's report.

Now Hunter knew that the *Queen Mary* had sailed on August 14, 1962. He would need to call the Cunard Lines headquarters in Santa Clarita, California, or better yet have Jim Riley drive down and check out the passenger list of the ship's crossing. There would be no certainty that a final destination was available from Cunard for the boys.

Hunter called Riley and explained what he needed him to do. "Their address is on the Internet, Jim," Hunter explained. "In the meantime, I have to get back to the Red Cross and see if I can find out about the James family in England. Perhaps they knew where the boys were going. If none of this works, we'll try the Social Security office to see if either one has a number." It was 10:00 a.m. Pacific time, and Jim thought if he left now, he could be there before 5:00 p.m. He quickly pulled up the Cunard office address and was on his way. As he headed south, he called Nancy at the flight school to cancel his lessons.

Jim took I-5 south to make the best time. He thought if he took 99 back, he could stop in Modesto and check on Mary. Perhaps sneak a little romantic interlude right in front of Windom's nose. He would call Mary when he left Santa Clarita and let her know what time to expect him. It would certainly be after 10:00 p.m.

* * *

RILEY ARRIVED IN SANTA CLARITA WITH TIME TO SPARE. He called the Cunard Lines from his car and got directions. Soon he was in the office and told the desk person what he was looking for.

"It will take a few minutes, Mr. Riley," the man told Jim.

"I'll wait," he responded. The man retired to another office, and Riley could hear him typing on the computer.

Soon the man returned with a printout of something.

"Here's what we're looking for, Mr. Riley," the man reported. Riley said nothing.

"According to our records, Isaiah and Myron Sukin were indeed on the manifest and had purchased tickets by train to Rochester while aboard our *Queen Mary*."

"Anything else?" Jim asked.

"No, sir, that is all we have."

Riley thanked the man and got into his car.

I'll wait until I get over the grapevine to call Mary, he thought.

Jim dialed Hunter's cell number. "Rolly," he said, "I found out that they ended up in Rochester. The record ended there."

"Okay, Jim. I'm trying to find the James family in Liverpool. No luck yet, but I'm sure I'll find them."

"All right, Rolly, talk to you later." Jim hit the "end" button and continued north on 99. He would soon be with Mary again. Riley was finding it more and more difficult to be away from her. He knew that no matter how this treasure hunt ended, he would ask her to marry him.

THIRTY-FIVE

HUNTER CONTACTED THE OVERSEAS OPERATOR for the local Red Cross office in Liverpool, England. Shortly he was on the phone to the Red Cross office. "Thank you for calling the Red Cross. We are presently closed," came the answer. The person on the other end announced the office hours.

Shit! thought Hunter, *It's eight o'clock there*. He would have to wait until morning.

* * *

RILEY CROSSED THE GRAPEVINE and was nearly to Bakersfield when he called Mary.

"Hi, kiddo!" he said.

"Hi, Jim. I was just looking out the window here at the guesthouse. I see a white Subaru pulling up to the front of Windom's house. I think it's the same one that we saw before, Jim!" Mary said with some panic in her voice.

"Mary, get the hell out of there right now! Windom must have found out about us!"

"But how would he know that?"

"Never mind now! Just get outta there. I want you to go to my place. I'll call the 'super' to let you in. I'll be there around midnight. Now go!"

She grabbed her coat and purse and headed for the front door. The doorbell rang as she touched the knob. She wheeled around and ran for the back door. As she opened the door, she was confronted by an Asian fellow with a scar on his face.

He smashed her in the mouth, sending her reeling across the room. Another man broke the front door open, entered quickly, and picked her up off the floor. The scar-faced man came at her again and this time slapped her across the face with his left hand and then repeated the action with his right. Again she tumbled to the floor, blood dripping from her mouth. On the second blow, the man had cut her above the eye. She was nearly unconscious, her face covered with blood. She could feel it running into her eye. Again, he picked her off the floor and pummeled her, this time in the stomach. She heard her own rib crack.

The second man grabbed a towel from the bathroom and threw it into her face. Hardly conscious, she tried to wipe the blood away. She was aware that she felt no pain. She also knew that she was about to pass out.

They are killing me! she thought. "Oh God, please help me!" she cried aloud.

The men picked Mary up from the floor and dragged her to her car. They wrapped her in a blanket from the guesthouse and roughly placed her in the trunk. They placed her purse in the trunk as well.

The man with the scar climbed behind the wheel and headed down the long lane to the 99 north entrance. He drove about five miles and stopped on the shoulder. The other man followed in the Subaru. He pulled in directly behind Mary's car to provide a shield from onlookers.

They opened the trunk and removed Mary's limp body, wiped as much blood from her face as possible, and moved her to the driver's seat. They took her purse and tipped it upside down onto the passenger's seat. One of the men opened the wallet and removed all of Mary's cash. He put the blanket into their vehicle. Just before leaving, the other man took out a sharp stiletto knife and jammed the point into the right rear tire. It whistled as the air expelled. It was a poor attempt at making the scene look like a robbery after a flat tire. Any crime-scene rookie would put the true picture together.

* * *

IT WAS NEARLY 9:00 as Jim pulled into Windom's driveway. He turned off his headlights as he drove up the long lane to the guesthouse. He shut the engine off several hundred yards away. He crept quietly up to the front door and saw at once that it had been broken into. The house was dark as he walked in.

"Mary? Mary? Are you in here?" He walked into every room. She was gone. The back door was open. Riley remembered that he had kept a small flashlight in one of the kitchen drawers while he had stayed there. It was still in place. He shined it around the living room. His heart stopped as he spotted blood stains on the floor.

"Oh, Jesus, no!" he said to himself as he bit his lip hard enough to draw blood. He ran out the rear door to see if her car was gone. It was. *Maybe she made it out of here toward my place!* he thought. He rushed back to his car and spun out down the lane and onto 99.

He almost missed it as he passed Mary's car at nearly eighty miles per hour. He had to drive to the next exit to return to her. After nearly fifteen minutes of maneuvering, he pulled up behind Mary. She was unconscious in the driver's seat.

"Mary! Mary! Honey, can you hear me?" Jim said with tears flowing down his cheeks.

"Jim?" she said softly. "Is that you? What kept you? Where are we? Where are those awful men?"

"Sweetheart, it's okay now. I'm here, Mary. I need to get you to a hospital right away. Those men hurt you pretty bad. Do you understand?"

Mary nodded her head as she passed out. Jim spotted her cell phone in the seat and dialed 911.

As he waited for the EMTs, he petted her gently and tried to wipe away the drying blood from her face. He kissed her on the forehead several times. Glancing around, he could see that the bastards were trying to make it look like some kind of a robbery.

Soon the CHP and the medics arrived. They would take her to the ER at one of the major hospitals in Modesto. Jim told the officer that he wanted to follow.

"Very well," said the officer. "I'll meet you there to get the report."

The medics told Jim that they were taking Mary to Modesto Memorial. "You won't be able to keep up with us, buddy!" said the medic in charge. "Just drive up to the emergency entrance. Okay?"

Jim nodded and returned to his car. The ambulance sped away with lights and siren blazing.

Jim followed the directions given to him by the medics.

"Those bastards!" he howled to himself. Tears flowed down his cheeks as he drove to the hospital. He had driven fast and was not far behind the ambulance. He arrived and ran into the emergency entrance. They had wheeled Mary into a cubicle with a bunch of medical staff all over her. Some doctor was barking orders about blood and X-rays.

Jim gave the clerk all the pertinent information that he was aware of. He did not know her birthday, and he silently cursed himself for that. He would not be that thoughtless again.

He opened her purse and withdrew her driver's license along with some medical insurance cards and all of the other information needed by the hospital.

"Does Miss Rison have a living will?" asked the lady.

"Ma'am, I wouldn't know that if I had to! Why in hell are you asking me that now?"

"It's standard procedure, Mr.?"

"Jim Riley," he answered. He was in no mood to give the James Bond response.

"I don't mean to suggest anything, Mr. Riley. The hospital is required to ask these questions of all patients."

"I'm sorry, ma'am. I'm just a little on edge right now."

"I'll tell you what, Mr. Riley. Why don't you go down this hall to the emergency waiting room. Just stop by after Miss Rison has been attended to."

"Thank you, I appreciate that." Jim hurried off down the hall, carrying Mary's belongings with him.

Damn it! he thought. *I need to call her parents, and I don't have a clue where they are or any number.*

He began looking through Mary's purse, which made him uncomfortable. He felt like he was spying on her, though he knew better. *She would not mind at all,* Jim thought.

Jim located Mary's mother's number in her cell phone contact list. He dialed the number and heard, "Hello, you've reached Helen Rison. Please leave a message and I'll get back to you. I promise!"

Riley left all the pertinent information and hung up the cell phone. Using Mary's phone, Jim dialed Jerry Dunne.

"Hi, this is Jerry."

"Jerry, Jim."

"Jim, where in the hell are you? What's going on with you and Windom? The bastard fired me and I think threatened to kill me! I told you how dangerous he was!"

"Yeah? Well he's not as dangerous as I am right now! He just had his goons beat the hell out of Mary. I don't even know if she's going to make it!"

"Where is she, Jim?" asked Jerry.

"She's in the hospital here in Modesto. I'm waiting for a report from the doctor now."

"So, is there anything I can do, Jim?" Jerry asked.

"Yes there is, Jerry. That's really why I called you. Now listen to me. Don't ask any questions. This will sound crazy!"

"What are you talking about?"

"I want you to call a big equipment rental place. Probably that one down 99 toward Fresno."

"And why am I going to do that, Jim?"

"I want you to rent a big-ass bulldozer and have it delivered to the entrance of Windom's lane."

"Holy shit!" Jerry whispered. "Sure, Jim. I'll just walk in and tell them I want to rent a D-9 Cat so I can destroy some guy's house!"

"No, Jerry! You tell them we have our own heavy-equipment operator and we're going to take an old barn down!"

"I don't know, Jim."

"Listen, Jerry, I promised that if Windom intimidated me again, I would tear his house down!"

"Jim, you can't be serious! For Christ's sake!"

"I am serious, Jerry. Now call the rental place and get me a dozer. Be sure it has a big front blade and a cage. Also have them throw in a hard hat!"

"Jim, I can't believe you're doing this. You sound like a junior high school kid talking!"

"Are you going to help me or not, Jerry?"

"Well, I guess I was never the sharpest knife in the drawer. Yeah, what the hell. Windom will probably have me killed anyway. I'll take care of it, Jim."

"Thanks, Jerry. Be sure to have the Cat there at 8:00 a.m."

"Okay, Jim; for your information, I heard that Windom drove up to Napa for a day or two. Bye."

Jim spent the remainder of the day in waiting rooms at the hospital. Eventually, one of the doctors called his name. "Mr. Riley?" he asked.

"Yes, I'm Jim Riley."

"We have Miss Rison pretty well stabilized. She has suffered some tissue damage to her face as well as a fractured jaw."

"Were there any other injuries?" Jim asked.

"Yes, she sustained a broken rib and a collapsed lung. We have treated her for these. If everything goes well throughout the night, she should come through fine. The healing will take a long time, however. I have made a police report. It is standard procedure for this kind of thing. They have asked me to have you remain here until someone can talk to you."

Jim thanked the doctor and found out where Mary was located. Her right eye was all that showed through the bandages. He kissed her gently and decided to sleep in the chair next to her bed. It was after midnight, and Mary's mother had not returned his call. *Oh well, I tried*, he thought to himself. The nurse brought him a blanket. It took him the better part of an hour to doze off.

* * *

IT WAS 6:30 WHEN JIM AWOKE WITH A START. Mary was moaning, obviously in pain. Jim ran to the nurses' station. The shifts were changing, and no one seemed in a hurry to attend to Mary Rison.

Jim raised his voice a bit. "Can I get someone to help my ... fiancée? She's in pain!"

One of the nurses looked up. With a look of irritation, she went into Mary's room, turned a small valve in the intravenous line, and within seconds, Mary settled down and slept.

Jim asked the nurse when to expect Mary to awaken. He was informed that she would be in and out of consciousness for most of the day. Jim made his way to the cafeteria for some breakfast before his appointed clash with Mr. Windom.

He had kept Mary's phone in his pocket for her mother's return call. It came as he was forcing down some oatmeal. There was panic in her voice and she wanted directions to the hospital. She told Jim that she was in San Diego and would catch a regional flight to Fresno. There she would rent a car and drive to the hospital in Modesto.

Jim informed her that he had some things to do and would be back in the afternoon. He said he was sorry to be meeting her under such unpleasant conditions. She too was regretful of the circumstances. Nevertheless, Mary had told her of Jim, and she looked forward to their meeting.

* * *

BY 7:30, JIM WAS ON HIS WAY back to the Windom mansion. As he drove down the frontage road off the 99 ramp, he saw the Caterpillar backing off the low-boy trailer.

Damn! That thing is big! he thought.

The driver parked the Cat at the edge of the lane, folded his ramps, and drove past Jim. He waved as he passed. Jim waved at the man, parked his car, and climbed aboard the big D-9 Caterpillar. He searched around until he found the start switch. He turned on the key and waited until the warning light went out. He engaged the clutch and hit start. The huge engine soon roared to life. He played with the hydraulic levers until his was able to move the blade up and down. He had only to find a low gear. It would not be necessary to shift.

With his left foot shaking violently on the clutch, he slipped into low gear. He let the clutch out too quickly and the big machine lurched forward and died. Jim repeated the process and got the thing moving slowly up the lane. As he zigzagged up the lane, he reached for his hard hat and slipped in on. He resisted the desire to chuckle as he imagined how this would look on camera.

Within a few minutes, he approached the portico but did not turn. He raised the blade two to three feet and made contact with the front of the mansion. The pillars creaked and cracked and began to fall on top of the cage. Small debris began falling through the cage, but nothing large enough to cause Riley any real concern.

The huge hand-carved doors, gleaming with the Windom crest, moved off their hinges with a tremendous complaining squeal and slid forward in front of the huge blade. The Cat moved without effort or change of momentum, plowing furniture and stair railings, walls and paintings, sinks and cabinets, dishes and glasses, a washing machine, a toilet, and a shower stall. Water was spewing everywhere.

Riley made a path straight through the mansion, avoiding the gas stove in the kitchen to the left. He did not want to be in the middle of an explosion. The electrical panel, however, shut down one breaker after another, following the first wall plug smashed.

Only the top six to eight feet of stair casing remained after the swath through the house. The back wall with a large cottage-type window inset with colored glass collapsed as the giant blade took out a portion of the back wall. He only hoped that the first crunch would send the servants scrambling for safety.

Riley made a large loop around the servants' quarters around the house and back down the lane. He could hear sounds of beams and rafters creaking. He continued to the end of the lane, still listening to falling debris.

"Well, the old fart has a real fixer-upper on his hands now!" Riley laughed aloud. He turned off the big Cat and jumped into his car, called the rental company to come pick up the machine, and headed back to the hospital and Mary.

My God! he thought to himself. *What is Windom going to do about Mary's dad? I'm sure the man has already been fired. Is Windom going to try to kill everybody? I know he's going to go absolutely nuts when he sees his house!*

Then his mind turned to his daughter, Julie. *God, how I miss her!* he thought. He had only seen her once since her mother's wedding. What a beautiful weekend that had been. Shirley was right. He did like Ted Foster. It made him a little jealous to see Julie pay so much attention to him, but he knew that she would have a full family life again. The man would be a good father. He also imagined Julie with himself and Mary. The idea worked. He knew Mary would love her too.

Jim's anger had subsided somewhat with his over-the-top act of vandalism. He now knew what road rage must feel like. A sudden wave of guilt hit him. Had he gone too far with this unpleasant act? How could he have let himself lose so much control? Now was not the time to be inviting more trouble. He must never let himself succumb to such ridiculous behavior again, though he had to admit there was a bit of satanic pleasure in his heart!

* * *

JIM WAS BACK AT THE HOSPITAL by noon. The lady in the room had to be Mary's mother. Jim was astounded at the resemblance. Her red hair and narrow hips were breathtaking. Jim's lusty thoughts were quickly quelled. *My God, Jim, it's her mother!* he reminded himself silently.

The two introduced themselves and began talking about Mary, who at this point remained unconscious.

Helen Rison began to tell the usual motherly stories about her child, beginning with the terrible birth pains and progressing through puberty, and unlike the old days, proceeded to glorify her daughter's first period. Jim was both amused and embarrassed. He could remember when such things were simply not discussed. He had remembered his mother mentioning something about a "curse," and had no idea what she meant until he was fully grown.

The two seemed to hit it off as they continued their discussions of Mary. Helen Rison gave a fairly complete autobiographical sketch, as did Jim. Both most certainly left out some private details.

Mary's mother was not a doting parent, but Jim could see that she loved her daughter. She moved to Mary's bedside and began petting her as best she could with all the bandages covering her face. The pain was such that Mary recoiled with each touch. Her mother stopped.

Mary's jaw had been wired shut, as is often the case with a fracture. Hers was slight and would heal quickly, according to her doctor.

"Jim," she said, "I understand that you are divorced."

"Yes, I am. My ex-wife recently married again."

"That's what Mary tells me. May I come right to the point, Mr. Riley ... Jim? Are you in love with my daughter?"

Without hesitation, he answered, "Yes, Mrs. Rison, I am!" He surprised himself with the quick answer.

"So, what are your plans when this is over?"

"I intend to marry her, if she'll have me."

"Oh, I don't think I'd be too worried about that, Mr. Riley. Now, if you don't mind, I would like to talk about this problem you seem to be having with Mr. Windom. It has involved my husband, which I'm sure you are aware."

"Yes, I am. I can only say I'm truly sorry it has come to this," Jim answered. "It was never my intention to cause trouble for anyone, especially Mary. And now her father."

"Is the matter so important that it can cause both to lose their jobs?" Mrs. Rison asked.

"Mrs. Rison, I'm afraid it is more serious than you know."

"Yes?" she asked.

"Mary would not be here if it were not for Oliver Windom's greed and anger!"

"What does he have to do with this?" she continued.

"It was upon his direct orders that Mary was hurt, and it was done primarily to get at me."

"You mean he actually tried to kill her?"

"I don't think so, Helen. I believe that he wanted her physically injured, just to get my attention."

"Oh, my God! What could be that damned important?" she asked with tears beginning to swell in her eyes.

"You would have to understand something about the man's entire life to realize what he is capable of doing! And I'm sorry that your husband became a casualty in this mess."

"That's the least of our worries. Mary's father does not particularly care for Windom and was already looking at other options. He is looking forward to meeting you, Jim. I think you two will get on."

Jim was relieved to hear those words.

"What is this all about, Jim? Mary has refused to discuss anything other than her actual job with Windom."

Jim answered as tactfully as he could without sounding like a child playing a game. He gave Rison a short history lesson, one that certainly showed the kind of person Windom had grown up to be in spite of his father's goodness and distaste for the fascists. Not only had he become an anti-Semite but a generally hateful man.

"Perhaps things would have turned out differently had he met someone to share his life," Jim continued. "But the man always seemed to turn people away after being around him for any length of time. I've always thought him to be a manic-depressive personality. I guess they call it bipolar now. One minute the man is the most engaging and likable person you could meet. Yet without warning, he can turn into a tyrant. A true Jekyll and Hyde."

The duty nurse entered the room and told Jim that a Mr. Windom was asking about Mary. "I have put him on hold. What would you like me to tell him, Mr. Riley?"

"Just tell him that she is resting and cannot be disturbed," Jim answered. The nurse turned and left the room. Jim felt a rush of panic. He said nothing.

Helen Rison's phone rang. It was Mary's father informing her that he was on his way and would be there that evening around 8:00 p.m. She touched the *end* button and returned to Mary's bedside. Mary did not move, other than the slight up-and-down signs of breathing. She remained unconscious. Jim sat beside her on the opposite side and reached for her hand. It seemed tiny and soft, and it felt cold. He rubbed it gently, trying to warm her. He thought she had squeezed his hand, but he wasn't sure. It prompted him to raise her small palm and kiss it softly. "I love you, Mary," he said with a whisper. It did not go without notice from Helen Rison.

"Jim, it is quite apparent how you feel toward our Mary. She has been a special treasure to her father and me her whole life. She has always been mature beyond her years, yet she maintains a childlike impishness that we do love so. I know that you will take care of her," Helen concluded.

Jim was beginning to get embarrassed and wished the subject would close. It did. Helen picked up her purse and jacket, walked over to Jim, and kissed him on the cheek. "Nice to meet you, Jim Riley," she said. "I'll be back in the morning. Tell Mary if she awakens."

"I will, thank you, and I've really enjoyed meeting you, Helen," he said as she departed Mary's room.

Jim sat for several hours, looking at Mary, petting and kissing her forehead through the gauze and tape.

THIRTY-SIX

HUNTER WAS ABLE TO REACH THE RED CROSS office in Liverpool. He found out that the James family was still living there. He was given a phone number, and he thanked the person at the other end.

He dialed the number and reached Mrs. James, now nearly 80 years old. He explained who he was and why he was calling. The lady told him that the boys left England for the Mayo Clinic in Rochester, Minnesota. Mrs. James told Hunter that the first born, Isaiah, had suffered severe epileptic seizures as often as three to four times a week, which continued through the day they left their home.

Myron, the younger boy, had determined as a small boy to get his brother to America, where he could be treated for his epilepsy. There could be no chance for him to live a normal life without treatment.

"I fully expected the boys to return," Mrs. James stated, "but we only received a single postcard from Myron."

"And you never heard from them again?" asked Hunter.

"No. The boys grew up bitter and, I think, godless. They blamed God for their parents' death and simply wanted to escape any connection to the past. The boys tolerated my husband and me, but we never felt any love emanating from either boy. We wept so often for them!" the woman said with a voice too weak to avoid showing the pain. Hunter surmised that she had been a good surrogate mother for the boys. He thanked her and wished her well.

Rolly Hunter would now need to track the boys from the Mayo Clinic. He only hoped that records still existed.

He called Jim Riley's cell phone and left him a text message. He didn't need to talk to him. He would do that later, when he found out what had become of the twins. He went directly to the airport to see what, if any, flights were leaving for Rochester in the next few hours. He thought he would try to get there and spend the night before contacting the clinic.

Northwest had a flight leaving in 30 minutes. He made his way to the ticket counter. Unfortunately, there was only one middle seat remaining. He hated the middle seat because he could rarely avoid sitting next to some obese man or woman who would surely hang over his armrest. In some cases, he had been trapped between two huge travelers. He felt guilty for discriminating, but that alone would make the ride uncomfortable. Hunter decided that the blame lay with the airlines for knowing better. Three people are never the size of three airline seats. He bought his ticket and waited to board.

* * *

HUNTER PULLED UP TO THE MAYO CLINIC information center. There he was directed to the clinic library, where he was able to research past case studies from the Epilepsy Department. They were numerous, but fortunately in alphabetical order.

It took a while for Hunter to complete his study of the file, but he found what he was looking for. The diagnosis, in simple form, suggested that the elder twin had what was described as an empty space roughly the size of a baby's thumb in his brain, which was devoid of tissue, and was caused by oxygen deprivation. The research suggested that it was in the area that controlled logic. The neurologist determined that the boy would have some difficulty with mathematical problems and difficulty in following normal logical patterns of thought in general.

The boys spent several days on an outpatient basis. Isaiah was given medication, and the boys remained for a week to see how it would work.

The records ended there.

Hunter could not leave it unresolved. He approached the central information area and began asking questions related to the boys' whereabouts. After talking to more than a dozen office personnel, he was referred to one retired male nurse who might have remembered the boys. The man did not live far away, and Hunter made his way to the man's home.

The elderly gentleman told Hunter, "I especially remember Myron, who was hell-bent on moving to Independence, Missouri. He admired President Truman and thought it would be a good place to live. He respected the man immensely."

"Do you remember anything else about the boys?" Hunter asked.

The man said that he didn't. Hunter thanked him, gave him his card, and left. He would now try for a phone listing of either man. He had spent a great deal of money thus far and felt he could not continue for long. He needed contact with a real live descendant of one of the original six.

Hunter spent the next several minutes trying to locate either a Myron or Isaiah Sukin in or near Independence. There were no listings for either man, but there were several Sukins listed. Hunter found a nearby coffee house, ordered a regular coffee, and seated himself in an overstuffed chair in the corner. He thought he might be there for some time. After three painful attempts at calls through information, he gave up and decided he needed access to an Independence phone book. What he needed was an Internet connection somewhere. He would head back to the airport and use a public-access terminal there. In an hour, he was sitting in a cubicle, searching USA Phone Book. There were no Sukins listed in Independence. He would have to go there.

Hunter was becoming quite exhausted and knew he must find something soon or he would be out of energy before he was out of money. He studied the departures until he found a Southwest flight to Kansas City. He purchased his ticket and sat for a good 40-minute snooze in the waiting area. He would need to do laundry soon. He was totally out of clean underwear, and his shirts did not smell too fresh. He decided he would check into a Marriott and get a quickie laundry job done. Besides, he needed a real room where he could rest comfortably. He had not been sleeping well.

It was late in the evening when his plane touched down in Kansas City. He would need to rent a car and drive to Independence. He figured it would be near midnight by the time he got settled. He did not miss it by more than a few minutes.

He spent an hour in the bar unwinding with a couple of Sapphire martinis. Tonight he would just sleep. In spite of his lack of success thus far, he did not doubt for a moment that his quest would be successful.

*   *   *

IT WAS NEARLY 10:00 A.M. WHEN HUNTER AWOKE. A knock at the door startled him.

"Maid service!" came the female voice from outside.

"Not now!" grumbled Hunter.

Without thinking, he jumped from bed and reached for his trousers. Then he stopped and realized there was no hurry.

He took time to make the little pot of tasteless coffee supplied by the hotel. He turned on the news and started to shave, but his razor quit before he could finish.

"Damn!" he grumbled. He reached for the charger from his bag and plugged it in. He would finish his shower, and perhaps it would be charged enough to finish his shave.

His cell phone rang a couple of times before he could find it.

"Hello, this is Rolly."

"Mr. Hunter?" came a voice.

"Yes, who is this?" asked Hunter.

"This is Homer Olsen, Mr. Hunter."

"Who?" Hunter asked.

"Homer Olsen, I'm the nurse you talked to about the Sukin twins."

"Oh, yes, Mr. Olsen, I'm sorry. I've met so many people lately that it's hard to remember everybody."

"Well, I just thought of something that might be helpful."

"Yes?" responded Hunter.

"When Myron was talking about going to Independence, he did mention that they had talked about Overland Park, Kansas, as well. I'm sorry, Mr. Hunter, I had forgotten about that. I just saw something about Overland Park on the television. It came back with a jolt!"

"Mr. Olsen, do you remember if they mentioned anyone's name?"

"No, I don't recall," Olsen answered.

"Mr. Olsen, I can't thank you enough. It so happens that I'm in the Kansas City area right now. I'll check it out. Thank you again. Goodbye!"

Without hesitation, Hunter grabbed the greater Kansas City phone book and opened it to the letter S. There it was, seven Sukins listed. One was Myron Sukin, near Prairie Village.

Hunter dialed the number.

"Hello?" came a child's voice.

"Yes, is Mr. or Mrs. Sukin home?"

"My grandma is here."

"May I speak to her, please?"

"Grandmaaaa!" shouted the boy.

"Hello?" came the response shortly.

Hunter introduced himself and gave his reason for calling. He asked the woman if Myron Sukin has or had a twin brother.

The woman, with some hesitation, said yes. "Why do you ask?" she inquired.

"Ma'am, are you Myron Sukin's wife?" asked Hunter.

"No, Isaiah Sukin is *my* husband. His brother Myron passed away three days ago. I am here with the family."

Hunter expressed his condolences and asked if he could meet with the family after a few days. The lady agreed that the next morning would be acceptable. She gave him directions and he agreed to meet them around 10:00 a.m. Hunter breathed a sigh of relief. He was getting close to his goal. He felt that it wouldn't be long now.

* * *

HUNTER WAS EARLY FOR HIS APPOINTMENT. He drove around the block several times before parking in front of a home that was rather modest compared to the general area. He shut off the engine, locked the car door, and walked up the driveway.

A lady who looked to be in her late sixties answered the door. Standing behind her were two children, a boy around 11 and a girl probably 8 or 9.

"Mr. Hunter?" she asked.

"Yes, Mrs. Sukin. I'm very pleased to meet you," Hunter said with some mild excitement.

"Please come in, Mr. Hunter," she continued. "Please call me Heddy."

Once inside, Hunter was introduced to the two grandchildren beside her and another woman in her thirties was introduced as Myron Sukin's daughter-in-law. Another elderly woman entered from the kitchen. She was stoic and looked confused.

"Mr. Hunter, this is my sister-in-law, Ruth Sukin."

Hunter was about to respond, when Heddy took him by the arm and pulled him aside.

"Mr. Hunter," she began, "I'm afraid that my sister-in-law is not well. She has been diagnosed with Alzheimer's. Her condition has been getting steadily worse in the last few months."

"I'm sorry, Mrs. Sukin. And now she has lost her husband. What are their plans?" asked Hunter.

"We have not had a moment to think about it. Her son Jacob has been making some calls, but nothing has developed."

"Pardon my asking, Mrs. Sukin, but what happened to Myron? Had he been ill?"

Heddy Sukin pursed her lips before beginning. "Not that any of us was aware. Last Thursday morning, I received a call from Myron's neighbor that a terrible accident had occurred. It seems that Ruth had covered the electric range top with paper towels and turned the knobs on to high heat. The papers flamed up. Myron ran to the kitchen and tried to pick up the burning towels with his bare hands, igniting his sleeves and burning his hands and arms and his face."

"My God!" said Hunter.

She continued. "I guess the pain and panic were too much for him. He suffered a massive heart attack. By the time the medics arrived, he was dead. Can you believe it?"

"No, ma'am, I can't! That is just too bizarre."

"That's it. It was over; Myron was gone," she concluded.

"Is Jacob at home?"

"Yes, he's out back. Would you like to talk to him?" she asked.

"Only if he feels like it," Hunter answered.

Helen Sukin went to the rear of the house and called for Jacob to come into the house. Shortly he entered and Hunter introduced himself. The man was thin and appeared to be in his late thirties. He seemed somewhat frail, but generally a neat, good-looking man, taller than Hunter had expected. He reminded Hunter of a taller James Dean. The man was soft-spoken with a pleasing voice. Hunter's idea of the typical Jew had been quite prejudicial. He had often visualized the men as short, often balding, and plump, with a tone of rudeness in their voice. *How did I get such a preconceived stereotype notion about a group of people?* he thought to himself. He was obviously impressed by the man's appearance and demeanor. It caught him off guard.

After several minutes of ice-breaking conversation, Hunter opened the door to explain his mission.

"Jacob," he began, "what do you know about your family background? I'm sorry; that's awkward. Let me start again. Are you aware of any details surrounding your father's background, his childhood, how he happened to come to America?"

"I know that my grandmother was in a concentration camp. I think she died there."

"Did he tell you about the James family in England?" Hunter asked.

"Yes, he and Uncle Isaiah were raised by them."

"Did your father or Uncle Isaiah ever tell about their time in the concentration camp?"

"No, it was never discussed. Well, I take that back. Uncle Isaiah brought it up once. My father yelled at him to stop it. 'That part of our life is over.

Do not bring it up in my house ever again!' my father told him."

"And that's all you know about you family history?" Hunter asked the son.

"I know that it left my father very bitter. It has caused much contention in the family."

"What kind of contention? Do you mind my asking?"

"No, I don't mind at all! My father was a complete atheist. Anytime Mother, Uncle Isaiah, or any member of the family would try to discuss religion, his answer was always the same: 'There is no God! Do not insult me with such gibberish. I'll hear no more of it.' That kind of talk."

The man continued, "He would not allow religious discussion of any kind in the house. He never attended synagogue. He did not participate in my bar mitzvah. Do you have any idea what that means to a Jewish boy?"

Hunter decided it was not his role to referee the family's religious disagreements. He wanted to move on to his true purpose.

He began, "If you'll allow me, I'd like to take you on a small journey in history. You see, I know much about your family, much more than you could possibly know."

The family sat in silence, all eyes glued on Hunter. For the next several hours, he told the whole story of the original six men and their plight. He told of the codebooks, bank accounts, and how he had a plan in mind for the heirs of the fortune. The family remained motionless. Even the two children sat still. For several moments following Hunter's story, the family sat quietly, the older ones wiping away tears, except for Myron's wife, who sat looking blankly at the floor. The children were simply fascinated by the good story told by Hunter.

"Jacob?" Hunter began. "Would you consider going to the West Coast with me for several days?"

"Yes, Mr. Hunter, if I can be of some value."

"You can, Jacob. In fact, it is almost necessary in order for us to continue. By the way, are there any other relatives of Isaiah or Myron that you are aware of?" Rolly asked.

"No," Jacob answered, "just those of us here, and Uncle Isaiah. He wants to be alone at home right now. My father's death has hit him pretty hard."

"I'm curious," said Hunter, "how has his epilepsy treatment been working over the years?"

Heddy spoke. "Partially. He still has localized seizures but no more of the grand-mal types."

"That's good to hear," Hunter responded. He continued, "Jacob, I want you to meet some very close friends of mine in San Jose, California. These two have placed themselves in a lot of danger trying to protect the codebooks. They are in this for the long run. You will like them, Jacob, I'm sure."

"I'm looking forward to it!" Jacob answered.

They agreed that Jacob would meet Hunter in San Jose the following Monday. Hunter gave his condolences once more and said goodbye to the family. He was anxious to return to the Bay Area. He knew nothing of Mary Rison's injuries or Riley's retaliation. Jim Riley saw no reason to tell him while he was traveling. Jim was hopeful that Mary would be well on the way to recovery by the time Hunter returned.

Hunter pulled into the airport car rental return area and proceeded to view the departures board on the main concourse. He would be back soon to what was beginning to feel like home.

THIRTY-SEVEN

OLIVER WINDOM REMAINED MOTIONLESS as he stood before the front door of his demolished home. His mouth gaped open, and he began to move his head slowly back and forth in total disbelief. Nearly a full minute passed before he could move. Deep in his throat, nearly inaudible, he began to emit a low, guttural sound. The volume increased and the tone changed to a higher pitch. The sound grew louder until it almost became a scream. The man's face turned from ashen to bright red. He collapsed to the ground and began to pound his fist on the walkway. Blood was soon oozing from his hand. He kept pounding until the chauffeur grasped the man and shouted for him to stop.

"Mr. Windom, I must help you to the guest house! Please, sir!"

Windom did not object but was unable to walk the short distance to the building without the man's help. Windom was escorted to the guest house living room and guided to the sofa.

"Can I do anything for you, sir?" the chauffeur asked.

"No! Just get out. Leave me!" Windom shouted.

The man left without a word.

Windom cried loudly and openly for nearly 10 minutes. Nothing in his life before, not even the loss of his father, Gino DiNapoli, had affected Windom as did this single act of terrorism against him. The mansion was his and his alone. It was his fortress against the world. It *was* his world. It was who he had become. It was his refuge against an evil society. It was supposed to be impenetrable. Yet, not once but twice, it had been violated.

"Riley, you're a dead man!" he shouted as though he expected Jim Riley to hear him.

One problem stood in his way: he had to have the codebooks and he did not have them. He must figure a way to get the books and have Jim Riley murdered. He must call the Asian assassins for one more attempt. He had no fear of the police. He knew Riley could not warn them anymore, now that he could have Riley arrested. This had to be handled without alerting the authorities. He was sure that the Santa Barbara file was still open. He didn't need any more police snooping around.

Windom rose to his feet and left the guest house to look again at the damage sustained by the mansion. It dawned on him that Riley had been selective in his destruction. *He could have totally destroyed the place,* Windom thought. *He deliberately avoided wrecking the whole damned place. Christ almighty! It was a message!* Windom knew it had to be in retaliation for what happened to Mary Rison.

"Well, Riley, that little bitch got what she deserved!" he said aloud. "You must have been getting into her pants to get so damned mad at me! Well, let me tell you something, Mr. Riley. I got your damned message! I'll have one of my own pretty soon! This isn't over by a long shot, you son of a bitch! You will be hearing from Oliver Windom again!"

As Windom surveyed the mansion, he made further observations. The ceiling trusses seemed to be intact. There was definitely floor and foundation damage, but most of the interior walls were not load bearing and could probably be repaired. The main loss was the furnishings, some expensive art pieces, a very exotic dining table, and a large Grecian statue of some obscure nymph that had adorned the huge entryway. It was costly, and Windom hated the thing anyway. So after a hurried inventory, the man determined that the situation looked worse than it was. He soon realized that the fact that he didn't see it coming galled him more than the actual damage.

Windom spent the next several hours plotting his next moves. How could he get the codebooks? He was sure that Riley had access to both. He had to devise a trap for Riley. Should he have him killed outright, it would be over. Windom himself would be the loser. There must be another way for him to punish Riley and regain possession of the books as well. He would have to be careful. Riley was becoming far too dangerous for back-and-forth game playing. He must hit hard and do it quickly. First he would have to be absolutely sure of the books' precise location. Who could he trust? He had burned his bridges leading to Riley. There must be another way to get Riley to relinquish the codebooks. He would need the services of his Asian gangsters, to be sure, but *how* was not a certainty at the moment. Now his anger and hate for one Jim Riley was fast blinding the man from his original purpose. Hate and revenge were quickly superseding greed and a childhood fantasy of how things should have been.

The need for money was never the motive for Windom's obsession with the codebooks and the treasure they bore. Windom was a man driven with a hunger for power, control, and some deep, distorted need to defile his father's original high purpose. He never forgave him for forcing him away from his fascist mentors. How could his own father have betrayed his country and made him appear to be a traitor as well? His real revenge was born in the realization that he might one day possess all the wealth of those hated Jews. In his darkened soul, he would as soon see the money burn in flames. This would satisfy him as much as actually possessing the money himself. The man could not comprehend the depth of his own hate. Yet he could not rid his mind of the picture of his father silently slipping away from his grasp in the icy sea. It would torture him for the remainder of his life. His guilt would not diminish.

THIRTY-EIGHT

MARY RISON LAY MOTIONLESS. Only the sound of light breathing could be heard. Jim sat beside her bed, gently rubbing her soft, slender hand.

"I love you, girl," he said softly. "Stay with me."

A small tear appeared and rolled slowly down her cheek. Jim knew that she heard. He kissed her hand and lifted the tear with his index finger. She could not awaken.

The nurse entered the room and explained to Jim that Mary had suffered severe pain during the night and was now on a combination of medications intended to ease the pain and make her quite drowsy. She was not expected to fully respond for another six to eight hours. The nurse saw the anxiety in his eyes. She told Jim that all of Mary's vital signs were normal and that once she got beyond the pain, she should recover quite well.

With that assurance, Jim turned his mind to what lay ahead. He would now call Hunter to explain what had happened and find out what progress was being made.

Jim was able to reach Hunter while he was on a short layover at Sky Harbor in Phoenix. They discussed Mary's run-in with Windom's thugs, and Hunter shared his discovery with Jim. They would both be looking toward their next meeting with Jacob Sukin the following week.

Since Mary would be out of it for a while, Jim decided to run back to

San Jose and complete a few things of his own. He would try to reach Jerry Dunne to plan their next move. Surely Windom would not sit still for the destruction derby.

* * *

HUNTER RETURNED TO SAN JOSE, where he rented a car and drove to his hotel. He unpacked his bag and immediately drove over to Jim's apartment. They were glad to be together once again. They had embarked upon a long journey of murder, attempted murder, burglary, and subterfuge. Both had paid a price to this point, and the path seemed as long ahead as it had been backward to the beginning. Without a doubt, there would be no looking back. They must continue. It was now time to decipher the codebooks.

Hunter obtained his safe-deposit key from Jim and made a quick trip to the bank. He removed the book and returned to Jim's apartment.

Together they opened the books side by side. Jim was holding the code reader, and Hunter held the accounts code. Both men had quickened breath as they opened the door into the past. Could it be happening? Sixty years after the Holocaust, two men should sit in an apartment and look into the hearts and minds of six men, long gone, caught in a web of genocide?

Jim and Rolly could not help but wonder if they were worthy. Jim suddenly felt like a peeping Tom looking into a stranger's bedroom. Could it be a violation of privacy?

It had not occurred to either man that these feelings might surface. Hunter was not ashamed of the feelings. It made him realize that he had a conscience. He was determined that what they were about to do would not shame the men whose legacy was printed here in two small books. The books were written such that decoded names of banks would have Italian spellings. It would be easy for Hunter to read the codebooks.

Within 30 minutes, the name of *First Bank of Zurich* was decoded. Shortly, *Account #84311 was translated*. It was obvious to Hunter that the deposit was at the "USD" against the *lire*. An amount of $143,000 U.S. dollars was deposited. Account #84311-1 represented an additional

$87,000 in stocks and securities surrendered and deposited in a sub-account by Professor DiNapoli. The codebooks showed that this account belonged to Sam Gold.

It was not clear to Jim or Hunter why DiNapoli had decided to use 24 banks when there were only six men. Their best guess was that DiNapoli had divided each man's money into four bank deposits. It would spread the assets around without raising undue suspicion among the Nazi hawk-eyes.

The work was rather monotonous, and the two could barely work for an hour at a time. How tedious this process must have been to the Jews and Professor DiNapoli.

Hunter wanted to see Mary. She had been on his mind all the while he and Jim were deciphering the codebooks. Jim, too, could not clear his mind completely. Truly the focus of their attention had turned to Mary.

Hunter folded the deciphered notes together with the codebooks and returned them to the safe-deposit box at the bank. Jim was parked outside the bank, waiting for Hunter. Soon he returned and they drove the two hours to Modesto.

* * *

MARY HAD BEEN AWAKE FOR A HALF HOUR before they arrived at the hospital. Her one uncovered eye was peering around the room with a look of confusion. Her surroundings were unfamiliar and stark. She could see the brightness emanating through the window. She determined that it must still be daylight. She had no idea of what day it was. Her breathing was strained, and she felt terrible pain in her left side. She thought it odd as well that her chin ached; something she had never experienced.

She tried to move, but the pain was sharp and electric. She settled back on her pillow and continued to gaze around the room. The pain subsided with her lack of movement.

Mary made no attempt to call the nurse. She took the time to evaluate her situation. She was unable to focus clearly on what had happened. Something had struck her, but she had no memory of what or who might have caused it.

Jim Riley and Rolly Hunter entered Mary's room and quietly eased toward her bedside. One wide green eye behind a maze of gauze turned to them, first to Hunter and then to Jim Riley. Mary was fully awake, and Jim could detect the smile in that beautiful eye.

The men spent the next hour telling Mary of everything that had been happening. Jim explained to Mary that she had been beaten severely by Windom's thugs. She no longer needed to wonder if Windom would realize that they were in collusion. When Jim told her of his vandalism at the mansion, Mary's eye widened to its extreme open position in a look of total disbelief. They revealed that their work had begun with the codebooks. She moved in a show of excitement.

Jim and Rolly spent another hour at Mary's bedside before the shift nurse entered to take the usual vital signs. Jim remembered how he hated the nonsensical interruption of the uninterested nurse. From slapping his arm, hoping to find a fertile vein, to extracting his badly needed blood, she would poke and prod most of his orifices. Satisfied that Jim was still alive, she would leave, promising to return in a few minutes with some orange juice or a Popsicle, never to be seen again. He was sure that the hospital had a system whereby the same nurse did not call on a patient more than once a shift.

Hunter squeezed Mary's hand and left the room while Jim took a few moments to brush back a few red hairs protruding from the gauze around her head. He kissed her forehead and promised to return in a couple of days. The smile was in her eye as he departed.

The two men headed back to San Jose to continue the code work and await Jacob Sukin's arrival. Jim had two lessons the following day that he could not cancel. He was definitely running short of resources.

One would be Howard Davies's final lesson before his FAA check ride. Jim was excited for the man and looked forward to his becoming a legal private pilot.

He was not looking forward to the other lesson. It was the infamous Donnie Friend returning. Jim had no idea of how to handle the situation. He did not want to embarrass the boy, and yet he must seriously tend to business.

He decided to let the chips fall where they may. He had more important things to think about.

* * *

THE PHONE RANG AT THE FLIGHT SCHOOL. "Flight school. This is Nancy."

"Yes, ma'am," said a male voice with a definite Asian accent, probably Korean. "I'm looking toward learning to fly. I've heard that Mr. Riley is a very good instructor. Can you tell me when he might be in?" asked the man.

"Yes, Mr. Riley has two lessons tomorrow morning. Let's see …" she muttered to herself. "Davies will be done at 10:00, and Donnie is next … Yes, sir, Jim will be doing touch-and-goes over in Livermore with a student from 10:00 to 11:30. He should be back in office by 11:45."

The man thanked her and hung up. Nancy gave the matter no further attention.

* * *

"MR. WINDOM? THIS IS MR. WI."

"Yes, Mr. Wi. Have you located Mr. Riley?" asked Windom.

"Better than that, Mr. Windom. I have his schedule for tomorrow morning. He will be flying over to Livermore with a student. We can take the helicopter and intercept Mr. Riley; that is, if you are sure that is what you wish," said Wi.

"Yes, Mr. Wi. I've had about all I can take from Mr. Riley. By all means, please intercept him!"

THIRTY-NINE

DONNIE FRIEND WAS FIVE MINUTES EARLY. He made eye contact with Jim Riley, smiled, but said nothing. The arrogance was gone from his demeanor and the cockiness gone from his swagger. He was a man on a mission in all seriousness. He signed in and walked out the back door to the flight line.

He was slow and deliberate in his pre-flight routine. Jim was impressed. Once completed, Donnie climbed the step into the cabin. He sat in the left seat and waited for Jim to appear from the office. He was nervous and still embarrassed from the last episode, but he was determined to put it behind him, as it were. Jim actually admired his courage to continue. *Hopefully things will be different,* he thought.

Jim climbed aboard. Donnie raised his side window and called, "Clear!" He brought the engine to life and contacted ground for taxi approval. "November-three-six-one-two-niner at flight school, for taxi," Donnie called with assurance. He was given instructions to continue to the active runway, followed by takeoff clearance.

It was a beautiful morning and the air was soft. Donnie climbed to 1,500 feet and took a left turn over the salt flats toward the 680 saddle over to Livermore. Traffic was heavy on the highway in both directions.

There were several planes in the air and one helicopter at the three o'clock position. Donnie called the Livermore tower and asked for clearance for touch-and-go landings. He was given wind conditions and approval. All went well, and Jim was pleased with Donnie's performance. Jim became aware that Donnie Friend showed a nice touch when he realized his limitations. Perhaps he would become a good pilot one day.

After 40 minutes of touch-and-go landings, Jim had Donnie turn back toward the San Jose area. They had flown to the top of the 680 saddle when a blue-and-white helicopter approached from the right rear of their Cessna. Jim glanced off his right shoulder in time to see someone sitting in the open side door, holding what looked like an old M-l rifle pointed directly at him. The man could tell that Jim had spotted him.

As calmly as he could, Jim looked straight ahead as he spoke to Donnie. "Donnie, I'm going to take the plane now. I want you to fold your hands in your lap. Do not touch the yoke or rudder pedals, no matter what. Do you understand?"

With a dumbfounded look on his face, he simply followed Jim's instruction. He barely had time to glance to the right to see what Jim was looking at. The shot nicked the passenger-side windscreen as Jim pulled the power off to idle and dropped the nose sharply. The helicopter shot ahead of the Cessna and took a high, sharp left turn to come around to face Riley's plane. The chopper was much faster, and shot past the 152, and in a matter of seconds was back on Jim's tail.

Jim Riley turned back toward Altamont Pass, zigzagging as much as possible. He knew that he could make these simple moves quicker than the chopper. Three more shots were fired. One caught the right wing strut. The bullet pierced through the strut and caught the very tip of the prop. It was enough to affect the propeller's balance and the plane began to vibrate. Jim pulled the power back a few rpms and the vibration subsided. It was still rough but manageable. The other two bullets missed their mark entirely. Jim and Donnie could only hear them.

Jim had no idea what he was going to do over Altamont Pass. There were lots of hills and an expansive windmill farm, perhaps five hundred units or more. Maybe he could weave around the windmills in order to play ditch 'em with the chopper long enough to get him short on fuel or make it too dangerous for him to continue. Jim felt that he had no other options open to him.

"All right, Windom, you son of a bitch! Now you're playing in my yard. Let's see how good your chopper pilot is!" Jim shouted.

He continued to stay low, trying to follow the terrain as much as he could. But he was flying too high. Jim knew that he would have to drop lower if he had any hope of evading the helicopter.

Flying closer to the gigantic windmills, Jim was able to see just how large the monsters were. He had never considered the immensity of these wildly odd machines.

Donnie's only comment was, "Holy Jesus!"

One gleaming white fan filled the entire windscreen almost too late for Jim to take evasive action with a 90-degree turn to the right. The chopper was on his tail but was able to pull up short of disaster. He shot up vertically for a hundred feet. Donnie sat motionless.

On his recovery, Jim noticed the large orange ball on the high power line crossing between two hilltops. Now was his chance to make an offensive move. He hit full power into a climbing left turn. The plane was vibrating almost uncontrollably. He continued his turn a thousand yards to the west of the line, with the stall warning screaming all the way. The chopper was right behind him. Just what he wanted.

Jim made a hard left turn. By now he was nearly a hundred feet above the power line. He slowed slightly until the chopper was directly behind him. Jim hit full power and the Cessna shuddered and peeled into a shallow dive toward the orange ball. He was sure that the chopper pilot would not see the ball, with his 152 blocking the man's view. Riley only hoped that the pilot would be glued to his tail.

At the very last second, Jim dropped the nose into a dive, just missing the power line. He had to pull up immediately to avoid the ground. The chopper pilot, however, was too close as the line filled his vision. He too tried to drop under the power line, but his tail rotor did not clear. Jim thought he could hear a dull ripping sound, followed by a high squeal. He had no time to maneuver. He was too low and too fast to avoid the swinging giant in front of him. The blades were turning slowly, and with nothing but pure reaction time, Jim put the Cessna between two blades of the enormous windmill. He pulled the stick back to his chest and hit the throttle in case there might be an ounce of needed power left in the little four-banger. He climbed steeply as the 152's stall warning sounded. The behemoth windmill was turning directly in front of him. Jim and Donnie thought they could hear the sound of the huge blades slicing the air.

Jim continued his climb until he cleared the turning giant. His stall warning continued its obnoxious blaring. He pulled the 152 into a left wing over almost on its back and into a steep dive. He pulled the power off and yanked back on the yoke. Donnie had never felt G forces on his body like this. The little Cessna was now pointed back to Livermore.

The chopper was spinning violently, rocking, and making large circular figures. At one point, Jim saw a person thrown out by the centrifugal force, arms and legs flailing as he fell to the ground. With a final thrust, the chopper entered the path of one of the big spinners. Its blade slammed the machine into the ground. A second of silence was followed by a tremendous explosion and ensuing grass fire.

Jim became aware of a horrible smell in the cabin. Donnie Friend looked straight ahead.

"Aw hell, Donnie. Don't worry about it. Some of that is mine!" Jim said. Both men began to laugh nervously as they departed the area as quickly as possible. Jim held his breath as much as possible. Donnie was quiet, and in spite of the terrible aroma, he sat with a smile, poring over his excellent adventure. He admired Jim's skill and was now determined to continue with his instruction. Perhaps one day he would be able to control his bowels in a high-speed wing over.

They returned to San Carlos Airport. Nancy was waiting to tell Jim of his new student-to-be.

"Yeah, Nancy, I just met him. I don't think he will be signing up for lessons after all!"

Jim and Donnie Friend smiled at each other as Donnie hurried toward the restroom.

"What is that awful smell, Jim?" asked Nancy.

"That, my dear, is the smell of heroism!" Jim responded.

Jim said goodbye to Nancy and headed for Modesto to be with Mary.

On his way, he dialed Rolly's number.

"Hi, Jim!" came Rolly's voice. It was a pleasant change of pace from the last hour or so.

"Hi, Rolly!" What are you up to?" Jim asked.

"I'm still working on the codes. What I can't figure out is where the stocks are located. So far I have discovered four banks with only two of the men's names."

"Yeah?" Jim asked.

"Well, I would have thought that there would be some mention of stocks or bonds or that kind of stuff," Hunter said.

"I'm sure that not all of the six men had bonds. Maybe you just haven't come across it yet."

"Yes, I suppose you're right. Jim, how do you think stocks would be valued that are 60-something years old?"

"I'm not sure what you mean," Jim answered.

"Well, suppose I had purchased a hundred shares of, say, IBM 60 years ago. I'm sure it has split at least a dozen times or more, wouldn't you think?"

"Yeah. What's your point?" Jim asked.

"Well, my point is this. Has that all continued to be recorded with IBM over the years, that they know a hundred shares of stock sixty years ago might now be thousands of shares today?"

"Yeah, Rolly, I'm sure they know that. I thought you were a financial wizard!"

"No, Jim, remember I said I was a spy. I never claimed to be a Wall Street brain. Anyway, I'll keep at it. Where are you?"

"On my way to see Mary. I'll be back tonight or in the morning. By the way, would you like to know what I've been doing?"

"No, not really. You can tell me when I see you. Bye!" Rolly said as he disconnected.

Jim hung up his cell phone and turned on the radio. He heard the announcer talking about an aircraft disaster on the Altamont Pass.

"We are here on the 205 Bypass. We are told that a helicopter belonging to Ben Wi Construction Company from the Bay Area has crashed into one of the large windmills. Reports indicate Mr. Wi himself was on board the craft. It is believed that at least one of the passengers was thrown from the craft. The word from a passerby is that the craft was spinning violently out of control and was unable to avoid the windmill. In addition, there was an explosion and fire. Much of the hillside is ablaze, damaging some of the other windmills. Fire crews are on scene as we speak. We do not know how many souls were aboard at this time. There was at least one other report of a fixed-wing aircraft in the same area. One eyewitness thought perhaps they collided, but there is no evidence of that. We will remain on site until we have more information. John Anderson, KMBR reporting."

Jim smiled and turned the radio to a jazz station.

* * *

HE PULLED INTO THE HOSPITAL PARKING lot around 2:00 p.m. The sun was shining. It was a beautiful day, not too hot as Modesto often gets. Jim was feeling somewhat vindicated for Mary. He thought that he would probably avoid telling her at all.

Mary was sitting up in bed when Jim entered. She was trying to sip some juice from a straw but was obviously having trouble. She raised her cup and waved when she saw Riley enter her room.

"Boy, am I glad to see you!" she muttered without moving her lips. "I feel like I'm in a cage!" Mary continued.

Jim touched her lips with his finger. He kissed her lips and the gauze that partially covered them.

"Me too!" he said. "How you feeling, sweetie?" Jim asked.

Again without lips moving she said, "I'd feel a lot better if I could go to the bathroom. It hurts my ribs if I try. The nurse just gave me a laxative. Maybe that will help. Where have you been?" she asked.

"Oh, just a couple of lessons this morning. You know, same old thing. Donnie Friend was one of them. Do you remember me telling you about him?" Jim asked.

Mary could not help laughing. "Damn it, don't make me laugh. It hurts too much," she said in her muffled voice.

"Well, the only other thing I was going to say was that he did it again!"

They both laughed for several minutes. Mary jabbed Jim on the arm in protest for making her laugh so much. She flinched from the quick jab of pain.

Jim then confessed that Donnie had done quite well and he was proud of him.

"I just did an unexpected wing over. Donnie wasn't quite ready for it," Jim said with a smile on his face.

Jim told Mary that he was going to the nurses' station to see what they were planning. Mary nodded slightly in agreement.

The nurse reported that she was waiting for the doctor to come in. He was planning to remove the bandaging. There were several stitches to be removed as well.

Holy crap! I sure didn't know about any stitches! Jim thought to himself. *I hope we're not looking at scarring!*

Jim and Mary spent the next several hours talking — or rather Jim talking and Mary listening. Jim explained what Rolly had discovered and what was to happen next.

Mary felt somewhat left out with her incapacitated state. However, she let Jim know that she would soon be back and able to help with the decoding.

The doctor arrived shortly before 5:00 p.m. He quickly removed the gauze bandages to reveal an ugly-looking shiner surrounding her right eye. A small cut below the eye had required only four stitches, and once the doctor removed them, there remained only a pinkish line. It appeared to Jim that she would not have any noticeable scar. Her jaw was quite swollen and would remain wired shut for another two weeks. As he moved her gown aside, Jim could see the bruised area on her rib cage. He thought her belly looked sexy, even with a bruise. He would be sure to buy her a belly button ring when she recovered.

Riley could see that Mary was getting tired. Her mother was going to come by later if she could connect with travel arrangements. Unfortunately, her dad was unable remain in Modesto. Jim would have to meet him later. Anyway, Mary would need to rest. "I'll see you tomorrow, honey!" Jim said after a light peck on her lips. "I love you!"

"I wove ooh too!" she answered.

FORTY

JIM CALLED ROLLY AS HE DROVE into San Jose. The men met for dinner at the 94th Aero Squadron. Jim revealed the details of his run-in with Windom's goons. Hunter sat utterly speechless, unable to believe what he was hearing.

Rolly announced that his day had not been nearly so exciting. He had made considerable headway with the decoding, however. He had found at least two banks where Samuel Gold's assets were deposited. Hunter had indeed found a safe-deposit number but no key.

The men returned to Hunter's hotel and continued on the codes for another three hours. They decoded all of Gold's deposits, totaling nearly 1.3 million lire.

The decoding showed that Wetzel and Cohen had combined their monies, which were deposited by DiNapoli into three separate accounts totaling $412,000 in U.S. currency.

Jim asked Rolly if he had any idea what that would have been in today's money.

"At least six times as much!" Hunter guessed. "Probably around $2,470,000, I suspect." he said with some authority, though he was simply guessing.

The men laughed as they sorted out the deposits. They had completed fourteen pages of the account codes. The whole process had, in some strange way, become a game.

"That's enough for one day," Jim said. "I guess I'll see you tomorrow. What time does Jacob Sukin arrive?"

"He's due in at noon. I'll pick him up. I've made reservations here at my hotel. I can give you a call as soon as he gets settled in."

Jim left Rolly's hotel and headed for his apartment. There were three messages on his phone.

"Hi, Daddy! It's Julie. I just wanted to talk to you and see when I can come to see you. We have Easter vacation in two weeks. Mommy says she can make special arrangements with the airline for me to travel. They have to talk to you first. Mommy said she would call you. Anyway that's all. Bye, Daddy. I love you!"

The second message was a blockbuster. "Hello, Mr. Riley. My name Dominic Windom. The last time we met is when you had your little accident with my brother's airplane. You may recall that I was on board the Baron? Could you please call me at 290-473-1811. That is the office of the place where I'm living. They can transfer your call to my room. I feel that I have something that should be of interest to you. I believe the time is now to share it, and I think that you are the right person. Thank you, Mr. Riley. I'll look forward to hearing from you. It is imperative that my brother is not aware of my contacting you. He monitors all my calls in and out. In fact I am calling from a pay phone across the street from my apartment now. When you call, please use a fictitious name."

Jim was shocked, to say the least. Of course he knew about Dominic, the drunken younger brother of Oliver Windom. He would call him first thing in the morning.

"What could he possibly have to say to me? I'll be damned. Maybe he wants to thank me for kicking his big brother's ass!"

The last message was from Mary's mother. "Jim, this is Helen Rison. I missed you by 30 minutes this afternoon. Anyway, I found out that they could release Mary tomorrow morning. I'm going to take her home with me. I need to take some time off anyway, and I can take care of her better at home. I know you have to work and so just let me handle things for a little while. Call if you need to talk. You have my cell number. Bye, Jim."

Jim felt somewhat relieved. She would be well taken care of by her mom. He had gotten behind in his lessons. There were three new students ready to begin. Jim needed the money, yet he wished to spend time with Rolly and finish the codebooks. He was also looking forward to meeting Jacob Sukin. Hunter had made a good first impression.

* * *

JIM WAS UP EARLY and wanted to call Dominic Windom but thought he should wait until nine or so. He was still dumbfounded at the thought of Oliver Windom's brother calling him. *What could the man possibly have to share with me?* he thought.

Jim ran over to Starbucks for a latté and a roll. He tried to read a newspaper that had been left there, but he could not concentrate. He finished his roll and went back to his apartment and dialed the number Dominic had left.

"Hello, this is Dominic Windom," came the answer immediately after the call had been transferred. The man must have been waiting for Jim's call.

"Yes!" Jim said. "This is Myron Jullif. I'm calling on behalf of the Roger Jacobson family. I understand you knew Mr. Jacobson?" Jim lied.

"Oh yes, Roger. Yes, I did know him well," Windom continued the game.

"Mr. Windom, would you be able to meet with me for a few minutes, say tomorrow afternoon?" Jim felt that his deception was going well. The call shouldn't alert Oliver Windom, he was sure.

"Yes that would be fine, say around two o'clock. There is a concrete bench in front of the building. I will meet you there."

"Excellent!" Jim responded. "See you tomorrow."

He hung up the phone and rubbed his hands together as though he had just won some minor acting award.

Jim dialed Shirley's number and discussed Julie's request to come for a short visit. They agreed on all the time schedules. Julie would not have to change planes. She would fly directly from Sky Harbor in Phoenix to San Jose.

He would pick her up on Wednesday and have her through Sunday. It would be a long time to be with her, and he was worried about keeping her entertained. Maybe he would take her flying. He reflected on the past few days and decided that would not be a good idea after all.

As the call ended, he heard the call-waiting signal. It was Hunter.

"Jim, it's Rolly. I'm with Jacob and we are going to Coleman's Still for lunch. Why don't you meet us there in about a half hour?"

"Sounds good to me. I'll see you there. Bye."

FORTY-ONE

JIM WAS IMMEDIATELY TAKEN WITH Jacob Sukin. He was quiet, unassuming, and sounded extremely intelligent. His handshake was strong and his smile genuine. He was thin and appeared taller than his six-foot frame. He was a clean-shaven and handsome young man, to say the least.

The men spent the next several hours over iced tea and hors d'oeuvres, recounting all that was known by Hunter about his great uncle and the others. Jacob sat motionless most of the time except for an occasional question.

"All that I had ever known," he stated, "was that my uncle joined with some others and deposited all their wealth in Switzerland. I knew nothing of Professor DiNapoli. Members of my family tried in vain to discover anything at all."

"That's not uncommon," Hunter interjected. "If one starts down the wrong road to begin with, it rarely ends up in success."

"So what part do I play in this treasure hunt?" asked Jacob.

"Well, Jacob," Hunter continued, "you are a bona fide descendant of one of the original six men. Now, if I've done my research correctly, you may act on behalf of them all and it will be perfectly legal and in line with the original directives."

Jim told the two men of his call from Dominic Windom and suggested that he had no clue what the man wanted. He would report back to Jacob and Rolly after his meeting with Dominic. The men parted company. Jim drove to San Carlos to meet one of his new students for a first lesson. Jacob and Rolly returned to their hotel.

* * *

JIM PULLED UP IN FRONT OF THE adult living quarters as Dominic had directed. He was anxious as he made his way to the front entrance. There sat a man he knew had to be Dominic Windom. His resemblance to his brother was uncanny.

"Mr. Windom?" Jim asked.

"Yes, Mr. Riley. How nice to finally meet you," Windom replied. "I know you must be full of questions!"

"That would be an understatement, Mr. Windom," Riley answered. "First of all, I am amazed at the resemblance to your brother Oliver. If I didn't know better, I'd say you were twins!"

"People have thought that for many years. It seems more so as we get older."

"I don't mean to pry," Jim said, "but I can't help wondering why you live in a place like this. It's very nice, but I would expect you to have a home like your brother."

"Well, we'd have to go back to the 1960s to understand all that. You see, I got quite caught up in the drug culture. I was drinking a lot and womanizing. Well, one thing led to another, and I totally lost control. I don't even remember the years from '65 to '75."

"What happened to you after that?" Jim asked.

"My brother had me locked up, more or less. I can come and go pretty much as I please, within reason. But I have no real means of support. He has always taken care of the two of us. I would love very much to be out of this place, but I don't have the courage to begin a new life at my age."

"Do you still drink or, you know, use any illegal drugs?" Jim continued.

"Oh no! I have been clean and sober for nearly 20 years. I don't think Oliver believes me, but that's neither here nor there. I really don't care what he thinks as long as he keeps sending money," the younger Windom continued.

"Were you or your brother ever married?" Jim asked.

"No. I wanted to, but my brother broke that up. All he could see was another person to support. I wanted to work at the winery, but he wouldn't hear of it. We had both learned winemaking from our father, Gino DiNapoli, but he and our mother decided I was to be taken care of financially but not involved."

"Why didn't you work for someone else?"

"Oliver threatened to cut me off if I even looked at another venue. By then, I was already beginning to lose control, what with the booze and drugs. I was simply afraid.

"As for Oliver, he had a fiancée years ago. He was deeply in love with her. Unfortunately, he found her in bed with his soon-to-be best man. Well, needless to say, the shit hit the fan there. That young man died in a car wreck three weeks later. The police said the car and the body smelled of alcohol. They called it an accident."

The man needed to talk. Jim sat and absorbed every word.

"It was all bullshit! I knew how to drink, and I'll tell you that guy didn't drink a drop."

"You think your brother had something to do with the man's death?"

"You know my brother; what do you think?" Windom asked.

"Yeah, I can guess that one!" Jim said.

"Now, Mr. Riley, I know you didn't come all this way to listen to small talk." The man reached down beside the bench and lifted a very old-looking briefcase. It looked as though it had been very wet at one time. Jim Riley's eyes widened as he considered that this might be the missing piece of the puzzle. Trying not to act overly anxious, he pretended to remain calm.

The man did not hand the case to Jim immediately but held it tightly to his chest as he began the narrative.

"A Jewish man by the name of Franz Steinmetz handed this case to me when we were in a lifeboat." He continued to relate the story of the sinking ship, which Jim was well aware of but he did not interrupt the man from his speech.

"I was asked by Mr. Steinmetz to hold on to this briefcase until he or his heirs would ask for it. They would be able to trace us from Ellis Island. The problem was that our mother changed our name and Franz Steinmetz was unable to track us. It was not until recently that the heir David Steinmetz discovered that we were the former DiNapolis living in Modesto, California. David Steinmetz was certain that my brother Oliver had the briefcase as well as some sort of codebook. And it was understandable why he would have expected Oliver to have the book. Franz Steinmetz told me aboard the lifeboat that he could not trust Oliver — Octavio — to take care of the briefcase. He told me that even though I was a young lad, he felt he could and must trust me.

"I was at the mansion when David showed up with a little black book of his own. He mistakenly thought that he merely had to show up at the Windom home and Oliver would gladly share *his* information. And together with the briefcase and book that Oliver possessed, the two would simply take care of business and retrieve the money out of Switzerland. Unfortunately, I did not know of David Steinmetz's existence until he showed up at my brother's mansion. I guess each thought the other had the briefcase."

"Now I know why David was so angry and afraid the day I flew him to Santa Barbara," Jim interjected.

"Yes, and he had reason to be. My brother Oliver was never very subtle about his feelings."

"Oh yes!" Jim said. "I've been on the wrong end of that lack of subtlety! More than once, I might add."

"Well, thank you, Mr. Riley, for coming. Here is the famous briefcase. Would you believe that I have never once opened it? Even in my drunken and drug days I was not tempted. I was so taken by Mr. Steinmetz's manner that I could not bring myself to violate his trust. I truly wish you well."

"And thank you, Mr. Windom. I don't think you will regret your helping us."

"Mr. Riley, please be careful. You have no idea just how dangerous my brother can be. On more than one occasion, I have seen what we used to call skinheads come to the mansion. He would send me to the guesthouse. However, I was not fooled. I know they were the group referred to as Neo-Nazis! Just watch your back, Mr. Riley."

Jim nodded that he understood, took the small briefcase, and returned to his car. He could almost feel the history in his hands as he rubbed the weathered case sitting in the seat next to him.

Jim was tempted to stop along the way and open it, but he realized it would be unfair to Hunter. He deserved the honor.

A thought suddenly struck him. *What if everything got soaked? Would they be able to read any information? Will the safe deposit key or keys be in there?* He could hardly contain himself. He needed to think of something else.

I wonder how Mary's doing with her mom. He would call her after Rolly and he were through snooping into the briefcase.

* * *

ROLLY AND JACOB HAD GOTTEN ON quite well while Jim had ventured to Modesto to see Dominic Windom. Both men were anxious for his return and were awaiting the surprise.

Hunter did not have to wonder long. He knew at first glance exactly what Jim held in his hand.

"My God, Jim! How did Windom's brother come by that?" Rolly blurted out.

"I'll tell you all about it later," Jim said. "Right now, I want to see what's in there before I piss my pants."

Rolly's fingers were shaking as he undid the two flaps. There was no key for the lock. It was flimsy, and Hunter unlocked the latch. He then realized that the honor of opening the case should belong only to an heir.

Jacob Sukin stepped forward and took the case from Hunter. He smiled and put his fingers on the flap.

A musty smell escaped as the young man slowly opened the flap. Jim Riley and Rolly Hunter sat motionless, trying to look over the flap and into the leather vault that had housed six men's financial destiny for more than half a century.

What they saw was stunning, to say the least. All of the contents appeared to be in a large, waxy paper sack that was somewhat rotted away, showing corners of documents and two small keys that had fallen from the sack. They showed evidence of rust.

Another heavy envelope was inside. Jacob extracted it. The envelope was intact. Jim handed him a pocketknife. He slit the flap and removed the note inside. In beautiful penmanship and perfect Italian was the writing of Professor Gino DiNapoli. The note was written on University of Milan stationery, dated June 16, 1938. It read as follows:

> *To the individual who shall read*
> *this document, I must assume the*
> *following. Neither I nor any of my friends*
> *are still alive. If you are a*
> *descendant of one of the six men*
> *to whom this case belongs together with*
> *the two codebooks required, then may*
> *I congratulate you and wish you the*
> *best. You should have very little difficulty*
> *in following the enclosed directions*
> *to retrieve your inheritance. I trust*
> *that you will see to it that all others*
> *also entitled shall receive their rightful*
> *shares as well.*
> *If you are not a legal heir, yet possess*
> *the required books, then it will require*
> *That you meet with the banks herein stated and*
> *make your case to each bank executive to*
> *show that you are entitled to retrieve*
> *all monies and securities in deposit.*

Should you not be a legal heir and are simply a fortune hunter, then I submit that you are wasting your time and effort to collect that to which you are not entitled, and I trust that the Swiss government will do all in its power to keep you at a distance until the Almighty Himself shall determine its fate.

If, on the other hand, the unthinkable has happened, then may God have mercy upon us all!

*Sincerely,
Gino DiNapoli
SOA Confidant*

The men sat motionless for several moments. Rolly Hunter felt as though he had personally known DiNapoli and that it was like hearing the man himself talking. He could not control the tears rolling down his cheeks. The trail had been so long. Now he felt that he was almost home. Perhaps the professor could soon rest in peace as well, knowing that his stewardship had been successfully completed.

Young Sukin handed the small keys to Jim Riley for no particular reason. Riley tried to wipe the rusty edges while Sukin slowly opened the sack, trying not to cause damage to the very old documents inside.

Hunter's fluent Italian required that he read the documents. At first glance, they appeared to be bank receipts of deposits. In fact, they were, and much more.

None of the bank names appeared on any documents. The only identifications were the bank account numbers. Each of the tiny keys had its own identification. One UB, the other TB. Somewhere the codes would have to identify a corresponding safe-deposit box number with the proper bank.

* * *

FOR THE NEXT SEVERAL WEEKS, things proceeded pretty normally. Jim met his new students, spent a great few days with Julie, called Mary several times, and spent his spare time with Jacob and Rolly.

They were able to determine the two bank safe-deposit box numbers. "UB" identified the Unterstarss Bank and "TB" identified the Tiefenbrennen Bank. All accounts and sub-accounts were identified, and all that remained was to collect the money. "Easier said than done!" Hunter announced with some trepidation. The mission from here on would be to doggedly follow the money.

Jim was missing Mary and wanted to have her near. He called her mother and announced that he was coming to get her and bring her to his apartment. Mary strongly approved of the plan, and her mother grudgingly agreed.

Her local doctor had removed the jaw wire, and her bruises were almost faded away. Her ribs continued to be somewhat painful, but all in all, Mary was feeling well and anxious to get back to Jim.

She had asked Jim how he felt about her getting into the instructor program at San Carlos. Jim was opposed to it simply because it had the effect of being a dead-end career move. He knew that she was too good at flying to become an instructor. She was in demand also because of her sex. She would have no trouble securing an interview. Men, on the other hand, were in hot competition for jobs.

Rolly Hunter spent most of his days cataloguing the Swiss banks and addresses. He learned that two of the 24 banks no longer existed. One was taken over by the First Commercial Bank of Zurich. The second was simply gone.

According to a local banking association, it seems that the Nazis had raped the bank to the point of financial destruction. This happened in the spring of 1944. It was reported that nearly $6 million was stolen or confiscated by the Nazis from that one bank alone. The bank manager was a known Nazi sympathizer, although a questionably respected Swiss citizen.

Though four of the original banks had gone through several buyouts and name changes, Hunter and Sukin were able to trace each back to its original name and location.

Another three banks had joined together to become the Conglomerated Citizens' Bank of Central Switzerland. This conglomeration was made up of a French consortium financed in part by the French government. The Swiss did not find the bank user friendly. It was known by the government that money was constantly being siphoned off to shady front companies from Russia, Brazil, South Africa, and some Middle Eastern companies. Rolly was sure he would have some trouble here. It would require him to warm up the French CEO in order to pull it off.

The other 16 banks in Zurich stood by their original names and locations, illustrating the stability of the Swiss banking industry. Nowhere else in world could one expect to see the degree of historical consistency as found in the banking industry here.

With the coding complete and the keys identified with their respective banks, Rolly determined it was time to move. He could not get Windom off his mind, however, and after much talking with Jim and Jacob, the men decided that they could not wait for Windom's next move. They would simply have to deal with it when it happened.

Jim left the two to work out the details of the next phase of their plan to retrieve the money while he slipped into his car and made his way to I-5 South. He would be with Mary in seven to eight hours. He missed her and needed her. He knew that she felt the same way about him.

Rolly and Jacob Sukin's next move called for the all-important trip to Zurich. They agreed that Jim and Mary should be a direct part of this excursion. It would be exciting and a great deal of hard work. All four would be needed to carry out the work ahead.

Rolly called Jim on his cell, and the two agreed. Rolly agreed to front the expenses for airfare, food, and lodging. Jim thanked him and said he was looking forward to the trip and was sure Mary would be as well.

FORTY-TWO

OLIVER WINDOM DROVE UP THE short entrance to the Sunny Dell Rest Home, planning his encounter with his younger brother Dominic. He had been informed by one of his local spies that Dominic had met recently with a stranger. The woman felt that Oliver should know about such an out-of-the-ordinary event. She was correct. Oliver was interested in anyone who approached his brother.

Dominic was waiting for Oliver. He took a deep breath and opened the door.

"Dominic," Oliver acknowledged.

"Oliver," the brother replied.

The two men made uncomfortable conversation for a few minutes until Oliver could stand no more of it.

"I understand you had a visitor the other day, Dominic?" Oliver began.

"Yes, that is correct. Just a casual acquaintance," Dominic answered.

"A casual acquaintance? Come on, Dominic, don't insult me! I'm sure I know with whom you met. I'd like to know why."

"It was Jim Riley, Oliver, as I'm sure you would find out somehow. But the reason is personal and private, and quite frankly none of your business," retorted the younger brother.

"How dare you talk to me like that, you ungrateful pup! After all these years and all that I have done for you, you have the nerve to disrespect me like this? How dare you?"

"All that you have done for me, Oliver? I should be grateful for you locking me in this cage? Turning me into a beggar in order to survive? Denying me a chance for real friends and, yes, perhaps even love? How do you want me to thank you, Oliver? Get on my knees and kiss your ring?"

"You bastard!" Oliver responded. "You damn drunkard! How many years and how much money have I wasted seeing to your needs and even your booze? And you're standing here ready to piss on my leg! I can't believe it!"

"Oliver, have you ever thought to ask me when I had my last drink? Has it ever occurred to you that I might like to help at the wineries? I was just a good as you, remember?"

"Now you're talking like an idiot. I couldn't trust you near anything alcoholic and you know that."

"Perhaps you're right, Oliver. You always are. You always have been. Understand this, though, big brother. Any shame or discredit which I may have borne upon our father's name is over. Yours never seems to end. I'm still not going to tell you about my meeting with Jim Riley. I suppose this means you are going to cut me off altogether."

"I cannot believe I'm hearing you talk like this. Where is it coming from?" asked Oliver.

"Well maybe I've decided it's time I grow some balls, Oliver. There's certainly got to be more to life than what I'm putting up with now. I am going to leave this place within a month. You can't stop me, and probably now you don't even want to. I've been saving from your allotment for some time, and I can make it outside for a while if I'm careful, not that you care."

"Dominic, I should just have you killed for the way you are talking to me, but you know what? You are on your own, and as far as I'm concerned, I no longer have a brother. I'm going to turn my back now, and I don't want to see your face again!"

With that, Oliver Windom turned away from his brother, walked to his waiting limo, and did not look back.

* * *

DOMINIC WINDOM IMMEDIATELY called Jim Riley's cell number to let him know what was coming. He reminded Jim that the man was ruthless and would continue trying to kill him.

Jim picked up the call as he was just arriving at Mary's family home. It didn't bother him, because he already knew that it would make little difference in Windom's attitude. The man would now become a wounded buffalo. There would be no end to his attempts on Jim's life and perhaps Mary's as well. He would need to keep her close.

To say that Mary was pleased to see Jim would be an understatement. She could not give him a hard kiss, but she clung to him and kissed him many times without pursing her lips. It would still be painful, to say the least.

Mary was finally able to introduce Jim to her father. The two men exchanged small talk for several minutes. Mary interrupted and said a quick goodbye to her parents while Jim put her bags in his car. They were off to San Carlos. Jim had already decided to stop over in Fresno so that they could make up for lost time in bed. He chuckled as he promised her that he would be gentle.

They checked into a hotel near the airport, had a light supper, and quickly walked arm in arm to their room. They embraced for many minutes as Jim unbuttoned her blouse to show her ever-so-pleasant breasts. Her bra seemed to barely cover her nipples. It was an easy matter to uncover their firm and upstanding beauty.

The two fondled each other for several minutes before the heat of passion took over. The last articles of clothing flew across the room.

Jim picked her up and gently placed her on the bed. She grimaced slightly as her rib dealt a tinge of pain. She simply ignored it. Jim let his hands roam her special place. He could tell she was ready. He felt like a raging bull trying to hold himself at bay. He did not want to hurt her. She smiled at his full erection and slowly spread her long, slender legs. The sight was almost too much for Jim to withhold his swimmers. It did not take long for either to explode. They continued to laugh and make love. When they finished, he kissed her black-and-blue rib cage. By midnight, with arms and legs entwined, they were sound asleep.

The next morning, they were up early and on their way. They stopped just north of Modesto to pick up Mary's car. They talked on their cell phones most of the way to Palo Alto.

Mary had given notice to her landlord and would only stay long enough to pack her things. Jim needed to clear his closet for her. He tried to rearrange his things but decided she would probably need the whole wardrobe area for her stuff. He moved his to the spare bedroom.

What treachery Windom might be stirring up was not far from either's mind. It was impossible to know if he was ready to let go or if he fully intended to try again to kill them. Dominic's warning suggested the latter.

* * *

HUNTER HAD MADE THE necessary reservations and they were scheduled to leave on the following Tuesday. It was late Friday morning when he completed all the arrangements.

Jacob Sukin tried to pay for passage for the four to Zurich, but Hunter would not hear of it. He knew the man could not afford such an expense, and should nothing be recovered, he would be out quite a sum of money. Hunter, on the other hand, had no family, and he thought of it as an investment toward his commission. With his percentage, he would not have to work another day of his life. Should he fail, he simply thought, *What the hell? Maybe I'll become a private investigator or a greeter at Wal-Mart.*

The excitement continued to build over the weekend. Nothing was heard or seen from Windom, and yet the feeling among the group — now including Jacob Sukin — was one of waiting for the other shoe to drop. They knew that Windom would not give up so easily. Neither side had any intentions of involving the police if at all possible. Even the investigation of Mary's suspicious robbery and assault was suddenly dropped by the CHP. Little things were always too conveniently forgotten to be considered coincidence.

Jim and Mary were at the San Francisco airport early. They would have time to eat something before boarding the plane. Rolly was running late. He and Jacob would just make the final boarding. The four settled into business class. With two adjoining aisle seats, they would be able to converse easily.

Rolly recapped his research and appointments. The first one would be the day after tomorrow. They settled down for the long flight to Zurich.

FORTY-THREE

AT 41,000 FEET AND 380 MILES WEST OF KEFLAVIK, ICELAND, the co-pilot's voice came over the speaker. "Ladies and gentlemen, we have encountered some minor electrical problems and I just want to let you know that we will be doing some very minor maneuvers as we try to locate the exact problem. Please try to relax and continue what you were doing. This should not take long."

Keflavik Flight Center called to Flight 754. "World International 754, did I hear you say *bomb aboard?*"

"Affirmative." By now the captain had donned his mask as standard operating procedure and sounded like Darth Vader. Talking was difficult.

"How do you know this, Captain?" came the response.

"Note left in aft lavatory. Passenger spotted it. Called the flight attendant."

"And what precisely does the note say, if I may ask?" came a new voice. By now, the flight center supervisor had taken charge.

"Stop bullshit! Declaring emergency; 240 souls aboard. Threat imminent. Roll out equipment. Request vector to runway one-one. Squawking emergency now!"

"Understood, 754. Squawk stand by," came the supervisor's steady voice. The pause was interminable.

Finally, a new voice came over the cockpit speaker. "How is your fuel, 754?"

"Seven hours," the captain replied.

"Seven-five-four, continue on present course and descend to flight level two-two zero," the supervisor announced.

"Roger! Four-five-zero for two-two-zero!"

The passengers continued reading and sleeping and munching on their blue-bag lunches.

"World Wide 754, this is Colonel Robert Moss, United States Air Force, Thule Air Force Base, Greenland. My unit is on temporary observation assignment here at the Keflavik flight center. Do you believe this to be terror-related?"

The second officer now placed the oxygen mask on his face. The captain reluctantly removed his and began speaking. "I'm not sure if this threat is even real. That's the first thing I must determine. I have the attendants quietly searching. As you know, we have a specific search program to follow. We're almost done. However, it will only tell us where the item isn't. We've got to cut into the cargo area, and that search becomes a hit and miss."

"Affirmative. What else do you know if anything?" the colonel asked.

"We already know that the culprit is either on board or hired some nut to place the note in the lavatory. I guess some non-English speaking person could have thought that he was passing a love note. I can't imagine that the author of this epistle wants to die."

"Captain, I know this isn't a good time, but can you read the note to me?"

"Very well, here it is: You people know who you are. You have pushed this thing too far. Now you must pay the full price. Lots of people will die with you."

"Thank you, Captain." the colonel responded.

Hunter expressed some concern for the plane's maneuver. *Why is the captain dropping altitude?* he asked himself. His suspicious nature and experience taught him not to believe anything on the surface. He decided that the cockpit would notify the passengers if they needed to worry.

Hunter dozed off. Mary had her head on Jim's shoulder, sound asleep.

Jim held a magazine in one hand and held Mary with the other. Soon, he too fell asleep. Jacob continued to look out the window. He enjoyed flying and didn't want to miss anything.

As the 777 dropped below 23,000, there was a pop that seemed to emanate from just under the plane's belly, beneath Hunter's seat. A tremendous shudder propelled passengers against the left side of the airplane. A second explosion shattered the right engine cowling, causing the engine to howl and scream to a sudden stop, followed by fire. The plane pitched upward nearly 30 degrees. Oxygen masks dropped from the overhead section. A few people began to scream. The majority sat in stunned silence. The pilot brought the nose down quickly before the stall warning sounded. The plane was shaking violently as the debris continued to fall away.

"Mayday! Mayday!" cried the captain from the flight deck.

Hunter managed to look out the window at the burning, naked engine, just as the extinguishers knocked down the flames. He could see small pieces of metal being blown away. More amazing were the dozens of suitcases and boxes of cargo flying out from the underbelly.

My God! he thought. *That was a damn bomb!* But Hunter's intuition told him that if it had been fatal, they would be nose-down by now, or at least the cabin blown open. *Obviously the pilot still has control!* he thought.

Jacob Sukin sat looking straight ahead with white-knuckled fingers fastened securely to the armrests. Hunter had to nudge him to place the mask over his face. Mary and Jim clung tightly together with masks in place. There was no doubt in their minds as to what had just happened.

Jim wanted to rush to the cabin to be of assistance, but he knew better than to interject himself without one of the flight officer's requesting it, at least at this point.

Jim, Mary, and Hunter were trying to assess the damage, using hand signals to communicate. It was their best guess that a bomb had been placed in a cargo bay, either planted by a ground person or smuggled through someone's luggage.

The question now was whether the plane was damaged enough to come apart shortly or at the very least cripple the landing gear.

Jim and Mary both knew that the 777 could fly safely on one engine. And for the moment, the captain had trimmed the plane enough to maintain control.

"Seven-five-four, this is Keflavik Control. We acknowledge your mayday. Sir, is your craft controllable for landing?"

"Unknown! I have control at the moment. Cargo fire indicator on. Have activated extinguishers. It is impossible to assess any of it with certainty."

"Are there any other fires aboard that you can determine, 754?" came the director's voice.

"Negative at this time!"

"Seven-five-four, turn to heading of zero-nine-zero and descend to one four thousand."

"Roger. Flight level two-two-zero. Descending to one four thousand. Steady zero-nine-zero."

The captain continued on the heading as he tried to control the rate of descent to 14,000 feet. As he neared the altitude, the flight center came back.

"Flight 754, turn right to heading of one-zero-zero and continue descent to 9,000 feet, maintain 280 knots."

"Roger, one zero-zero, 280 knots, passing one-four thousand for 9,000," replied the captain.

Jim and Rolly were already analyzing the situation in their own minds. Rolly began, "That damn thing was an altitude bomb set to go off at a designated height."

"That means it had to have been armed after reaching altitude. The son of a bitch is on board!" Jim concluded.

Their eyes began to wander up and down the aisles with no idea of who they were looking for.

Obviously the captain and the Keflavik crew had determined the same thing after the bomb had exploded. But why hadn't the thing blown the plane apart? Even a small bomb would have had more devastating results. The question would have to be answered later. For now, the pilot had his hands full. Time was not on his side.

"Seven-five-four, descend to 6,000 feet and turn right to heading of one-one-zero."

"Six thousand on one-one-zero," the captain responded.

"Seven-five-four, we're turning you over to Keflavik tower. Switch to 125.8 for vector into Keflavik. Good luck, Captain!"

"Roger, 125.8."

"Keflavik tower, this is World Wide 754 inbound with an emergency."

"Seven-five-four, roger. We have you. Maintain heading of one-one-zero for visual approach to active runway one-one. Wind out of east zero-eight-five at ten knots, visibility fifteen miles, high thin scattered."

"Roger, wind zero-eight-five at ten for runway one-one."

"Seven-five-four, would you like a go-around for visual inspection of underbelly?"

"Negative. I need straight in! It's rockin'!"

"Roger. Straight in for runway one-one. We have you in sight, 754. Cleared for landing."

"Keflavik, this is 754. Can you get visual of my gear position?"

"Affirmative, 754, your gear appears to be down. What is your indication?"

"Indicator shows nose and left down and locked. Right gear indicator negative."

"Roger, 754. Emergency equipment standing by."

Mary, Jacob, Jim, and Rolly sat quietly as the captain came over the intercom, "Ladies and gentlemen, I need not tell you that we have encountered some difficulty with the aircraft and will be landing in a few minutes at Keflavik International Airport. Please keep your seatbelts fastened and your masks in place for landing. There is some indication that the right-side landing gear may not be locked. As a precaution, please follow instructions of the flight personnel for a possible rough landing." It was obvious that the captain did not want to alarm the passengers any more than necessary and still get them into the crash position.

The captain eased the big bird slowly toward the center line of runway eleven. He bled off his speed to the very minimum required for safe landing. The cabin was like a tomb. Not a sound could be heard except for a single crying child.

The captain cringed as the main gear touched the ground. His cringe turned to a smile as he eased the nose wheel softly onto the runway.

The captain immediately pulled off the power but did not reverse his remaining engine, in order to avoid a violent swerve that could end in disaster. The runway was more than 10,000-feet long, and he touched down within the first thousand. He let her slow down with the assistance from the right amount of braking pressure.

The entire cabin erupted with loud whistling and applause as the huge airplane rolled to a stop just a few hundred feet short of the runway's end. Many strangers were hugging and kissing one another with tears of joy flowing freely.

Mary gave hugs to Jim, Rolly, and Jacob. They were glad to be in the arms of good old Mother Earth.

"Thank God the hydraulics held!" remarked the second officer to the pilot as the slides reeled out from the sides of the airplane.

"Let's get these people out of here!" replied the captain.

As the people were quietly exiting the aircraft, the pilot announced, "Would passenger Rolland Hunter and party please report to the small green shuttle bus now sitting on the taxiway next to your aircraft?"

The four looked quizzically at one another as they made their way down the air slides. They proceeded to the shuttle awaiting them. Hunter recognized his old colleague Earl Collins. He hadn't seen him in more than 30 years. The men shook hands and gave the "guy hug."

"Good to see you, Rolly!" Collins said.

"What in the hell are you doing here, Earl?" Rolly responded. "You can't still be working! Shit, you must be 80 by now."

"Eighty-one, and I can whip your ass right now!" came Collins's retort.

"You know, I think you might be right. Anyway, what's all this with the special treatment?"

"Well, first of all, the whole business of our meeting is purely a coincidence. I wasn't sure it was you on the passenger list. I was about to check you out before the shit hit the fan up there! I'm a security officer of sorts for an air cargo shipper, and my job is to monitor sensitive stuff crossing the pole. I've been here at Keflavik for the last five years. It beats working!"

"We must be carrying something damned sensitive for someone to blow up the damned plane!"

"Well, Rolly, not really that sensitive. What my company was shipping probably saved your lives."

"What do you mean, Earl?" asked Rolly. The others were listening intently.

"Well, as you must have already guessed, there was a bomb on board," Collins continued.

"Yes, but look at that little hole over there in the plane. It must have been a big firecracker just to scare someone!" Rolly added.

"No, Rolly. It was a big boy! Can you imagine this? My company was shipping six specially manufactured gymnastic floor mats from Casper, Wyoming. We are routing them through several countries to Beijing for the '08 Olympics. We'll verify as we inspect further, but lucky for flight 754 we had to leave out several cargo containers because we had to ship them rolled up. I can guarantee you that they were riding beside and on top of the bomb. This caused the blast to blow out the right side. I doubt that the mats are worth shit now, but I'm also sure that they saved your lives!"

"Wow!" Jim said. "I'm now starting to think a very unpleasant thought. Lord, I hope I'm wrong."

Mary jumped in. "Jim, I'm thinking the same thing! Can you believe that bastard had anything to do with this?"

"Yes, I can believe it, but why would any idiot deliberately commit suicide to do such a thing?" asked Jacob.

"That could have been easy!" Rolly chimed in. "All you have to do is get someone who doesn't speak or read any English and tell him or her in their own language that this is a personal note, or pay someone enough money and you can get anything done."

Collins interjected that he had heard the reading of the note in the tower. He related the contents to the group.

"Now I know that was meant for us!" Jim said. "I'm sure that I'm going to have to kill that madman before this is over! Nothing else will ever be likely to stop him."

Collins told Rolly that it would be necessary for everyone to come into the tower office and give statements related to the note. "We'll go over all departures that can get you to London or Berlin. Since your flight was bound for Zurich, you'll have to make connections from one of those two locations. I doubt that World Wide can pick you up from here."

The shuttle drove them to the office, where they spent nearly two hours trying to convince the authorities that the threat was personally directed toward them and was not an act of terror against anyone else.

Upon completion of the interviews, the group made their way to the departure board. There were three flights to London in 10 hours and one to Berlin departing within six hours. Rolly approached the Lufthansa counter and made arrangements for the flight.

The four sat in one of the airport pubs, recounting almost everything that had happened since Jim met David Steinmetz. Jacob Sukin said very little. He merely shook his head slowly from time to time until all was revealed by the others.

Unbelievably, not one of the four had thought seriously as to what they would do with their share of any money extracted from Zurich. They would chuckle from time to time about the implausibility of getting any money at all out of the country.

They concluded their layover with a decent dinner before boarding the Lufthansa flight to Berlin.

FORTY-FOUR

IT WAS A BEAUTIFUL SUNDAY morning when the group landed in Zurich. Boulevards were in full bloom and cleanliness the byword as they proceeded down Highway Switzerland past Oberhusen on to Steinackerstrasse to the Rosengarten Restaurant. They were all famished.

They had decided to have a good breakfast before checking into the Swiss Quality Hotel located on Falkenstrasse 6. Hunter had stayed in the hotel twice when he was stationed in Italy. He liked the hotel because it was a four-star and because it was in the center of the business district. It stood next door to the opera house on the Lake of Zurich.

It suddenly hit Jim and Mary. "This is it. This is what it's all been about." Now the real test was about to begin. They had already decided that first on the list would be the Unterstarss Bank of Zurich. It dated back to 1910 and was about to become their first target. It was also the first of the two banks with safe-deposit keys.

Hunter and Jacob would go in. Hunter would pose as Jacob's attorney without actually saying so. He would not set himself up to lie.

Jim and Mary spent the evening making love and trying to watch television. They giggled at John Wayne speaking in High German. The dubbed voice was half the strength of the Duke's. They thought he sounded like Doogie Howser. The two were thoroughly entertained.

Hunter and Jacob spent the evening rehearsing their presentation. By 11:00 p.m., all had settled in for the night.

* * *

THE BANK DOORS OPENED PROMPTLY at 9:00 a.m. A very pompous-looking guard stood at the entrance. Jacob and Rolly walked to the first window and asked the clerk to see the bank manager. She tried to pry into their motive for seeing an executive, not that it was uncommon. Screening was part of the modus operandi of Swiss banks in general.

"Good morning, gentlemen!" came the voice of a neatly trimmed man with an old-fashioned turned-up collar. He gave the appearance of a speakeasy proprietor of the roaring twenties. "I am Jacque Fournier, president of the Unterstrass Bank. How may I serve you?"

Jacob was prepared. "I am Jacob Sukin, a direct descendant of one of your depositors in 1938."

The man raised his eyebrows to the point of eye-popping surprise. "Yes, yes of course. What is it that the Unterstrass staff can do for you then?" he asked with a suspicious tone.

"First of all, I would like to extract the contents of my safe-deposit box, number 214," stated Jacob.

"Well, gentlemen, you must understand that we are talking about more than six decades. I'm not sure how to respond."

"Well, how about if I take my key here along with yours and open the box?"

"May I ask Mr. Sukin if you have identification with you to verify that you are indeed an heir to contents of the safe deposit and any accounts that may be claimed?"

"Here, Mr. Fournier, is my birth certificate, my Kansas driver's license, and my social security card. Will that be sufficient?"

"Yes, Monsieur, that is sufficient. Now, if you will excuse me for a moment. Would you like some coffee or tea perhaps?"

Both men waved off the drink offer. They sat quietly.

* * *

JIM AND MARY HAD A leisurely breakfast as Mary looked through the local attractions guide, but first they had an assignment to locate a U.S. bank that would become the holding station for the collections made by Hunter and Sukin.

As they scanned the phone directory, to their pleasant amazement, there was a branch of the Bank of America just three blocks down Falkenstrasse.

The day was clear and warm, so they walked to the bank. With the help of the assistant manager, Jim and Mary set up a holding account for what they told the man would be perhaps millions of dollars.

He reacted with an air of suspicion. Nevertheless, he made no move to suggest his distrust and dutifully set up the account.

The bank noted that all monies were to eventually end up at the Third National Bank of San Francisco. Under no circumstances were any amounts to be diverted to any other entity or institution without the signatures of both Mary Rison and James Riley. This was Hunter's idea, in case something was to happen to him or Sukin as they proceeded with their collections.

* * *

MR. FOURNIER RETURNED after nearly 20 minutes, accompanied by another gentleman and a very attractive middle-aged woman.

"Mr. Sukin, Mr. Hunter, may I introduce Mr. Otto Perrier, one of our board members, and Ms. Touché, our attorney."

Jacob and Rolly rose to their feet and shook hands with the two.

"Why, may I ask," began Jacob, "do we need the presence of a lawyer?"

"A mere formality, Mr. Sukin. In matters such as this, it is imperative that there are no misstatements or misrepresentations on either side," Fournier explained.

Rolly could sense the frustration beginning to build in Jacob. He nudged him and moved his head ever so slightly in the "no" position. Jacob understood.

"Mr. Sukin," Touché began, "I'm sure you have with you some sort of directions, a copy of which would have been given to the bank manager at the time of deposit. Is that not true?"

To her complete surprise, Jacob extracted from a new briefcase the original directions given to the bank president at the time of deposit. It was signed by Heinrich Corbel, Bank President. The board member excused himself to research the history of the bank presidents to determine if Jacob Sukin was telling the truth. He was.

"Gentlemen, this is going to take some time to sort this out. In the meantime, I suggest that we proceed to the safe-deposit vault. Number 214 will be in the old vault, below the first basement. It is rather musty down there, so please be aware."

The board member and the lawyer retreated into the main conference room and dialed the other board members to report immediately to an emergency conference.

Fournier extracted the appropriate key from an old storage closet and asked Jacob and Rolly to follow him down three flights of stairs to the old vault. They would certainly be in violation of the disabilities act in good old America. Upon their arrival, the ornate door to the vault immediately startled them. They could not imagine the cost of such scribing, color, and countless hours of labor it must have taken to design such a magnificent structure.

The tumbler was not locked, another amazement to the two men. Fournier wiped the cobwebs out of the way and turned the handle. Near-total blackness greeted them.

A small, bare light bulb expelled the darkness. As their eyes became accustomed to the dim light, their eyes caught the countless rows of elegantly inscribed numbers on elaborate small doors. Almost at once, both men's eyes were drawn to number 214. Jacob felt his knees beginning to quiver. Hunter felt the hair stand up on the back of his neck. He felt his own goose bumps on his arm.

Fournier stepped to the safe-deposit box and inserted and turned his key. "Gentlemen, I shall return to my office. Please press this button when you are finished." He left the two men to their business.

With nervous anticipation, Jacob placed his key into the slot. It did not want to turn, but he jiggled until it opened. He pulled out an extremely heavy 4"x12" box from where it had rested for 70 years.

He handled it with great reverence as he set the box on the table. He and Rolly sat down and looked at it for a few moments. Rolly wanted Jacob to open it quickly, but he said nothing.

The shining gold caught the light of the single bulb and made the vault seem suddenly brighter. Two flat bars of what looked to be pure gold rested in the box. Rolly lifted each and thought that they weighed about a pound. He had no idea of what that would be in troy ounces. They had obviously been poured into some makeshift mold to approximate something close to a pound.

This deposit belonged to Isaiah Cohen. It must have required the meltdown of jewelry, gold coins, and trinkets of all sorts. Perhaps it had been a hobby that he kept to himself. "It would have taken him years to gather enough gold to make nearly two bullions weighing roughly a pound each," Jacob concluded. "Must be worth over $30,000 at today's price," he surmised.

"Yeah, Jacob, but what would it be worth for the historical value, do you suppose?" asked Rolly.

"I don't know. Maybe 10 times that much to a rich art or history buff!"

Jacob set the heavy gold bars on the table and picked up a large, worn envelope that had been folded over lengthwise to fit the safe-deposit box. He unwound the string and reached inside for the contents. As he withdrew the papers, he saw *International Business Machines*. He could see that it was a stock certificate for 100 shares.

The men immediately knew the implications of this find.

"We've got to be looking at millions here, Rolly!" said Jacob almost breathlessly.

"My God! How many times do you think that stock has split since 1938?" Rolly asked.

By now, Jacob's hands were shaking. He could not believe the potential wealth sitting in this old safe-deposit box.

He removed five silver Morgan dollars that were in mint condition. "They will be valuable to a coin collector, I'm sure," Jacob announced.

In a second envelope was a certificate for 200 shares of Standard Oil of New Jersey. They could not even begin to imagine its worth after all this time.

Another certificate for 40 shares of Packard Motor Car Company stock was withdrawn from the box by Jacob, which the men immediately determined to be worthless except to some collector of that sort of thing. Nothing else was in the box.

Rolly placed the items into their briefcase and pushed the button to call Fournier. Jacob locked the lid to the safe-deposit box and left the box on the table. They would not need it further.

Fournier ushered the men up the three flights of stairs and into the conference room. There sat the board representative and Ms. Touché.

"Gentlemen," she began, "Mr. Fournier informs me that you have a numbered account with us. Is that not correct?"

"Yes, ma'am, we do. That account number is 11485." Sukin answered.

"I see. Mr. Sukin, is it? Mr. Fournier will verify that information, but it seems we have a minor problem."

"And that is?" Sukin responded.

Fournier headed off to his office with the account number. He would return before Ms. Touché continued.

He nodded affirmatively to her.

"Here is the problem, gentlemen. It seems that a Mr. Oliver Windom from California has filed a petition with the Swiss government for an injunction against anyone withdrawing any monies under the names of Franz Steinmetz, Isaiah Cohen, Benjamin Wetzel, Samuel Gold, Peter Dussell, or Harry Sukin. Do you know Mr. Windom?"

"Not personally," Jacob responded. "But Ms. Touché, I'm confused. Mr. Windom could not have known of an account here for one of the names you mentioned."

"You are right, Mr. Sukin. This petition came down from what you in America would call a superior court to every bank in Switzerland. Until a panel of three judges hands down a ruling, we cannot act."

Rolly turned to Jacob. "Windom is shooting at us with a scatter gun,

Jacob. He has no idea where the accounts are!"

"In case you are curious, which you appear to be, Mr. Windom has made no less than nine visits to this bank over the last 35 years. He insists that it was his father who made the deposit and received the receipt for same. However, he showed no evidence beyond the original directions to the bank that his father, a Mr. Gino DiNapoli, had any claim whatsoever. His petition was filed only two days ago. Therefore, we have been expecting you," the lawyer concluded. "We didn't think it would be so soon."

Mr. Fournier looked over at the woman. She nodded.

"Gentlemen," he began, "an amount of 270,000 U.S. dollars was deposited. Without going into detail, the account has earned an average of 5.3 percent interest for 70 years, for a total of $9,288,080.95."

Jacob and Rolly looked at each other in disbelief.

"So do I understand that when the court decides that Mr. Sukin is the rightful receiver, you will issue him something like a cashier's check?" Rolly asked.

"Well, yes, that is correct. Or if you wish, our bank can make a direct electronic deposit to any bank of your choosing," answered Mr. Fournier.

It was obvious to Jacob and Rolly that this would not be the first time that such a huge amount was either deposited or withdrawn. To the bank, they were just numbers.

"Now, of course," the female attorney began, "the matter of the court must take place. I have requested a decision regarding this bank as soon as possible. Your circumstances should trump any complaint of Mr. Windom's, I would think."

Rolly looked directly at Fournier and asked him why the bank was not reluctant to release such an amount of money. Fournier answered with an explanation of the $5 billion Holocaust fund recently authorized by the Swiss government. His bank would be supported by that fund.

He explained to Rolly and Jacob that the bank would have to verify his identification before releasing any money, however. "We are doing that as we speak," Fournier concluded.

The men were quite pleased with the attitude of the bank personnel, as well they should be. They believed it would be a matter of a few days until a decision could be handed down. In the meantime, they would continue to make their rounds of the other banks identified in the codebooks. The men were quite pleased with their initial progress. Hunter surmised that the money meant nothing to the bankers. It was all simply paperwork to them.

Sukin and Hunter left the bank and hailed a cab for der Erste Oberhausen Bank just off the Steinackerstrasse. They stopped for a quick lunch before going into the bank.

* * *

JIM AND MARY ANXIOUSLY awaited Rolly's call to report on his progress. They were sure that the men had finished their first appointment by now. Perhaps Rolly would call before continuing, unless of course they had hit a snag.

Jim's cell phone rang.

"Jim, this is Rolly!"

"Rolly, we were just wondering how it's going. Where are you?"

"Well, I think we're doing fine. It looks like we have over $9 million from the Unterstrass Bank!"

Rolly could hear Jim relate the information. He could hear her answer: "Oh, Jesus!"

Rolly chuckled and explained to Jim how Windom was trying to stop the whole process. "I don't think he can get away with it! Professor DiNapoli made sure that no one but a rightful heir can get anything. It's apparent to me now that without Jacob, it would have been impossible."

"Yeah, thank God you found him, Rolly! How is he taking all of this?"

"Well, we're both like a couple fifth-grade boys at recess!"

Jim told Hunter that they had completed all the setup for a holding account at B of A.

"We'll meet you back at the hotel for cocktails around five!" Jim told Rolly.

"Jim, you might do something for me while you're waiting."

"Sure, Rolly, what do you need?" Jim asked.

"Either call or stop in to one of the stockbroker offices in the city and ask them what 200 shares of IBM stock purchased in 1938 would be worth today. I'm sure it will knock your socks off!"

"You got it, Bubba! We'll see you this evening."

* * *

THE MEN ENTERED THE BANK at 1:00 sharp and repeated their request to see the manager, as they did at the first location. Following the same routine, Jacob introduced himself. This time, a very casually dressed man, short with balding hair, approached and introduced himself. "I am Joseph Richer, president of the bank. May I help you?"

They introduced themselves, and Jacob repeated the same routine with the man, who offered no expression whatsoever. He had obviously heard some strange stories. It was impossible to tell whether he believed Sukin or not. He barely glanced at the birth certificate and driver's license. He did pay some attention to the social security card. No doubt he would check it out as well as the birth certificate, if it came to that.

This man was not as friendly as Fournier. He was an unemotional businessman doing his job.

Rolly was trying to guess whether he was German or Swiss. Since everyone spoke High German, he could not tell. His accent, while he spoke clear English, sounded German to Rolly.

The men retired to the manager's office.

"Gentlemen, if I may … I, er … the bank will not be able to act on your request. You see, the national government has already set aside almost $5 billion for these kinds of claims, and …"

Rolly interrupted the man. "Yes, Mr. Richer, we know about that. It was set aside for general Holocaust survivors, not depositors. May I suggest that you read the directions and note the bank executive who signed the receipt? And by the way, we are aware of the petition filed to disallow withdrawals. You will see that Samuel Gold, one of the names mentioned in the petition, was the holder of the deposit here."

Without showing any emotion, the bank president said, "First of all, let me check this numbered account, ah … 442507. I shall return in a moment."

"Not another damned board member or attorney, I hope!" Jacob muttered to himself.

The man returned in less than two minutes. "Mr. Sukin, it appears that everything is in order. It shows in the record that Mr. Gold's deposit was 1 million and 42 dollars. Gentlemen, have you any idea what we are talking about here?"

"At least 10 to 15 times that, I'm sure," Jacob stated.

"Much more than that, my friends. As of today, the total worth of Mr. Gold's deposit is $37,153,884.00!" The man actually had a smile on his face as he relayed the number.

"Do you mind my asking how you calculated that so fast, Mr. Richer?" Rolly asked.

"Well, Mr. Hunter, as you pointed out, you knew about the petition to stop payments. You should know as well that every bank in Switzerland reviewed their accounts to see if they were included. Gentlemen, this is not a rare event. The banking industry in this country is extremely volatile and has been since the beginning of World War II, in spite of our laissez-faire attitude. Hundreds of millions of dollars are entering and leaving the county every hour of every day. I am happy for you, Mr. Sukin, but to me it is all in a day's work. Let us hope that the petition is denied."

They were informed that it would be necessary for them to return to close the account, should the petition be denied. Their money could then be electronically deposited wherever they desired.

The men could hardly wait to share their information with Jim and Mary.

FORTY-FIVE

THE FOUR LAUGHED AND DINED on lobster as they reviewed their first day's work. They discussed tomorrow's schedule. A second bank carrying Samuel Gold's final deposit would be the first stop. It would also include the second safe-deposit box.

Already they had uncovered nearly $50 million in accounts alone, not counting the 200 shares of IBM stock. Jim reported that information to the group. "Are you ready?" Jim asked. Jacob and Rolly leaned forward and rested their arms on the table.

"Two hundred shares of IBM purchased in 1938 is now worth $55,770,582.00 … and change!"

"That brings our total to somewhere near 150 million U.S. dollars!" Rolly announced.

"This is not real!" Jacob interrupted. "There is no way that this country is going to let us walk away with the kind of money we're dealing with!"

"I'm not so sure that they can stop it, Jacob," Rolly said. "Remember that Richer said it's all in a day's work?"

"Yes, but this is a little more than a day's work." Mary chuckled.

"We know they can't do anything about the stocks. There was nothing in Windom's petition that dealt with safe-deposit boxes. Fournier and Richer had no problem accepting Jacob's identification either," Rolly added.

"Well, I guess we should just continue our schedule and see what happens," Jacob concluded.

The four left the table, and each settled in to make a phone call or two. Mary called her mother. Jim called Julie. Jacob talked for almost an hour with his wife. Rolly returned to his room and reviewed all the account numbers and bank names. He randomly checked information against the codebooks. They had done well. All that he reviewed was in order and correctly decoded. He anticipated that tomorrow would bring the court decision on Windom's petition.

* * *

JIM AND MARY PREPARED TO CASH in the IBM certificate and have the money electronically deposited directly to San Francisco, while Jacob and Rolly rented a small car and drove the 16 miles to Bern.

They pulled into the parking lot of The Tiefenbrennen Bank of Bern. Here they would close the final account of Sam Gold, which included a deposit of $12,000.00 and a safe deposit key.

The men were not surprised that Gold's $12,000.00 had grown to $445,827.89. They were surprised at safe-deposit box number 1217, however. It contained three military medals from World War I, all from the French government, including the impressive Legion of Merit and a couple of foreign service medals. There were two insurance policies that certainly had expired due to default in premiums. There were five stock certificates, four in Italian companies that had long since ceased to exist. One, however, was for Standard Oil Company of New Jersey for 100 shares.

Following their visit, Rolly called Jim and asked him to research Standard Oil of New Jersey for one hundred shares bought in 1908. Jim would talk to him at dinner and hopefully have an answer. The bank gave Jacob the same answer as the other banks regarding the petition.

Their next adventure was the Riesbach der Zwite Bank of Bern. "I think that means the second bank, for whatever that's worth," Rolly told Jacob. And so it continued.

At dinner, Jim reported that Standard Oil of New Jersey was sued by the

U.S. government under the Sherman Anti-trust Act in 1911. They were forced to split into 38 companies. "Your boy ended up owning Exxon-Mobil stock. His 100 shares are worth $37,153,884.00. Not a bad profit for 15 minutes' work!" Jim said with a laugh.

"Isn't this fun?" Mary chimed in. "We dropped off the IBM certificate at Morgan Stanley here in Zurich. Everything seemed okay. The money should be in San Francisco by tomorrow morning."

They all agreed that there was no further need for Jim and Mary to remain in Zurich. No one had any idea when the petition might be settled. It would be better for them to be near San Francisco.

After their evening meeting, Mary called a local travel agency for tickets back to the Bay Area. They were scheduled to leave Zurich the next afternoon. Jacob insisted that they fly first class. Mary did not object. She still had some continuous pain in her rib area. Jim picked up a copy of Tom Clancy's *Patriot Games*. He had been meaning to read it. Now was a good opportunity.

* * *

ROLLY AND JACOB CONTINUED their banking adventures for the next several days. A single bank called the Kusnacht Commercial Bank of Switzerland had ceased to exist. According to Rolly's information from one of the neighboring banks, a dozen Nazi SS troopers had ransacked it in 1944, following D-Day. All accounting reports had been burned on site and the vaults emptied. It was considered to have been owned by a Jewish consortium and therefore marked by the Nazis for destruction. There had been deposits under the names of Isaiah Cohen, Benjamin Wetzel, and Peter Dussell.

Jacob could not avoid tearing up as he heard the story. There were three other banks that still existed that *did* have his money. Their goal was three banks per day, but there were snags. Two more of the banks identified in the codebooks no longer existed. It was impossible to track them beyond the date of their closing. In the months to come, they could use some of the acquired resources to follow whatever trails may exist. For now, they needed to act quickly.

Pressure was being applied by Windom's people to stop any further intrusion into the banks. It was to their credit that the banks refused to be intimidated. They had become experts at resisting that sort of thing. It was not difficult to understand what Windom was doing. Besides that, the eyes of the world were on the Swiss banking industry. Reputation trumped all other attempts to meddle in their business. Rolly realized that the timing was right for their own activities.

"DiNapoli may not have been a genius," Rolly told Jacob, "but he sure knew what the hell he was doing!" Jacob smiled in agreement.

To date, should the petition be rejected, the two had completed the necessary paperwork to withdraw a total of more than $104 million, not counting the stock sales. With nine banks remaining, they counted another million dollars in initial deposits. They presumed this would bring the total to well over $200 million from deposits alone.

The two men settled into a routine of contacting bank after bank until their job was finished. Oliver Windom had other ideas, however. His crony lawyers added an addendum to his petition. Every bank in Switzerland would be required to report to Central Banking each and every request to withdraw funds under the names of the original six Jews.

Rolly was not comforted by this new twist. He was sure the Swiss government was not anxious to release hundreds of millions of dollars from its gold mines. They also knew that Windom would have a very weak case in trying to prove that he alone was entitled to the inheritance. Confusion and delays were great tools for the postwar banking industry in Switzerland. Every day they could hold on to an extra $100 million meant lining someone's pocket.

After each bank reported attempted withdrawals by Hunter and Sukin, Windom was to be given a chance to present his case to them. Once all the reports were in, then, and only then, would the petition be approved or denied. Rolly knew that this was nothing more than a delaying tactic. Nonetheless, they must continue.

Jacob was sure that it was just a matter of time until Windom's petition would be thrown out. The men were having a good time considering the bumps in the road.

FORTY-SIX

JIM AND MARY WERE EXHAUSTED when they arrived in San Francisco. The plane had been hot and stuffy inside, and they could hardly wait to breathe the fresh, cool air outside the SFO airport. They hurried to the baggage claim and unfortunately had to wait until nearly the last bags appeared. "Par for the course!" Jim commented.

They left the airport and got into the next awaiting cab. The cabbie was less than happy that his fare was heading south for six miles rather than the city to the north. He was prepared to have driven extra unnecessary miles to up his fare, a common practice of cab drivers everywhere.

The two didn't bother to unpack but fell into bed and quickly fell asleep, Jim in his boxers and she in her panties and one of Jim's T-shirts.

They heard nothing until the door flew open at 1:30 a.m. The ripping of the woodwork told them it was not a silent burglar.

By reflex, Jim rolled onto his right side and grabbed for the top drawer of his nightstand. With one move, he opened and retrieved his .22-caliber, cocked it, and sat upright in bed. Mary moved to his side, holding her pillow over her upper body.

"All right, Jim, I've had all I can take from you. It's time to settle this once and for all!" shouted a very familiar voice to both Jim and Mary. "Just turn on the light and walk out here where I can see you," the voice commanded.

Jim knew it would not be wise to remain on the bed. He stood and motioned for Mary to stand behind him. They walked slowly toward the bedroom door. Jim reached over and switched on the light. As they entered the living room, the intruder turned on the lamp. Windom's goon immediately took direct aim at Jim Riley. Riley fired and hit the man in his right arm. This caused him to drop his weapon. He lunged toward it and Jim fired a second shot. The man froze.

Jim and Mary stood motionless. Windom stood glaring at Riley.

"You have no idea what you have gotten yourselves into. I belong to a new world order. We have been growing for over 50 years. Our strength is increasing. Your power as a nation is becoming weak and lazy. You think terrorism is your enemy. I say it is your own socialistic society that panders to the human debris of this world. The mixed blood of races and the handouts to the weak instead of their elimination will destroy your nation! But don't worry, we will clean up the mess!"

The arrogance of this insane man did not surprise Jim. What did surprise him was what the man was wearing as he pointed what looked to be a WWII German Luger.

"Holy shit!" Jim exclaimed. "You son of a bitch! You took the ribbon from a Medal of Honor badge and replaced the medal with a fucking swastika? And you've got the nerve to wear it? You're crazy!"

"I thought it might upset you a little, my boy. But I want you to know when I pull this trigger, you'll have no doubt about the new world order behind your death. This is just a beginning!"

"You loony bastard, you haven't got the guts to be a real Nazi!" Jim said as he stepped toward Windom.

The shot rang out and Jim sank to the floor. Mary fell on top of Jim as if to protect him. She took the gun from Jim's hand and aimed and fired at Windom with one quick motion. The bullet struck him just above the left nostril, killing him instantly. He fell to the floor like a sack of concrete.

Jim felt the burning in his right hip. It was bleeding profusely, but his pain was minor. As Mary lowered his trousers, she could see that he had been only slightly grazed. She kissed him and reached for a pillow, which she placed under his head. Windom lay in a pool of blood across the room. Mary dialed 911.

* * *

THE POLICE HAD ONLY TO LOOK at the swastika to surmise what had happened. Jim presented the entire back-story to his relationship with Windom. All the necessary statements were taken from Jim and Mary. Windom's hitman was patched and hauled away by ambulance under police accompaniment.

The police sergeant took Mary aside, and as he rested his hand on her shoulder, he said, "Miss, I'm going to give you my card. I want you to call me in the morning. I will put you in touch with a lady who will talk to you about what has happened tonight. Believe me, you need to talk to her. You may not feel it important now, but I assure you, you will not regret it. Even experienced officers who face similar situations need to talk to someone sooner or later. This lady is trained to deal with your feelings, which will certainly surface."

The story was on the United Press and around the world by the time the 6:00 p.m. news hit the airwaves.

Somehow, the Swiss were listening. Within an hour of the news report, a decision to reject Windom's petition was issued to Central Bank. It was apparent to Hunter and Sukin that the Swiss government wanted no part in this story. The men began their collections the following morning. Within three days, all monies were transferred to the Bank of America in Zurich and made ready for wire to San Francisco. The total deposit was $105,212,123.00. Together with the stocks and sale of the gold, the grand total came to $197,366,971.00.

The money was in San Francisco the following Tuesday morning. Uncle Sam was not far away. It appeared that the IRS had no claim on any of the money until the day it began earning interest in San Francisco.

Upon their return to the City by the Bay, the four met once again for a final celebration. They knew that the federal government was busy clamoring for ways to get its hands into the pie, and Dominic Windom was already taking care of his brother's affairs. He had left a message on Jim's phone to call him. Riley procrastinated, unsure of how to handle a conversation regarding Dominic's brother.

After a certain amount of trepidation, Jim called him. He was indeed surprised that Dominic harbored no ill will against him for Oliver's death. Jim thanked the man for his concern and wished him well. Dominic did likewise.

It was now time for a major decision. Should the group conclude that they had done everything to find any remaining heirs to this gigantic fortune or was the discovering of Jacob Sukin enough? No, they all agreed, it was not enough. They must exhaust every avenue in the search for others. The finances were there to do it right.

After much discussion, it was determined that Rolly and Jacob would return to Washington, D.C., to the Holocaust Museum to search for possible heirs. Mary would work the Internet to fish for any connections that might be fruitful. Jim was determined to find out what the Wi Construction Company had to do with the Neo-Nazis, if anything. They would keep in contact with one another.

Jacob and Rolly made a stopover in Kansas so that Jacob could spend a night with his family, then they went on to D.C.

Mary soon realized that the sergeant was right. Feelings of guilt at the awful memory of shooting Windom began to well up in her mind. She called the number on the card given to her and met on three separate occasions with the counselor. She was encouraged, because of her innocence, to put the matter to rest. Her strong character allowed her to do that. She thought of it no more and was able to turn her attention to the task at hand.

After two days of constant work on the Internet, Mary came across the name of a freshman girl at Cornell University. The girl had a hyphenated name that caught Mary's attention. Her name was Laverne Wetzel-Glazer from Milan, Italy. Mary had searched for foreign exchange students from Milan specifically. Her inquiry seemed to pay off. She decided to contact the school and leave a message for the girl to call her. She waited two days for the call to come in.

Mary explained why she was calling. The girl was less than enthused. She told Mary that they had changed their last name to avoid being associated with the Holocaust victims. Mary was stunned. She could not imagine why.

Mary persisted, and the girl agreed to meet with her in the Libe Café in the Olin Library on the following Wednesday. She had three finals to take and did not want to be interrupted. Mary understood and set the appointment. The girl said she would be wearing a yellow blouse and would place a black fanny pack on the table in front of her. It was all set.

Jim drove to Sacramento to the Contractor's License Board. He knew that to get any information on Wi Construction, he would have to file some sort of a complaint.

When the agent approached, Jim gave him the story regarding the windmill incident and explained that the craft had tried to make him crash. He left out the sniper part.

The agent was thrilled. He had read the story in the *Sacramento Bee*. "What can I do for you, Mr. Riley?" he asked.

Jim explained that he wanted to know more about the people and why they tried to kill him. The two men retired to one of the conference rooms.

"Now, let's see," the man began, "Wi Construction is owned by J. Wi and Oliver Windom. Windom has 51 percent, Wi owns 30, and four others own the rest. That's odd," the man said.

"Odd in what way?" Jim asked.

"Their names sound kinda English and German, Schwenk, Hardisty, Singlar, and Brown."

"I knew it!" Jim exclaimed. "Do you know where Wi came from?"

"His home address was in Hong Kong. That's why Windom owned 51 percent. Wi was the qualifying partner. The license is under Windom's name."

"I have reason to believe that this company was merely a front for a Nazi group. Is there any way of stopping these guys from continuing business? Both Windom and Wi are dead!"

"Absolutely! I'll pull the license right now. They're out of business today!"

* * *

ROLLY AND JACOB WERE UNABLE to uncover any useful information. They informed Jim and Mary that they would continue for another few days.

Mary hopped a red-eye flight to Ithaca via New York City on Tuesday. The girl was waiting for Mary in the library café when she arrived. They introduced themselves, after which the girl sat back in her chair with folded arms. The ball was in Mary's court.

"Miss Glazer, or do you prefer Wetzel-Glazer?"

"Glazer. The Wetzel was my idea when I enrolled. Just call me Laverne," she said.

"Laverne, may I ask how you came to use the Wetzel name?"

"Well, I was told by my mother that her grandfather was one of the Holocaust victims. Nothing more was ever said, and whenever I tried to find out more, I was put off. No one in my family wanted to talk about it. I think they were somehow ashamed. Can you believe that?"

"Yes and no, Laverne. Survivors *have* been ridiculed and disbelieved over the years. Some have even suffered physical abuse. And I guess you know that there are forces at work all over the world to convince the world that it never happened. And because of these prejudices, I can see why some do not want their stories brought to light."

"Well, I'm not going to be one of them!"

"And I honor you for that, Laverne. That is precisely why I'm here. Tell me about your family," Mary asked.

"Well, my father is a jewelry repairman at a shop near our home. My mother works four days a week as an assistant in a senior care home, you know, helping old ladies take a bath and that kind of stuff. My little brother is eleven. He was born with cerebral palsy and is unable to walk or feed himself. My older sister Tamara is married, and she and her husband live with us and she takes care of our brother, Antonio. Her husband Roberto is a city bus driver."

"So your mother's family traces back to Benjamin Wetzel?" Mary asked.

"Yes, but how did you know the first name of Benjamin? I didn't mention it!"

"I know, Laverne. Let me explain. I need to tell you a story."

Mary continued for the next two hours revealing to the young girl the whole background of her ancestors and the other five Jews. The young Jewish girl had never been privy to such information. She was delighted.

"How are you able to attend such an expensive and prestigious school, Laverne?" Mary asked her.

"A combination of Italian government and scholastic achievement scholarships," she answered. "My family couldn't afford it, that's for sure!" she chuckled.

"Laverne, I want to tell you right now. Your family will never again face financial troubles … ever!"

"What are you talking about?" the girl asked.

"Your family will inherit nearly one sixth of … are you ready?" The girl nodded her head in amazement. "Nearly $205 million!"

Laverne clasped her hands across her breasts. Her face went from a blushing red to a colorless white. It was unbelievable. The girl could not speak. Finally she said one word. "Antonio!"

Mary explained to the young woman that it would require some decisions between her parents and Jacob Sukin as to the exact dispensation of the money.

"I'm sure that Mr. Sukin will agree to fly your parents into San Francisco to meet with him. Mr. Hunter, whom I told you about, is advising Mr. Sukin. Together you can all come to common ground on what happens next."

"What about you and this Mr. Riley whom you discussed? Certainly you are entitled to something for what you have both been through?" asked Laverne.

"That will be up to your family and Jacob Sukin's family. There is something else, Laverne."

"Yes?"

"In a relatively short time, Mr. Hunter, Jim Riley, and I have uncovered two direct descendants of the original six men. Now it seems to me with enough concerted effort, others can be located. I cannot believe there are only two."

The girl listened and said nothing.

"My point is this, Laverne: you and Mr. Sukin will have to decide if you want to keep looking or simply end it here. You can do that, you know! Quite a serious decision. I do not envy your family and Mr. Sukin, who is a total stranger to you, having to determine together what you wish to do with 200 million-plus dollars. The thought must be mind-boggling."

"Mind-boggling? I can't even comprehend the amount you are talking about, let alone what to do with it! I cannot believe you're serious about this!"

"Laverne, I would not have come clear across the country just to meet a young woman from Italy. Believe me, it's true."

"So what happens next?"

"Give me your parents' full names and address and we'll contact them and get back to you," Mary continued.

Mary hugged the young woman and returned to California on the next flight out of La Guardia.

FORTY-SEVEN

IT WAS 5:30 WHEN THE GLAZERS ARRIVED at the San Francisco airport. Jacob and Rolly were there to meet them. They would meet Jim and Mary at Gulliver's in Millbrae, across from the Marriott where they would be staying.

* * *

As the Glazers were introduced to Jim and Mary, it was obvious to Mary that they seemed confused. They both spoke English quite clearly, with some broken English. They were reluctant to offer any more information than asked.

Mary sat beside the woman and held her hand, smiling and doing everything to make her feel at ease. Soon a comfortable feeling of friendship filled the air. The Glazers became satisfied that this was not a scheme to rob them of their life savings.

Jacob took the lead and began the full story behind this meeting. He explained the roles of Rolly, Jim, and Mary.

Mrs. Glazer apologized to both Jim and Mary for being hurt physically in the midst of the journey, as though it was somehow her fault. Mary smiled and patted her hand. Mr. Glazer sat and listened, displaying very little body language.

Jim detected that the couple was getting weary and tired. He suggested that they continue in the morning.

After breakfast, it was decided that the Glazers and Jacob Sukin needed to have their own private meeting. They all agreed that they would meet at 2:00 p.m. and discuss further plans.

* * *

JIM, MARY, AND ROLLY waited for 15 minutes past the appointed time, until the Glazers and Jacob appeared. Everyone was polite but only small talk ensued.

At 2:30 p.m., they all retired to the large lobby overlooking the bay and the San Francisco airport.

Jacob began, "We have been talking since we left you this morning about everything and we've come to an agreement on what should be done."

Mary, Jim, and Rolly sat at full attention like children waiting to hear their grandfather's last will and testament.

"First of all," he continued, "we have all been overwhelmed by all of this, which I'm sure you can understand, but we want to do the right thing. How many people do you imagine are hit with something of this magnitude like a bolt of lightning? The feeling is indescribable!"

Everyone sat looking intently at Jacob. He went on, "From everything you have told us, we are to consider ourselves the RIGHTFUL HEIRS. Is that not correct, Rolly?"

"Yes, that is correct," Rolly responded.

"Then it is our sole responsibility to decide what happens to all the money?"

"Yes!"

"Very well then. Here is our decision. Rolly, you are to receive $15 million for your years of effort and we'll call it finder's fee!"

"I am more than grateful, Jacob. I'm sure you know that!"

"Yes, Rolly, I do! We will all be eternally grateful to you for never giving up, and for finding me!"

"Mary and Jim, we can only imagine what you have endured to make all of this happen. We wish to give you each $5 million as a token of our gratitude!"

Jim and Mary looked at each other and smiled broadly.

Jacob continued, "Now, I'm sure you are wondering what we plan to do with the rest." They nodded that they would like to know.

"Our families will each take one-sixth of the remaining money. Two-thirds will be set up in a trust for three years to sponsor a worldwide search for any heirs of the other four families. If any are found, their shares will be given to them. After three years, all remaining money will be given to the National Holocaust Foundation for general reparations."

The group continued to discuss details of the distribution of monies and agreed to meet at the Bank of America main branch in San Francisco the following day to obtain cashier's checks for the amounts agreed upon.

EPILOGUE

JIM, MARY, AND ROLLY SPENT an extra two days in the city to celebrate their success in finding the rightful heirs. Jim proposed an idea that he and Mary had discussed earlier.

"Rolly, Mary and I are going to purchase a good used Cessna Citation jet and begin a charter service. We would like to offer you an opportunity to be part of it. Are you interested?"

"Wow! I think that would be an outstanding business venture. I would be willing to invest a few million bucks. How about if we buy two new Citations? I could be a hell of a dispatcher and office manager!"

Jim and Mary contacted Jerry Dunne and offered him a $100,000 signing bonus to become the maintenance foreman, an offer he couldn't refuse.

While Rolly made arrangements for office and hangar space, Jim and Mary went to St. Louis for safety certification and checkout on the Cessna Citation while placing an order for two new planes with custom painting showing *J&M Charters* high on the tail.

The planes were delivered on their wedding day. The ceremony was held at the new hangar, as Jim and Mary stood between the shiny new birds, facing the altar.

Rolly honored Jim as his best man. Jim's daughter Julie stood as Mary's miniature maid of honor. The two had hit it off at once. Upon meeting at the airport, Julie hugged Mary and said, "Thank you for taking care of my daddy!" Mary immediately fell in love with the young lady.

The wedding party included Mary's parents, Jim's ex-wife Shirley and her new husband, as well as Nancy, Donnie Friend, and other guests of the bride and groom.

The first contract was signed the following day. Windom Wineries signed J&M Charters for their valley transportation travel. They shook hands with the new CEO, Dominic Windom.

For their honeymoon, Jim and Mary decided on a cross-country flight in one of their new Citations.

"Hello, Roger, this is Jerry Dunne. I would like you to install a wall safe here at our new hangar office in San Carlos … How much you ask? How about time and materials plus a little bonus of $10,000? Hello, hello, Roger? Are you there?"

ABOUT THE AUTHOR

Mr. Schuyler is a native Montanan who moved to the warmer climate of California to complete his B.A. and M.S. degrees from San Jose State University.

Completing a major in English and Speech arts, he spent the next 22 years as a high school English and drama teacher. After leaving the education field he shifted gears and became a sales representative for several companies involved in the FAA airport noise abatement programs.

He now makes his retirement home in the lovely foothills of the Sierra Nevada near Sacramento, CA. He and his wife Barbara are celebrating their 54th year of marriage. Mr. Schuyler has written his first novel at the age of 74.